THE GIRL IN THE MOSS

OTHER TITLES BY LORETH ANNE WHITE

LORETH ANNE WHITE

THE GIRL
IN THE
MOSS

Montlake
Romance

Text copyright © 2018 by Cheakamus House Publishing
All rights reserved.

Published by Montlake Romance, Seattle

www.apub.com

Amazon, the Amazon logo, and Montlake Romance are trademarks of Amazon.com, Inc., or its affiliates.

ISBN-13: 9781503901636
ISBN-10: 1503901637

Cover design by Rex Bonomelli

Printed in the United States of America

For those who search for the missing.

A SECRET RUNS THROUGH IT

And out of the ground made the Lord God to grow every tree that is pleasant to the sight, and good for food; the tree of life also in the midst of the garden, and the tree of knowledge of good and evil.

—Genesis 2:9

SEPTEMBER 1994

Twilight lingers at the fifty-first parallel, painting the sky deep indigo as tiny stars begin to prick and shiver like gold dust in the heavens. It's cold, winter's frost already crisp upon the breath of the late-September evening. Mist rises wraithlike above the crashing white water of Plunge Falls, and fog hangs densely over the forest, playing peekaboo with the ragged peaks of the surrounding mountains. She moves carefully along the slime-covered rocks at the edge of the deep-green eddies and pools of the Nahamish River.

Stopping for a moment, she watches a cloud of small insects that have begun to dart just above the water's mercurial surface. Peace is complete, a tangible thing that feels akin to a gentle blanket wrapped about her shoulders. She's in the moment as she crouches down to her haunches and removes a wallet-size fly box from the front pocket of her fishing vest. She opens the silver box, listening to the thunder of the falls downriver. The wind hushes through the forest up along the ridge at her back. She selects a tiny dry fly that best matches the insects hatching over the water. Gripping the fly between clenched front teeth, she draws the line from her rod with her fist. With practiced movements she knots her fly onto the tippet attached to the leader at the end of her dry line. A silver hook nestles in the feathers, which are designed to fool the trout into thinking the fly is food. A smile curves her mouth.

Rising to her feet, she begins to cast—a great big balletic sequence of loops, her line sending diamond droplets shimmering into the cool air. She feels a punch of satisfaction in her belly as she settles her fly right at the edge of a deep, calm eddy, just where the current begins to riffle along the surface, where she's seen fish rising for the hatch.

But as her fly begins to drift downriver, she senses something. A sentience. As if she's being watched. With intent. She stills, but her pulse quickens. Her hearing becomes acute.

Bear?

Wolf?

Cougar?

She can no longer hear the others, she realizes. They're upriver at a camping area near the boat pullout. She left them gathering around the fire, sipping drinks, waiting for their two male guides to prepare dinner, getting ready to laugh and eat and tell tall tales into the night. But she'd been hungry for a few last casts before full dark on this second-to-last day of their trip. It was a failing of hers—always wanting just one more of everything, not being able to stop. Perhaps it was not a good idea. She swallows, turns her head, looks up at the rocky bank. Nothing moves in the darkening shadows between the trees that grow shoulder to shoulder along the ridge. Yet she can feel it—a presence. Tangible. Watching. Malevolent. Something is hunting her—weighing her as prospective prey. Just as she is hunting the trout. Just as the fish are hunting the insects. Nerves tighten. She squints into the gloam, trying to discern movement in the shadows. A rock dislodges suddenly. It clatters down the bank, disrupting more stones, which rattle and knock their way down to the river and splash into the water. Fear strikes a hatchet into her heart. Her blood thuds against her eardrums. Then she sees it—a form. It shifts forward, becoming distinct from the forest. Human. Red woolen hat.

Relief slices through her chest.

"Hey!" she calls out with a wave.

But the person remains silent while continuing forward, picking a determined route down the bank, heading directly for her, something heavy in hand. A log. Or a metal bar. About the size and heft of a base-ball bat. Unease slams back into her chest. She takes an involuntary step backward, closer to the water's edge. Her wading boots slip on greasy moss despite the studded soles. She wobbles, steadies herself, and laughs nervously.

"You spooked me," she says as the person reaches her. "I was just wrapping up here, and—"

The blow comes fast. So fast. She spins away, trying to duck out of the weapon's reach, but her quick twisting motion sends her boots out from under her. Her rod shoots into the air. She lands with a hard smash on rocks and tumbles instantly into the river, entering with a splash.

The shock of cold water explodes through her body. It steals her breath. Icy water rushes into her chest-high stocking-foot waders; seeps into her studded wading boots; saturates her vest, her woolen shirt, her thermal underwear—the weight of it all dragging her down. She flails at the surface with her hands, trying to keep her head above water, strug-gling to grab at slippery rocks as the current moves her downstream. But her fingers fail to find purchase.

She gains momentum as the river sucks her toward its heart, where its currents muscle deep and strong toward the thundering boom of Plunge Falls, where mist boils thick above the tumbling water. She tries to kick, to swim, to angle back toward shore. But the Nahamish has other plans. It clutches at her with newfound glee, with impossible strength, tossing her about like a toy, drawing her down and into its churning bowels. Just as her lungs begin to burst, the current shoots her teasingly to the surface.

"Help!" she screams and gulps as her head pops out. She thrusts her hand up high out of the foam, pleading.

"Help!" She goes under again, swallowing water, gagging. Again, the river gives her false hope and shows her the surface. For a moment she manages to keep her chin above water. She can see the person on the bank growing smaller, face white under the red hat, dark holes where there are eyes. Behind the figure an army of black spruce marches along the ridge, sharp tips like warrior spears piercing the fog.

Why? It's all she can think. It makes no sense.

The Nahamish tugs her back under, smashes her into a subsurface boulder. Pain explodes through her left shoulder. She knows it will take seconds before hypothermia completely steals her brain function, before she loses all motor coordination, all ability to fight, to swim. Wildly, clumsily, she struggles against the current. She must halt her ride downriver before she reaches the falls. But her hands have frozen into cramped claws. Her waders and boots drag her down as if a monster is pulling her by the legs from below, down, down, down into its lair, into a watery grave.

Lungs burning, she is roiled and bashed against more rocks. She no longer knows which way is up or down, which way to fight for air. As she starts to pass out, the river once more tosses her to the foaming surface and swirls her into a small bay. Her head rises, and she gasps maniacally for air. Water enters her mouth. She chokes as she is sucked under again. But she grabs for a fallen log wedged into the bank. This time her claw-hands find purchase.

Hold. Hold, dammit . . . Hold.

Her heart pounds against her ribs. She digs her nails into soaked bark as branches trap her like a thing caught in a strainer. She can feel the spindly branches breaking, her grip slipping in the rotten log detritus. The river yanks insistently at her waterlogged waders.

Should've worn a life vest. Would it have even helped?

She manages to draw a breath, then another. Absurdly, she notices the indigo sky—the brighter points of two evening stars that hover like emergency flares. Planets, really. *Jupiter? Venus? No idea.* But they give her a sense of the universe, of her tiny place in it. A sense of hope.

Star light, star bright, first star I see tonight . . . It was nights like this—sitting at a campfire with her dad, who taught her to fly-fish when she was a little girl—that were the beginning of a journey that had led her to this point, to this river where she is now going to die. *Life is like a river. Life is absurd. The only constant is the water of change.*

She takes another breath, then manages to move her hands along the log. She gains a better grip, pulls herself toward the bank.

Time is strange how it slows, stretches. She had a similar experience once before during a head-on collision on a snowy highway. Under extreme life-and-death stress, one really does have occasion to observe things in slow, protracted motion that in real time occur in a smashing blink of an eye. Claw upon frozen claw, she inches closer to the bank. She gropes for the sticks of leafless scrub growing along the river's edge. The bank is very steep here. For a while she lies panting, half in and half out of the water, the side of her face resting in slimy green moss and black loam. It smells like compost, like mushrooms. Like a garden pond with koi.

A sound reaches into her consciousness—a raven. Cawing. It must be close, right above her somewhere in the trees on the bank. Otherwise she wouldn't hear it above the boom of Plunge Falls. The raven is a scavenger. It's smart. It knows she is dying. It will go for her eyes first, the soft parts of her body. Her mind begins to go dark.

No. No!

I must keep my brain alive. It's all I've got now. My mind. Use it. To command my body to live.

She lies there panting in the slippery mulch of soil and moss and dead leaves, struggling to comprehend her situation, the sequence of events that sent her into the river. Her brain fades to black again. It's almost a relief now. She welcomes it. But a stray little spark in the blackness does not die. It flares slightly. Flickers. Then bursts to hot life as fear strikes a jumper cable to her heart.

You.

I think of You. My fear is suddenly for You, who I once thought didn't matter.

Her eyes flare open wide. Her pulse races. Adrenaline pounds through her blood.

You matter now. Now that I see death. What do they say about people who survive against all odds when others would surely perish? About that man who sawed off his own arm to free himself from the rock jaws that trapped him; the young woman who descended a snowy mountain after a plane crash wearing a miniskirt and no panties; the female teen who survived feverish, insect-ridden months in the Amazon jungle after falling like a whirling seedpod from the sky while strapped into the passenger seat of a commercial airplane; the man who drifted for months on a raft in the ocean? They all returned to civilization with one common refrain. They say they lived, survived, did it for someone. A loved one. The thought of that loved one infused them with a superhuman strength to fight death, because they had to go home. To that loved one. *I must go home for You. I must live for You. This changes everything. Everything. I can't let You down. I'm all You have.*

Slowly she reaches for a clump of roots, drags herself up the bank an inch. She gathers breath, strains to grab a higher clump, pulls. Pain screams into her body. She relishes it. She's still alive. She fights death knowing that one slip, one lost grip, will shoot her back down the slick bank into the water. And over the falls.

She's almost at the crest of the bank. She stops, gathering breath, marshaling reserves, retching. Fog creeps over her, thick with moisture and gathering darkness. She senses something again. She's not alone. A strange combination of hope and dread sinks through her. Slowly, very slowly, terrified of what she might find, she looks up. Her heart stalls.

A black shape among the trees. Standing deadly still. Silent. Watching from the gloom. Observing her struggle.

Or is she hallucinating? Wind stirs boughs, branches twist, and the shape moves. Coming closer? Or is it just shadows in the wind?

Painfully, slowly, she releases a fist-hold on grass, making precarious her position on the slick bank. She raises her free hand, stretching her arm out toward the shape.

"Help," she whispers.

No movement.

"Please. Help . . . me." She lifts her hand higher, giving gravity more power. No response.

Confusion chases through her. Then it hits. Like a bolt from the blue. And as she realizes what is going on, why this is happening, all hope is sucked out of her body. It robs her last vestiges of strength. Her outreached hand has tipped the balance, and she begins to slip. She gathers speed suddenly, gravity thrilled to have her back, tumbling and sliding her in her waterlogged waders and boots all the way back down to the river. She lands with a splosh. The current grabs at her with delight as the human figure continues to study her in silence from the trees above. A final thought cuts through her mind as she goes under.

It's impossible to suffer without making someone pay for it.
But who will pay if I drown?
How will You get justice? How will anyone know?
Because the dead cannot tell.

CHAPTER 1

SUNDAY, OCTOBER 28
TWENTY-FOUR YEARS LATER

Sixty-five-year-old Budge Hargreaves spotted the mushrooms the moment he entered the grove—golden funnels pushing up through a carpet of pine needles and twigs, crumbs of black loam still fresh upon their lips like bits of chocolate cake yet to be wiped off.

Excitement crackled through him. Finally, he'd lucked onto a good spot. He could harvest these beauties before the light faded completely. He clambered over a moss-covered log thick as his torso, wincing as his arthritic knee gave an audible click.

Rain dripped from the bill of his cap as he crouched down among the ferns. Using his knife, he gently prized a large chanterelle free from the soil. He wiped off the wet pine needles, sniffed the fungus—fruity, like apricots. A little peppery. Unlike the toxic false chanterelle, this was the real deal.

Carefully, he placed his find into the airy bag he wore slung across his blaze-orange vest. His dog, Tucker, a wirehaired pointer, sported a blaze-orange vest, too. And a bell hung on his collar. They were into the dying days of October—killing season in these parts. Budge had no intention of either him or Tuck being mistaken for deer in this dark section of the Nahamish woods. Just last fall a couple of hunters had put a slug into the heart of a black Lab a few miles east. They'd claimed they'd thought the dog was a black bear.

Fuckers. No bear hunting allowed in these parts, ever. And all they had was permits for deer, so why in the hell was they using shotgun slug for deer? He glanced up suddenly as it struck him. He hadn't heard Tuck's bell in a while. His dog liked to go on ahead, nose around a bit on his own, but usually he wasn't out of sight or earshot for long.

Budge whistled—three short blasts, one long—Tuck's special call. But no hound came crashing through the forest. No *chinkle* of Tuck's bear bell sounded. Tension clumped in Budge's chest. He whistled again, then listened carefully to the noise of the rain forest.

Water drummed steadily onto the sleeves of his Gore-Tex jacket. It leaked down the back of his neck. All about him droplets quivered and plopped down from the canopy and fell from the plate-size leaves of the primordial-looking devil's club that grew over a meter tall around him. The smell was of wet soil, fecund. He caught a distant snatch of voices carrying up from the river, which widened into a delta maybe two hundred meters down a thickly forested slope from where Budge squatted. Must be the fly-fishers he'd seen drifting the currents in jet boats earlier.

A chipmunk exploded into a machine-gun barrage of chirping as Tuck burst abruptly through the ferns. Fright punched through Budge, followed quickly by a wave of relief. Tuck was panting, his eyes bright, his snout caked with black mud. Budge grabbed Tuck's collar and ruffled the animal's coat.

"Where's your bear bell gone, eh boy? You snag it loose on a branch or something? And whatcha been ferreting out with that filthy ol' snout yours, eh, you old goof? You found something good and rotten? Rootin' out that chipmunk's stash, were ya?"

Tuck wiggled and whirled his stumped tail, trying to lick Budge's cheek.

"Whoa, back up there, bud. You're gonna squish my chanterelles." He slapped Tuck on the rump and allowed his hound to scurry back into the bush to continue digging at whatever had snared his attention. Light was fading fast under the old-growth canopy, and they still had a fair trek back to where he'd parked his truck off an old forestry road. Yesterday Budge had scored only about six pounds of goldens. Today would prove a much better haul if he got cracking before darkness fell.

Rapidly harvesting the chanterelles, Budge moved deeper and deeper into the woods. Vegetation grew denser around him, mossier, more primal. Sound became hushed. Witch's hair trailed from massive cedars, and black lichen smothered bark. A chill trickled down his spine suddenly. He stilled. It felt creepy in there, the fog sifting through the trunks like ghosts. Something *thwocked* onto the bill of his cap. He jumped and fell back on his butt. The object flopped from his cap onto the ground.

Budge's heart hammered as he stared at what had hit him. A rotted fish carcass. Adrenaline thumped through his veins. He looked up. Another carcass dangled from the branches above, slimy white and glistening. Eagles, he thought. The bloody scavengers. They flocked north each year when the salmon came up the Nahamish to spawn. When the fish died, the eagles plucked them from the river with their talons and carried them high into the trees, where they fed on the ripe flesh.

Bears also brought the carcasses up into the woods. Budge had been a logger. He could always tell a good salmon year from the rings in trees—lots of nitrogen in the soil those years. But a rotten carcass smacking him on the head in the goddamn spooky twilight like this? *Too much for an old dude's ticker.* He snatched up the knife he'd dropped, swore out loud for good measure, and decided he was done.

He creaked back up onto his feet.

"Tuck?" he yelled.

No response.

"*Tucker!* Where in the hell are you, boy? We gotta go!" Budge pushed his way deeper into the brambles and ferns. A rustle and growl sounded along the far edge of the clearing, beneath some wild blueberry and salmonberry scrub. Budge stilled. Unease crawled deeper into him. "Tuck?" He moved closer toward the snuffling, hand fisting around his knife. "What is it, boy?"

He edged aside fern fronds and then froze. Tuck looked up at him, eyes aglow. He growled again, teeth clamped around a long, dirt-encrusted bone.

"Jeezus, give me that! We're leaving." Budge snatched for the bone. But Tuck backed away, jaw tightening around his prize as he dropped his head, his growl deepening as his hackles rose.

"Fucksakes, Tuck! You know not to do that. Drop it. *Now.*"

The hound lowered his head even farther but acquiesced, reluctantly releasing the bone. Budge leaned in to see what animal the bone might have come from. That's when he caught sight of the clawed-back carpet of moss behind Tuck. His blood turned to ice.

Protruding from the moist black earth was part of a large rib cage. Budge swallowed. His gaze tracked up from the ribs. A skull lay sideways in the loam, as if in sleep, the exposed eye cavity caked with dirt. The left side of the skull had been bashed inward.

Blood began to boom in Budge's ears. This was no hunter's kill. This was not a moose or big buck that had perished in the rain forest.

This skull was human.

CHAPTER 2

Angie Pallorino flicked her wrist, trying with sheer force of will to land her fly exactly where she intended. It fell short in a snarl of fishing line. She cursed, pulling her tangled line back into the boat. She and her boyfriend, Detective James Maddocks, were into the last hours of their four-day guided trip down the Nahamish, and today they were fishing in the flats below the Plunge Falls. She'd hoped to have nailed this fly-fishing gig by now, but it eluded her, this apparently esoteric art. Angie didn't like failing at anything. Irritably, she wound the dry line back onto her fly reel and got set to attempt another cast.

"Try not to aim directly into the wind—it's picking up," their young female guide called from the back of the jet boat, where she sat steering their drift down the river.

Yeah, yeah, do this, don't do that, try again. But Claire Tollet was right. The breeze was turning testy, shooting riffles across the smooth surface of this flat section of water. Every now and then a sharper gust brought an icy chill down from the snow-dusted peaks to the north. Angie yanked her woolen hat down lower over her ears and proceeded to cast her line out. She muttered a curse as her fly settled barely a few meters out from the boat. She seated herself in the boat to watch her line.

"Hey, that one wasn't so bad," Maddocks said. Angie still called him Maddocks rather than James. They'd worked together, and not only was it police department custom to use last names, the tag had filtered over into his social life decades ago. No one called him James, let alone himself.

"You'll be surprised how much easier it'll be next time." He stood above her in the boat, holding his rod as he slowly stripped in his line, making his fly dart atop the water like the real thing.

"*Next* time?" she said.

"Sure, there'll be a next time." He grinned. It put light into his dark-blue eyes and creased his face in a way that warmed her heart. In his wading gear and fishing vest, his jet-black hair ruffled by wind, he looked all mountain man—a far cry from the sharp homicide cop in suit and tie she'd fallen so hard and fast for almost a year ago. But the words he'd spoken in the car on their drive up the island to the remote lodge sneaked back into her mind.

She broke eye contact and returned to watching her fly, a disquiet settling into her chest. Autumn on the Nahamish—it had sounded so romantic when he'd suggested it. And their trip was designed to be just that: a romantic getaway to rekindle their relationship away from cell phones and the stresses of their respective new work commitments.

But his words—that one question—had somehow sent everything off-kilter before they'd even arrived at the river.

Have you ever thought about having kids?

Angie's line developed slack. She pulled some of it in as she'd been instructed. The water was shallow here. She could see the slime-covered stones along the river bottom. Above the stones a school of salmon carcasses held steady in the soft current. The weight of their skulls pinned the dead fish in place and kept them facing upstream as the current swung their bodies gently to and fro, making it appear as though they were still swimming. Zombie fish, Angie thought, doomed to perpetually fight their ghostly way upriver as shreds of rotting flesh peeled off their bodies. Or until they were plucked from the water by scavenging bald eagles. Or taken by bears, or the wolves that ventured down to the river's edge at night.

It was a ritual that played out each year as millions of chum, pinks, chinook, and coho in the Pacific Ocean were triggered by some biological cue to suddenly scent out the fresh water of the one river they were born in and to then swim into that river mouth and fight their way back to their birth home, bashing and beating themselves into shreds upon rocks and in white water. Just to spawn. To fertilize the eggs. And then die. So that the cycle could begin again.

Angie and Maddocks weren't angling for the aged salmon, though. They were hunting the muscled and silvery trout that swam among them. But Angie was having trouble moving mentally beyond the bloated carcasses hovering beneath their boat, the stench of dead fish washed up on the shores. This whole birth-death cycle made her ponder the futility of it all, the merits of bashing one's way against the currents of life just to propagate and die. It darkly underscored Maddocks's question at every turn, and she didn't have an answer.

Have you ever thought about having kids?

With quick, jerky movements, Angie started reeling her line back in.

"You okay?" Maddocks said.

"Fine," she said as she came to her feet, wobbling the boat. She cast out her line one more time. "But if there is a next time, it better be someplace warmer."

"Come on, you love it. Admit it."

"Yeah, right." She avoided his gaze by turning her attention to the second boat in their drift party. Hugh Carmanagh was the guide at the helm, his clients a long-married couple from Dallas. Seniors with the zest of teenagers. Over the past four days, Angie had witnessed the septuagenarians attacking this trip as though they were trying to bleed every last drop out of the few years they had left on this earth. Again, she wondered about the merits of it all—this gathering into your chest all these life experiences right before you kicked the bucket and went to the grave, where memories meant zip to the dead. She'd seen Maddocks watching the couple, too. She could tell from the look on his face that he was envious of them, that he perhaps wanted himself and Angie to be like that couple one day, aging together. Laughing together. Having sex in tents and fun and adventure to the very end. Making up for lost time—him for a failed first marriage, her for a traumatic past.

But to Angie those septuagenarians just seemed desperate, like they were panicking now that they'd glimpsed the finish line. She wasn't 100 percent certain about the future of her relationship with James, either. Right now all she wanted was to get back to the city where she could continue clocking up hours toward her full private investigator's license. Once she had the legislated hours under her belt, she could think about opening her own agency. She was done working for assholes. She couldn't wait to call her own shots, pick her own cases. Everything until then felt like a waste of time.

Light faded and shadows lengthened across the water. It made the dead fish beneath the boat appear more real. Rain started to softly fall. Angie's thoughts turned to the scalding shower and hot dinner waiting at the lodge. Plus a real bed after three nights in a tent—she couldn't wait. Tomorrow morning, early, she and Maddocks would start the return drive to Victoria.

"Time to pack it in," Claire said, drawing her rain hood over her head. "Start bringing in the lines." She reached for her radio and keyed it. "Claire for Rex, Claire for Rex." She released the key.

The radio crackled. "Rex here. Come in, Claire."

"We're bringing in the boats. What's your ETA with the trailer at the pullout?"

"Almost there now."

"Good timing," she said cheerily. "Light's fading fast. See at you the pullout."

"Copy that. Over."

Claire waved to the other boat. "Yo, Hugh!" Her voice carried over the water as she made a winding motion with her hand high in the air. "Wrapping it up here. Rig's almost at the pullout."

He gave a thumbs-up. His clients started bringing in their lines.

Claire fired the motor. It coughed to life with a puff of blue smoke. But as Claire steered the boat around, Angie caught movement on the opposite bank. She squinted toward the thick line of trees, unsure of what she was seeing in the fading light and fog. It looked like a man gesticulating wildly along the bank. He had a dog at his side. Both wore blaze-orange hunting vests.

"Whoa!" Angie yelled over the engine, shooting her hand up to stop Claire. She pointed. "What's that over there?"

Claire killed her motor. Silence descended once more over the river. And they heard him.

"Help! Over here! Need help! No phone reception!"

Quickly, Claire keyed her radio. "Hugh, do you copy? Hugh?"

"Hugh here. Whassup, Claire?"

"Guy on south shore. He's calling for help. We're heading over."

"Copy that. I'll take clients to pullout. Yell if you need me."

She fired the engine back to life. "Sit steady!" She gave it full throttle. The boat nose lifted from the water, and they sped for the far shore, a smooth wake surging out behind them.

As they neared, she slowed their craft. An old man hobbled hurriedly down the pebbly beach toward the water's edge, his dog in tow. He carried a bag slung across his torso. As Claire nuzzled the prow gently against the gravelly shore, the man waded into the water and grabbed hold of the gunwale. He was breathing hard. Angie judged him to be in his late sixties. He had a big paunch, gray whiskers, and a weather-beaten face that was ruddy with cold—or from years of drinking. Or both.

"Budge?" Claire said as she raised the back of the engine out of the water so the props wouldn't catch the shallow bottom. "What's going on?"

"I . . . I—" He was seized by a bout of coughing. Releasing the gunwale, he doubled over, hands bracing on his knees as he hacked and wheezed.

Maddocks hopped out of the boat, boots splashing into water. Angie followed suit, her waders and boots keeping her feet dry as she walked through the shallows and placed her palm on the man's shoulder.

"You okay, sir?" she said.

He raised his hand, indicating he was fine as he coughed out his fit. Coming erect, he thumped his chest with his fist and cleared his throat, eyes watering. "Damn cigarettes. I got no cell reception on this side, but I saw the Predator Lodge logos on the boats, and I know you guys got radios and can relay a message back to the lodge. The folk up there can call the cops down in Port Ferris. I . . . I—" He was racked by more coughs.

"Take a few breaths, sir. Relax a moment," Angie said.

He nodded, wheezing as he drew in a slow, deep breath. He came slowly upright again. "I found a body—a skeleton."

CHAPTER 3

Angie took up the rear as the old-timer who'd identified himself as Jim "Budge" Hargreaves led them single-file into the darkening forest. Each held a flashlight taken from the boat, and their haloed beams bounced off shifting fog, making shadows dart and loom then vanish. Tucker the dog strained against his lead up front. Primeval ferns grew large, and water dripped everywhere as rain fell with a soft patter atop the tree canopy.

A sound reached them. They all stilled. Even Tucker fell silent.

It came again—a distant howl, rising in pitch then dying in a series of yips that echoed into the snow-capped hills.

"Wolves," Claire whispered. "They're getting bolder. They come closer and closer to the lodge each fall."

Goose bumps shivered over Angie's skin as a vestigial childhood memory stirred to life. And suddenly she was back in the forested grove where her biological father had held her and her identical twin sister captive as children. Where he'd murdered Angie's twin and their mother. There'd been wolves on those islands where he'd imprisoned them. Angie had heard them some nights, their howls coming through the bars on their high windows. Fear curled into her; old neural responses reawakened. She fisted her hands at her sides in an effort to marshal control, to remain present. PTSD was the pits. It rose its hooded serpent head and struck when she least expected it.

The wolves quieted. As if on cue, Tucker resumed panting and yanking on his leash to reach the human remains. Yet as they resumed their trek through the woods, Angie found her mood had shifted. A wet branch snapped back, smacking her in the face. She jumped and froze solid in her tracks.

Breathe.

Breathe. It's fine.

It's going to be fine. Just memories. Keep moving.

"You okay?" Claire said, turning to wait for Angie as the others continued ahead. Claire sounded cool. Composed. On familiar ground. This frustrated Angie. Not because the woman was young and naturally beautiful with thick black hair and moss-green eyes, or because she was skilled in the wilds where Angie was not, but because Angie hated her own fear. She resented what her buried past could still do to her. She *detested* that she couldn't shake this post-traumatic shit that still dogged her and probably always would.

"How do you know Budge Hargreaves?" she asked Claire, her voice clipped as she resumed walking. The question was in part to deflect the tension she felt. As an ex–sex crimes and then homicide detective with the Metro Victoria Police Department, interrogating people had been Angie's forte. Even though she was no longer a cop, defaulting to old police procedure at a potential crime scene was an easy coping mechanism, a way of guarding her emotions from others.

"Everyone around here knows Budge," Claire said. "He worked as a logger in this region for over two decades before retiring. I feel bad for him. He lost his wife in a tragic accident about twenty-six years ago and went off the rails, started drinking heavily. Sold his place in town and built a homestead in the woods just east of here on land he rents from my family. Pretty much keeps to himself now. When he's not wandering around in the bush, you'll find him at the Hook and Gaffe tavern in town."

"Your family owns parts of this forest on the south side of the Nahamish? I thought all this area inland from Port Ferris was Crown land."

"Big tracts of it are Crown, but we've got private pockets from when my great-granddad settled this area and opened a mill."

Up ahead Budge and Maddocks came to a stop, Tucker going nuts barking and jerking against his collar. As Angie and Claire joined them, Budge pointed his flashlight into a dim grove. "The skeleton's in there, behind all that devil's club growth."

"*Oplopanax horridus,*" Claire said quietly. "You don't want to let that stuff touch bare skin."

"Claire, Budge, why don't you guys wait here?" Maddocks said. "Angie, you come with me."

"Yes, sir," she muttered. "*You're* the cop."

He shot her a glance, eyes glinting in the twilight. Tension quickened between them. This edge was never far from the surface since Angie had been fired from the MVPD.

"That is, if you *want* to come with me," he said quietly.

She didn't reply. Parting a hedge of ferns, they entered the grove. The moss was springy beneath their wading boots. A heavy hush pressed over the area. Even the dog had quieted. It was as if a reverence was owed by those entering this grove of ancient trees.

Maddocks panned his beam across the moist ground behind the devil's club bushes. What was once a uniform carpet of emerald-green bryophyte growth had been peeled back like slabs of commercial turf, exposing the glistening black loam beneath. Sticking out of the recently disturbed soil was a section of rib cage. Above the ribs lay a half-buried human skull. A fecund smell rose from the grave. Tendrils of mist sifted through the trees like ectoplasmic fingers reaching out to caress the bones.

"Spooked the crap outta me when I first saw it!" Budge called from the outskirts of the clearing. "Like I said, I'd have called the cops right away, but there's no cell reception in these parts."

Maddocks squatted down. Angie crouched beside him. Slowly, they ran their beams over the exposed parts of the skeleton. Angie's pulse quickened at the familiar rush of coming upon a possible major crime scene. Right on the back of that rush rode a sharp whip of reality. Never again would she be officially tasked with managing her own crime scene.

Mouth tightening at the overwhelming impact of this thought, she said, "Coroner will need to get a full team in here. It's going to take a while to excavate this." She leaned in closer to examine the skull. It was encrusted with dirt, no remaining flesh discernible. A mud-filled eye socket stared back at her. "Some kind of compression fracture." She pointed to the hole in the left side of the skull where bone caved inward, cracks radiating out like a starburst. "This person took a hard blow to the left side of the head."

"Won't know if that's post-, ante-, or perimortem until a forensic anthropologist gets a good look," Maddocks said.

"Some ribs are missing." Angie aimed her beam at the exposed portion of encrusted rib cage.

"Maybe the dog did that," Maddocks said. "Or other scavengers—" His hand stilled as his beam settled on something poking out of the moss near the base of the rib cage. "Some kind of dark fabric, maybe?"

"What fabric lasts longer than it takes for a body to become fully skeletonized?"

He glanced at her. "Gore-Tex? Neoprene? Stuff like that doesn't biodegrade."

"Like neoprene waders?"

"Hmm." He looked up. "Seems a bit far from the river to be a stray angler."

"We're still wearing waders," she said. "This person could've walked up here, like us. We came via that circuitous trail from the beach, but I reckon the river is only a few hundred meters north of this grave as the crow flies."

"Yeah, but it's all old growth and dense scrub from here to the water as the crow flies. Some serious bushwhacking if anyone wanted to come that way from the beach."

Angie repositioned herself as Maddocks spoke. She was getting stiff, her own neoprene waders doing only so much to ward off the evening's creeping cold. As she moved she noticed another bone sticking out of the disturbed moss carpet at her feet.

"Oh shit!" She moved back farther. "Another one. Right here, under my boots."

They both stared down at the bone. It was long with white marks at the rounded end, as if recently gnawed.

"Humerus, maybe," she said.

"What's that beside it?" Maddocks pointed at a round object encrusted with black muck.

Angie zeroed her flashlight onto the object. "Looks like some kind of cuff bracelet or a piece of machinery. We need to move back, get out of here. This is a crime scene until proven otherwise. We should cordon off this whole area until the coroner and local law enforcement can get in."

"The closest RCMP detachment is in Port Ferris," Maddocks said, coming to his feet. He and Angie backtracked carefully along their path of entry to where Budge and Claire waited patiently in the dripping rain and encroaching darkness. Tucker whimpered softly and wiggled on his lead as they neared.

"Can you radio it in to the lodge, Claire?" Maddocks said. "Someone from there will need to call the Port Ferris RCMP and inform them a clandestine grave has been unearthed by a dog. Give them the GPS location. And tell them Sergeant James Maddocks from MVPD major crimes in Victoria is on scene and will attempt to secure the area until they can get in with a coroner."

Claire keyed her radio, stepping aside to make her dispatch.

Angie turned to Budge and said, "Is there a road up from Port Ferris on this side of the Nahamish?"

"Just a deactivated logging track, not used much apart from hunters and me and Axel Tollet, who also has a homestead on this side. His spread is farther west, though."

Maddocks said quietly to Angie, "There's no way the coroner and law enforcement will be getting in here tonight. Not much can be done until first light anyway—those remains aren't going anywhere. Not after all these years."

"What about scavengers, now that it's been exposed?" Budge pointed to a dark mudlike mound near his boots. "Bear's been here already. This scat is fresh, dumped since I left here to go to the river to call you guys for help."

The radio crackled as a message came in from Rex on the other side of the Nahamish. "Gotcha, Claire. Message has been relayed to the lodge. You guys coming back over?"

She turned and looked expectantly at Maddocks and Angie.

Maddocks said, "I'll stay out here for the night, secure the scene until the local authorities can get in. Can we get some supplies from the lodge? I'll need a tent, sleeping bag. Radio. A supply of dry wood for a fire to help keep wildlife away. Some bear spray, pencil flares, just in case. And some rope. Or line, or tape—something I can use to run a rough perimeter around the grave site."

Angie stared at him, her skin going hot. He was making her feel like a spare part, hammering home that she'd been fired, was no longer a police officer let alone a sex crimes or homicide detective.

Claire said, "That shouldn't be a problem. I'll go and collect the gear from the lodge myself and ferry it back over the river. Are you coming with me, Angie?"

"I'll camp out here. With him."

His gaze ticked sharply to her. "You sure?"

"Of course I'm sure," she snapped. "What do you think? I'm just going to leave you out here alone?" So much for that anticipated shower, hot meal, good mattress. "It'll be fine as long as I'm back in town for my job at the airport tomorrow evening, because Brixton will fire my ass if I'm not."

Jock Brixton, who ran Coastal Investigations, had been reluctant to hire Angie in the first place because of her notorious dismissal from the MVPD and the subsequent media frenzy after she'd shot and killed a serial sex murderer known as the Baptist.

The media had also gone to town over the discovery that Angie was the mysterious little Jane Doe found in an angel's cradle over thirty years ago and that her biological father was a sex trafficker who'd killed her mother and sister, among others. Angie had begged Brixton to give her a chance because no other PI firm had come even close to offering her a job, and by law she had to work for a registered company in order to accrue the hours required to graduate to an unsupervised PI license. Once she had her unsupervised license, she could think about starting her own boutique-style agency. She'd even offered to take a lower-than-average rate of pay.

Brixton had finally relented and offered a probationary period of employment. Which meant Angie had been left scraping the bottom of the PI barrel, her case load consisting mostly of following adulterous spouses or the children of rich parents who wanted to spy on their kids. It sucked; no two ways about it. But she just had to keep her eye on the prize—running her own business. Screwing up her probationary employment would cost her that prize.

"Hey, look, if you guys don't need me," Budge said, "would you mind if I headed back to my truck? Port Ferris cops know where to find me if they have questions or anything."

Maddocks said, "You okay to find your way back? It's almost dark."

"Got my GPS. Got my headlamp. Got Tuck. We know our way. Done it plenty times in far worse conditions. Don't live that far away, neither." The old guy positioned his headlamp atop his ball cap and clicked it on. He gave a nod and, wheezing, made his way off into the woods. They watched his light bobbing into the mist, then it disappeared.

"Do you want to come help me get the gear while Maddocks waits here?" Claire said to Angie.

She nodded and started to follow Claire down the trail toward the beach, but Maddocks reached for Angie's arm and held her back a moment.

"You okay?" he said.

"Why shouldn't I be okay?"

He angled his head, his skin pale under the beam of her flashlight. "Because you're reacting like this. Getting all snippy. What is it? The wolves? Are they prodding old memories?"

She glowered at him, a cocktail of feelings stirring into her heart. He cared. He was a good guy. She loved him with all her heart, and a part of her resented him because he was so goddamn perfect. Because he was still a big-shot detective, and she wasn't. Because his success—his recent promotion to head a new major incident unit—just offset her own failures. Because something buried deep down inside her was still resisting committing fully to a relationship with him, and she didn't know why, and it saddened and confused her. More than anything she did not want him to treat her like a victim. She wanted his respect. To be his equal. She wanted his admiration, not pity.

"You've been treating me like fragile china ever since I found out my father was a killer. Do you know that?" she whispered so Claire would not hear. "And while I appreciate the sentiment—I really do— I'm made of tougher stuff than you're giving me credit for right now, okay? I don't like being cosseted. I want you to lay off."

An owl hooted somewhere. Wind rustled through the tops of the trees. His gaze held hers, and a deeper subtext layered into the chill between them.

You ever thought of kids . . .

"I'm a survivor, Maddocks," she reiterated. "*Not* a victim."

Something shifted in his face. He stepped back, his shoulders squaring. "Fine," he said. "Are you sure you want to stay out here with me tonight?"

"Do you *want* me to stay?"

"You know the answer to that, Angie." He paused, eyes glinting. "I always want you. It's what *you* want right now that worries me."

Her jaw tightened as she held his eyes a second longer. Then she turned and followed Claire into the woods, heart thumping against her ribs.

CHAPTER 4

James Maddocks poked a log into the campfire, shooting small orange sparks into the night. Angie was snugged up beside him, a blanket around her shoulders. A tarp strung between branches kept rain from their heads as water plopped and fizzed into the flames. She handed him a hip flask of brandy. He took it and sipped in silence as they listened to the wolves howling in the mountains. The ominous roar of Plunge Falls seemed to creep closer in the black cold of the night.

Angie shivered and drew her blanket up tighter around her shoulders.

"Chilly?" he said.

"It's the sound of those wolves," she said. "You were right. It does send me back into the past." She shot him a wry smile. "Doesn't help to be camping next to exposed human remains."

"Claire said the pack stays mostly on the other side of the river."

"Hope so. I haven't practiced defense with OC in a while," she said, using the police term for bear or pepper spray that contained extraction of oleoresin capsicum.

He studied her face, the way the firelight played over her pale complexion. He loved her features, her strong lines, her haunting pale-gray eyes, even the crooked scar across her mouth. The glow from the flames cast a rich copper hue on her red hair, which hung loose and thick over her shoulders. He thought of sex and turned away to look into the fire.

All he'd wanted was a quiet, rustic, romantic getaway, far from the city, far from the stresses of work, a chance to try to rekindle their nascent relationship, which was taking strain under the demands of Angie's new line of private investigative work. He'd been under additional pressure himself as he took charge of and shaped the MVPD's new integrated major incident team—or iMIT, as it was being called.

Instead they were here, camped in a freezing cold rain forest beside a skeletonized corpse. A wry smile tugged at his mouth. Perhaps it was fitting.

Perhaps the wobble in their relationship was his fault.

He'd suggested marriage at a bad time nine months ago, right on the back of Angie having narrowly escaped with her life when her father had abducted her and tried to kill her a second time. Just prior to that she'd lost her old partner and mentor, Hash Hashowsky, while on a call that had cost a toddler's life. She was undergoing therapy for it all, working hard to cope with the PTSD, as she'd promised him she would, making every show of addressing it all head-on, grabbing hold with both hands and trying to beat it into submission, Angie style. Yet she remained scarred and probably always would be. You couldn't just "get over" a past like hers. But it was her emotional distance—this subtle wall he could feel rising between them—that worried Maddocks. It was as though Angie was struggling with an insidious tension between her desire to be alone and her need for intimacy. Maddocks believed this inner battle was what had lain at the heart of her addiction to aggressive, anonymous sex.

"It was supposed to go down differently," he said.

"What was?"

"This trip. Tonight." He hesitated, then thought, *What the hell. If this all blows up in my face, it's better I know now rather than later.* He reached into the inside pocket of his down jacket, and his fingers touched the slim fly box he'd been keeping there. It was warm against his body, under the down, near his heart. He took out the box and inhaled deeply, nerves suddenly fierce. "I . . . wanted to make it official."

Her gaze dropped to the little tackle box. She frowned. "What are you talking about?"

He opened the fly box. Nestled in foam that would ordinarily hold flies with hooks was a simple blue-white solitaire diamond set in platinum. The stone glinted in the firelight.

Her jaw dropped. Her gaze shot up to his face. Shock registered in her eyes.

"Marry me, Angie Pallorino."

"You . . . I . . . you already asked me."

"And you said you'd think about it. I don't recall a proper hard-and-fast *yes*." He sucked in another deep breath. "We've both been so busy we haven't really managed to discuss it or make plans. That's why I wanted some time away with you. I wanted to make it special, Ange. Official. With a ring. Set a wedding date." He gave a soft snort. "I asked the chef at the lodge to prep a special dinner for us on this last night, to be served with that French wine you like. A fire was to be lit in our room, hot tub bubbling on the deck. Some real lodge luxury after three nights of riverside camping. But here we are instead, guarding a decaying corpse." He smiled. "Typical, eh?"

She stared at the diamond nestled in the foam. Emotion glittered into her eyes. Wind gusted, fluttering the strips of flagging tape they'd secured to the cordon around the grave site.

"I . . . don't know what to say."

Disquiet feathered into him. He remained silent as he watched her study the ring without touching it. Tension tightened her features, and her lips pressed into a thin line as though she was struggling to keep her emotions in check, battling with what to say next. And all over again he felt he was going to lose her. He felt vulnerable, laid bare, raw to the wind.

Afraid.

You could say yes.

He cleared his throat and said slowly, "You wanted this trip, right? Some romantic time together?"

"Yes, yes, of course. Something romantic, but . . . I . . . I didn't know you had *this* in mind."

"I've upset you."

She swallowed, her nose going pink. She wiped her hand across her mouth.

"Look at me, Angie. *Talk* to me."

Carefully, she raised her eyes. What he saw in them clutched at his heart.

"Maybe we should wait, Maddocks," she said. "Until I've got enough supervised hours under my belt, until I start my own PI agency."

"Why? Why wait?"

Silence.

"Angie?"

"Once I've got it all squared away, you know? I'll be in a better place to plan for this. Once—"

"You're running," he said. "You've been avoiding me ever since I first posed the question, avoiding talking about *this*, us, setting a date. Wedding plans. You've been using all that shit about hours, needing to work around the clock, seven days a week, no weekends, as a—"

"I *told* you! I fucking *hate* what I'm doing right now, sneaking around in the dead of night, hanging out in cheap clubs and motels tailing couples indulging in sordid affairs, trying to catch them in flagrante to prove their infidelity to a sad and jealous spouse who then detests *me*"—she jabbed her fingers against her chest—"for rubbing their noses in the photographic proof." She swore softly. "But I *need* to accrue those hours as fast as possible so I can get out from under that jackass Brixton's control and go out on my own. I—"

"Don't. Do not mess with me, Angie," he said firmly. "This has less to do with Jock Brixton than what I asked you in the car on the drive up. I saw your reaction. That question set the tone for the weekend. It goes right to the heart of this, of us, doesn't it?"

She turned her face away from him, away from the diamond ring in the box he was still holding, the ring she had not touched. She glared into the flames. He watched her carotid pulse at her neck.

"It was just a simple question about whether you'd ever thought about having kids, Angie."

She swung to face him. "Listen—"

"No, you listen to me. I don't *care* about having children if you don't want them. I have Ginny—I've been there. I don't *need* to start parenting all over again. I just wanted to know what you want. Because I care about understanding what's going on inside the woman I love, the woman in my life. The woman I want to spend the *rest* of my life with. It's a normal question, one of the things normal people discuss when they're going to spend the rest of their lives together."

A tear escaped her eye and leaked down her cheek.

Maddocks cursed inwardly. Wrong thing to say. How could Angie Pallorino be "normal"? Her childhood, her past, was violent and bloody and abusive. She was a textbook case for some victim psych study. And yeah, a true crime book on her life story would be out soon, written by forensic shrink Dr. Reinhold Grablowski against Angie's wishes and without her cooperation. It was a miracle she was even functional.

"I miss it," she said eventually, still not meeting his gaze. "The job. Sex crimes. Homicide. Being a cop. Carrying a gun. Having some authority around a crime scene. Running an investigation."

"I know."

She turned sharply to face him, her features raw. "I'm struggling. I don't know how *not* to be a cop, Maddocks. I feel like I'm something . . . less. And making such a big life commitment at a time when I can't even figure out who I am, who I want to be—I don't know if that's the right thing to do." Her gaze bored into his. "Because most of all, I never want to disappoint you. I don't want to let you down and have you think one day down that road that you made a terrible mistake."

"*This* was a mistake," he said, closing the lid on the box and shutting the diamond away from the light. "My mistake."

He'd forced his girl's hand, and she'd rejected him. This was it—plain as day: it wasn't going to work out with Angie. Maddocks was almost shaking with the reality of the blow. It made him realize how badly he'd wanted her in his life, at his side, always, forever. "I should have waited," he whispered, more to himself than her. "Done this another time. I just wanted to confirm we were moving forward, but—"

She placed two fingers over his lips and shook her head, tears beginning to spill down her cheeks. She removed the box from his hands. In silence, she opened the lid and took the ring from the foam. She slipped it onto her ring finger and held her hand out to the firelight.

Emotion balled in his throat as he watched her face.

"It's too big," he said, voice hoarse. "I can see it's too big." He cleared his throat. "I used a ring I found on your dresser for size."

"That was my adoptive mom's ring. My dad gave it to me after she went into the home. It doesn't fit me. I just keep it on my dresser . . . to think about her. About things."

"Give it back to me," he said. "I'll have it resized. We . . . we can try another time." How could he stick this genie back into the bottle? It would be like putting smoke back into a fire, impossible now to retract.

"It's beautiful," she whispered, still staring at the ring. "Elegant. Pure. Simple."

"Let me take it. I'll get it fixed."

"No, James Maddocks," she said softly as she unclasped a silver chain she wore around her neck. She threaded the diamond onto the chain.

"Here, help me fasten it." She flipped her hair over her shoulder and bent her head forward.

He closed the link at the nape of her neck. She slipped the diamond ring on the chain under her shirt. "I'm wearing it until we can have it resized. Together."

Emotion slammed his chest. He took a shaky breath. "Does that mean what I think it means?"

She cupped the side of his face. "Yes," she whispered. "A hundred times over, yes. I love you, James Maddocks. I didn't even know it was possible to love someone like I love you. Didn't know it was in me." She paused. "Or how scary and vulnerable that would make me feel. And how badly I don't want to let you down."

Tears blurred his vision. "Let's do it before the end of next year, before Christmas. Maybe this spring or summer?"

"I like spring," she whispered. "I've always loved the streets of Victoria when they're filled with cherry blossoms and petals litter the pavement." She leaned in, kissed his mouth. Her lips and cheeks were cold and damp. Her scent was her, and he loved it. He slid his hand under her fall of hair, cupping the back of her neck. He deepened the kiss, desire stirring hot and low in his groin.

She moaned, and her body softened against his as his tongue tangled with hers. She moved her hand up the inside of his thigh, cupped his hardening erection.

"Tent," he murmured against her mouth.

They made love in the dark tent in the wilderness, affirming life with a raw sexual ferocity as if to defy the death that slumbered in the shallow grave nearby.

But as they lay there sated, their down sleeping bags zipped together, limbs entangled, Angie's hair soft against his cheek, Maddocks heard the wolves again. Hunting something, calling, mating. A sense filled him that something was still not on the right track with Angie and him. A subtext lingered beneath her acceptance. Quietly, he extricated himself from his lover's sleeping embrace. He unzipped his bag and pulled on his gear.

"Where are you going?" she murmured, turning over, reaching for him.

"To feed the fire."

He crawled out of the tent and zipped up the flap. He sat alone under the tarp, staring into the flames for a long, long while as the earth turned under the heavens. He sensed that Angie, too, was lying awake in the tent.

His thoughts turned to his previous failed marriage. Nothing in life was a guarantee. An "I do" might be a promise of forever, until death do us part, but it didn't mean things would be so. Hell, he'd tried the whole shebang with Brie, his ex, Ginny's mom. He'd thought he was getting it right the first time around—providing for his family, being a dad, trying to advance his career as a Mountie. So what made him want to do it again? Why on earth did he think it *would* work out this time?

Especially with a woman like Angie.

Live in the moment. One step at a time. That's all we can do. The skeleton decaying in the shallow grave nearby underscored the temporary nature of it all. He reached for a log and shoved it onto the fire. Flames flared and crackled, warming his face. He wondered about the body in the moss, who it was, where the person had come from. How he or she had died and why no one had found the remains. Until now.

A lone wolf's wail rose higher and higher in pitch, echoing through the endless cold wilderness. A sense of winter approached.

CHAPTER 5

Monday, October 29

Angie woke to a strange, pale luminescent dome over her head. She realized almost instantly she was in the tent, a silvery-gray dawn illuminating the fabric. She turned in her sleeping bag. Maddocks was not there. She listened for a moment to the ambient sounds of the forest. Birds, lots and lots of tiny chirps. The sharp staccato call of a squirrel or chipmunk. The soft roar from the falls upriver. She pulled her woolen hat down low over her ears—she'd slept in both her hat and her down jacket. She unzipped the tent, opened the flap, and peered out.

Mist swirled thick. Smoke tendrils snaked from coals. Maddocks lay asleep in front of the dying fire beneath the tarp.

Angie ducked back inside the tent, wriggled her jeans over her thermal leggings, and belted her sheathed knife to her hip. It was a habit, carrying the knife. She pulled on her boots and crawled out of the tent.

Her footfalls were silent on the springy underfloor as she approached Maddocks. Judging by the last two smoldering logs, he'd stayed up most of the night feeding the fire to keep animals at bay while she'd slumbered like a baby. Unusual for her. He'd drawn the hood of his sleeping bag over his head. She studied his profile—strong brow, defined jaw.

He was a beautiful man, this top homicide cop. Driven. Just. He commanded authority. Was patient against her impatience. Cool against her volatility. A pang of poignancy cut through her heart followed by that disquieting and oft-felt sensation that she wasn't good enough for him, didn't deserve his love. How could she even begin to entertain the idea of bearing his children? She'd make the world's most terrible mother.

Or was that her buried shame speaking?

Shame for who her father was, for having been conceived in violence by a teenage sex slave. For the fact she'd been abandoned—the so-called "lucky one" who'd survived where her twin had perished. Angie's therapist had raised the possibility of buried shame. Until that point she'd never entertained the notion that she suffered from some kind of subterranean humiliation or sense of degradation. She'd *never* identified with being a victim, but then he'd said it: "buried shame."

You need to forgive yourself, not blame yourself. Let it go. Give it time. Time.

It was only ten months ago she'd first learned her entire life had been a lie. But Maddocks wanted a commitment now. A vise of anxiety clamped her chest. She sucked air in deep and left him to sleep while she made her way toward the grave site.

From behind their makeshift crime scene cordon, Angie studied the skull and the partial rib cage poking out of the soil. In proper daylight she could see that a much larger area would likely need to be secured. Buried remains discovered this close to the surface could be either totally localized or scattered over a vast distance due to scavenger activity or environmental forces.

Imagining it was her own crime scene, Angie ran through the steps that would come next. The exact dimensions of the perimeter would need to be established in a systematic fashion, using trained K9s or soil probes if necessary, working carefully outward from the discovery. A forensic anthropologist would need to be brought in to look for surface irregularities, inconsistencies in vegetation patterns, changes in the moss and fungi, signs of soil compaction, and additional indication of animal activity until no more remains or related evidence was found.

Once the extent of that area was established, it would have to be mapped. Each bit of evidence would need to be bagged, labeled, and correlated with a GPS position on a map. Next would come the meticulous excavation. Additional evidence collected would again be documented and then transported to a facility where it could all be fully described, photographed, and labeled under secure and confidential conditions. An autopsy would be done, and the process of identification would begin. An attempt would be made to determine cause and manner of death.

She rubbed her brow.

She did miss it. Like a physical hole gnawing her stomach from the inside out. She reached into the neck of her jacket and pulled out the chain with the diamond ring. The stone glinted in the silvery dawn light, flawless to her naked eye, set into a simple band of platinum. Nothing frilly or fancy. He knew her well. Too well. She clasped her hand around the ring and returned her attention to the disturbed grave. *Your life is different now. Accept it. This is not your case.*

"Hey."

Angie jumped and spun round.

Maddocks emerged through the mist and tree trunks, boots silent on moss. He wore his big down jacket, and his hair was ruffled and stood up in a way that endeared him to her.

She smiled. "Jesus, you startled me."

"Me big bear." He raised his hands like paws above his head and swayed from foot to foot, making like a grizzly up on its hind legs. He growled.

"Idiot." She smacked at his arm with a laugh.

He grabbed her face with both hands, kissed her hard on the mouth, then leaned back to study her eyes. "Sleep well?"

"Too damn well. Wolves could have entered the tent and taken a bite out of me before I even noticed they were there. Don't know what came over me—I never sleep that soundly. And you? Fast asleep like that out in the open?"

He angled his head and gave a lopsided grin. "What makes you think I was asleep? I saw you come out of the tent."

She slapped the side of his arm again.

He stuffed his hands deep into his pockets and regarded the scene.

"Going to need a larger perimeter," he said.

"That's what I was thinking."

Silence fell as they studied the disturbed loam, the clawed-back carpet of moss, the exposed bones of some loved one.

"What else were you thinking?" Maddocks said. A gravitas had entered his voice.

"I thought it was the female in a relationship who always asked that question?"

He cast her a sideways glance. "Didn't know stereotyping was your thing, Pallorino."

She snorted and stuffed her cold hands into her own pockets. "I was thinking that this is not my case."

"It's not mine, either."

"You know what I mean."

A kestrel shrieked somewhere high above the canopy, and wind rustled through the treetops, releasing a shower of droplets from boughs.

"Doesn't stop me wanting to know what happened to this decedent, though," she said with a tilt of her chin toward the body. "How long do you figure he or she has been lying there?"

He pursed his lips. "Could be decades. Depends on the chemical composition of the soil, of course, weather patterns, how cold the winters, how wet. How dry the summers." As he spoke the distant sound of engines reached them. They turned to face the direction of the noise. The engines grew louder as they neared.

"Sounds like quads," he said. "Coming from the direction Hargreaves went last night, along that small track." They began to retrace their steps, moving toward the sound in order to meet the vehicles and head them off before they encroached too close upon the scene.

Two mud-caked ATVs emerged through the trees bearing three people with helmets. The two drivers wore RCMP jackets and pants with yellow stripes down the sides. The third, a passenger, sported a black jacket emblazoned with the word CORONER.

The quads came to a halt. The engines were killed. The larger of the two Mounties dismounted first. Pulling off his helmet and gloves, he came forward and held out his hand. "Constable Darnell Jacobi," he said. "Port Ferris RCMP."

Angie and Maddocks shook his hand, introducing themselves. Jacobi was bald with an aggressive face, hawkish brows over pale-hazel eyes. Leonine eyes, thought Angie. Intense man. With a wrestler's grip that he declined to soften for a female. She judged him to be in his mid to late fifties.

"And this is Constable Erick Watt," Jacobi said. "And on-call coroner Robin Pett."

Officer Watt removed his helmet and shook their hands. He was much younger than Darnell Jacobi, over six feet tall with a clean-faced, buzz-cut, Germanic look. Fresh out of depot division training was Angie's guess, a newly minted rookie still wet behind the ears and posted to a nice small detachment up the coast to find his feet.

Robin Pett removed her helmet, exposing short dark hair that framed a tiny face with large brown eyes. "I hear you cordoned the area off?" she said.

As the on-call coroner for this region, the body was Pett's responsibility—she'd take custody of the remains. But if there was evidence of foul play, the criminal investigation would fall initially to the Port Ferris cops.

"Roped it off as best we could in the dark," Maddocks said. "You're probably going to want to cordon off a much wider perimeter." He led the team in single file along their original path of entry. Angie took up the rear. They came to a stop in front of the cordon. The flagging tape fluttered in a gust of wind.

"It was Budge Hargreaves who found the remains?" Pett said as she extracted her camera from her bag.

"Yeah," Maddocks said, hands in pockets. "Hargreaves alerted us from the riverbank. If he'd had cell reception, he'd have called it in himself."

The two cops exchanged a glance. The rookie turned in a slow circle, surveying the scene, the monstrous, ancient trees, the fish flesh hanging from dead boughs, the primeval ferns, the devil's club, the lichen and moss smothering the rocks and trunks, the witch's hair lifting in the cold breeze. "So Hargreaves just happened to come this way? He walked right into this remote grove?" Watt said. "There's no discernible trail or anything leading into it."

Angie said, "Hargreaves told us he was foraging for mushrooms when his dog located the remains. He had a bag full of chanterelles across his body when he flagged us down from the riverbank."

Another glance passed quickly between the two Mounties. Angie noticed. So did Maddocks, because his brow crooked up slightly.

"Is Hargreaves known to police?" she asked, curious.

The coroner's gaze ticked briefly to her. But Pett said nothing. Neither did the officers. Clearly, to them, Angie was a civilian, and this was not her purview.

A cool irritation filtered into her chest. "Well, if you don't need me"—she checked her watch—"I have a job in the city this evening. I need to get back."

"Corporal Watt will take a full statement from both of you along with contact details," Jacobi said. "Then you're free to go."

CHAPTER 6

Angie paced up and down the water's edge, checking and rechecking her watch. It started to rain again, a soft, insidious drizzle falling on the camping equipment she and Maddocks had piled up on the bank. Tension wound tighter inside her. They'd given their statements to the Port Ferris cops, packed up their gear, called the lodge on the satellite phone Claire had brought them, and made their way down the trail to the beach to await pickup by boat.

But the boat was taking its sweet time to arrive.

"What's the problem?" Maddocks said. "You're starting to wear a track right through those rocks."

"Look at the time. I need to be in my vehicle and waiting outside the Victoria airport by 7:00 p.m., and we're not even across the water yet," she said. "This is Brixton's 'major client' who 'we cannot lose.'" Angie made giant air quotes. "This client is out of town for five days, and he told Brixton his wife was likely going to collect her lover at the Vic airport when Lover Boy flies in from Seattle on some business pretext. I'm supposed to tail Wifey and Lover Boy from the airport, get photographic evidence of their liaison—catch them having sex on camera if at all possible. It's a big-deal account for Coastal Investigations. If I screw this up—"

"You won't. We'll be back in time."

She smoothed a hand over her dampening hair. "I'm on thin ice with Brixton. If I miss this opportunity to nail this couple on camera—" She checked her watch again. "Did the lodge guys give an ETA?"

"Angie, relax. Jock Brixton knows he's got a good thing with you in his employ."

"He's a jackass," she snapped. "An aging ex-detective who was first demoted for insubordination, then fired for using police databases for personal reasons while driving his demotion desk."

Maddocks crooked a brow and angled his head.

"What? You're not saying what *I* did—" She cursed. "What I did was different, okay."

"You went rogue. You used your badge without authorization." He raised both hands, palms out in self-defense. "Hey, I'm not passing judgment. Just saying it like it is. I totally understand why you did what you did. We all do. Even the MVPD brass. I'm just saying, maybe cut Brixton a little slack. He had his reasons."

She regarded him steadily, her temperature rising. Wind gusted, sending raindrops skittering over the river surface. "I'm sorry," she said after a while. "I know I made mistakes. I . . . just want to be better than that—than *him*. I want to transcend my past, not hang out with a bunch of fat old failed cops and retired detectives." A pause. "His is the only agency that offered me a job. I've just got to get through my hours there. I *need* those fucking hours."

Maddocks did her the favor of not answering. Angie plunked her butt down on a wet log and watched an eagle take flight from a towering snag. It flew up, higher, higher, where it began to drift on invisible thermals, wings outstretched, its eagle eyes scanning for tiny things below. Scavengers. Killers. Angie's thoughts turned to the ghost fish swimming beneath the mercurial surface of the river and to the futility of beating oneself to death for a goal. Just to die.

"One day at a time," he said.

"Yeah. Right." He'd said that before. Maddocks was constantly reminding her to live in the moment, to enjoy the small pleasures. She knew she needed to hear it, but it didn't sit easy. She inhaled deeply.

"I can hear the rig," Maddocks said suddenly. Angie lifted her head. She heard it, too, a distant diesel engine growling along the logging road on the far side of the river.

Angie pulled up her hood against the increasing rain as she settled in to wait. She checked her watch again, and her mind turned back to the body in the moss.

"Did you see the way those cops looked at each other when we spoke about Budge Hargreaves?" she said.

Maddocks grunted. He was crouched down on the gravel, busy retying the dry bags to keep rain out.

"Wonder how Hargreaves lost his wife?" she said. "Claire mentioned he went off the rails after her death, started drinking heavily, sold their house in town, and moved out into the remote woods. Bit of a loner, she said."

Maddocks peered up, his eyes catching the light as droplets formed little diamonds on his thick black hair. "What? You think Hargreaves knew those remains were there? That he wanted to reveal them to someone? Like he's some kind of killer revisiting his crime scene?"

"Just keeping an open mind."

A grin crumpled his face, and he laughed.

"What's so funny?"

"You. Not being a cop. It looks just the same as you being a cop."

She playfully kicked some small stones at him with her boot. His hands stilled. His eyes darkened as his gaze held hers.

Angie swallowed as a soft rush of desire filled her belly. The specter of their future rose into the silence between them. Yeah, she thought as she looked into Maddocks's dark-blue eyes, she was going to make this work. She'd pull back from her crazy work hours a little, pace herself.

Try to enjoy life and this man along the way. Because before she knew it, she could be a body in some grave, just like those bones in the grove.

"We could buy a place, you know," he said, standing up and dusting off his pants. "Start house hunting when we get back. Move in together."

Surprise washed through her. "I . . . what about your yacht? I thought you liked living at the marina."

He laughed. "Not big enough for two. We could keep it, though, and use the old schooner as your office, maybe."

"*Office?*"

"Yeah. You know, when you open your new 'boutique investigations agency.'" He made his own air quotes, a big grin on his face. "Jack-O would make a great office mascot, don't you think? There are other small businesses at the marina. The place is set up for it, got parking. It's close to downtown yet kinda private. Got its own cachet. It'd be a good fit, I think."

Speechless, she stared at her fiancé. The image of his wooden character-filled schooner and his little three-legged rescue mutt filled her mind. She could actually visualize it. Jesus, it *was* attractive. It was like he'd just this very minute given her a tangible picture of what her goal could look like, something she could hold in her mind while she raked muck for Jock Brixton. But before she could speak, a honk sounded from across the river, and a big red Ford truck with a trailer and jet boat in tow started backing down, trailer clattering toward the water.

Angie and Maddocks watched as the crew—it looked like Claire Tollet and Hugh Carmanagh—worked to get the boat into the river. Behind them a third person alighted from the truck. A big male in a bright-blue jacket and red ball cap. Slung around his neck was what appeared to be camera equipment with a massive telephoto lens.

"Fuck," Angie whispered, shading her eyes against the rain as she squinted at the big male ambling down to the water's edge. The man stopped, looked directly at them, and raised his lens to his face.

"Is that what I think it is?" she said. "Media?"

"Could be," Maddocks said, watching.

Angie swore again, tension rising to a boiling point in her chest. "So much for a nice remote location away from city stresses," she snapped.

Once the boat was in the water, Claire and the big guy climbed inside. Claire took the helm, and the craft wobbled as Hugh pushed them out into the current. The engine growled to life. Claire turned the prow to face Angie and Maddocks. The boat surged up onto a wake as it gunned toward them across the wide expanse of water.

As the boat neared, Blue Jacket raised his camera lens again and appeared to shoot more images of Angie and Maddocks waiting with their gear on the bank.

"Fuckit," Angie whispered, fury riding hard in her. "That's all I need. To be in the press again. Brixton won't tolerate it—he just won't. He made it clear as glass that I need to stay low-key and under the radar if I want to keep working for him. He wants his investigators incognito, to have the ability to blend in anywhere."

As the jet boat reached the south shore, Claire eased up on the engine, slowing the craft until it nudged gently against the shale incline of the beach. Claire tossed Maddocks a line. He caught it and pulled the boat ashore.

Angie marched straight up to the massive guy in the blue jacket as he clambered out of the boat, sloshed through the water, and strode onto the bank.

"What are you doing with that camera?" she demanded.

"Hey." He smiled and proffered a big ham of a hand. "I'm Dave Falcon. Reporter with the *Port Ferris Beacon* as well as a stringer for CBC. You must be Angie Pallorino."

She glowered at him, ignoring his hand. "How do you know who I am?"

His smile turned hesitant. He diverted his hand to adjust the bill of his cap against the rain. "Was listening to the scanner early this morning. Heard human remains had been found in the Nahamish old growth. I called the lodge." His gaze ticked briefly to Claire, who was helping Maddocks load the camping gear into the boat. "I know the folk up at Predator Lodge. They told me that you—Angie Pallorino— and a Detective James Maddocks of the new MVPD iMIT unit found the grave." Dave nodded a greeting to Maddocks as he spoke. Maddocks ignored him as he loaded the last dry bag into the jet craft.

"We did not find anything," Angie said coolly. "A mushroom picker found something. Nothing to do with us."

"But you guys camped out here last night, right? Secured the scene, waited for the RCMP and the coroner." He wiped rain from his chin. It was pummeling down hard now. "Claire said if I got up to the lodge pronto, she'd bring me over. I'm headed into the grove now to see if I can catch up with Darnell and Erick while they're still out there."

"Darnell? Erick? Friends of yours?"

"The Mounties?" He shrugged a meaty shoulder. "Sure. Small town, you know? Everyone knows everyone. We all go back, and our parents before that." He turned to study the trees growing tight along the bank. A scraggy red ponytail hung out the back of his ball cap. "So you're the angel's cradle baby," he said, regarding the forest.

Angie's pulse quickened. She saw Maddocks fire a hot glare at her, reminding her to tread carefully.

"Such a cool story," he said louder, still facing the trees. "I recognized your name instantly from all the recent media coverage." He looked down at her. A hard glint entered his eyes. He smiled, showing sharp little canines. "I'm looking forward to reading Dr. Reinhold Grablowski's book when it releases next month. You worked with him at the MVPD, didn't you? On the Baptist case. Before you were terminated."

She bit her tongue hard, her gaze lasering his, her temper spiking red hot.

"That forensic psychologist sure was on the ball with getting that one to press so fast." His gaze lowered and lingered pointedly on the scar across her lips. "And the fact that it was *you* who found this skeleton in the moss? Already a notorious celeb? Talk about a lucky break—my editor at CBC is all over this. The *Sun* and *Colonist* want pics and a feature story, too. Been several missing persons in these parts over the decades. Those remains could be any one of—"

"You can't use my photo," she said, voice tight and very quiet. "Or my name."

He angled his head, his eyes continuing to hold hers, unblinking. Blue eyes, Angie noted. Pale blue. He had dirt beneath his nails. The hair on the backs of his hands was red. A bracelet of tiny colored beads nestled beside his Garmin watch strap, like an African tourist trinket. Angie pinned him as a pseudo liberal, an asshole who pegged himself as a global traveler, but she'd bet her ass he'd never venture alone off established tourism tracks. A wannabe who'd missed the international journalism boat and would try to make up for it by going full bore with a story on her because she was a sitting duck.

"I'd really like to interview both you and Detective Mad—"

"Go fuck yourself," she whispered.

Something shifted in his pale, flaccid features. "I don't need your permission, Ms. Pallorino," he said. "Just like Dr. Grablowski didn't need your permission to write his true crime book. Your finding that body is public record now. *You* are public record."

CHAPTER 7

Jilly Monaghan reached for the television remote and hefted her arthritic feet onto the ottoman. She clicked on the CBC channel to wait for the nightly 10:00 p.m. news broadcast, a routine that marked the end of each day. Days that felt too long and too damn dull. Retirement was not what it was bloody cracked up to be.

Just before the newscast was about to begin, her in-home caregiver, Gudrun Reimer, brought Jilly's nightly tot of brandy on a tray.

Jilly lifted the brandy snifter without taking her eyes off the television. "Thanks, Gudrun."

"Anything else?"

"Nope."

Like Swiss-German clockwork, Gudrun exited the living room at precisely 10:00 p.m. Jilly supposed that if she had to have help, Gudrun was probably the best kind for the job. Not young—midsixties. But solid in body and mind. Her five kids all grown and flown the coop, Gudrun had nothing better to do than look after some old woman who could afford the privilege. In that way Jilly and Gudrun were a team—two female seniors heading down the twilight road of their lives, Gudrun assisting Jilly with a steady hand at the elbow and a nonjudgmental reminder when Jilly forgot things. And Jilly was easing Gudrun's golden years with a hefty paycheck each month. Functional partnership. Plus the German Frau wasn't a half-bad chef, and Jilly liked to eat well.

She bumped up the volume. The recap of the day's current affairs proved boring. Possibly that was a good thing. Dull news meant things were going well. She sipped her brandy as the footage cut back to the anchor for a local segment.

"And on Vancouver Island, a decades-old mystery has just been unearthed with the discovery of human remains buried in a shallow grave. The remains were dug up by a mushroom picker's dog late yesterday afternoon about two hundred meters from the banks of the Nahamish River, north of the small town of Port Ferris."

Jilly shot bolt upright, spilling her drink. She grabbed the remote and blasted up the sound.

"Port Ferris coroner Robin Pett has taken jurisdiction of the skeletonized remains. Once the remains have been excavated, a postmortem will be performed, and the process of identification will start. Local reporter Dave Falcon was on-site. What can you tell us, Dave?" The footage cut to a big dough-faced reporter with red hair.

"I'm here near the grave site with Budge Hargreaves, whose dog, Tucker, discovered the bones yesterday." Dave Falcon held his mike toward a whiskered, red-faced old man with nervous eyes. "Can you tell us what happened, Mr. Hargreaves?"

"My dog, Tuck, dug it up. The skeleton, or rather, some of the bones. Right over there." The camera panned to yellow crime scene tape fluttering between old-growth trees. "There's no cell reception here, so I ran down to the river where I'd seen some boats from Predator Lodge. I yelled for help. In one of the boats was a detective from Victoria. He came on land and took charge of the scene until the local guys could get in."

The image cut back to Dave Falcon. "The detective in the boat was Sergeant James Maddocks of the MVPD," he told viewers. "Sergeant Maddocks was on a fishing trip with his partner, Angie Pallorino.

Pallorino is an ex-cop who recently made headlines as being both the angel's cradle baby and the MVPD officer who shot and killed serial killer Spencer Addams, also known as the Baptist."

A woman's face filled Jilly's screen. Long red hair, pale complexion, a vicious scar across the left side of her mouth. Jilly knew how Angie Pallorino had acquired that scar. She'd watched and read everything on Pallorino. And the Nahamish? A skeleton? If a body had become skeletonized, it meant it had been in the ground for quite some time. Excitement pounded through Jilly.

"Gudrun!" she yelled. "Gudrun! Come here, *quick*!"

Gudrun burst through the door, panic on her face. "Is everything all right?"

"Pass me that framed photo on the shelf there. Yes, that one."

Gudrun hurried over with a framed image of a young woman. Jilly snatched it from Gudrun and stared at the photo. The young woman gazed back at her with almond-shaped eyes so dark they were almost black. A thick fall of hair the color of ebony hung below her slender shoulders. Her smile was broad and white and alluring, as was the coquettish tilt of her head as she looked directly at the photographer. She was wearing chest-high waders, and she held a fly-fishing rod in her hand. Around the wrist of her hand that held the rod was a silver cuff bracelet. Jilly had bought it for her in Egypt.

Is it you? Can it be? After all these years?

"What is it?" Gudrun said, reaching for the remote and turning down the blaring volume.

Jilly looked up, her eyes misting with emotion. "It's her," she whispered. "I *know* it's her, Gudrun, it has to be. They've finally found her."

CHAPTER 8

Tuesday, October 30

Angie pulled into the lot and parked in front of a two-story brick-faced building. It was 8:55 a.m. She sat in her car, letting the engine run, keeping the air warm as she regarded the nondescript structure through rain-streaked windows. The sign on the glass door said COASTAL INVESTIGATIONS (CI). The building was flanked by a Howard Johnson inn on the left and a twenty-four-hour Tim Hortons restaurant on the right. The Tim Hortons was a magnet for after-hours police incidents, Angie knew from her time with the MVPD.

She dragged her hands over her hair, tightened her ponytail, and got out of her car to face the music.

On their way home from the Nahamish River, she and Maddocks had run into a serious logging truck accident on the highway. There'd been two deaths. Logs had spilled across all the lanes. Traffic along the Malahat pass had been stopped in both directions for over five hours while survivors had been medevaced out and police had gathered evidence. She'd called Jock Brixton to explain she wouldn't make the airport in time. He'd instructed her to be in his office by nine the following morning. Angie expected the worst.

She entered the building, climbed the wooden stairs to the second floor, and opened the door to the bullpen office. Most of the desks were still empty at this hour, but she found Jock Brixton's door ajar. Angie knocked on the treated glass.

"Enter!"

She pushed open the door. The interior was small and warm. It smelled of coffee and sweet pastry. A Tim Hortons bag rested on Brixton's desk. He stood silhouetted against the gray window, holding a take-out cup of coffee, watching the rain against his windowpane. The ex-cop was an inch or so shorter than Angie, but he was broad in the shoulders with a hard, protruding belly that stretched his shirts at the seams. Jock Brixton liked his drink. He liked junk food. And he liked cheap women. The irony was not lost on Angie—the adulterer who made his living trapping other adulterers was himself married. Angie kept tally. One never knew when chips might need to be called in.

On his desk next to the Tim Hortons bag lay a copy of the *Times Colonist* newspaper. Beside that newspaper was a white envelope with her name on it in bold caps.

"Sit," he said without facing her.

She remained standing. He turned, reached for the envelope, and tossed it closer to her. She made no move to pick it up.

"What is that?" she said.

"Letter of termination."

Her pulse kicked up a notch. "You can't fire me because a logging truck lost its load into oncoming traffic, Jock. There was no way we could get through. Half the city was backed up along that highway when it shut down yesterday afternoon. By the time the road reopened, it was 6:45 p.m. and one lane only."

He set his coffee down and spun the newspaper around to face her. He jabbed his fat finger on the big black headline.

Human Remains Found in Clandestine Grave

Beneath the headline, above the fold, was a photograph of Angie looking bedraggled and haunted in the mist along the Nahamish riverbank. Gingerly, she reached out, drew the paper closer, and read the cutline.

> Ex-MVPD cop Angie Pallorino and MVPD Detective James Maddocks guarded the grave site through the night. Pallorino, who was recently fired from the MVPD in connection with the shooting death of serial killer Spencer Addams, a.k.a. the Baptist, has also made media for being the angel's cradle child—

"I told you to keep a low profile," he said.

Anger tightened her face. She looked up. "I didn't even find the damn body. My fiancé is a major crimes detective. He took the initiative to protect the integrity of a scene that a mushroom picker stumbled across. As *you* would have were *you* still on the job, Jock. As any detective would. I was just there—"

"My point," he said, his face darkening at Angie's underscoring his own ex-detective status. "You can't scratch your damn butt without someone taking a photo and printing headlines, Pallorino. It's what happens to famous—or rather, infamous—people. Not only that, but you're also dating the city's top cop, a guy who's just been put in charge of a high-profile new unit being micromanaged by our new mayor and police board. All eyes are on James Maddocks and his major incident team right now and watching to see how he cooperates with the other jurisdictions. This makes *you*"—he poked his finger toward her—"a liability to *me*."

"You hired me knowing who I am."

"With reservation, and I told you so. I warned you to lay low, to try to keep under the media radar."

"I didn't *do* anything, for Chrissakes."

"You don't have to. That's the shitty deal with being infamous. Like Angelina-fucking-Jolie, everything a celeb touches becomes a fucking front-page story. You're a local notoriety. This is a small city, not a terribly heavily populated island, so I appreciate your struggles in getting around incognito—but this island is also *my* jurisdiction. It's Coastal Investigations' livelihood. My entire staff depends on this livelihood. The CI motto is 'Discreet, confidential.'" He pointed. "It's written right on the door. These are the cornerstones of my firm. Good luck to your boyfriend and iMIT, because he and his team are going to be dragged through the media circus behind you wherever you go."

Her voice turned low, quiet, cool. "You know about that media circus, don't you, Jock? Because you've been there, too."

It was as though she'd dropped an invisible electromagnetic pulse bomb into the small office. Angie could feel the waves of hot energy radiating off him.

"What, exactly, is that supposed to mean?"

Mistake. Back up. I need this job. Flatter him. He likes to be flattered.

"I'm just saying that you overcame a hot run in the media yourself. And look at what you've built with CI in spite of it. Please, let me try. Give me one last chance. Just one."

His eyes flickered.

"Look," she said, coming forward quickly, taking the gap. "I might have missed the client's wife picking up Lover Boy at the airport, but her affair with him is clearly a long-term thing. And your big-shot client is always traveling out of town. It's going to happen again. Next time I'll be there waiting. I'll get them on camera."

"My clients will make you, Angie. It'll just be a matter of time. Look at you. You've got distinct looks. That scar. That hair. That face. You're all over the front pages and on television. If Norton finds out I put someone like you on his case, if his wife or her high-profile lover make you . . ." He ran his hand over his balding pate. "Norton is our biggest client right now. He's huge. If I can keep him happy, he will recommend CI. I just can't let you fuck this up for everyone else."

"I won't. I've worked UC. I'll wear cover, buy wigs. Change clothes. I can *do* this, Jock. Please. I'm better than half the guys you have on your crew, and you know it."

He inhaled deeply.

"One." She held up her index finger. "Just one last chance."

He turned to the window and looked down to where her car was parked. A nice new Mini Cooper she was paying off. Creamy white with distinctive stripes down the side.

"I'll get another vehicle," she said quickly. "I'll use rentals that suit the job in question. On my own dime."

She saw his shoulders dip as he released his chestful of air, and she almost began to breathe, anticipating him relenting.

"I'm sorry," he said. "That *was* your last chance."

Her heart plummeted. "Jeezus, Jock, it was a motor vehicle accident. It—"

He turned. "It's the headlines, Pallorino." He jerked his fat chin toward the newspaper. "That story is just winding up, believe me. It's got legs, and it's gonna run for weeks. No way you're flying under the radar now. No way I'm putting you on another of my top cases."

A wave of gut-sickening reality crashed through her. She reached for the back of a chair, still hearing a *but* buried somewhere deep in his words.

It didn't come.

"How about you let me work the admin shit, the grunt cases? Behind-the-desk stuff."

"I'm sorry. I really am. I tried to give you a chance; you know that. But it was my mistake. You're a fucking shit magnet, Pallorino. Your probation is up. You're done."

Tension fisted in her stomach. She continued to face him, not quite believing her ears even though she'd seen this coming the second she'd spotted Dave Falcon and his camera on the other side of the Nahamish River. Angie wanted to kill that big-ass reporter for this. She wanted to shoot him dead, in the face. Like she'd shot the Baptist.

"Go on, take your letter of termination and get outta here."

"You'll be sorry, Jock."

"Yeah, I am sorry. You're a good investigator. Hope you find something." He turned his back on her and stared once more out the window.

Angie snatched the envelope off his desk and stomped out of Jock Brixton's office, her heart burning with rage and hurt and frustration.

She exited the building, rammed her black ball cap onto her head to ward off the rain, and felt her old self beginning to bubble and fester inside—the bad Angie who wanted to punch someone. Anyone. For just being in her fucking way.

Use the old schooner as your office, maybe . . . when you open your new "boutique investigations agency . . ."

Yeah, well, that wasn't going to happen now.

Jock Brixton had just robbed her of her dream.

CHAPTER 9

FRIDAY, NOVEMBER 16

Angie ducked sideways, barely avoiding the blow from Chai Bui's gloved fist. Breathing hard, slick with sweat, she took a step backward on the mat as Chai, her Muay Thai coach, came at her again.

"Hands higher!" Chai commanded. "Protect your face. Keep the marching stance, keep moving, foot to foot. Balls forward. Body square. Face me—" The roundhouse kick came fast, swiping toward Angie from the side. She jerked up her knee to block the strike, but she was too late. Chai's leg whopped hard into Angie's side, forcing air to explode from her lungs. At the same time, his hands whipped up, and he grabbed hold of her head. Yanking her body forward, he brought his other knee to her face. He stopped short of connecting and let her go.

She backed away and wiped her wrist across her brow.

"Got it?" Chai said.

"Yeah, yeah, I got it, I got it. It's putting it all into practice that's the problem."

A grin cut Chai Bui's face. He was a small, tattooed, and sinewy ex–Muay Thai champ from Malaysia, and he taught the historic art of Thai combat in his gritty little martial arts studio near Chinatown.

Angie had spent almost every afternoon or evening since the fishing trip getting beaten up by Chai on the mats or by one of his students as Chai showed her how to spar, parry, block, kick. It was making her lean and strong in body.

Angie was hoping it would also forge strength of mind, because she was on a dangerous edge since Brixton had axed her. Either it was Bui's Boxing Gym or she'd be hitting the bar or, worse, the sex club. She'd been feeling the nip of the old dog at her heels and her brain—that desperate desire to block everything out, to resort to her old coping mechanism of both numbing and exciting herself with hot, anonymous sex.

She could not do that to Maddocks.

Or herself.

So she was here. Safe from temptation while she tried to fight and box and kick and elbow her demons into submission.

And there was another reason. The only damn job interviews she'd managed to score in the past three and a half weeks included one for a security guard at a high-end gated community where she'd basically be sitting in a guard booth at the gates. Another was for a close-protection detail. She'd been offered both positions and was considering taking the bodyguard job because she'd run out of options—no local PI firm was interested in hiring her. The close-protection job would involve being fit and fight-ready. It would also mean extensive foreign travel and being away from home for months at a time.

The job required protecting a female pop star in her midtwenties, a talented but irascible and foul-mouthed prima donna fast gaining international traction, a young woman who flaunted her sex appeal and had issues staying out of booze, boys, and trouble. Glorified babysitting was what it would be. Angie detested the idea. Even so, part of her deep down wondered if it might be a good idea to take a break from this city, from the media, from seeing MVPD members at every turn and being reminded of her failed career. But taking the job would wobble her relationship with Maddocks. It might mean putting the wedding and house-hunting plans on hold.

"You'll be ready for the ring soon," Chai quipped as his impish grin widened.

"Yeah, right." Angie took a deep glug from her water bottle, allowing liquid to spill down her neck and cool her chest. "More like ready to kick at the marauding superfans of a little pop diva." She wiped her face with her towel and tossed it onto her gym bag, which rested on the floor against the wall.

"Good to go?" Chai said, starting his Muay Thai march, hands up in front of his face, his head held low, his black eyes fixed on hers.

She nodded and stepped onto the mat. Raising her hands in loose fists in front of her face, she began to shift from foot to foot, meeting his gaze.

"You're still angling your hips, Angie. You still got the boxing stance."

"Habit. Protecting my gun, offering smaller body target to my opponent."

"Yeah." He threw a kick. It caught her hard before she could get her knee up to check him.

"See? That's why. You stand with one hip leading like that, and you can't get into position fast enough to check my kicks," he said, shuffling toward her, backing her up, aggression in his stance. He punched suddenly, swung, elbowed, swung, kicked, and flipped her down onto the mat with a thud. Air whooshed from her as her back slammed the ground.

"Jeezus." She scrambled rapidly to her feet, breathing hard, a fresh rush of adrenaline dumping into her blood.

"Like I said, balls forward. Face me squarely. You want to tempt and bait your opponent with a wide body target. When he moves in, you attack, parry, block. Strike."

"Yeah, I got balls to put forward. What's your problem, Chai, you never taught a woman?" He kicked fast. She sidestepped and threw a kick of her own. High. He ducked. She spun through the movement, landed her foot, brought her other leg up and kicked fast from the other side while raising her opposite hand to protect her ear and the side of her head from the strike she knew Chai would retaliate with. She landed her kick, spun, and hit him with her elbow.

"Good! Good." He laughed, stepping back. "Now *that's* the way to do it—eight points of contact. Use 'em all. Elbows, knees, hands, feet." He resumed the classic Muay Thai stance and so did Angie, her gaze locked on his, her body square this time, hips forward. She moved quickly. *Attack, kick, jack, parry, step, knee, kick.* They continued like that in a hot trance, a dance of combat, sweat gleaming on their limbs. Angie was deep in the zone when she heard her phone ringing in her gym bag.

It distracted her momentarily, and Chai took the gap, landing a kick to her head.

The blow dazed her, and she stumbled sideways.

He laughed again. "That was just a tap, Ange. Keep focus at all times, hear me?" He reached for his own towel and hooked it around the back of his neck, using the ends to wipe his face. "Next time we'll get you squared up with an opponent in the ring. You'll wear full protective gear and let rip a bit."

She snorted, chest heaving as she made for her bag and scrabbled inside for her phone. She frowned as she checked the caller ID. Unknown number.

Connecting the call, she put her phone to her ear that wasn't ringing from a kick.

"Yeah?" she said, voice coming out in a breathy croak. Hot, she dabbed sweat from her neck with a towel.

"Angela Pallorino?"

Angie stilled. The voice was female, strident. Something about the tone quickened her pulse. Her first thought was *reporter*. She glanced at Chai, who was now prepping to spar with another student, and she turned her back.

"Who is this?"

"If that's Angela Pallorino speaking, I want to hire you. For a case."

Surprise, then caution, whispered through Angie. "Who am I speaking to?"

"Name's Jilly Monaghan. The case is an old one, a cold one. You know about it. Be at my house at four fifteen tomorrow afternoon. I'll have returned from my walk by then, and that's the time I take tea. We can discuss the case and payment over tea. My address is—"

"Whoa, hey, hold on a minute," she said quickly, bending down to snag her bag. She moved toward the changerooms where it was quieter. "I'm not taking any new cases. I—"

"I'll make it worthwhile. Financially. *Very* worth your while."

Angie stopped in the passageway near a water fountain, her curiosity now ignited. "Ms. Monaghan, I do need to inform you that I'm no longer with Coastal Investigations. And I'm not—"

"Well, who *are* you with then? Last I saw on the news is that you were with Coastal."

"I . . . I'm between firms. I—"

"Fine. You work for me direct."

"That's not poss—"

"Everything is possible, Angela."

Irritation began to rustle. "Angie. My name is Angie, and I like to finish my sentences."

"Yes, of course, whatever you wish. Angie. Be at my house at four fifteen tomorrow afternoon, and we will discuss. I'm at 3579 Seafront Road off Harling Point. That's just past Gonzales Bay. Four fifteen. Saturday." The phone went dead.

Angie stared at the phone in her hand. *What the . . . ?* Jilly Monaghan? Who in the hell was Jilly Monaghan? There was something vaguely familiar about the name. The woman had sounded older, a senior perhaps, yet forceful, confident. Like someone accustomed to getting her way.

Angie made for the changeroom. She peeled off her damp gear, and while she showered she chewed over Jilly Monaghan's odd call.

Admittedly, the woman had snared Angie by the short ones with two words: *cold* and *case*.

The promise of financial reward was simply a bonus.

Even though Angie could not work a case without a PI license, not legally, and she could not get a full license until a firm hired her and gave her enough supervised hours to qualify for one, she knew she would show up if only to hear Jilly Monaghan out. Curiosity had gotten the better of her.

Harling Point. It was a pricey subdivision, Angie thought as she grabbed a clean towel and dried off. She opened her locker, running through her mind what she knew of the area. It was a waterfront promontory steeped in the history of Victoria, once home to rumrunners, bathhouses, tearooms, and dance halls. Now it was the residence of choice for old money and multimillionaires with a penchant for sleek designer houses. Intrigued, she dressed, shrugged into her leather jacket, grabbed her bag, and slung it over her shoulder.

She waved goodbye to Chai as she exited the gym and stepped out into the cool Friday afternoon rain. It was already dark this time of year with the low cloud. She got into her car, started her engine, and reversed out of her parking space. She called Maddocks via Bluetooth hands-free, wanting to catch him before he headed with the guys to the Flying Pig, which she knew he would on this Friday evening, especially since they'd just wrapped up a big case.

His new team had arrested and charged a serial rapist who'd been preying on women in the Harris Park area for the last five months. It was a major coup for iMIT and for the new mayor and police board. It proved this special integrated major investigations approach could work. And it was a personal feather in Maddocks's cap—he'd hand-selected his crew of top investigators.

It was also a case Angie would have been working had she still been with the MVPD. Sex crimes was her wheelhouse. This *should* have been hers.

"Hey," she said as soon as he answered. "Thought I'd check in before you guys hit the Pig for the big celebration."

He asked her to hold on a second, and she heard noise in the background, someone speaking to Maddocks. "Sorry about that," he said as he came back on. "Just tying up some loose ends in the Harris Park case with Crown counsel here. What did you say?"

"Nothing. Just checking in, saying hi."

"We're headed to the Pig for happy hour. Want to join us?"

"Not a snowball's chance will you find me in drinking hell with Leo and those old guys while they sit all smug and gloating about me being fired." She paused, feeling irked and yes, sidelined, even if it was her own choice not to go. Those old deadwood detectives had tried to block and oust her from the force during her entire career with MVPD, and in the end, in many ways, they'd won. At least, that's how Leo and some of the others saw it. Angie couldn't help saying the words that came next. "You know better than to ask me that."

"Sorry, Ange. I . . . the only reason I'm going myself is—"

"I know, I know. Your team. Your case. The arrest and charges are your big win. You need to do this. I'm going to catch some Netflix and an early night."

"How'd the job hunt go today?"

Her mood dipped even further. Once again he was asking about her daily slog to find work. Once again, she had little to report.

"I'm considering that close-protection detail," she said, stopping at a red light, wipers going.

"That involves months of travel at a time."

"Yeah." The light turned green, and she moved forward. "But it might be good to get out of town now and then."

He was quiet a moment. When he spoke again, the shift in his tone was clear. "It'll mean putting the wedding plans and house hunting on hold."

"Just for a while, maybe. At least it's work, Maddocks, until something better comes up."

Silence.

"You there?" she said.

"Yeah, listen, Ange, there has *got* to be something else. There's no rush, is there? We can go ahead with our plans, move in together. I have a job. I can—"

"You can what? *Support* me?"

"Of course."

Frustration burned hot into her chest. It was her worst nightmare in a way, going from complete independence to tying the knot and depending fully on a partner. It undercut everything she'd been striving for her whole adult life. "I need to work, Maddocks," she said.

"You don't."

"Yes. I do." She turned down her street near the Gorge. "For so many reasons. On so many levels."

"Just . . . listen, just don't rush into anything, okay? Just . . . look awhile longer. And talk to me before you make any big decisions. You're a damn fine investigator—something *will* come up. We'll find a way to make this work. Together."

"Yeah."

"What about a late dinner or a drink after?"

"I'm beat. Rain check?"

Another silence. She pulled up at her underground parking garage gate and scanned her access card. The gate began to rise.

"We're spending even less time together now that we're engaged," he said. "I've hardly seen you since the fishing trip."

Now that we're engaged.

Guilt pinged through Angie. She'd been avoiding him, that much was true. On the few occasions they had gotten together over the past three and a half weeks, things had felt progressively strained. Angie believed Maddocks had also been consciously limiting spending time with her. It was as though both of them feared that the more time they spent together at this juncture in their lives, the more strain they'd put on what was looking like an increasingly fragile relationship. Neither wanted to push things to the point of destruction, so avoidance was safer.

"Yeah, well, you've been really busy with the Harris Park case and the new unit." Which was true. "And I really haven't got much to report on the job front." Which was making her feel increasingly worthless and frustrated.

"A partnership isn't supposed to be about reporting, Ange."

She inhaled deeply and drove into the garage. "I know. I know."

"How about tomorrow afternoon, Saturday—you busy?"

"I . . . I've got an appointment."

"On Saturday?"

"Yeah, some woman wanting to talk about possible PI work."

"She's hiring?"

"Sorta." Angie cleared her throat and reversed into her parking bay. Technically, it wasn't a lie. But if she told Maddocks some woman wanted her to work independently on a cold case, he'd remind her that as attractive as working an investigation might sound right now, there was one major problem. She couldn't do it legally. Not if she wanted her full license. Not if she wanted to open her own firm someday.

"What about Saturday dinner?" she said.

"You've forgotten. I have dinner plans with Flint tomorrow. Then I fly out early Sunday morning. I'm going to be out of town until Monday evening for that law enforcement seminar on the mainland."

"Oh shit, yes, I did forget. Do . . . d'you want me to take you to the airport on Sunday?" Angie killed the Mini Cooper's engine and felt an odd, sinking resignation leaching into her belly. She knew what she was doing—what they were both doing—but she couldn't shift gears and get off this one-way track they seemed to be on now.

Maddocks seemed unable to shift gears, either, because his tone was cool and crisp as he said, "No. I'm sorted for the airport. I'll call you when I get there."

The phone clicked.

CHAPTER 10

Maddocks killed his call with Angie, a dark mood settling in his gut as he pushed open the door and entered the newly renovated iMIT section. The unit was buzzing, everyone excited about the arrest of the so-called Harris Park Rapist, a serial sexual offender who'd graduated to murder. Mustering his enthusiasm for his team, Maddocks threw a victory punch into the air. "Crown is charging him on all counts!" Cheers erupted.

"First round of drinks on me at the Pig tonight," he declared as he made his way through the bullpen of metal desks toward his glassed-in office.

But as he passed Harvey Leo's desk, the old detective said in a loud stage mutter, "Funny how Pallorino is *still* managing to undercut the MVPD in the news, though. You'd think *she* just saved the entire city by discovering that skeleton in the moss by the way those reporters are covering that story. They're using it to drag up all the old crap about police brutality and how she overkilled the Baptist in a fit of rage and all that. Moves the dialogue completely away from what really matters—the fact *we* have shut down another serial killer. Without killing him first."

Maddocks stilled in his tracks. He turned to face the old cop.

Silence fell as the men's gazes locked. Tension swelled in the room. Rain ticked against the windows. A heating vent made cracking noises, and the smell of the new carpet became noticeable.

"You say something, Detective Leo?"

Leo folded his arms across his large chest and leaned back in his chair behind his desk cluttered with overstuffed files. "I'm just noting what the media is still saying about us city cops. Pallorino continues to taint us all with her brush. Doesn't help that she's your significant other, sir, because, respectfully, whatever you do as boss of the iMIT now, she's hanging there like a negative stone around our collective neck. If she goes crossing paths with cases that belong squarely on law enforcement books, the next thing the newspapers are going to be saying is that she's getting personal information from the inside. Just noting we gotta keep those personal affiliations separate."

Pressure torqued rocket-tight in Maddocks's chest. "You're right, Leo," he said very quietly. "Personal feelings—like long-held animosity, jealousy—you need to let it go because it can cloud judgment, make an officer do and say very stupid things. Things that beg to have him kicked off this unit." Maddocks faced the crowd in the room.

"Let me make one thing crystal clear. To all of you. Whatever happens in this unit, whatever is discussed in this unit, it stays right here." He jabbed his index finger onto Leo's desk, his jaw tight, anger simmering beneath his skin. "Nothing, and I mean nothing, is said to the press or to anyone who is even vaguely affiliated to the media. You don't talk to your spouses about ongoing investigations; you don't talk to your girlfriends or boyfriends; you don't talk to your kids or your grandparents. You talk to no one." He turned and met the eyes of each and every person in the section.

"That goes for me, too. Do you all understand this? I don't divulge sensitive information to my partner, and neither do you. If anyone—*anyone*—has a problem with this or with me or with my relationship with Pallorino, speak up now."

He waited.

Silence met him. Some members shuffled in their seats. Someone cleared his throat.

"Good. Because we're all professionals here. We know how to keep work separate. I trust you. You're going to trust me. And the minute I don't"—he pointed to the door—"there's the exit. I've got a dozen other highly qualified MVPD members banging on that door to be let in here, to be part of this new and elite team. But Inspector Flint and I picked you. I vouched for every one of you, because I believe you each have what it takes, a unique skill to contribute to major incident investigations. Prove me wrong, I pull you. No warning. No second chance. Understand?"

No one moved.

He turned to the old detective. "Your skill, Leo, given your very long history with the force, is required for a new sub unit I'm initiating. There's an incident room being set up one door down as we speak. Get out. Go wait for me there."

Leo's clear blue eyes flickered. His brow furrowed, confusion showing on his rugged face.

"Move it. Now."

Leo unfolded his arms, picked up his notebook and pen off the table, came slowly to his feet, and made his way through the desks. All eyes followed him.

"Holgersen," Maddocks said, jerking his head toward his office. "A word?"

Holgersen followed Maddocks into the glass office. Maddocks shut the door, trying not to look at the framed photo of Angie on his desk. She was running again in considering that bodyguard job. He knew it. She knew it. But he didn't know what to do about it or even when to stop trying. A quote from an old poster he once had pinned up on his bedroom wall as a kid entered his brain.

If you love something, set it free. If it comes back to you, it's yours . . .
That was the part he got stuck on. He wondered *if* Angie would actually come back to him if she took that job away from home. And whether he should maybe just let it be.

"I've got something new for you," he told Holgersen. "I'm starting a cold case unit. Unsolved homicides and suspicious missing persons incidents. This will be a small subsection under the iMIT umbrella. There's new money for it, and it's a direction the new police board wants. There's also been considerable political pressure for an increase in our closure rates. Reopening some of these old cases and applying new forensic technology, plus using new computerized databases and social media, could go a long way to addressing those rates. You'll have a dedicated cold case tip line operational within the next few days, along with social media accounts and support staff. And you'll have access to additional resources and personnel as you need them. You'll bring your requests to me." He paused.

Holgersen started shuffling foot to foot, his brown eyes darting around the room like a junkie jonesing for a fix. "How big is this unit—how many on the team?"

"Two detectives. To start. You and Harvey Leo."

Holgersen's gaze snapped to Maddocks. "What the fuck—you kidding me?"

Maddocks held his gaze.

"Oh no. No fucking way. I . . . Jeezus, is *that* why you brought him onto iMIT? To stick him on some lost cause sub unit? We was all wondering what in the hell when you named him. What about me then, huh? What's your beef with me, boss?" He ferreted into his pocket and pulled out his pack of nicotine gum. He struggled to free a tablet as he started shuffling again.

"This unit has potential, Holgersen. Your goal will be to prioritize the MVPD backlog of unsolved cases and earmark those that have a higher solve rate probability. Like triage. You then focus on those cases with the most potential, get some results we can take to brass. Depending on how you run with it, this sub unit can be your baby. We're talking career advancement here."

Holgersen managed to liberate his gum from the packaging. He popped the green tablet into his mouth, began chewing furiously as he shook his head. "Nope. I's not working solo with Harvey-ass Leo. No way, José."

Maddocks glanced through the window at his officers behind their desks, and he lowered his voice. "Yes, you are. And I want you to watch Detective Leo," he said. "Like a hawk."

Holgersen stilled and met his boss's eyes. "So . . . what d'ya mean? I'm, like, *spying* on Harvey Leo? Is *that* what you're saying?"

"Just watch him for me. Watch how he handles and prioritizes cases."

Holgersen frowned. "I don't follow."

Maddocks reached for his door. "Let's go. I'll get you set up so you can start Monday. Leo is already waiting." He began to open the door.

But Holgersen balked. "Oh man, Jeezus fuck, boss," he whispered. "You can't be serious?"

"Dead serious."

He cursed again, scuffed his boot, and looked down at the floor as he considered this. "Keeper of lost causes," he muttered. "Cold cases and fucking Harvey Leo." Holgersen looked up. "So you gonna tell me what's the deal with Leo? What exactly am I looking for?"

"If you see it, you'll know it."

"You messing with me, sir?"

Maddocks gave a rueful smile. "If I had something to give you, I would. Get my drift?"

Holgersen angled his head. "Fishing expedition? You suspect something but have no proof?"

Maddocks said nothing.

"Is internal behind this? Am I working for internal affairs or some shit without my knowing it? Because—"

"You get weekends, Holgersen, a regular workweek, for the most part."

"I don't like weekends."

"You'll learn."

CHAPTER 11

SATURDAY, NOVEMBER 17

Angie pulled up at the gates in front of the home on Harling Point.

The residence was one of those clean-lined, modern affairs with lots of glass and spiked plants posing as rather hostile-looking landscaping. The early twilight added to the bleak and brooding atmosphere. Intrigue rustled through her as she powered down her window and reached for an intercom button set into one of the stone pillars flanking the gates.

Finding Internet references to Jilly Monaghan had been child's play—Angie had realized almost immediately why the woman's name had seemed familiar. She was a retired justice of the BC Supreme Court, and plenty had been written about her.

Justice Monaghan had been notoriously brazen and outspoken throughout her long career. A media scandal had erupted when Justice Monaghan had been brought before the federal Canadian Judicial Council for misconduct after "mistakenly" referring to a complainant as "the accused" several times during a domestic assault trial. Justice Monaghan had also asked the complainant in court why the complainant hadn't left her husband after she'd realized she was pregnant by him, especially given her husband's history of her violence toward her. This had sparked speculation that the old justice might be suffering from age-related mental deterioration. But before any action became necessary, Justice Monaghan retired on her seventy-fifth birthday.

Angie depressed the button on the intercom.

"Who is it?" came a female voice.

"Angie Pallorino to see Justice Monaghan."

The gates began to slide open. Angie closed her window and drove slowly through the entrance. The gates shut automatically behind her. She parked outside the front door. A stout gray-haired woman opened the door.

Angie exited her car and ducked through the rain.

"I'm Gudrun Reimer," the woman said, holding out her hand as Angie approached. "I'm Justice Monaghan's housekeeper."

Angie was shocked by the power in the older woman's grip. Rough, dry hands. Brutally short nails—no polish. Her accent was German.

"You're early," Gudrun stated.

"By four minutes," Angie said, consulting her watch.

"The judge will be back in four minutes. She's punctual if anything. She's presently taking her constitutional down along the beach. Tide is low right now. Come on through. You can await her on the deck out front if you like or in the living room. If you do want to go outside, leave your shoes and coat on."

Yes, ma'am, sir.

Angie followed Gudrun from the mudroom into an open-plan and starkly bright home. White walls and cream furnishings were punctuated with dark leather pieces and splashes of violent color in the modern art adorning the walls. Glass ran the length of the building facing the sea. Angie imagined the view across the Juan de Fuca Strait to the snow-capped Olympic Peninsula of Washington State must be spectacular in clear weather.

Gudrun opened the glass slider. Angie stepped onto the deck and went to the railing. The home had been built in three levels. The top deck on which she stood looked down over another deck that housed an infinity pool.

"There she comes now," Gudrun said from inside the doorway.

Angie looked to where the housekeeper pointed. Far below on the beach, a squat figure bent her head into the wind and rain as she pulled herself forward with walking sticks, a brown coat flapping behind her. The figure reminded Angie of a dung beetle soldiering determinedly forward under a low bruised sky. The old judge was clearly fighting both age and weather in her passage home.

The image of this lone old female figure in the storm against the backdrop of gray ocean tugged at something in Angie. The justice had to be in her early eighties by now. She reached the stairs at the bottom of the property, and Angie faced Gudrun. "That's a lot of stairs. Doesn't she need help?"

"She needs only to reach the elevator at the bottom. She's independent. If she wants help, she'll ask for it. Come inside. Let me take your coat. I'll get the tea ready."

Gudrun settled Angie in the living room and disappeared to rustle up the tea.

Angie sat facing the sea and checked her watch again. Four fifteen.

"Good afternoon, Angela!"

She jolted, came sharply to her feet, and spun to face the voice. The judge had ditched her coat and boots for a large sweater and slippers. She hobbled determinedly into the living room, a look of ferocity on her face. But after having witnessed the old woman struggling along the beach Angie recognized the set in her features for what it was—grit against pain, against showing vulnerability. The woman had pride. Oddly, this warmed Angie to the retired justice. It gave her a peek into the woman's psyche, and Angie understood something about pain and pride. And fear of displaying her vulnerabilities.

"Angie," she reminded the judge as she stepped forward and held out her hand. "Angie Pallorino. Not Angela."

"Yes, of course." The judge shook Angie's hand with a man's grip. Her eyes bored into Angie's. "Very good to meet you. I've seen you look worse, on television and in the papers. Sit. Gudrun is bringing tea, unless you want coffee."

"Whatever you're having."

"Tea." The judge winced as she lowered herself into a chair diagonally across from Angie's seat, a glass coffee table between them. Gudrun appeared and set a tray on the table. The housekeeper poured tea into china cups with saucers, and she offered around a plate of gingersnaps. Victoria was like that—the legacy of British colonial tradition lingered. High tea at the Empress Hotel on the harbor had become a draw for US tourists, as had the *olde sweet shoppes* and other Brit idiosyncrasies in the historical quarter of the city. Gudrun then fetched a leather file box from a cabinet across the living room. She placed the box on the floor at the judge's side.

Raising her cup to her lips with a slightly trembling hand, the judge sipped and eyed Gudrun until the woman exited the room. Then she said, "I'll come straight to the point. I want to hire you for a cold case. An old one."

"Well, as I mentioned on the phone, I'm no longer taking cases."

"Yet you are here."

Angie readjusted her position on the sofa. "I'll admit, I'm curious."

The judge gave a small smile. "Which opens a window. All I have to do now is twist your arm and get you through that window."

Angie opened her mouth, but the judge shook her head. "No. Wait. Hear me out. Twenty-four years ago my granddaughter, Jasmine Gulati, went on an all-female angling trip. The group consisted of nine women and their two male guides. Jasmine was twenty-five at the time, a UVic master's student, English literature. Expert angler—learned from her dad, my son-in-law."

She leaned forward and set her cup and saucer on the table with a wobble and chinking of china. "The trip was organized by a woman named Rachel Hart. Rachel is a fly-fisher and filmmaker who was making a documentary of the trip. It was tentatively titled *Women in the Stream*. The project was being sponsored by *OutsideLife* magazine and by Kinabulu, which is an outdoor apparel enterprise catering to enthusiasts of the 'silent sports.'" The judge made air quotes. "Sports like climbing, trail running, fishing, surfing, skiing. My Jasmine vanished on that trip." She paused, holding Angie's eyes.

"Jasmine was last seen washing over Plunge Falls on the Nahamish River on the second-to-last day of the trip. She'd been fishing alone in a small bay just upstream of the falls. It was presumed that she slipped on slick rocks and fell into the river. Her body was never found."

A chill rippled over Angie's skin. "The *Nahamish*?" she said.

The judge angled her head, assessing Angie. "I saw you on the news," she said. "That shallow grave, those human remains, it's my Jasmine."

Angie leaned forward sharply. She placed her cup and saucer on the table. "The skeletal remains have been positively identified?"

"DNA, dental records, and jewelry have confirmed that the body in the grove is that of my missing granddaughter. I got the call from the coroner's service yesterday morning." The judge paused, continuing to watch her. Angie felt as though she was being played on some level.

"So . . . you saw me on the news and decided to call me?"

"Things happen for a reason, Angela. I firmly believe this. And one needs to seize the opportunities where they present. You found her. You're an investigator—you presented to me."

"I didn't find her."

The judge dismissed the comment with a flutter of her hand. "I know, I know. But you *were* there, on that very same river as my Jasmine. You stayed in the same lodge where she and those eight other women stayed. You camped along the same beaches. You were right there on the water at the exact time the mushroom picker's dog unearthed Jasmine's grave after all these years. He called for help, and *you* responded. You saw her lying there, her bones. You saw her with your own two eyes." She stopped as if to gather her breath or possibly to marshal emotion.

"The way I see it, you have a personal connection now to my Jasmine. I also know something about your background from the news, Angela."

"Angie," she said quietly.

"Yes, of course. Angie. From what I have learned on the news about your past, I think you are very well equipped to answer some questions about what really happened to Jasmine on that river twenty-four years ago."

Angie stared at the woman, a sense of unease and disbelief deepening inside her.

"What do you know about my past?"

"I watch television news and read the papers religiously. I've been intrigued by your angel's cradle story and the Baptist killing. I know you investigated your own cold case. I know how you discovered who your biological father is. I await his trial with interest, and I have preordered Dr. Grablowski's unauthorized biography on you." She bent forward. "All of that"—she motioned her hand to the windows as if to indicate a wealth of information lying out somewhere over the ocean—"tells me one thing. You are stubborn. When you want something, you go after it irrespective of personal cost. You don't give up in the face of roadblocks." She fell silent, held Angie's gaze. "I like you."

Angie blinked.

"You're a pit bull. I like pit bulls."

Angie cleared her throat. "You say your granddaughter was—"

"Jasmine. Her name is Jasmine. Let's call her by her name."

"You say that Jasmine was last seen washing over Plunge Falls, that she might have slipped into the river?"

"Yes."

"So she was presumed drowned?"

"Yes."

"Then what questions do you have about what happened twenty-four years ago?" Angie immediately had a question of her own—if the judge's granddaughter had gone over Plunge Falls, why were her remains found in a grove almost two hundred meters away from the river?

Justice Monaghan picked up a gingersnap and bit into it. She chewed carefully, swallowed, and wiped her mouth with a napkin. "Let me show you something." She reached down into the leather-sided file box beside her chair and pulled out a file followed by a framed photograph. She set the file on the table and held the frame out to Angie.

Angie reached for it. The photo was a close-up of an attractive young woman. Dusky skin. Liquid black eyes fringed with dense lashes. A broad smile with all the white wattage of a toothpaste advertisement. Dark hair tumbled about slender shoulders. She wore waders and a fly-fishing vest, and she held a fly rod.

"See that bracelet?" the judge said.

Angie peered closer, and her pulse quickened as she recalled the blackened, dirt-encrusted, metal-looking cuff that had been lying next to the long gnawed bone.

"This is what it looks like cleaned up." From the file folder on the table, the judge extracted a photo. She slid it across the glass surface toward Angie. "I gave Jasmine that silver cuff. I bought it on a trip to Egypt. It fitted nice and snugly with a solid clasp, which is why it probably stayed on her wrist when she went over the falls. That cuff was found with her body. It was our first clue it could be Jasmine. This was also in her grave." The judge slid another photo over to Angie. "That ring. It was still on her ring finger or, rather, the bone that was her ring finger."

Angie studied the image. "Engagement ring?" she said. Her skin went hot suddenly as she recalled her own diamond on the chain. She'd removed the chain and ring before her Muay Thai session. She'd secreted the jewelry in the glove compartment of her car and forgotten she'd done so. Angie made a quick mental note to check it was still there when she got back into her vehicle.

"That's one of my questions."

Angie looked up, distracted. "What is?"

"Is that an engagement ring? The coroner's service still has possession of the ring, along with the cuff bracelet. They haven't yet released Jaz's remains or finalized their official report. But I still have connections, and I managed to obtain a copy of the pathologist's preliminary postmortem findings." The judge pointed at the photo in Angie's hand. "Those diamonds are real. High-end. It's a very expensive ring. I'd like to know where Jasmine got it—who might have given it to her. Or whether she bought it for herself."

"Was she involved with anyone at the time of her accident?"

"Not to her parents' knowledge nor mine. None of her friends mentioned a significant other from what I know. And no one came forward when she went missing."

"So maybe she did buy it herself."

"Then I want to know that. That's my first question. My second is, where is her journal? Jasmine was a compulsive recorder of events, a born storyteller. She'd been keeping journals since she was nine years old. She has one in her hand in this photo here." The judge dug into her file box and found another picture, which she held out to Angie.

"This is the group of them together at the campsite on the second evening of their trip."

Angie studied the image. Jasmine Gulati sat on a log. She was laughing, her eyes sparkling. In her hand was a purple book. Standing behind her and seated alongside her on the log were eight females who varied significantly in age. The youngest looked as though she was barely a teenager. The oldest Angie guessed to be in her seventies. The group was flanked by two males. One of the men was tall and slender with sandy hair. The other was slightly shorter and built like wrestler. He sported

81

a shock of thick black hair and a trimmed black beard. Blue eyes. Blue like cornflowers, and piercing. He looked eerily familiar. "Is . . . is this a young Garrison Tollet?" Angie said, pointing to the dark-haired man.

"That was the guide's name, yes."

"He owns and runs Predator Lodge now," Angie said. "It was his daughter, Claire, who guided our boat."

The judge held Angie's gaze. Quietly, she said, "See? You are the right choice for this."

"Who's the other guide?"

"Jessie Carmanagh."

"Carmanagh? Our other guide was a Hugh Carmanagh. Is he related?"

"I have no idea."

"There's a Carmanagh Lake up near the lodge. I was told it was named after a family that settled the area a long time ago. Who took this group shot?"

"Garrison Tollet's wife, I believe."

"She was on the trip, too?"

"No, just brought some supplies to one or two of their camps."

Angie set the photos back on the table. "You want to know where Jasmine's ring came from and where her journal went?"

"Yes. I have an inventory of her belongings that were returned to her parents. There is no journal listed. I believe Jasmine was hiding something. I think there was indeed a special man in her life. I want to know why he never showed his face when she went missing. I want to know exactly what was happening in her life during the months leading up to her drowning. And I want to know exactly how she came to go over those falls."

Angie regarded the judge. Rain gusted against the large windows, sending watery spatters across the panes.

"You don't think it was an accident."

"I don't."

"You know, sometimes it's hard to accept the news when it finally comes. Sometimes people need to find someone to blame—"

"No." The judge leaned in, eyes turning hot and beady like an eagle. "This is *not* like that. When I learned it was Jasmine in that shallow grave, I got out this file box, and I went through the contents. I had not done this before. That box came to me after the death of Jasmine's parents. My daughter and son-in-law died in a car accident seven years ago, and by the time the box came to me, Jasmine had been gone for almost two decades, so I didn't give it much thought until I saw the news and the coroner's service confirmed for me that it was my grand-daughter who'd been found. In this box are copies of the original police interviews with witnesses from the river trip, plus the search and rescue report on the search for Jasmine's body and some photos of the group. Going through it all now, something just doesn't *feel* right to me."

"Feel?"

"Oh, don't tell me you've never acted on gut feelings or followed hunches as a detective, Angie. Do not deny to me that the best investigators out there develop a sixth sense that tells them when something is off or when someone is hiding something. Even if I am wrong, I'm Jasmine's only remaining kin. Her going missing near killed my daughter and her marriage. I just want some answers before I lay my grand-child's remains properly, and finally, to rest." She paused, catching her breath. "As long as you do your best to paint me a picture of Jasmine Gulati's life and her acquaintances in the months leading up to her death, as long as you interview whoever was connected to that trip who is still alive, as long as you try your level best to find that journal and discover who her secret fiancé might have been, this is what I will pay." She scribbled some numbers onto a piece of paper, folded the paper in half, and shunted it across the table along with a signed check.

Angie picked up the piece of paper. As she unfolded it, the judge said, "The first figure is an advance—a retainer. The second figure is what I will pay per hour before expenses if I am satisfied with your progress. The third figure is the bonus if I'm satisfied with the results."

Angie dropped her gaze to the numbers the judge had scrawled, and then she glanced at the check. She had to focus on not blinking or catching her breath.

"This would be taking advantage of you," Angie said, carefully refolding the paper.

The justice held up both hands as Angie tried to give it back. "No. It's me who is taking advantage of your expertise and your time. I can afford to. Indulge me, Angela. Indulge an old woman with some answers before she dies."

"I can't. By law you cannot hire me to work directly for you. I really am sorry."

"Just take it, take this box, take the reports, take the retainer check. Find a way." She creaked to her feet, wincing as she pressed her hand to her back.

"Did it ever air?" Angie said.

"What?"

"The documentary."

"What documentary?"

"*Women in the Stream*, the film Rachel Hart was making on the river."

The justice looked confused suddenly. Then her eyes showed panic. "Gudrun! Where are you?"

The housekeeper came bustling in.

"Show . . . uh . . . Ms. Pallor . . . Palloridio the way out. Make sure she takes that . . . that box with her." The judge shuffled hurriedly toward a door that led off the living room. "If you have questions, Angela, give me a call." She began to sing as she reached the door, her words soft at first, then rising in strident tenor. Her voice was remarkable. Stunned, Angie stared at the judge's back. She recognized the tune—a song about being in the arms of an angel and finding comfort there.

Angie stared after the judge as she disappeared through the door.

Gudrun said, "A song for an angel's cradle child."

Angie faced the housekeeper, confused.

"She's losing her mind," Gudrun said. "When she gets tired, her memory suddenly goes. It's a terrible thing for a woman with a formidable intellect to lose. She's bored. She has the money to pay you. You should do this for her."

"So I'm to be paid entertainment?"

"There are worse things to be." The woman paused. "Like unemployed."

She'd been listening at the door.

Gudrun replaced the photos and files in the box and picked it up. "Come, I'll show you out." She carried the box as she escorted Angie back to the front door.

In the mudroom, as Angie shrugged into her coat, Gudrun said, "Rachel Hart, the filmmaker, is still alive, if you're interested. She's in her seventies, lives in Metchosin now. There's a list of everyone who was on the trip in the original SAR and coroner's reports from twenty-four years ago. And no, the documentary never aired. The sponsors killed the film after the tragedy. Just take a look at it." She held the box out to Angie. "Please."

Inside her car, engine running, heater on full blast to clear the fogged windows, Angie rummaged quickly in the glove compartment. Relief sliced through her as she found her engagement ring where she'd secreted it. Angie stared at the ring, thinking of Maddocks, of their last phone call. Anxiety twisted in her stomach.

She fastened the chain and ring around her neck and hesitated, her hand wrapped around the ring. She wanted to call him. Yet she didn't want to call him.

Reaching forward, she put her Mini Cooper in gear. She'd wait until he returned from his trip. It would give them both a bit of a breather. It would give her time to decide what to do about the bodyguard job offer. Because she really couldn't even begin to consider taking the old judge's money.

For one, it would not be legal, and she could jeopardize any chance of ever being able to open her own PI firm. For another, Angie had pride—she was a good investigator, not hired entertainment. For another, taking money from an old woman going senile was a kind of abuse.

But as Angie drove through the gates of the Monaghan residence, she cast a fast glance at the leather-sided file box on the passenger seat.

Maybe she'd take a quick look at the files when she got home. If anything, it would keep her mind off her own problems on a Saturday night alone in her apartment.

CHAPTER 12

The makeshift whiteboard Angie had glued to a wall in her apartment to investigate her own cold case was still in place, her computer and printer still neatly positioned to the side of it. And as she laid out the contents of Justice Jilly Monaghan's box on her dining room table, the act of embarking on a fresh investigation felt comforting and familiar. An escape.

In the box was the initial coroner's report into the investigation of Jasmine Gulati's disappearance twenty-four years ago. Also in the box was the Port Ferris police report complete with witness interviews and a SAR manager's report on the search for Jasmine's body.

Angie set these reports to one side and took out a pile of photos. She sorted through them, spreading them out on the table. Several were close-ups of Jasmine Gulati, clearly a striking young woman. With a surname like Gulati, Angie surmised that Jasmine's father—the judge's son-in-law—had been of South Asian heritage.

Among the photos were several group shots of the nine women on the river. One had been taken outside a wood-sided building, where the women stood laughing beneath a sign that read HOOK AND GAFFE PUB. One the back of this photo was an inscription that read: *Day One. Port Ferris. The Gathering.*

The trip participants were listed as *Rachel Hart, Eden Hart, Trish Shattuck, Willow McDonnell, Jasmine Gulati, Irene Mallard, Donna Gill, Kathi Daly, Hannah Vogel.*

Angie flipped the photo around again and studied the faces, wondering if the teenager pictured with the group was Eden Hart and if Eden was Rachel Hart's daughter. A few more photos included the male guides, Garrison Tollet and Jessie Carmanagh.

The last photo in the bunch showed Jasmine with two women of similar age. This one had not been taken on the river trip. It had been shot on a sunny beach, and all wore bikinis. The two young women with Jasmine were not among those pictured on the Nahamish River trip, either. Angie flipped the photo over. On the back was written: *The three amigas—Jasmine Gulati, Mia Smith, Sophie Sinovich—Hornby Island, Summer 1993.*

Angie glanced at her watch, surprised at the time. And relieved. This case was providing a desperately needed distraction for her. She was pleasantly famished. She set the photos down and went into her kitchen, where she put some Italian leftovers from Mario's in the microwave.

While her food warmed, she opened a bottle of merlot that Maddocks had left in her apartment. She turned up the gas fire, and when her food was ready, she took her meal and wine along with the SAR and coroner's reports and settled on her sofa. She read the reports as she forked pasta into her mouth and sipped the wine. Wind whistled around her balcony balustrade outside, and foghorns sounded out at sea, but inside she finally felt warm.

According to statements made to the Port Ferris RCMP, the group of nine women and their two guides had brought their boats ashore near a campsite above Plunge Falls on what was to be their second-to-last night on the river. It was the same camp where she and Maddocks had overnighted before portaging around the falls to fish downstream in the Nahamish Flats, where Budge Hargreaves had called them from the bank.

According to the statements, Jasmine Gulati had told the group she'd seen a hatch and fish rising in the eddy of a small bay just downriver from the camp. She said she was going to try a few last casts before nightfall. Jasmine then left the campsite with her fishing gear. Tollet and Carmanagh built a fire. The other women settled in with drinks, and the two guides then left to gather more firewood for the night.

A short while later, Garrison Tollet had been collecting wood above a talus scree when he saw a woman he believed was Jasmine thrashing about in the river and then going over the falls.

Jessie Carmanagh had been lower down on the slope. His view of the river obscured by trees, he'd had no visual of the falls. Garrison Tollet had screamed for Jessie Carmanagh to radio for help. Jessie Carmanagh ran back to camp for his radio while Garrison Tollet clambered down the scree and descended a treacherous cliff alongside the falls to see if he could find Gulati at the bottom of the waterfall.

Carmanagh radioed for help from the camp. By the time RCMP and search and rescue volunteers had arrived, it was dark. A night search using hunting spotlights was conducted along the banks below the falls. The search intensified at first light. SAR dog teams were brought in to assist. Gulati's fishing vest and a small silver box containing her flies were found downstream of the plunge pools at the base of the falls. But nothing else.

Eventually what had been a search and rescue mission shifted into a search and recovery effort. Nothing more of Gulati was ever found.

When the winter had come and gone, and the snows had finally melted and the river was low again the following year, another recovery mission was attempted. It yielded nothing. Efforts were called off. The coroner's service ruled that Jasmine Gulati was likely deceased from accidental drowning.

The coroner's report noted that over a period of fifteen years prior to Jasmine Gulati's accident, there had been five deaths at Plunge Falls. Two were classified as accidents, three as possible suicides. It appeared

Plunge Falls had been something of a go-to for killing oneself. In three of those cases, the bodies were never found. The water pressure below the falls was described as intense, and there were underwater caverns at the base of the falls that divers were unable to safely access.

Jasmine Gulati's fly rod had been located on an extremely slippery section of the rocky bank where she said she'd been going to fish. There were marks in the slimy moss near the water's edge where her wading boots appeared to have slipped.

Angie reached for her glass of wine and sipped. This was clearly believed to have been a simple but unfortunate accident where Gulati had fallen into the river. She'd been wearing waders, which would have quickly filled with water. The river was also extremely cold—fed by the glacial waters of Carmanagh Lake—and the currents swift in sections. Even a good swimmer would have been dragged over the falls in those circumstances.

Jasmine's body had probably been trapped by water pressure deep below the falls or hooked and held beneath rocks in icy temperatures for years. So why had she popped out and ended up buried beneath a shallow layer of soil almost two hundred meters away from the riverbank?

Angie set down her wine and reached for the current pathologist findings on the remains from the shallow grave.

Everything from the grave site had been first carefully documented in situ, and then the remains had been excavated and taken to a morgue. The body was skeletonized, so the autopsy was more of an anthropological exam with both the pathologist and anthropologist present.

Clothing and other items found with the remains had been documented, including the ring and the cuff bracelet, which had been photographed before being cleaned up and photographed again afterward.

The ring was described as white gold with a princess-cut diamond set among a halo of smaller diamonds. Angie peered more closely at the image of the cleaned ring. The design was definitely that of a classic engagement piece, although it might have been nothing of the sort. It had, however, been found on the left ring finger of the skeleton. Angie reflexively fingered her own engagement ring on the chain around her neck.

The silver cuff bore an Egyptian insignia, which fitted with Jilly Monaghan's claim she'd bought the bracelet for her granddaughter in Egypt.

The only clothing found on the body that had not biodegraded in what appeared to be highly acidic soil was a pair of chest-high booted neoprene waders. The brand was Kinabulu. It was noted in the report that Kinabulu was a sponsor of the trip and that the outdoor clothing company had provided all the participants and guides with complimentary gear, including wool hats, waders, fleece vests, and jackets.

Angie turned the page and read further. According to the report, the waders were made of neoprene—or polychloroprene—a synthetic rubber produced through the polymerization of chloroprene. The material exhibited good chemical stability and maintained flexibility over a wide temperature range. The waders were five millimeters in thickness, and the attached boots were a composition of rubber and Gore-Tex. The report noted that both neoprene and Gore-Tex were nonbiodegradable.

Angie studied the image of the rubber boot soles. Good, deep tread. But they had not stopped Jasmine from slipping off the slick rocks along the water's edge.

She turned to the image of the skeleton laid out on the examination table in an anatomical position. All bones were accounted for. Nonhuman bones that had been found with the body, including those of small rodents, had been segregated. Skeletal abnormalities listed included a spiral fracture of the left arm, typical of wrenching force. There was no sign of healing, which indicated the fracture had occurred perimortem—at or around the time of death. This could have happened when Jasmine Gulati went over the falls.

Radiographs also showed shallow depressions on the dorsal surface of the pubic bones near the symphyseal border. Angie leaned forward with interest as she read the anthropologist's description:

While the presence of these dorsal pits is strongly suggestive of a full-term pregnancy, the number and size of pits is only weakly correlated with pregnancies. Current research has shown these pits do occur in males and in females known to have never given birth.

Angie chewed the inside of her cheek, thinking. Justice Monaghan had said she was Jasmine's only remaining next of kin. If Jasmine had had a child, where was it? Angie reached for her notepad and jotted a note down:

Had Jasmine given birth? If so, what happened to the baby?

She returned her attention to the report. The anthropologist had documented another skeletal anomaly—scarring at the left shoulder joint that was reportedly consistent with a chronic dislocation of the shoulder. Angie frowned. A dislocated shoulder that had not been properly slotted back into place would have been extremely painful, surely? Or at the least, it would have been uncomfortable. It seemed strange that someone of Jasmine Gulati's socioeconomic demographic would not have received immediate and effective medical treatment.

Angie wrote in her notebook:

Had Jasmine ever dislocated a shoulder for which she was not properly treated? Possibly as a child?

She turned the page and studied the images of the fractured skull.

The blunt-force trauma was clearly evident—a hole the size of a golf ball with concentric and starburst cracks radiating out from it. According to the report, although the outer table of the skull was broken, a portion of the inner table was bent inward in a greenstick effect. Angie had seen something similar in a homicide case where the victim had been struck and killed with a hammer.

According to the anthropologist, this skull trauma was perimortem and a possible cause of death. Unless the victim drowned first, thought

Angie. Or simultaneously, as might happen if the decedent was thrust headfirst over a waterfall and the force of the water had smashed her skull into a sharp rock.

She reached for her glass, leaned back, and sipped absently as she ran a hypothetical scenario through her mind: Jasmine casting her line as she stands in her waders too close against the water's edge. Jasmine overreaching perhaps, the imbalance causing her boots to slip on those rocks. She drops her rod, her boots scraping through the slimy moss as she goes down. Once she falls into the river, her waders fill quickly with cold water and drag her down, where the current snatches her and carries her faster and faster toward the booming falls. She perhaps goes over headfirst, smashing her skull into rocks on the way down, her body twisting through rocks and her arm wrenching. She's then submerged by the sheer volume of water powering over the falls, possibly trapping her in an underwater cavity for years until water volume and pressure and currents suddenly change enough to release her back to the river and she washes into the flat delta area.

But again, how had her body ended up two hundred meters from the shore?

Flipping through the rest of the coroner's preliminary report, Angie found the answer. There had been two significant flooding events over the past quarter century that had caused the Nahamish to break its banks in the flat delta area below the falls. The water had spread over a distance of more than two hundred meters through the forest along the south shore. That could explain it. A flooding event could have switched up currents and flow pressure enough to release Jasmine Gulati's remains from where she'd been trapped underwater. The flood surge could have floated her into the trees. When the water receded, she'd have been deposited there, possibly in a layer of muck over which moss and other vegetation had grown over the years.

Angie picked up a photo of Jasmine, the diamond cluster clearly visible on her left hand. Had no one on the river trip asked her about it? What about those two friends in bikinis? If so, what had she told them? Angie reached for the photo of Jasmine with Mia Smith and Sophie Sinovich on Hornby Island. She studied it closely. Jasmine was not wearing the ring in this photo, which had been taken the previous summer. How recently had she acquired it?

Angie finished the last of her wine and got up from the sofa, chastising herself. Because here she was already trying to answer Justice Monaghan's questions. But she could *not* take this case.

Not legally, not if she ever wanted to reach her big dream of getting a full license and opening her own boutique investigations agency.

She rinsed her glass, set it in the rack to dry, and then went back to the table and picked up the retainer check. Twenty-five thousand dollars, nonrefundable, simply for agreeing to investigate. On top of that, the judge was offering three hundred dollars per hour plus expenses and a bonus bigger than the advance upon satisfactory completion. It was ridiculous. Just for finding out where that ring came from? Whether a man gave it to her? What Jasmine Gulati's life was like in the months prior to her death? Simply because a retired justice who was going senile had a *feeling* something was wrong?

She flicked the check back onto the table. Justice Monaghan was in denial. Angie had seen this kind of behavior among relatives of crime victims. They wanted to *do* something, to feel they were taking control. They wanted to apportion blame. They wanted revenge. If they were wealthy, they always thought they could throw money at the problem.

Her cell rang, and Angie started. She grabbed it off the table and felt a clutch in her chest as she saw it was Maddocks calling. She hesitated, thinking of their last stilted conversation, then engaged the call.

"Hey," she said.

"You all right?" His voice was cool, distant, as if he was making an obligatory call to check in on her mental well-being.

Angie inhaled. "Yeah, I'm fine, thanks. You all done with Flint? You guys have a good evening?"

"Yeah. Was good. Caught up on some iMIT stuff. How'd it go with your appointment—that woman with the PI job you mentioned?"

He was fishing. "I don't think it's anything that will pan out," Angie said, purposefully remaining vague. She wasn't ready for a lecture over having brought Jilly Monaghan's box of files and photos home.

"You busy now?"

"Now? Why?"

"I thought it might be too late to come over and see you, but then I drove past, saw your lights on."

"Where are you?"

"Outside. In my car."

She hurried to the window, moved the blinds aside. She couldn't make out his vehicle in the parking lot below. It was dark. Rain smeared the lights. Black water glinted in the adjacent Gorge.

"Can I come up?" he said.

Her stomach fisted with sudden tension, and her heart started to beat fast. She shot a glance at the files and photos littering her tables. She didn't want him to see them—didn't want to have to explain, hear his questions, listen to his admonishments, which she knew would come, albeit cloaked in well-meaning advice. She checked her watch. It *was* late—11:45 p.m. She'd lost track of time. Blissfully so. In immersing herself in the Jasmine Gulati files, she'd had some respite from her own screwed-up life. It struck her suddenly—a bolt from the blue—an idea.

She knew how she could do it, how to take the Gulati case legally. But she needed to get up early, and in order to swing it she needed to be in top form.

"Maybe it's not a good idea, Maddocks. I . . . it is late. And—"

"And I'm on a plane tomorrow morning."

"I know. I—" She dragged her hand over her hair, conflict ratcheting tighter inside her chest. "I'll see you when you get back." By then she might have her plan in action. She'd be on a really solid footing. She'd be able to think forward, think about planning her life with him.

A beat of silence. Rain ticked against the windows.

"What are you thinking about that close-protection job?"

"I . . . I'm just considering options right now."

"Fuck it, Angie," he whispered. Another soft curse. "Is this what you want? D'you want to take a break? From us, from our relationship? Because it sure as hell sounds like it."

"No, of course not. It's—"

"I think it is. I think you were getting cold feet before we even went on the Nahamish trip. Or claustrophobia or commitment phobia or whatever it was that you were getting, and then I went and mentioned kids, and on top of that I gave you the ring and pressured you for a wedding date and spoke about moving in together . . . It spooked you, didn't it? It scared the stuffing right out you, and now you need to think about it all because you don't know if you can spend the rest of your life with me."

"Maddocks—"

"Christ, Angie, I'm not a fool. Give me some respect, here. This is not about your employment opportunities; this is about us."

"Listen, come on up. We'll talk. I'll buzz the parking gate open—"

"No. Forget it. Have your break."

"Wait, Maddocks, I—"

"Maybe I really need one, too. I don't want a one-sided relationship. I don't want to be the one doing all the pushing." His voice grew husky, then hitched. The sound of his emotion gutted her. She began to shake.

"Please, Maddocks, don't do this now."

"Now? Angie, I've been trying to talk to you for the last four weeks, ever since the fishing trip."

"It's the job hunt. It's—"

"It's that you need time. I know, you've been telling me for weeks. You need time to think it all through. Well, take your time, Ange. Get your space, whatever in the hell you want. Take the bodyguard job. Fill your boots. Sow your oats. I'm done trying to prop you up and support you and tiptoe around your emotions without getting anything back. I know you've had a ton to deal with, and PTSD doesn't just go away, but I want your *love*. I want it honest and full, and I want acknowledgment that you know I'm there for you, that you *trust* me. Maybe I just have to face the fact you don't love me back. Maybe I just need to face the fact you're not into the same dreams as I am. Maybe you don't need what I need."

"Maddocks, please—"

"No, don't talk. I'm done talking. You figure it out. Just know one thing, Angie—I love you. If you want to stay engaged, if you want what I want, to get married—I'm here. I'm yours. But it's your call. You pick up that phone only if and when you're good and ready. Until you make that call, we're over." Her phone went dead.

Angie stared at her phone and realized her hands were trembling.

She'd done it. She'd pushed the man she loved too far. Deep down she knew she'd been doing it. She'd seen this coming, and she'd not been able to stop herself from sliding. Perhaps she'd even wanted it.

But now he'd drawn the line.

He'd lobbed the ball squarely into her court. If they were going to get married, she had to be fully on board. *She* had to make that move. Angie had to respect him for that. Maddocks was not some mat to be walked over. Right at this moment, she hated herself for even having tried to take for granted that he'd always be there for her.

He knew her well. Too well. Well enough to know this was what she needed if they were ever going to make a relationship work.

CHAPTER 13

SUNDAY, NOVEMBER 18

"Who the *fuck* let you in here?" Jock Brixton's face turned florid as he stood rooted to the spot in his doorway at the sight of Angie awaiting him in his office.

Angie surged to her feet. She'd been waiting for Brixton since 8:00 a.m. She knew he liked to come into his office and work quietly, catch up on admin on Sunday mornings, and that there would be a skeleton staff along with someone to admit her. "One of your staff let me in," she said.

"I thought I told you we were done here." He strode to his desk and depressed the buzzer on his phone. "Debbie! Get security. I want this woman out. Now."

"Wait," Angie said, raising her hands, palms out. "Please, just wait. I have a proposition."

"Jeezus, Pallorino, you have effing balls coming in here like this, I'll hand you that, but—"

Two burly security guys appeared in the doorway. "Sir, you called?"

"Get this woman outta here." Brixton rounded his desk and dumped his briefcase on top. "She's trespassing."

"Hold it," Angie instructed the guards. "Jock, you're gonna want to hear this."

The guards moved in and took her by the arms. Brixton opened the Tim Hortons bag he'd brought with him and took out his breakfast sandwich. He set it on his desk, ignoring her.

"Just hear me out, and then I'm gone. I swear."

"You've done your begging. I'm done listening. I've already had a nervy, media-shy, and extremely wealthy client back out of a contract because of all the publicity you and that damn body in the moss have gone and heaped all over CI. Frankly, I'd like to kill you, Pallorino. I can't even begin to tell you."

"See that?" She jerked her chin to the check she'd set on his desk. "It's a retainer. There's a fee of three hundred dollars per hour coming on top of that. Plus a bonus. Plus expenses. All yours, apart from fifty percent of the bonus, which goes to me if the client is satisfied."

He looked down. Confusion chased across his broad features as he read the amount on the check. "What client? What is this?"

"It's yours—it all goes to Coastal Investigations if you allow me to take this case under your agency umbrella. Client wants me specifically, no one else."

"What in the hell are you talking about?"

"Call your guards off me, and I'll explain."

He jerked his head to the door. "Let her go. Give us a minute. Wait outside and shut the door."

Angie waited until the security guys had departed Brixton's office. Once they were alone, she said, "I've been offered a case. High-profile client. Like I said, the money is all yours, minus expenses and part of the bonus. But only if you hire me back purely on a contract-by-contract basis."

"Three hundred per *hour*?"

"Yup."

He snatched the check off his desk. "And this retainer is against the hourly fee?"

"On top of."

"Who's the client?"

"Connected in the right places. If we do good by this client, the client will recommend us. There'll be more work like this coming in."

"Us? There's no freaking *us*, Pallorino."

"Fine." She reached across his desk for the check in his hand. But he snatched it out of her reach.

"What kind of case?" he said. "Is this going to get us in more trouble?"

"Cold case. Old one. Nothing suspicious so far as I can see. Client just wants information about the victim leading up to an accidental death. Victim is a family member. It's a personal, closure thing."

He looked dubious. He rubbed his chin hard, then flicked a glance at the window as if seeking a way out while still hanging on to that fee. He inhaled deeply.

"I'll tell you something else, Jock. My exposure in the media, my notoriety, is *exactly* what brought me this case." Angie slowly took a seat, expanding her presence in his office, taking up his space, projecting confidence, a relaxed demeanor. She felt anything but. It had an instant calming effect on Brixton. She'd learned how to work him.

"Meaning?"

"Some people are actually pleased I took a serial killer off the streets. They sympathize with my history. They can see I got a raw deal as a kid and that I fought against it every step of the way to become a cop and fight for justice. Thanks to the media coverage, they're aware of the dogged way in which I worked my own cold case. And they see all of this as a plus for a private investigator. They want me to do the same for them and for their loved ones." She bent forward. "See? My notoriety—my so-called abrasive pit-bull personality—can actually *bring* you contracts. Certain kinds of contracts. You could benefit from keeping me on the side. If you do hire me back, I will not have CI on my business cards. I will not even mention Coastal Investigations. I will just be your quiet Pallorino Special Investigations arm. No commitment on your end other than allowing me to work on your firm's books and giving me access to the CI databases and tech support staff."

"You just want CI as an umbrella under which you can earn your under-supervision hours."

"Yes. So? You get the bulk of my fee for it."

"And then when you've banked all the requisite hours, you'll walk. After using our name."

"No, Jock, you're not hearing me. I won't use your name. It'll be my own name. New business cards. I just work through your infrastructure. Sure, if CI wants to throw additional cases my way, we can discuss." She leaned back. "Why are you even worried about me walking? You wanted me out, remember. Now you want to *tie me down*?"

He scratched the back of his neck. "Let me think about it, okay?"

"Nope." She started to rise from the chair. "There are other firms who'll be interested in this kind of deal with me. Client wants me on this right away."

Justice Monaghan had opened Angie's eyes to a hot possibility—where her notoriety, her past, could be a commodity and not a millstone.

"Okay, okay. Just . . . sit."

She reseated herself. Waited.

He looked once more at the check. "Okay," he said. He met her eyes. "We have a deal."

"Good. I won't need office space or anything, but like I said, I'll need to avail myself of some of your systems and personnel for vehicle registration searches, criminal record and background checks, that sort of thing."

She reached into the inside pocket of her jacket and extracted a document she'd prepared during the night. A sleepless night after the call from Maddocks. But this was Angie's way forward, her only way of coping right now. She would focus on the Jasmine Gulati case. Sure, she might be providing Justice Monaghan with a diversion, a form of entertainment in her twilight years, but Justice Monaghan was providing Angie a similar service in return—distraction from her own problems. Plus a path toward her goal of opening her own firm. Which in turn was a path back to Maddocks. It made Angie feel better about taking the judge's money.

"So who is the client?" Brixton said. "What's the job?"

Angie unfolded the document and slid the sheaf of papers over his desk toward him. "First, the contract. We need to sign it."

His eyes narrowed. "I'll need our lawyer to—"

"No, Jock. No time. It's simple. I work for CI on this case. I call all the shots on this case. The fee goes to Coastal, minus expenses, which I expect will be minimal. And minus fifty percent of the bonus if I earn it. At no time do I use your company name. Whether or not you want to mention my name or offer my individualized services to your clients—that's up to you. This contract is solely in connection with this one job. We can go case by case in the future if you like. Or if this arrangement ends up meeting your satisfaction, we can write up something longer term."

He inhaled deeply, then pulled out his chair and took a seat. He dragged the document over to his side of the desk. The old clock on his filing cabinet ticked as he read the contract draft carefully. Rain fell outside, and a siren sounded in the distance.

He reached for his pen, signed his name next to Angie's.

"And sign the copy underneath, one copy each."

He signed the duplicate, looked up. "So who's the client?"

"Retired justice Jilly Monaghan."

"Senator Blackford's widow?" he said, a dark gleam beginning to light his eyes.

"Yes. The human remains discovered along the Nahamish River have been identified as Jasmine Gulati, a UVic master's student presumed drowned in 1994. She was Justice Monaghan's granddaughter. Monaghan wants me to fill in some missing pieces around the final months of Jasmine Gulati's life leading up to the accident."

His gaze dropped to the check. "For *this* kind fee?"

Angie gave a shrug. "She saw me on the news. She knows I was on that same river and that I saw her granddaughter's grave and remains with my own eyes. She's also followed my past in the news. She wanted to make sure she got me. See? My being on the news brought me that case."

He grinned and leaned back in his chair. "I might get to like you yet, Pallorino."

"Feeling's mutual, Jock," she lied with a smile.

"I'll take the case," Angie said into the phone. "At the terms discussed."

"I thought you couldn't. What changed?" Justice Monaghan's voice boomed into Angie's ear. Angie moved her cell farther away from her head to save her eardrums. She'd called the judge from her car outside Brixton's office, wasting no time.

"I got my old job back. I'm working this case in conjunction with Coastal Investigations." She hesitated, then said it anyway. "Your check did the trick. Thank you for that."

"Hah, glad to hear I'm still worth something! I like that you don't mince your words, Angela. That's *exactly* what I want, for you to say it like it is, no matter what you find out about my granddaughter."

Angie let the judge's misuse of her name slide this time, especially after hearing Gudrun's explanation that Jilly Monaghan was losing her memory. "But I've got a few questions before I proceed," she said. "We can do it over the phone if that works?"

"Fire away."

"There's a photograph among the files you gave me. On the back it says, 'The three amigas.' Who—"

"Jasmine's closest friends. Those three were tight. Mia Smith went all the way back to grade three with Jasmine. Sophie Sinovich made a threesome of the group from their first year in junior high. The three attended UVic together."

"Are Sophie Sinovich and Mia Smith still around?"

"I don't know. I haven't thought about them in years."

"So you wouldn't know if they married and whether they're using married names?"

"No."

"What about the other women on the river trip? Anything you can tell me about them or their whereabouts before I start a search?"

"Rachel Hart lives in Metchosin with her husband, Doug. I don't know where their daughter, Eden, is, or where any of the others are now. There was a septuagenarian on the trip. She's probably dead by now."

"So Eden is Rachel Hart's daughter?"

"Yes."

"And to confirm, the documentary was quashed by sponsors and never aired?"

"Correct. My son-in-law, Rahoul Gulati, threatened to sue the sponsors if they aired the footage in any way, which resulted in them spiking the project. Rahoul did not want Rachel Hart or her sponsors sensationalizing Jasmine's death or capitalizing on it. I figure Rachel would've turned it into some adventure drama doc if she'd had half a chance."

"So what happened to the raw unedited footage Rachel Hart shot? Did you ever see any of that?"

"No. Rachel offered to compile a montage of Jasmine's final days along the river for her parents, but my daughter, Kitt, declined. She felt it would be too painful. Kitt had a really rough time of it all."

"How did you come to have such an old granddaughter?" Angie said. "Jasmine was twenty-five years old twenty-four years ago. That would have made you—"

"Kitt was my husband's daughter from his first marriage. I married my husband, Logan Blackford, after he'd been widowed for some time. He was quite a bit older than me. I was thirty-one on my wedding day. Kitt Blackford was twenty-three years old when she technically became my stepdaughter. It was a rocky period for both Kitt and me. But we grew closer over the years. Even more so after Logan died."

"So for the record, Jasmine was not a blood relative of yours."

"She was my granddaughter, blood or no. I doted on her as a baby. She was the child I never had, never could have. I'm the only family Jasmine has left. It falls to me to ensure she's laid properly to rest in memory, with her parents."

"I understand." Angie started her car and put on her windshield wipers as rain came down more heavily. "Two more questions, if you don't mind. To your knowledge did Jasmine ever dislocate her left shoulder?"

"Not to my knowledge. I saw the mention of shoulder scarring in the pathologist's report, and I feel I *would* have known about such an injury if it had been at all serious. The coroner did ask me about it. But no, I cannot recall any shoulder injury."

"Okay, and did Jasmine ever give birth?"

"I also saw the mention about the post parturition scars. No. She'd never given birth."

"Would you have known if she had?"

"Of course. I was close to Kitt. She was close to Jaz. Kitt would have known."

"Would Kitt have told you? Even if it was something Jasmine might have told her mother?"

The judge hesitated. "Possibly not. But you know, I've thought about it, and I can honestly recall no period in Jasmine's life where she looked pregnant or where she disappeared for any great length of time that would have allowed her to have a baby and give it away. But people keep secrets, I know this. I'm also aware from the pathologist's report that post parturition pits are not unequivocal evidence that a woman gave birth. This is in part why I hired you, Angie. I don't know those answers, and I need you to find it all out and tell me."

"And if I find nothing suspicious? If Jasmine was leading an ordinary life and simply had a terrible accident?"

"Then I will know that, too. Then I can bury her feeling I've done right by her."

Angie killed the call, put her head back, and closed her eyes as Maddocks's words from last night looped through her brain yet again.

Just know one thing, Angie—I love you. If you want to stay engaged, if you want what I want, to get married—I'm here. I'm yours. But it's your call. You pick up that phone only if and when you're good and ready. Until you make that call, we're over.

She opened her eyes. This was it. This case, this job—it was her way back to Maddocks. To that dream.

She wanted to marry Sergeant James Maddocks, find a house, and make it warm with a sense of family inside. She wanted to open her own PI agency and run it from the schooner down at the marina, with three-legged Jack-O as the office mascot. She could *see* it, *taste* it. All of it. She was going to hold this vision clear as glass in her mind as she went forward. She was not going to let it drop and shatter. Ever. She'd show him. She'd find a way, find something concrete to prove to him that she wanted the same things he did.

Putting her vehicle into gear, she exited the parking lot.

CHAPTER 14

Kjel Holgersen dumped two more file boxes onto a table in the small incident room. Leo entered the room behind Kjel and hefted his own load onto the table. Swearing, Leo slapped dust off his pants. He'd loosened his tie, and his face was red, beads of perspiration glinting along his upper lip. He smelled like old liquor.

"So you was late at the Pig again yesterday?" Kjel said as he lifted the top off one of the boxes.

"Drowning my sorrows, yeah. Why in the fuck did Maddocks pull me from homicide into iMIT anyways?" Leo flung his arm at the mounting stack of boxes. "Just to stick me in this shithole? These cases are dead, I tell you. Stone-cold dead. While the rest of the team is out there working the hot major incident stuff, we gotta go through *this* crap?" He shoved a metal desk into position under the window as he spoke, bagging the best spot in the room. "Maddocks is fucking getting back at me for talking to Grablowski about Pallorino being the cradle baby. He figures I leaked Pallorino's story and that *I* am responsible for the book Grablowski's written."

"You did leak it," Kjel said.

"Well, I'll tell ya something—I didn't write that goddamn book. That forensic head shrink would've been all over Pallorino's true crime story with or without me. I just facilitated it, sped things up a bit."

"For a fee."

Leo ignored the jab and ambled over to the coffee machine. "Question is, why is Maddocks sidelining *you*, eh, Holgersen? What have *you* done to earn this special treatment from the new boss man, eh?"

Kjel shunted his own metal desk into position against the wall next to the whiteboard. "Because he figures I gots what it takes to boost the entire department's homicide and missing persons solve rates. But hey, if we do score, if we makes some of these cases hot again, we gets more staff, a higher profile. Not a bad gig."

"Dream on, buddy." Leo poured himself a mug of coffee and set it on his desk. He went back to the boxes, took the lid off one, and began rummaging through old homicide files. "Where in the hell do we even start with this shit?"

"Right there. Like you're doing," Kjel said. "We go through each cold case, document it in our new computer system—"

"System's not even up and running yet."

"Will be by the end of today. Techs are due in an hour. Once we've entered a case, we gives it a rating in terms of solvability, public interest, potential to generate new leads via social media, potential to apply new DNA tech, potential links between other old cases, potential witnesses who might still exist and who have decided to talk, and so forth. Then once we's ranked the priority—like applying triage—we starts running the top cases past the crime analyst. We starts feeding those to the soc media unit, and we starts getting DNA and fingerprint evidence into the crime lab queue. When and if we get hits, we run with them hits. When and if we need more staff, we ask. Simple."

Leo snorted and opened a murder book. He scanned the contents. "Well, for starters, we can ditch some of these."

"Some of what?"

"Dead junkies." Leo jabbed his hairy finger on a young woman's mug shot. "Deceased homeless vics like this useless tweaker here. Found overdosed down a bank near the Gorge five years ago."

Kjel went over to look. He read the victim's name. Seema Solomon. Someone's daughter. Maybe a sister. Maybe even a young mother. A human being who'd deserved respect. A human being who'd ended up in a bad place and was now dead. Under suspicious circumstances.

Leo shut the file and put it to one side on the table. He returned to ferreting in the box.

"So what you gonna do with that dead tweaker file, then?" Kjel said.

"Nada. That's going on the dismissal pile."

"Just 'cause the vic was part of a marginalized population?"

Leo stilled and shot Kjel a glance. "You kidding me? Ever since pig farmer Robert Pickton started hunting street workers in Vancouver's Downtown Eastside, now every missing or murdered street person could be a victim of some serial murderer?"

"Don't know until we look."

Leo snorted. "On the one hand you got linkage blindness, but on the other there's overkill, buddy."

Kjel opened another box and took out a file. This one contained details of a missing persons investigation from last December. He flicked through the file contents.

"Hey, this is the Annelise Janssen case," he said. "Remember that student who went missing from the UVic campus last winter?" He peered up from the file. "She's still missing. Her father is that big-shot industrialist. Pots of money." Kjel tapped the file. "This one's high profile and high on the public-interest scale. A pretty young blonde from a good family just vanishes off campus, poof, gone? No one has a clue where she went? If we can solve one or two like this, we gots it made." Kjel ambled over to his new workstation and sat at his desk as he continued to peruse the file.

"Yeah, I remember this one," he said. "I was partnered with Pallorino in sex crimes when a woman's body floated up in the Gorge last winter. Everyone's first thoughts was that the floater was Annelise Janssen. It was the first question reporters asked me and Pallorino." He glanced up. "I reckon this one goes to the top of our pile. I reckon for starters we get this onto the social media desk and put word out again that we's still looking for tips on Janssen."

"It was all over social media last December."

"Yeah, but you knows how it goes. Sometimes peeps is scared to come forward at the time. Then circumstances change in their lives, and they're ready to talk. Or maybe someone never saw those posts last winter." As Kjel returned his attention to the file, out of the corner of his eye he saw Leo snag the tweaker murder book off the table and take it back to his desk.

An odd feeling quirked through Kjel as he thought of Maddocks's words.

Just watch him for me. Watch how he handles and prioritizes cases.

CHAPTER 15

It was almost noon on Monday when Angie knocked on the door of the Hart residence, a rambling estate on the ocean near Metchosin, a semirural area about a half-hour drive from the city. Finding Rachel Hart's address had been easy. The documentary filmmaker, now seventy-two, had a website with contact details. Angie had called ahead to explain her investigation and to ask for an appointment.

A man in his early seventies opened the door. He was tall, rangy limbs, a long face with playful light-blue eyes. "Angie Pallorino?"

"Yes, I—"

"Rachel is expecting you. Come on in. I'm Doug, her husband."

Angie shook his hand. He had a solid grip, and the smile in his eyes remained warm. She liked him on the spot. She'd done a bit of digging before coming out and learned that Rachel was married to Dr. Douglas J. Hart, a recently retired dean of humanities at the University of Victoria. It was the same university that Maddocks's daughter, Ginny, now attended, and where Angie's father had been a professor of anthropology. Before turning to law enforcement, Angie had once thought she might pursue an academic career of her own.

"Come through this way. Don't worry about your shoes—Rachel is out back, down by the water, fly casting." He led Angie through an open-plan living room to sliding glass doors that looked over a lawn that rolled down to a bay. The Hart home was all clean architectural lines and plenty of natural light. A series of black-and-white photographic portraits filled one wall. Angie slowed to examine them. Some studies were of Doug and Rachel, others of a small boy with a young girl. Then the girl alone at various ages as the years progressed.

"Is that Eden, your daughter?" she asked Doug. "I think I recognize her from some of the river trip photos."

"Yes. And that's our boy, Jimmy. We lost him when he was four."

"I'm so sorry." She glanced at Doug.

"Jimmy was riding his tricycle and went off the edge of the dock at a lake house we were renting over the summer. By the time we realized he was gone, it was too late. It was a rough time." He opened the door, letting in the fresh autumn air. "I'll take you down to the beach. Rachel likes to practice casting down there when she needs to think or relax." He shot another easy smile over his shoulder. "Rachel hasn't thought about the river trip in a long while. She was rather deeply shocked when you told her about Jasmine's remains being identified."

They walked over the lawn. The ocean danced and sparkled in the sunlight. Along the boundary of the property, deciduous trees were still aflame in fall color, leaves ruffling in the breeze. It was a glorious day.

Doug stopped on a grassy knoll, his hands going into his pockets. "There she is." He titled his chin toward the water.

Down at the bottom of the incline, at the water's edge, a lithe woman with long silvery hair in a ponytail cast her line in balletic arcs, water droplets glinting in the sun. Her physique and movements belied her age.

Angie and Doug watched in silence. It was a sort of poetry in motion, thought Angie, an esoteric ribbon dance with a fine filament of line. She knew firsthand from her recent trip with Maddocks just how goddamn difficult it was to pull off that kind of grace with a fly line.

"What's she trying to catch?" Angie said.

"Nothing. She has a fly without a hook. It's just practice. Her Xanax." He fell quiet, seemingly lost in his own mind as he watched his wife at the water's edge.

"Is it okay to talk to her about Jasmine and what happened on the trip?" Angie asked quietly.

Doug seemed to snap back from wherever he'd journeyed in his brain and said, "No. Well, yes, of course she's fine to talk. It's just that it was a long time ago, losing Jasmine. Your phone call—the sudden revelation that those human remains belong to Jaz—it brought it all back. Rachel took it very hard at the time. It was her trip. She organized it. She invited Jasmine, and she felt responsible for everyone's safety."

"Did Rachel know Jasmine well?"

His gaze ticked to hers. "Well enough. Maybe it'll help seal the wounds now that Jasmine's remains have been found. Why don't you go down and introduce yourself while I put some coffee on? I'll bring it out to the table on the patio—it'd be a shame to waste a day like today."

Angie and Rachel sat nursing coffees at a small round table in the balmy, low-angled sunshine. The golden light was flattering on the older woman's features. Angie liked her face. It was angled with interesting lines, a firm set to her jaw, sharp gray eyes. Her wrinkles seemed to map a history of intense thought, laughter. Sadness, too. Strands of silver hair escaped a thick ponytail that brought Jane Goodall to Angie's mind.

"Do you mind if I record this?" Angie set her digital recording device on the table between them.

Rachel eyed the device. "Why record?"

"Just for my reference. I can be more present, listen more completely if I'm not taking notes." She smiled.

Rachel nodded, lifted her coffee mug, then stilled. "Run by me again why Justice Monaghan hired you? Does the postmortem on Jasmine show something suspicious?"

"No. Jasmine's death is being ruled accidental. I suspect engaging my services is Jilly Monaghan's way of dealing with the news. She feels a need to *do* something, anything."

"She's losing her memory, you know? Word is that she has some kind of dementia."

"I heard. I suspect for a woman of her considerable intellect, a woman who once wielded the power to lock people away, to take away their freedom—this makes her feel in control again. Possibly it's just her way of finding closure."

Rachel held Angie's gaze, her mug midair as she considered this. Something softened in the older woman's countenance, and Angie felt as though she'd passed some arcane test.

Rachel took a sip. "I was going on forty-eight when I got the idea for the documentary," she said. "At the time, perimenopause was a slap in my face. I wasn't dealing well with the changes to my body or mind—the irritability, shortness of temper, thinning skin, the sudden aches in my joints, sleepless nights, bad dreams, hot flushes, exhaustion. The list is endless. It felt cruel and sudden." She paused. "The worst, I think, was the mood swings. I felt almost homicidal at times." She met Angie's eyes.

"My fly rod and the river became my only salvation. Fishing in the wilderness brought peace. It drove home to me how angling had brought me happiness during the many stages of my life, starting from when I was a little girl on my granddad's knee, watching his big hands tie impossibly delicate little flies that would lure esoteric creatures up from their watery depths. He showed me how to study nature, mimic it, quietly. To be strong yet work with a gentle touch that registered every nuance of movement in the line. To not be afraid of the wilderness but to embrace its vagaries, to find solace and meaning in Mother

Nature's arms." She sipped her coffee, her eyes going distant as they caught autumn sunlight.

"Fishing and camping trips got me through puberty, through being bullied at school. Through my first real relationship and subsequent heartaches. It helped me through my son's death, brought me close to my own daughter. It gave me my profession—a desire to document outdoor life and sport on film from a female perspective. So, facing menopause, I once again turned to the river, to angling, to my passion for film, and I decided to document a story of women at various stages of their lives using the river as a metaphor for life. I wanted to show how they all came to angling and how they individually used fishing and nature to define their roles and understanding of being female in a man's world."

Angie liked this woman even more. "Hence the *Women in the Stream* title?"

Rachel nodded. "I invited an angler in her seventies, one in her sixties, one divorcée who was also a single mum, another angler married yet childless by choice, two lesbians seeking to adopt a child of their own, all the way down to my own daughter, Eden, entering the difficult teen period." She looked away, as if remembering.

"All of us were dealing with our sexuality and femininity in our own ways. Jaz, for example, was the flighty temptress with the world still lying fresh at her feet. Her life had not yet been molded by partnership commitments or motherhood. Choices still dangled tantalizingly in front of her." She cleared her throat. "I pitched the idea, got sponsors, and started planning. We set off in September of '94."

Angie eyed her recorder, checking that the red light was still on.

"It must have hit hard to have Jasmine die on that trip."

Emotion filled Rachel's gray eyes. She nodded and once more looked away at the ocean. "It crushed me," she said. "I saw in Jasmine the epitome of femaleness in full, lush, glorious bloom. Could have any man she wanted. Wasn't choosing to settle yet. She represented what we'd all been once and what we'd lost: choices." Rachel met Angie's gaze. "Jasmine would have been going on fifty now, had she lived."

Angie felt a sudden paradigm shift. Realizing that Jasmine would now be older than she was herself hit home. It made Angie realize she'd have been Eden Hart's age at the time of the fateful trip. Just fourteen. At that time Angie had been blissfully unaware of her own tragic and brutal childhood or true identity.

She reached down into her sling bag hanging over her chair and took out a file. From the file she extracted the photos Justice Monaghan had given her. Angie placed on the table the picture of the group of women laughing under the Hook and Gaffe sign.

"Can you point out who's who in this photo and tell me a little bit about each?"

Rachel nodded. "That was shot outside the motel and pub in Port Ferris where we all met the first night. Our guides met us there, too. We left our cars at the motel, and the guides drove us up to Predator Lodge in their big four-wheel-drive vehicles the following morning. That there is me, obviously." She pointed. "And that's my daughter, Eden. This is Willow McDonnell. She was thirty-nine at the time, gay, a criminal defense lawyer. This is her partner, Trish Shattuck, forty-two, a landscape architect. They were trying to adopt a child from Korea at the time of the trip, but the process was dragging and they'd faced several disappointments. Both were—still are—keen fly-fishers. Both had come off rough relationships, one with a man, the other with a woman. They were each other's second chances and working hard not to blow what they had left of life."

She pointed to the blonde in the photo. "Kathi Daly, thirty-nine at the time. My good mate." Rachel smiled a little wistfully. "Foul mouth and a sharp wit. She was recently divorced, a single mother of four who felt that she was never enough. Her ex was going through a midlife crisis in hackneyed fashion—new sports car and a string of nubile young pussies, many of whom he paid for in one way or another, which left him nothing for child support. This redhead here is Irene Mallard, forty-two. Married. No kids. Believed her husband was having an affair because her 'vagina was no longer tight.'" Rachel snorted. "Like she was a disposable cock sheath past her sell-by date. Irene constantly fretted over whether she should've had kids, whether that might have kept her philandering husband close. But the reason she'd opted not to have children in the first place was because she figured they aged a woman." Rachel glanced up. "Yeah, yeah, don't tell me, I know. I didn't get Irene at all. But she gave a different perspective on the female journey. Plus, she was a brilliant angler. Fishing was the one thing that took her out of herself and away from self-recrimination."

Angie's thoughts turned to Maddocks's question in the car, about whether she wanted kids, and her chest felt tight. "What about the other two?"

"Donna Gill. Sixty-one. A triathlete. Single by choice. She claimed she was too self-centered for a committed relationship—didn't want to be a slave to a guy, she said. Donna was a wellness coach, taught gym classes for seniors, led a hiking group in the summer, and did snow-shoe and cross-country ski tours in the winter. Über health conscious. Ironically she died five years after the trip—cardiac arrest. Cholesterol apparently off the charts. And this is Hannah Vogel. She's passed, too. Septuagenarian. German background. Fished the European rivers as a child and forged new frontiers in female fly-casting competition in North America. Widowed at the time of the trip and her children grown. She was a writer—narrative nonfiction. Part of me wanted to be like Hannah."

"It's good to put faces to the names in Justice Monaghan's file," Angie said. "She gave me a list, and I did manage to make contact with Willow McDonnell and Trish Shattuck last night," Angie said. "They're in the phone directory and live not far from here. I'm seeing them on my return to Victoria. I guess I can cross Donna Hill and Hannah Vogel off my list now, since they're deceased. What about Irene Mallard and Kathi Daly? Do you know where they are?" Angie asked.

"Why do you want to speak to any of them?"

"To get a feeling of what Jasmine's final days were like, hear what they thought of Jasmine and what she might have told them."

Rachel eyed her. "Kathi lives up island, in Ladysmith, not far from where my daughter, Eden, now lives. Eden's a psychotherapist. She has a practice in downtown Nanaimo. Irene lives in Australia now. Do you really have to interview them all?"

"Is there a problem with asking them?"

"No, no, I just . . . I feel responsible for what happened in some ways, and I don't want them feeling harassed now because of my trip."

"When I spoke with Willow and Trish on the phone, they told me they were more than happy to meet with me. It's completely voluntary of course." Angie offered a smile that she hoped was warm and encouraging. "I'm not a cop anymore. I'm not in the business of forcing anyone to do anything. I'm just trying to paint for myself a picture of the trip and of Jasmine's last months leading up to it."

"You're indulging Justice Monaghan. Do you know that?" Rachel's gaze locked with Angie's, and Angie detected hostility.

"She has questions. She offered me a fee to try to answer them."

Rachel gave a soft snort. "So maybe it's more a case of you taking advantage of her, taking money from an old woman losing her mind."

Angie crooked up a brow. "That's rather harsh."

Wind gusted, and Rachel pushed wisps of silver hair off her face. "I'm sorry. But the justice has . . . she has a reputation for being a self-centered rabble-rouser. She was like that throughout her career. A pontificating bear on her bench. Ask Willow. She's a defense lawyer and has had the misfortune of appearing in Monaghan's courtroom. She'll tell you Justice Monaghan is probably doing this just because she can, to cause trouble and entertain herself."

"You don't like her?"

"I don't like that she's digging all this up again. It was hard enough for us to get over it the first time around."

"I think I can relate to what the judge is doing," Angie said. "I'll be discreet with your friends. I just have a few simple questions. Beyond that I really don't want to upset anyone."

Rachel looked away. She exhaled deeply. "Fine. What else do you want to know from me?"

"Can you tell me how you first met Jasmine Gulati?"

Rachel moistened her lips. "Jaz took one of my script-writing courses. I used to give a summer series at the University of Victoria. She was an English major, was doing her master's at the time of the trip, so I knew her as one my husband's students as well. Doug was an English professor before becoming faculty dean."

"Doug probably knew my father," Angie said. "My dad was an anthropology prof at UVic."

"I know."

Their gazes met. And it struck Angie just how correct Jock Brixton was—she was infamous. Strangers knew personal things about her life. It would be nigh impossible to conduct future investigations without people knowing who she was, what her past was. What she'd done. But she was determined to use this to her advantage, cut her other losses. It was her only choice if she wanted her own agency and to get onto solid footing with her man.

"Can you tell me briefly your recollection of those last hours before Jasmine disappeared?"

Rachel took a sip from her mug as she cast her mind back. "We'd pulled out the boats in a camping area upstream from Plunge Falls, and we'd moved our gear up to what was to be our campsite for the night. The two guides—Garrison and . . ."

"Jessie," Angie promoted.

"Yes, Jessie. Jessie Carmanagh and Garrison Tollet. They pitched the tents and put out snacks. The rest of the group had gotten themselves set up with drinks. Jaz said she'd seen a hatch in a cove just downriver, and she was going to try a few more casts before it got dark. She left while Garrison and Jessie lit a fire, but they needed more wood. So they left the campsite right after Jaz to gather some."

"And everyone else stayed put?"

"I also left the camp. After the guides. I followed the bank upriver along a promontory of land that jutted out into the Nahamish. From the point I filmed some footage looking back at the campsite. I wanted the ambience of the fire and smoke in the gathering dusk. I was there filming when I heard men screaming. I hurried back as fast as I could through the trees. When I got back to camp—" She paused, gathered herself. "That's when I learned Garrison had seen Jasmine's body going over Plunge Falls. He'd seen her from high above, where he was standing on a shale slope. He had a good view down to the waterfall."

"You say 'body.' Was there a sense Jasmine was not alive at that point?"

Rachel set her mug down carefully. "No. I suppose I say that in retrospect, knowing now that she's gone."

Angie put another photo of the women in front of Rachel. She pointed. "In this image Jasmine is holding a purple book. Justice Monaghan believes it was her journal. She says Jasmine journaled compulsively for most of her life."

"Yes. She was writing in it on the trip. Usually in the early evenings by the fire."

"Any idea what happened to that book? It was not with the belongings returned to Jasmine's family."

"It wasn't?"

"I have a copy of the itemized list. There's no journal on it. Any idea what could have happened to that book?"

Rachel pursed her lips, then shook her head. "I can only surmise that it got lost among all the other camping gear at some point."

"So someone else might have it?"

"They'd have returned it in that case, surely?"

"One would think."

"Unless . . . it's a wild stab, but when the guides asked Jaz what she was always writing in her book, she intimated the diary contained erotica—too hot for them to handle, she said." Rachel gave an apologetic shrug. "That was Jaz. A tease. All about sex. Maybe one of the guys tried to sneak a peek and was too embarrassed to return it once the heat was on after her disappearance."

Angie mentally filed this away as she set the photo of the diamond ring on the table. "Did Jasmine mention where she got this ring?"

Rachel pulled the photo closer. "No. She wouldn't tell us. We asked, but she came across like it was some 'big secret.'"

"Do you know if Jasmine had a significant other in her life? If she was perhaps engaged to this person?"

"No. Again. Big secret."

"Why was it a secret, do you think?"

Rachel gave a derisive snort. "Hell knows. Maybe this mystery man wasn't real. Maybe Jasmine bought the ring herself and was playing her own game with us all. Maybe she was pathologically needy. Maybe she even believed in her own fake engagement. Didn't stop her flirting with the guides, though."

"She was capable of believing in her own fantasies?"

"Jasmine was like that. She was a bit . . . odd."

"Yet you invited her on the trip."

Rachel's lips curved into a wry smile. "Back in '94, the TV show *Survivor* was still just a gleam in Mark Burnett's eye, but the concept was at play in my idea for *Women in the Stream*. I wanted conflict, some edge to my women forced into close proximity and away from civilization. My hope was to see the trip participants working through their conflict on film. If they'd clashed and burned, it would have made even better television."

"The documentary never aired in the end?"

"Nope. Jasmine's father, Rahoul Gulati, threatened to sue if it ever saw the light of day. In the end the sponsors pulled the plug, and I just stuck all the unedited tapes into storage."

"You still have the uncut footage?"

"Stashed it all in boxes in our basement. The tapes are still there, buried at the back somewhere."

"Any chance I can view the footage?"

"It's in old VHS format. And there's a whole bunch of tapes."

"I'd like to see the footage if possible."

"Technically it belongs to the sponsors, but it can't hurt if you don't intend to use any of it. You'd need a VHS system to view the footage, or you'd have to get it all digitized."

"That I can do."

Rachel regarded Angie, a look of distrust entering her features. "Am I missing something here? All this trouble just to give Jilly Monaghan a picture of Jasmine's last days? Because watching all those unedited tapes is going to take you a long time."

"Justice Monaghan is paying me well for my time."

Rachel moistened her lips and nodded slowly. Again, that wry smile. "I see. One wonders who is indulging whom." She came to her feet. "They call her Jukebox Jill, do you know that?"

"No."

"And do you know why? Because when her memory suddenly gives up on her, she breaks out in song to deflect attention from her illness. She can sing just about every request you might think to make, like a real live human jukebox. Her memory of the lyrics is genius, but it's a pure diversion tactic. It spooks people, makes them forget what they were talking to her about."

"She's a damn fine singer."

"Right. I'll get Doug to fetch the boxes of tapes out of the crawl space." Rachel checked her watch. "But you'll have to excuse me. I have a Skype meeting I need to prepare for." She opened the sliding door into the living room and stood waiting for Angie.

Angie clicked off her recorder and gathered up her photos and file. She put everything into her bag, came to her feet, and slung her bag over her shoulder. "Do you know if Jasmine ever gave birth to a baby?"

Rachel blinked. "Excuse me?"

"Had Jasmine ever had a child?"

Rachel stared. "No. I . . . Heavens, no, not that I'm aware of."

"In retrospect, was there anything she said that might support the notion she'd given birth?"

"No. I . . ." The mistrust on her face turned to a look of suspicion. "I just wouldn't have dreamed that possible. Why do you ask this?"

"Just a question that came up."

"How did it come up? In the postmortem?"

"Nothing unequivocal."

Rachel held Angie's gaze, weighing her. Wind rustled fall leaves across the patio paving, and the air turned cool. "I just don't see it."

Doug appeared from the direction of the kitchen, wiping his hands on a dishcloth. Rachel glanced at him. "I've got to get ready for my call. Doug, could you fetch those documentary tapes for Angie?" She faced Angie. "It was nice meeting you." But as she turned to leave, she hesitated, then swung back. "It's probably irrelevant, but you'll see it mentioned in some of the footage. There were three men following our boats. Up on the bank. They spooked some of the women. I believe that was their intention."

"*Following* you?"

"I think they were part of a group of guys we met in the Hook and Gaffe pub on our first night. Bunch of drunk rednecks. Jaz antagonized them, and I think they decided to come mess with her, or all of us, as payback. I believe it was harmless, though. Just thought I'd mention it."

"Jaz antagonized them? How?"

She gave a snort. "You'll see on the footage. I managed to capture Jaz in full-blown action." A pause. "It would have been a damn fine female-focused documentary. You'll see that when you watch the tapes. The cassettes are all marked, and the scenes are listed on an accompanying inventory list."

With that, Rachel disappeared down the hall, presumably making for her office.

CHAPTER 16

On her way to Colwood, a city that lay within the greater Victoria metropolitan area, Angie phoned Eden Hart and set up an appointment at her practice in Nanaimo. Doug had given Angie his daughter's number along with the boxes of VHS tapes now on the back seat of her car.

She slowed her vehicle as she checked the numbers on the houses. She found the one she was searching for and pulled into the driveway. Neat lawn. Manicured flowerbeds. The kind of orderliness and subjugation of nature that seemed at odds with a lesbian couple who loved the wilderness and fishing untamed rivers. Or maybe that's exactly why people like Willow McDonnell and Trish Shattuck did love the wilderness. It provided escape from the constraints of suburbia and social expectations.

Doug had told Angie that Willow and Trish, now sixty-three and sixty-six, had eventually managed to adopt a five-year-old girl from Korea. The adoption had come through about six months after the tragic Nahamish trip. They were now proud grandparents, which was evident by the toys littering their yard. Trish, Angie had learned, was retired but used her architectural landscape design skills for charity work. Willow still worked as a criminal defense lawyer for a legal aid clinic; much of her work these days was pro bono.

The front door opened before Angie had fully exited her vehicle. A compact woman in a red fleece, cargo shorts, socks, and Birkenstocks stepped onto the porch. As Angie climbed the wooden stairs to the porch, the woman came forward, her hand extended.

"Trish Shattuck," she said, shaking Angie's hand up and down heartily. Her smile was broad, her teeth square and bright against a face weathered and tan from the outdoors. Her silver brush cut grew slightly longer on top of her head and was spiked up with gel. She wore glasses with red-rimmed plastic frames. "Come on in."

Inside, Angie removed her jacket and shoes and padded in socks along the hardwood floors as Trish led her into a large kitchen. Steaks marinated in a dish on the counter, and the room smelled of freshly brewed coffee and baking. Through the window Angie could see a small garden with a pool and a neat lawn. Two bug-eyed King Charles spaniels peered in through the slider, snouts smearing the glass. Trish opened the door and let the dogs in. They wiggled and sniffed around Angie's jeans. She petted them, fur soft as silk.

"Willow will be through in a sec," Trish said. "She's in her office just finishing up a legal brief. Coffee? I have freshly baked oatmeal choc-chip cookies."

"You bet," Angie said with a grin. She'd had coffee at the Harts', but the cookies and this coffee smelled too good to pass up.

"Take a seat." Trish motioned to a stool at the granite counter. She took pottery mugs down from a cupboard and poured three cups of fresh brew. She set a mug in front of Angie along with cream and sugar followed by a plate of cookies. Angie snagged one, bit, closed her eyes.

"Oh, this is heaven. Did you bake them?"

"Heh, it's about all I'm good for these days," Trish said with a chuckle. "Amazing what having grandkids around can teach you. Ah, here's Willow."

Angie did a double take as the woman in her sixties entered the kitchen. She had the physique of an ex–ballet dancer, her movements liquid grace. Her features were fine, and her eyes were a clear, pale amber. She smiled, nabbed a cookie. "You must be Angie Pallorino?"

Angie got up and shook the lawyer's hand. Willow bit into her cookie, assessing Angie in a way that made her feel a little naked. "Do you suspect foul play in Jasmine Gulati's death?" she said, cutting right to the chase.

Angie explained to them what Justice Jilly Monaghan was seeking. They listened attentively.

Willow pulled up a stool and reached for her mug. "I can understand where Justice Monaghan is coming from. She was—is—a formidable woman. I've had my share of professional encounters with her in the past. One didn't dare go into Justice Monaghan's courtroom ungirded."

Angie cupped the pottery mug in her hands, the shape comfortable. Warm. Like this couple, like this home. This was the kind of home she wanted with Maddocks one day. A place that exuded this same kind of geniality. The thought—the visual image, the feeling of it—blindsided her. Angie's heart beat faster. She set her mug down quickly and cleared her throat, refocusing on why she was here. "Do you mind if I record this interview, just for my own reference later?"

The couple exchanged a glance. "Fine by me," Trish said.

"I'm good," Willow added.

Angie took her digital recorder from her bag, activated it, and set it beside the plate of cookies.

"Did you guys get to know Jasmine on the trip?" she asked.

Trish's features turned serious. She eyed Willow again. Willow seemed to give an almost imperceptible nod.

"We didn't like her," Trish said. "I'm just going to say it straight because maybe that'll help you paint the picture you're looking for." She reached for her mug. "Jasmine was probably a good kid at heart, and maybe she was just going through a phase, but on the trip she came across as self-centered. Arrogant. Provocative." She looked at Willow again. "I leave anything out?"

A crooked smile curved Willow's mouth. "She wasn't easy to warm to, unless she felt she needed something from you. Then Jasmine was all smiles and irresistible, cajoling charm. Under her facade I believe lay real depth. She was intelligent, well read. Philosophical at times. I got a sense she was really trying to find who she was, testing ground, pushing boundaries to see just how far she could get. Maybe she was a lot like her grandmother, in truth. Jilly Monaghan had—probably still has—an abrasiveness both in and out of her robes."

"Did any of the others on the trip warm to Jaz at all?" Angie said, intrigued at this picture of Jasmine Gulati that was emerging.

Another exchange of glances. "Maybe that Kathi woman?" Willow said to Trish.

"Nah, that was more a kinship in the bottle." Trish met Angie's eyes. "Those two liked to get drunk and talk shit around the fire before crawling into their sleeping bags and passing out."

"So Jasmine drank fairly heavily on the trip?" Angie said.

"She sure didn't hold back. Damn fine fly-fisher, though. She showed me a thing or two on the water." Willow sipped her coffee as she appeared to cast her memory back. "Eden seemed to get on relatively well with her. They chatted a lot, usually earlier in the evenings around the fire while Jasmine was writing in her journal. Before she got drunk for the night."

"What about Rachel? Did she like Jasmine?" Angie asked, poking at the perimeters of what Rachel had told her.

"Rachel was in work mode," Trish said. "She played the role of nonjudgmental observer. She wanted to encourage natural interaction. She has a real knack of sticking a camera in your face and making it seem like she isn't even there."

"Rachel said Jasmine made an issue of having some big secret."

Trish gave a laugh. "Yes. Some clandestine lover who'd given her that diamond ring she was flashing about. Then she'd go on about how everyone held some deep dark secret, each one of us on that river, she said."

The words of the old nurse who'd found Angie stuffed into the baby box at Saint Peter's Hospital on Christmas Eve over thirty years ago sifted through her mind . . . *Sometimes we think we're keeping secrets. But really, those secrets are keeping us.*

Angie set the photo of Jasmine's diamond ring on the counter. "This was the ring she mentioned?"

They nodded.

"Did you get the sense she was promised to someone? Or just messing with you all?"

"By the way she was flirting with the guides?" Willow said, her voice quieter, a guarded look entering her eyes. "Someone engaged to be married doesn't . . . behave like she did."

Angie said, "There's no forensics evidence to support this question, but it is a question that has nevertheless come up." She paused. "Did Jasmine at any point lead you to believe she might have given birth in the past, perhaps to a baby she'd surrendered for adoption?"

Surprise cut through both their faces.

"No," Willow said.

"You both reacted quite sharply. Why?"

Trish raked her fingers through her silver-gray spikes. "It's just that one evening we'd all been discussing adoption. It was in relation to what Willow and I were trying to do with an orphanage in Korea. Jaz came across as vehemently negative about our efforts to adopt a Korean baby. She said it was stupid, that we had no idea what we might be getting with a baby from an orphanage."

"She was incredibly harsh," Willow added. "She said we might end up with a kid with fetal alcohol syndrome or brain damage or ADD challenges. Admittedly, she'd made fair inroads into her wine by that point, but—" Willow paused. "It would certainly not lead me to conclude in any way that she was sympathetic to the notion of adoption. Or that she might have gone down that road herself."

"Unless, in retrospect, she was disturbed by having done this in her own past," said Trish, "and it was her way of lashing out and burying it. Maybe *that* was her big dark secret."

"Then why her apparent smugness?" Willow countered. She turned to Angie. "See, that was the thing. Whatever big secret Jaz was on about, it was cloaked in a cocky superiority. It was something she was happy about or at least positive. She was waving it about like a red flag."

"Why would she do that?" Angie said.

"Hell knows. She was twenty-five. World at her feet. We were old bags. Maybe that's all it was. Animalistic superiority of youth. Put the old crones down."

Angie held their eyes. "One more question," she said. "Rachel mentioned that a group of males taunted you from the shore while you were drifting downriver."

"Oh, that." Another dry laugh from Trish. "We figured that was Jaz's fault, too. She affronted a group of local males in a pub at Port Ferris. We'd all gathered there for a meal and briefing with the two guides the night before heading up to Predator Lodge. We'd booked into the adjacent motel for the night. But in the pub side of the restaurant, there was some game on television, and it seemed like the whole town had come out to cheer on a local hero. Plenty of drink flowing."

"So the place was raucous, patrons really drunk?"

"We weren't doing so badly ourselves," Trish said. "It was our big pretrip sendoff. Some of us, including Jaz, filtered over to the pub side and joined the locals in celebration of the big win."

"How did Jaz offend these guys?"

"Well, most the guys in the pub were really big dark-haired logger types, a lot of them wearing the Kamloops tux—"

"Kamloops tux?" Angie asked.

"Oh, just a name for those padded plaid jacket things everyone out in the rural areas of BC seems to wear, from loggers to hunters to mechanics," Willow said.

Angie's mind shot to Garrison Tollet, now current owner of Predator Lodge. He fit the mold—big, built like a logger, thighs the size of her waist. He'd been wearing his padded plaid jacket on both occasions that Angie and Maddocks had interacted with him at the lodge.

"What did Jaz say to these guys?" Angie prodded.

"Something about them being interrelated. She asked if they were all cousins and whether they forwent dental hygiene and played banjos in the woods," Trish said.

"Oh jeez," Angie said. "You're kidding me?"

"'Fraid not. So we think some of the guys from the pub figured it would be a lark to follow us along the river. There were three of them in the woods, following us, we think. Two big men. One with black hair, one who wore a red toque and a plaid jacket. The third man was shorter and skinny. They'd appear in the trees along the riverbank, just standing there. Sometimes we'd see them silhouetted up along the talus ridges. Then one afternoon we heard a banjo. We heard it again that night near our camp."

"And one of the big guys was always carrying something," Willow added. "It was long. Could have been a rifle or shotgun."

"So you think they were just out to spook you, or did you actually feel threatened? Did you feel they could be dangerous?"

"It felt tense to me," Willow said. "Bottom line, Jaz asked for it. If Garrison and Jessie hadn't stepped in and defused things in the pub that night, I suspect things could have gone seriously sideways. Garrison took Jaz aside, bought her another drink, and cozied up to her in a booth at the back of the bar while Jessie talked the other blokes down."

Trish and Willow exchanged another look, as if weighing something. Then Trish said, "We weren't going to say anything because it was personal, but we're pretty sure Garrison Tollet got into Jaz's pants that night. She was booked into the motel room next to ours, and we . . . heard her with someone."

"Heard?"

"Banging headboards kinda heard."

"So she slept with Garrison Tollet, her guide, on the first night?"

"Yes."

Angie's mind shot back to her and Maddocks's trip. They'd met Sheila Tollet, Garrison's wife. Sheila had mentioned at the time that she and Garrison were going on twenty-six years of marriage. They would have been married only two years the night Garrison allegedly slept with his client, Jasmine Gulati.

"Are you *certain* it was him in the next room with her?"

"No. That's also why we didn't really want to mention it, because she *could* have been with someone else entirely. But if you look at the footage Rachel shot in the pub that night, you might learn more."

"Not exactly the behavior of a woman promised to another man," Angie said quietly.

"Nope," Trish said. "That you'll certainly see from the tapes."

CHAPTER 17

Dusk was settling over the city, thick fog rolling in off the ocean as Angie went up a small stone path to the door of what she hoped was Sophie Sinovich's house.

Sophie was one of the "three amigas" pictured with Jasmine Gulati on a Hornby Island beach twenty-six years ago.

Angie had looked up both Mia Smith and Sophie Sinovich after dropping off Rachel Hart's VHS tapes to be digitized at Mayang Photo Place, a specialty store run by Daniel Mayang, a guy used by Coastal Investigations for all manner of photographic restoration, enhancement, and old film advice in general.

Turned out there was more than one Mia Smith living in Victoria, and if Mia had married and was using her husband's name, Angie was likely to hit several dead ends before making any progress. Sinovich, however, was a surname that narrowed the field, so Angie had focused on looking for Sophie first.

She'd found a social media profile for a Sophie Sinovich Rosenblum that named the University of Victoria as one of the schools she'd attended. The profile photos of Sophie Rosenblum showed a brunette in her early fifties. She looked like she could be a match.

As Angie raised her hand to knock, the door opened, startling both Angie and a tiny woman holding a Great Dane on a lead. The woman stepped back in fright, her hand shooting to her chest. The hound began to bark.

"I'm looking for Sophie Sinovich Rosenblum," Angie said loudly over the sound of the barking dog.

"Oh, Bella, shut up. Hold on, please," the flustered woman told Angie. She scooted Bella-the-Dane back inside and stepped out, shutting the door behind her. "Sorry about that. I was just about to take Bella for her walk. We didn't expect to see anyone right at the door. You scared the daylights out of me."

Disappointment flushed through Angie as she regarded this tiny black-haired woman with pinched features. She was not the Sophie in the photos.

"My apologies. I think I might have the wrong address," Angie said. "I was hoping to find Sophie Sinovich Rosenblum who attended UVic about twenty-five years back."

Hesitancy crossed the tiny woman's features, followed by suspicion. Inside, the barking intensified. The woman looked back at the door as if reassessing the wisdom of locking her guard dog away.

"Here—" Angie quickly dug out her card and held it out to the woman. "My name is Angie Pallorino. I'm a private investigator, and I'm looking into a cold case that Sophie Sinovich might be able to help me with."

The woman studied the card in the porch light, looked up. "You have the right address. Sophie is away with her family, trekking in Nepal. They'll not be in cell range much until they return. I'm Lacey Richards. I'm housesitting, or rather"—she jerked her head back to the door—"Great Dane sitting."

"When will Sophie be back?"

"Not for another few days."

"Can you give her my card, ask her to call me when she returns?"

"Sure."

Angie thanked the woman and started down the path to her car, but Lacey called out into the misty twilight. "Can I perhaps help? I was also at UVic with Sophie."

Angie stilled. Hope flared. She turned and hurried back up the path, ducking under cover of the eaves out of the fine drizzle. She took out the photo she'd put in her jacket pocket. "Do you know who this friend of Sophie's was?" She showed the print to Lacey.

"That's Jasmine—" Her gaze ticked up to Angie. "Is this about Jaz? She disappeared the year after this was taken, presumed drowned in the Nahamish River. No one ever knew for sure what happened to her. There were all sorts of rumors."

"Rumors like?"

"So this *is* about Jaz?"

"It is, yes. Her remains were recently discovered and positively identified. Her grandmother has asked me to paint a picture of Jasmine's final months and days leading up to the accident. I was hoping Sophie could fill in some details."

"Wow," Lacey said, her attention returning to the photo. She fell silent. Inside the house the dog stopped barking, as if listening for her voice now. A foghorn sounded across the water. Darkness seeped in with the mist, wrapping the city in a claustrophobic cape of cold moisture and casting ghostly halos around the streetlights.

"What were the rumors?" Angie probed gently.

Her gaze still riveted on Jaz's smiling image, Lacey said, "The usual stuff that comes up when people vanish without a trace. That she'd faked her own death. That she'd gone south, crossed the border into Mexico, had been seen in Puerto Vallarta. Someone claimed they'd seen Jaz in Oaxaca and that she was living with some man there." Lacey peered up. "Where was her body found?"

"Next to the river, in a shallow grave where she likely washed up in a high-water event."

"And all this time people thought she could be cavorting around the globe. Meanwhile she was lying right there . . ."

"Was there any reason you'd be inclined to believe any of those rumors?" Angie asked. "For example, was there anything Jasmine Gulati might have wanted to escape?"

"I never did believe the rumors," Lacey said. "It's a way of filling a void. The human mind doesn't like unanswered questions. The instinct is to fill the unknown gaps with something, anything, even if it's bizarre. That's why closure is so important. Knowing, even when the truth hurts, you know?"

Angie knew. All too intimately.

"How well did you know Jasmine?"

She gave a shrug. "As well as most people. Jaz had a way of being super friendly to everyone but at the same time not really letting anyone in. Sophie was very close to her, though, and Mia." She nodded to the pic. "The three amigas, we used to call them."

"Does Mia Smith still live in town?"

"She's Mia Monroe now. And yes. She owns a boutique near Chinatown called Candescence. She studied law and went straight into clothing design. Go figure."

Angie thanked Lacey and reminded her to pass a message to Sophie to call upon her return.

"Oh," Lacey said, halting Angie once more. "Mia and Jasmine kinda fell out shortly before that river trip. I remember now—I haven't thought about it all for such a long time."

"Fell out? How so?"

"Big argument about something. I mean, really big. They'd had their spats, but this one? It was for real."

CHAPTER 18

Maddocks poured hot water over a tea bag. He set the mug of steeping tea on the small galley table in front of Holgersen. The quirky detective had come to visit Maddocks at his yacht. It was 8:30 p.m. on Monday night, and Maddocks had just returned from his law enforcement seminar. He'd showered, fixed himself a double whiskey, and was settling in to read some case files when a bedraggled Holgersen had come knocking on the hatch of his schooner.

"Thanks," Holgersen said. He began dunking the bag of green tea in and out of the hot water, presumably to make it steep faster. Maddocks watched him. It was dark, raining, and windy out, and the old schooner rocked gently on a swell, hanging lanterns outside swinging in the mist. Jack-O snoozed on the sofa.

"You sure you don't want something stronger?" Maddocks said, holding up his glass. "Got some good whiskey."

"Nah. Had two beers at the Pig already."

Maddocks sat opposite his detective and took a sip of his drink. "So what's on your mind? What brought you all the way down to the marina?"

He inhaled. "Jeezus, boss, what in the hells do you want from me? What you looking for in Harvey Leo?" His gaze locked with Maddocks's. "What fucking game you playing with me here?"

"You got something?"

Holgersen looked away, chewing on whatever was bothering him.

"Okay. So maybe Leo's showing a particular interest in some particular cold cases."

Maddocks's pulse quickened. "What do you mean, 'interest'?"

Holgersen dumped his tea bag on a saucer with a small spatter of water. "You gonna tell me what you's looking for specifically?"

"Tell me what cases, Holgersen. Tell me how he's showing interest."

The detective ran his tongue over his teeth. "First day on the cold case job, and he's chosen to siphon off dead tweaker cases—them homeless kids who's ended up overdosed or who's died from exposure or things like that. But there's been some suspicious circumstances around their deaths, so files were opened, but nothing came of them."

"All female vics?"

"Some male kids in there as well."

"And he's prioritizing these cases?"

"No way, José. He's spiking them. Claiming them's lost causes. Just junkies and a waste of our time." Holgersen brought his mug to his mouth, sipped. "Leo reckons ever since pig farmer Pickton started hunting and killing street workers in Vancouver's Downtown Eastside, every missing or murdered street person is now seen as a potential serial killer vic. He said it's overkill. Waste of our time."

Maddocks eyed Holgersen. "Leo *said* that?"

The detective began shuffling in his seat as this question hung between them.

"Let's get one thing straight here, boss. I's not comfortable right now. Spying on a fellow cop—not my shtick. You gotta tell me what's going down, or I ain't coming here with tattletales that mean shit. I's not some tool for some McCarthy witch hunt, 'cause the way I sees it, anyone can make a meal out of nothing if theys really want to. Maybe you gots an axe to grind with Leo over what he did to Pallorino."

Maddocks snorted and sat back. He took another sip of his scotch, watching Holgersen closely. "You have a way with words."

"Yeah. Well."

"All right," Maddocks said. "Off the books. What I say stays here. You okay with that?"

Holgersen's eyes ticked up. "Yeah. Okay."

Maddocks inhaled, circling around something he was not really able to pin down himself. "During the Baptist investigation, I got a sense something was off with Leo. I think you did, too."

"Maybe."

"I'm not just talking about him drinking on the job and working under the influence. I'm talking something bigger, and it's not just me. Word came from the top that I was to watch him. I was given a directive to pull him in from homicide and give him some rope in this new unit, where he'd be confronted with some of his own old and unsolved cases. And to see where he ran with that."

Holgersen regarded him steadily, his dun-colored irises almost quivering. Nothing about this guy was ever truly still. "You saying he's a dirty cop?"

Maddocks sipped his drink, said nothing.

"Fuck," Holgersen whispered. "So you want some kinda proof." He swore again. "I feel like a fucking shit-pawn. Why me?"

"Because you're good. You've partnered with him before, so you know him—you have a baseline. Putting you together again won't raise suspicions." Maddocks paused. "I meant what I said, Holgersen, about the potential for growing the cold case division within iMIT. You close some cases, it'll get you noticed by the right people. You could make sergeant. This could take you where you want to go."

Holgersen lurched up from his bench. He took a step across the small cabin, as if considering bolting. But he spun around, returned to the table, and sat back down. He started rapping his fingers on the table. "As long as it doesn't just fast-track me into internal."

"You're playing the Leo angle for me, technically off the books. That's it. You bring me something solid, and I'll pursue it through other channels. Official ones. This is just a start."

"Maybe you really are just gunning for hairy-ass Leo because he dropped Pallorino in the shit."

"It's got nothing to do with her relationship to me. He dropped a fellow officer in the shit. Any cop should care about that."

Holgersen eyed him, and Maddocks felt an air of challenge rise between them.

"I don't like dirty cops," Maddocks added quietly. "If he's dirty, I want him."

Holgersen nodded. Behind him, on the sofa, Jack-O suddenly lifted his head and cocked an ear.

Maddocks watched his dog's nostrils twitch as the animal turned his head and stared at the stairs that led up to the deck. Maddocks eyed the stairs, then got up and went to the window in his galley.

He squinted out at the dimly lit dock. Nothing but lanterns swinging in the wind and halyards chinking against masts. His heart sank a little. Even though he'd drawn his line in the sand with Angie and told her not to call until she was ready, his heart quickened at every sound as every molecule in his body willed her to appear.

Perhaps she'd never call. Perhaps he'd been an ass. Maybe he should be worried about her well-being instead of drawing battle lines.

"Company?" Holgersen said.

"No. Just wind." Maddocks went to scratch Jack-O's ear. "It's okay, boy."

I know you miss her, too. Another day. She might come around again another day. We need to let her be for now.

"I should go," Holgersen said, coming to his feet again and reaching for his wet jacket that hung by the stairs.

"You going to be okay with all this?" Maddocks said.

He shrugged into his jacket. "I don't like dirty cops, neither."

Maddocks nodded. Holgersen began to head up the stairs.

"You heard from Angie?" Maddocks said, unable to stop himself, worried about her, wondering what wild career moves she might make after his phone call.

Holgersen stopped on the stairs, regarded him. "Why?" he said slowly.

Maddocks inhaled deeply and dug his hands into his pockets. "Just . . . wondering."

"You guys broken up or something?"

"Taking a bit of a breather."

Holgersen's gaze locked with Maddocks's, his features unreadable. He hesitated, then said, "Want me to check in on her?"

Maddocks snorted. "I wouldn't mind knowing if she's doing okay. Keeping busy with . . . work and all."

Holgersen nodded slowly. "Sure's a thing, boss. I'll call her in the morning."

CHAPTER 19

"What do you mean, 'the last ones are missing'?" Angie said as Daniel Mayang handed her a digital storage device over the counter. Daniel had said he could have some digital footage ready for her by 9:00 p.m. So after her visit to Sophie Sinovich Rosenblum's house, Angie had grabbed a bite to eat and headed to the gym for another Muay Thai session with Chai Bui. Both to kill time until 9:00 p.m. and because she was unable to rest, to be still, for stillness turned her thoughts to her screwup with Maddocks.

He'd be back from his seminar by now, and Angie was antsy to get this investigation ball rolling. If she could nail this gig and find more like it, she could begin to see a way forward. In her life. And with Maddocks.

"I mean, the VHS tapes listed at the end of Rachel Hart's inventory are missing," Daniel said. "The ones you asked to have converted first—those tapes are not in the boxes you gave me."

"The footage filmed of the campsite from afar on the final night of the river trip is gone?"

"I don't know how many other ways I can say it, Angie—those tapes are not there."

"Rachel said all the tapes were in boxes."

"Hey, I can't make them appear, okay? *They are not there.*"

Frustration clipped at Angie. She reached into her pocket for her cell. It was just after 9:00 p.m.—not too late to call the Hart residence.

Doug answered, and Angie cut right to the chase. "Can I speak with Rachel? I'm having her tapes digitized, and the final footage from the trip is missing."

Rachel came onto the phone. "What is it?" Her tone was sharp.

Angie explained that the last three tapes listed on her inventory had not been in the boxes Doug had handed over. "Were they perhaps misplaced? Could you look for them? I can come by tomorrow and collect them. I need to see those last hours in camp."

"You don't *need* to see anything. You *want* to see it. Critical difference there, Angie. You're making money off me and the judge with this investigation. Just keep that in focus. You're not a police officer, and I'm not at your beck and call. I'm under no obligation to even talk to you. Even if you were law enforcement, you'd need a warrant to force any of us to cooperate and dredge up all those awful memories."

Angie shot a glance at Daniel, who was watching her intently from his side of the counter. She turned her back on him and lowered her voice, her heart beating a steady, angry drum in her chest. Her shortness of temper, her frustration with Rachel, had more to do with her situation with Maddocks than these missing tapes. Angie needed to rein herself in if she wanted to make this damn PI gig work. She had to learn to be nice in order to get what she wanted because her days of waving search warrants were over.

"My apologies, Rachel," she said more quietly. She smoothed her hand over her hair, marshaling her composure. "That was uncalled for. I'm very grateful for your help. Justice Monaghan is grateful, too. Anything you can give us that will help lay Jasmine Gulati's memory to rest and allow her grandmother some peace will be appreciated. I was just wondering if there might still be another box of tapes in your crawl space, something Doug perhaps missed. Or if those final tapes somehow ended up outside the boxes and are lying loose down there."

"No. There is nothing more in our crawl space. I went down there myself after you left. Doug gave you everything."

"Any idea what might have happened to that final footage, then?" she prompted gently.

"I'm sorry. I really don't know. Those tapes have been down in storage for almost a quarter of a century. Things might have been mislaid or thrown away in error. I really am sorry," she said again.

"It's okay. I appreciate your help."

Angie hung up and swore softly. She slipped the external drive into her pocket, wondering if Rachel was lying and, if so, why. Or it could be a totally innocent misplacement, but it just further piqued Angie's curiosity to see them.

"Thanks, Dan, seems they've vanished into thin air. Is it okay if I settle with you when I pick up the rest tomorrow?"

"No problem, Ange, but one more thing. While I managed to convert those first three cassettes on your list, I'm not sure I'll have the same luck with the rest. The quality of the others has been compromised to various degrees. Judging by old watermarks on the sides of the storage boxes, the tapes have likely seen water damage."

"You mean . . . these first few might be all there is?"

He gave a shrug. "Old magnetic tapes need to be properly stored in a controlled environment in order to extend the life of the media. High temps, humidity, water, dust, corrosive elements in the air—they can all result in a loss of readable data through decreasing the magnetic capability and damaging the binders, the backs of the tapes. I'll do what I can."

Angie thanked Daniel and left Mayang Photo Place. As she made her way back to her vehicle parked down the street, she checked her watch again and dialed the number for Trish Shattuck and Willow McDonnell.

Willow answered as Angie reached her vehicle.

"It's Angie Pallorino," she said as she beeped her car lock. She climbed into her Mini Cooper and started the ignition. "I apologize for calling at this hour, but I was hoping I could ask you guys one more question?"

"Oh, it's not late, not for me," Willow said. "I usually work at least until midnight most nights. Shoot."

"That last evening in the campsite, after Jasmine left to fish downriver, who all remained in camp?"

A moment of silence. "It was a long time ago. Let me think . . . the two guides, they left shortly after Jasmine to collect more firewood."

"So there were eight of you at the camp? You and Trish, Eden, Rachel, Kathi, Irene, Hannah, and Donna?"

Another long pause. Angie turned up the heater in her car in an effort to demist the windows.

"Oh, wait, I believe Rachel then left with her equipment."

"To shoot footage of the camp? From a nearby promontory upriver?" This was what Rachel had told Angie, and she wanted to see if it meshed with Willow's and Trish's recollections.

"I . . . thought she said was going downriver to see if she could film Jasmine fishing from a higher vantage point along a ridge."

"Rachel *said* that—downriver?"

"Oh, Angie, you know, it was such a long time ago, I cannot be sure. Irrespective of what she might have said, I didn't actually see with my own eyes which way Rachel went. Even if she did say she wanted footage of Jaz, she might have decided otherwise when she saw the light, the time, caught a good aspect, a potential visual. She was doing that all the time. She'd head into each day of shooting with a plan, but if the light shifted or something changed, she'd go with the fresh cues. It's what made her good at her job, being responsive, watching things unfold, seeing a potential story in the patterns evolving in front of her."

"Thanks, Willow. I really appreciate this."

"Anytime. I'm happy to help." A pause. "Why is this important?"

"It's probably not," Angie said, putting her car into gear. "But that final VHS footage Rachel shot on the last night has gone missing. I was hoping to see it for myself."

"Maybe it'll show up yet."

"Maybe."

Angie killed the call and drove home through a quiet city on this Monday night, an edginess crackling through her, a sense that something felt slightly off about the Jasmine Gulati story. The November wind gusted, and a fine drizzle plastered fallen leaves to the sidewalks.

Who were those three men who'd followed the women down the river?

Had Rachel lied?

What had Jasmine meant about the women on the trip all having secrets? Angie's thoughts circled around what the old nurse who'd rescued her from the angel's cradle had said.

We all tell lies. We all have secrets. A secret can own a person. A secret is powerful. But only to the degree that the truth threatens someone.

If there were indeed secrets being kept about the river trip, who would be most threatened should the truth be revealed?

CHAPTER 20

Back in her apartment, Angie downloaded the digitized files onto her laptop. Daniel Mayang had labeled each file to match the VHS tapes listed on Rachel Hart's inventory—"Arrival in Port Ferris," "Gathering in Hook and Gaffe," "Camp Moments: Second Night."

She checked her watch. She might be able to get through watching most of this footage tonight if she pushed through. She knew sleep would elude her anyway, given her anxiety over her relationship.

She turned up the gas fireplace—temperatures outside were dropping fast, the wind howling—and made a mug of cocoa. Gathering her hot drink, notepad, and pen, she settled in front of her laptop. Before she hit PLAY, she brought to mind the parameters of her investigative brief:

Jasmine Gulati's death was being ruled an accidental drowning. So far no crime nor criminal intent was evident. Yet there were interesting questions around Jasmine herself. Her mystery engagement ring. A possible secret fiancé, one who'd never stepped forward after she vanished over the falls. A missing journal with possible erotic content. There were the three men stalking the women along the river. And there were the anomalies in the pathologist's report—healing scars from an improperly treated shoulder injury, scars on the decedent's pelvis. Even with an accidental death, there were always human factors at play, interrelationships that could have led to the events that culminated in a mishap.

She clicked PLAY, reached for her steaming mug of cocoa, and settled back to watch the unedited footage.

The first scene came to life on her monitor as an image of a younger Rachel Hart filled the screen. Rachel had turned the camera on herself somehow. In her late forties, she was striking, her gray eyes sharp, strands of loose blonde hair blowing across her face in a breeze. She stood in front of a wood-sided building, cheeks and the tip of her nose pinked from cold.

The sign above the door read HOOK AND GAFFE. She pointed up at the sign.

"Looks like Eden and I are the first to arrive. The nine of us are gathering here at this pub and restaurant in downtown Port Ferris just across from Ferris Bay. Eden's handling the camera for me." She smiled and gave two thumbs-up. "Great job, kiddo."

The image jiggled as the camera girl laughed. It made Angie smile, this concept of a mother and daughter team, this adventure they'd embarked on, those happy hours they were enjoying before tragedy would strike. Angie's thoughts darted to her own adoptive mother. It had been a while since she'd visited Miriam Pallorino in the home. She should go with her dad. She should catch up on a few family things. Filing the thoughts away, Angie refocused on the footage.

Rachel held a contour map up to the camera and pointed to a twisting blue line that ran through the mountains. "The Nahamish is here, this blue line. A static feature on this map, a constant, yet the very definition of a river is change. If you step into the waters of the Nahamish today, it's not the same water as yesterday, and the water flowing through the river will be different tomorrow. The water changes by the second, yet it remains the same river. Like a woman. She bears a constant identity throughout her life, yet her very nature, her function, is one of change. She's a toddler before she becomes a young girl, then a teen, like my Eden here. She's sister, aunt, and friend. She matures into a siren to attract a mate. She becomes mother, menopausal broad, divorcée, widow, a senior, the crone. But always, inside, she's the same girl carried along the river of life. In the name of that metaphor, we nine women, all at different points in our own river, will gather here today at the Hook and Gaffe." She grinned and pointed at the sign again.

"Over the next seven days as we drift the Nahamish, we may clash or bond, but one thing we all bring to this trip is a common love and understanding for fly-fishing and the outdoors."

Angie sipped her hot drink, thinking the idea was cool but way too New Agey for her. She reminded herself it was raw footage, unedited. But in spite of herself, it made her think about her own place in that life stream. And Maddocks. And the choices she now faced.

The camera panned across the parking lot to the attached motel, then across the street to show a row of small stores snugged along a stretch of what Angie presumed was Ferris Bay. The footage ended on an image of the Mariner's Diner directly across from the hotel.

Angie hit PLAY on the next file.

The interior of the Hook and Gaffe came alive on her screen. The footage was grainy, the color off, and the images were scratched with shapes that flickered across her monitor like floaters in her vision. It was reminiscent of an old film reel.

The restaurant interior was done in deep paneling, low lighting. A burnished metal-topped bar counter jutted out, dividing the restaurant from a more informal pub section that housed a pool table and several TV screens. The pub side was packed, mostly with men in outdoor work gear and logging-style jackets. An odd assortment of hunting, fishing, and sports memorabilia adorned the walls, including hockey sticks, a lacrosse net, fishing rods, crab pots, faded buoys, and glass fishing floats. An ice hockey game played across the television screens.

The camera panned back to the restaurant section and zeroed in on two women seated at a wooden table, bottles of ketchup, mustard, hot sauce, and beer in front of them. Angie leaned forward as she recognized the faces of Trish Shattuck and Willow McDonnell. Trish's hair had not yet turned gray. Willow was even more attractive around the age of forty than she was now.

"So, ladies"—Rachel's voice—"in your opinion, what's the most significant difference between male and female anglers?"

Trish raised her beer bottle to the camera. "For one thing, women don't lie about size!" She laughed and took a long, deep swallow of her beer.

"No way," countered Willow. "It's the reaction you get from sales clerks in angling stores." She faced the camera. "When a woman peruses the tackle section, the clerks are nowhere to be found. It's like you're invisible. But as soon as you leave the rod and reel section and cross some unseen line into the clothing department, bam, you materialize, and the clerk rushes over to you."

"Yeah, you're suddenly a viable customer," said Trish. "That never happens to guys." She lowered her voice and drew out her words theatrically. "Clerks handle a male in the tackle section with gravitas." She lifted her bottle and took another swallow.

Willow laughed, showing bright-white teeth.

"So it's still a man's sport, a man's world out on the river?" Rachel said.

"Funny thing that," Trish said, pointing the neck of her beer bottle toward the camera like a wagging finger. "Since it was a female, a nun, who supposedly wrote the first 'Treatise of Fishing with an Angle' in the fourteen hundreds."

"Who was this nun?" Rachel said.

"Dame Juliana Berners. A prioress," Trish said. "That woman could show the men a thing or two with her angle."

Willow leaned forward, eyes alight with drink and mirth. She lowered her voice in mock conspiracy with the camera. "Truth is, I'd be worried if I was a man on the river with all of us women around."

"Why?" Rachel asked.

"Because we're of a certain age," she whispered. "Nothing quite like hot flashes, lack of sleep, food cravings, bloat, and mood swings to turn a woman murderous." Her face turned serious, and she crossed her arms, sitting back as their server arrived and set more bottles of beer on the table.

When the server left, Willow said to the camera, "In honesty, it's why I still fish. Nothing calms me like the river. Nothing takes my mind off things like being silent, still, watching the insects, trying to read the fish, the sky, the water, listening to wind in trees."

"Trish," Rachel said from behind her camera. "Why do you fish?"

"I used to drink," she said matter-of-factly. "And I swallowed all manner of drugs. I figured my guy friends thought I was cool, that they admired my stamina, my ability to put them all under the table." She paused. Her face changed. "It almost cost me my life one day." She glanced at Willow. "But I got a second chance. I met someone who reminded me of my fly-fishing roots, my love of nature, and what was real. And how to be true to myself—true to my sexual orientation especially. I've never looked back since, only upriver."

Eden came suddenly into camera view. She wore a light down jacket and a woolen hat with a small Kinabulu logo on the side. Her long hair hung in two thick braids over her shoulders. She took a seat at the table across from Trish and Willow. The server set a cola and a plate of nachos in front of her.

"Why do you fish, Eden?" Willow said.

Eden looked directly at the camera. No smile. "Because my mom makes me."

Willow appeared uncertain. But Trish guffawed and tilted her beer bottle at Eden. "Yeah, and you will thank your mom for that because that's how I started. My mom. After I lost my way I realized that my mother—who I used to hate, mind you—had actually given me something to fall back on. An anchor. I realized I was not that much unlike her."

Eden reached for her glass and sipped. She came across as a sullen and rebellious fourteen-year-old. Angie remembered her own mood swings at that age. Oh, the joys of hormonal shifts on either end of the age spectrum.

A raucous series of whoops and banging erupted from the pub side of the establishment, and the camera swung abruptly around to the source of the sound. Beer bottles and glasses were being raised and chinked, high-fives exchanged as fresh rounds of drinks were yelled for.

Rachel panned over to their server. "What's all the excitement on the pub side?" she asked the woman.

"Robbie Tollet," said a male voice. The camera angled to find the voice.

Angie blinked as a man came into view. She was looking through a time warp at the owner of Predator Lodge, Claire Tollet's father, Garrison. He sure was built back in the day—broad shoulders, thick neck, a swath of black hair, dense beard, pale-green eyes that danced with a wicked mirth beneath a dark thatch of brows.

"Ah, meet Garrison Tollet, one of our guides," Rachel said for the camera. "Who's Robbie?"

"My little brother. Twenty-one. Plays for the Winnipeg Jets. Half the village is watching their home boy tonight."

"I thought union negotiations had resulted in this being an NHL lockout year," Trish said.

"Ah, this isn't an NHL game," Garrison said. "It's in Helsinki. Jets won their first against Tappara, and now they're up against HIFK in the final. Could be one of the last hurrahs for the Jets—there's talk of moving them to Minnesota. Oh, here's Jessie the Man. Come on over, Jess. Meet the girls."

A tall sandy-haired male joined Garrison, his smile boyish, his cheeks slightly flushed.

"Ladies, your second guide, Jessie Carmanagh," Garrison said with flourish.

Jessie's flush deepened. Angie found his shyness charming. According to the reports she'd read, Jessie Carmanagh had been thirty-three the year of the fateful trip. He was also the father of the young male guide on Angie and Maddocks's trip.

"When everyone else has arrived and after we've had dinner, we'll get set up with the safety briefing and run through the schedule for tomorrow," Garrison said, raising his hand to summon the server. He motioned for another round of drinks as he and Jessie seated themselves at the restaurant table.

"What made you become a fishing guide, Garrison?" Rachel zoomed in on his face.

He paused, his green eyes holding the camera. Angie swallowed. His intensity was stark, raw. Masculinity oozed from him. The lightness of his eyes against his black hair and beard was startling. A woman couldn't help but imagine what he'd be like in bed. Big. Hard. Rough. Satisfying.

"My grandfather homesteaded along the Nahamish," he said, looking directly into Rachel's lens. "He bought up huge tracts of forest along Carmanagh Lake, stretching way back into the north mountains, and the land was dirt cheap because no one wanted to live out here at the time. He also started logging an area of Crown land on the south side of the river. He built a mill to process the lumber, and he began shipping it across Canada and into the States. With those original logs, he built Predator Lodge, which my father now runs. We were born there, raised there, and still live in and around the lodge. Hunting and fishing and living off the land is our family's way of life. I was homeschooled out there. We have extended family living in those mountains to this day. And given the changes in the economy, we're moving away from the resource industries and segueing more into tourism—guided angling, backcountry skiing, guided hikes, hunting—it's a natural move."

"Jessie, how 'bout you?"

Jessie cleared his throat, looking embarrassed. "My family's into aquaculture—oysters, clams, scallops. Commercial fishing is my thing. But I like to guide on the side. Both ocean and river. We—the Carmanaghs—go back with the Tollets."

A man of few words, thought Angie as the clip ended abruptly.

The next file showed the other females arriving, tables being pushed together, dinner and more drinks being ordered, introductions being shared. Jasmine Gulati entered the frame. Angie hit PAUSE, took a screenshot, and saved and printed the image.

The woman was stunning. As she entered the room, every face seemed to turn to her like sunflowers to the sun. Angie rewound and played the moment again.

Jaz entering the restaurant was like a magnet being set among metal shavings that began to vibrate along her magnetic poles. The alpha male of the group—Garrison—immediately moved his chair over to make a gap for another chair to be brought in for her. But Jaz declined to sit there, choosing instead to seat herself beside Jessie. An immediate little power play, thought Angie. Jaz said her hellos all around. Garrison eyed Jessie, who looked suddenly flustered.

Rachel took a seat, now including herself in the footage. She must have set her camera on a tripod and left it running. More food and drinks arrived. Hand gestures turned expansive, voices rose, complexions grew flushed, and eyes turned bright and animated as fishing adventures were shared.

Catching any particular thread of conversation was impossible, but among the group Angie identified the German septuagenarian, Hannah Vogel. Now deceased. The woman closest to Hannah in age was Donna Gill, sixty-one, the triathlete. Also deceased. The redhead with freckles Angie pegged as Irene Mallard, forty-two, unmarried, husband having an affair—the "loose vagina" woman now living abroad. The bottle blonde with the hard face and foul mouth Angie identified as Kathi, bitter divorcée, single mother. No child support. Ex paying for sex in his sports car.

Jaz left the table. Angie noted both Garrison's and Jessie's gazes following her ass. Kathi moved her chair closer to Garrison. She leaned drunkenly toward him. This caught Jessie's attention. A strange look entered his eyes as he watched Garrison listening politely to whatever Kathi was saying in his ear. Eden came suddenly and sharply to her feet, a look of disgust on her face. She muttered something, and Hannah reached out and placed her hand on Eden's arm. Hannah then also rose from her chair and said good night to the group. She and Eden left the establishment together, Hannah with her arm around Eden's shoulders.

Donna also left as Jasmine returned to the table with a new drink in her hand. Jasmine angled her head, smiled at Garrison, and pointed to the pub section. Kathi's face darkened. Booze had clearly removed the filter that controlled Kathi's facial expressions. The men were no longer even trying to hide their overt sexual attraction to Jasmine Gulati. The other women were noticing, too. The footage ended.

The next clip opened in the pub area. Angie presumed Rachel was once more behind the camera, and the filmmaker was clearly pursuing the Jasmine-sexual-interest angle. Her lens was focused tightly on Jaz's face. Jaz's black eyes glittered with drink and apparent amusement. But her stance was combative as she pointed her long-nailed finger into the face of a big man with strawberry-blond hair. The male was missing two front teeth. He was flanked by three equally robust males, and they all looked tanked. Two of the men appeared identical. Angie paused, rewound, and watched the segment again. She figured the two could be twins. She took some screenshots of the males, which she printed. She hit PLAY again.

Noise and cheering was loud, but Jaz's voice came across clear. "So—what? You're like *all* related to that hockey player kid? Like, the whole town?"

The camera lowered slightly, capturing her cleavage. Jaz had loosened her top buttons to expose a dusky swell of breasts. Yeah, she was sexy. Exotic. Apparently worldly. Jaz Gulati was something these rural dudes might not have come across in some time.

"Is the hockey kid the reason for this whole rabid turnout thing?" She waved her finger in a circle, indicating the raucous crowd in the bar. The diamonds on her ring finger glittered in the light.

Angie could almost feel the tension rising off the men—a mix of lust, resentment, anger. She leaned forward with increasing interest.

"Whaddya mean, *rabid*?" The big toothless man with strawberry-blond hair spat his words at Jaz, getting closer, in her face. He wore what Trish had referred to as a Kamloops tux—a lined plaid shirt-cum-jacket. Angie took another screenshot of him and jotted a note in her book: *Toothless male. Strawberry-blond. Shirt matches description of males on ridge. Who is he? Who are other three men with him? Two are identical twins?*

Jaz did not back down from Mr. Toothless. Instead, she took a step closer to him, and Angie realized she was actually getting a kick out of turning these guys on while humiliating them at the same time. "Come on, sweethearts, you *gotta* all be interrelated. Just look at *you* two guys." She gestured to the identical-looking men with black hair and green eyes.

"What're your names, handsomes—you guys twins? You look kinda like our guide, Garrison Tollet. Same eyes and hair and build and"—her gaze brazenly dropped down to their crotches—"size and all."

Garrison suddenly appeared at her side. He took Jasmine's arm firmly. "This is Beau and Joey. My cousins," he said. "Come with me."

She resisted, trying to shake off Garrison's hold. "Beau and Joe? No way!" She threw back her head and laughed, showing the smooth column of her throat. "See? I told you!" She wagged her finger between the men. "All related. Do you also live in the woods? Got no dentists out there?" She tilted her chin toward Mr. Toothless. "You guys play banjos, too?"

"Fuck you," said one of the twins, stepping forward.

"Come. Now," Garrison growled to Jaz. "See that booth over there? Go wait for me there."

"Nope, I need to go fetch another a drink." She slurred the edges of her words as she turned to aim for the bar.

"I'll bring you a drink. Go wait."

"Really? You'll bring me booze? Oh, okay then, yessir, boss guide, sir. I'll wait for you in the booth." She wove her way through the crowd toward the booth, calling over her shoulder as she went, "Make mine a dirty martini. I *like* dirty."

Garrison shot a hot warning glare at the men. "Play nice with the tourists, okay? Port Ferris needs their money. *We* need their money."

"We don't need to be fucked over by them for the price," said the big blond. "What're you now? A fucking prostitute, Garry Boy? Selling yourself out for some fucking city clitty?"

Garrison lowered his voice, eyes turning cold. "There's a camera on you right now. This documentary could be real good or real bad for our town. Play nice, and I'll ask that this footage never sees the screen. Got it?"

"What're *you* going to do, try to get into her pants?" said Mr. Toothless. A fifth male joined the group. He was older. Smaller. Pale. Freckled complexion. Also fair-haired. *Scrawny* was the word that came to Angie's mind. She grabbed a screenshot of him and printed it.

"Fuck you, Wally," Garrison said.

Angie scribbled in her book: *Mr. Toothless—name is Wally?*

"What's going on?" said the scrawny male.

"Nothing," Wally muttered as they all watched Garrison head to the booth where Jasmine waited.

One of the twins—Beau—flipped a bird at the booth. "Fuck you, cunt, bitch."

"Fucking bitch," repeated his brother, Joey.

The footage ended abruptly. Angie scribbled: *Wally who? Who is the older scrawny, freckled guy? Twins—Beau and Joey who? Cousins to Garrison Tollet how?*

She sat back a moment, chewing on her pen. Talk about antagonizing the locals—Jaz had been like gasoline to fire. Shit. Angie rewound and watched again, absorbing the nuances and taking more screenshots, which she printed out. She'd use the prints for interview purposes when she drove up to Port Ferris.

After she'd watched the altercation between Jaz and the men one more time, Angie pulled up the final file that Daniel had converted for her. She hit PLAY.

This file showed general footage of the bar, Rachel presumably trying to capture the deteriorating ambience as the night wore on. Angie had to hand it to the filmmaker. She did have a way of putting a camera into people's faces without inhibiting them. Or perhaps that was the booze. But clearly Rachel had been careful to maintain her role as an objective recorder because at no point had she intervened in Jaz's altercation with those massive men.

Angie watched the crowd footage carefully, trying to identify faces. The camera lingered slightly on Kathi, her cheeks red as she stood drinking at a high table with Jessie, Irene, and two other guys. Kathi's gaze shot daggers in Jaz's direction. Jessie also cast the occasional look over his shoulder at the booth where Jaz and Garrison huddled over drinks. His features showed displeasure. Understandably—Jasmine Gulati was a client of his and of Garrison's, and this was ground zero for their trip. It did not bode well for the next seven days.

Angie paused the footage in several places and grabbed additional screenshots of faces. She saved them to her hard drive and hit PRINT on several. She paused suddenly as she noticed a woman entering the rear door of the pub. Slight with reddish-blonde hair. Could it be? Angie froze the scene and enlarged the image.

Shelley Tollet.

Now, there's a thing.

The pale and fragile Sissy Spacek look was undeniable. It was definitely Garrison's wife. She looked barely thirty. Angie hit PLAY and watched intently as Shelley entered the bar, her gaze searching the crowd.

Jessie noticed Shelley almost immediately. He left his table and hurried through the crowd toward her. He put his arm around her, turning her around, trying to shield her from sighting her husband with Jasmine in the booth. He guided her back toward the exit. But it was too late. Shelley looked over her shoulder and froze as she saw Garrison cuddling up close to Jasmine.

Shelley's body stiffened. Her jaw sagged, and her eyes went wide as she shot a desperate look at Jessie. Jessie bent his head to hers, said something. She shook her head. He spoke some more. She considered his words, then handed him a package. She looked once more toward the back booth and rushed out.

The scrawny older dude who'd earlier joined the men arguing with Jasmine saw Shelley leaving. His gaze shot to Jessie. Something unspoken passed between the two men. Mr. Scrawny then hurried out of the pub after Shelley.

Angie sat back, feeling exhausted. There was enough motive emerging here for any number of people to have wanted to hurt Jaz Gulati.

Was her accident really just an accident? Or could someone have helped it along?

Or worse.

Could someone have pushed her into the water above the falls with intent to kill?

CHAPTER 21

TUESDAY, NOVEMBER 20

Kjel Holgersen stood in a bus shelter smoking his cigarette. It was almost 3:00 a.m., and the road near the university campus was dark, misty, and deserted. Silence had a weight at this hour. It pressed in with the fog. People were asleep in their little houses, hearing not even the wail of a distant siren.

As much as Kjel resented being partnered with Leo in what Leo called the Unit of Lost Causes, his curiosity was piqued. He'd had his own suspicions about Detective Harvey Leo. Mostly they'd involved a belief that Leo was paying young female addicts on the street for blow jobs. And the guy was a mean asshole. He'd dropped Pallorino in the shit for sure. But a dirty cop?

He sucked in another deep chestful of smoke, exhaled slowly, and checked his watch. This was his fifth night in a row with no sleep, so he'd come here at this hour to focus on his case. It was either that or wander the dark streets looking into doorways for the familiar, ravaged face of his father, searching for a way to stay one step ahead of his memories, his guilt.

He and Leo had gotten a tip via the social media blurb that Kjel had asked to be posted on Annelise Janssen in an effort to revive her missing persons case.

A male had called into the soc media desk shortly before Kjel and Leo had punched out for the day. The man claimed he'd seen Annelise at this bus shelter on the night she'd disappeared. Kjel had asked him to come into the station to make a proper statement. The guy claimed to have been leaving one of these small houses behind this bus shelter around 3:00 a.m. last December—a full ten hours after Annelise Janssen was believed to have last been seen on the university campus.

The man said he'd seen the young woman huddled in this bus shelter. She'd been soaked, he'd said, and looked drunk. No coat. It had been extremely cold that December night. While he'd watched, debating whether to approach her, a white Mercedes van had come up the road. It had pulled up to the shelter, stopped. The van had a logo on the side—maybe dark blue or black or olive green. The witness couldn't be certain given the rain and mist and the dull street lighting. But he'd described the logo as a simplistic, blocky graphic, like First Nations art. The design had reminded him of a stylized animal, like something you'd find on top of a totem pole. The woman had climbed into that van. It had been headed north, he'd said.

Kjel looked northward up the glistening, deserted street, trying to bring the scene to life in his mind in these similar conditions. Once that van had reached the top of this road, it would have hit a traffic circle. From there it could have traveled in any of three opposing directions.

Kjel killed his smoke and yanked up his collar. The self-proclaimed witness maintained the reason he'd not come forward until this time was because he'd been having an affair and had been sneaking out of his lover's house that night. He hadn't wanted his wife to find out where he'd been. But he was divorced now, so it no longer mattered what his ex knew. Kjel had checked. The man's ex had corroborated the affair and divorce. Kjel had then run this new Annelise Janssen information through the crime analyst, and something very interesting had popped up. It was possible they'd scored a major break on more than just the Annelise Janssen cold case. This case could be linked to others.

Ducking out of the shelter, Kjel made for his vehicle parked a short way up the road. His plan was to grab a coffee at the twenty-four-hour Tim's, maybe a couple of jelly doughnuts. And wait until it was a decent enough hour to call Pallorino. His reason was twofold—to check on her for Maddocks, and to sound his theory out on her, because one of those potentially linked cold cases had been hers.

But as he drove toward the Tim Hortons, Kjel found himself near the bottom end of the city by the water. Wipers going, he slowed his vehicle to a crawl as he peered into the shadowed doorways and alleys. Searching. Always searching. For the man he'd once believed he'd find on these streets. That belief was wearing thin like tired, ragged cloth.

He hit the brakes as something caught his eye. He reversed, stopped. It was nothing.

Just wet cardboard flapping in the wind.

A persistent buzzing entered Angie's consciousness. She yanked a pillow over her head, trying to muffle the noise. Her brain was pounding. Then it struck her as she became more aware—the intercom. Someone was calling up for her. She sat bolt upright in her bed.

Maddocks?

She swung her feet over the side of the bed and stumbled blindly to her front door before it dawned on her that Maddocks would have used his key. Frowning, she grabbed her phone from the wall near the door. "Yeah, who is it?"

"Heya, top-o-the mornin' to ya, Palloreeeno."

She shut her eyes, cursed, and shoved a tangle of hair off her face. Holding her hair in place on the top of her head, she glanced at the clock in the kitchen. "What do you want, Holgersen? Everything okay?"

"For sures. Wanna go grabba jabba? I needs to pick your brain on a case that crossed your desk last winter."

"Excuse me?"

"I said, I needs to pick your brain."

"Have you seen the time? It's not even six thirty."

"Figured I didn't wanna miss you or nothing."

She swore again and almost told him to beat it, but intrigue won. "What case?"

"UVic student who went missing last December. Annelise Janssen."

"That wasn't mine."

"Yeah, but she might be linked to one of your old ones. Can we talk?"

Damn him. He'd hooked her, and he was reeling her in. Had to give the guy credit where it was due.

"I'll be down in fifteen. Coffee shop on the corner—it opens early. Order me the full breakfast when you get there, okay? On your dime." She hung up and eyed her computer. She needed coffee and food anyway. She'd find out what Holgersen wanted and then come back here to transfer the rest of her files to her laptop and pack while she tried to set up appointments in Port Ferris and, along the way, Ladysmith, because that's where Kathi Daly lived. Before going to bed, she'd made a list of "persons of interest" in the Jasmine Gulati case.

If all went to plan, she could be checked in at the Port Ferris motel by late this afternoon and doing her first interviews this evening. Once she'd packed she'd swing by Mia Monroe's clothing boutique, Candescence, and see what Mia had to say about her long-term friendship with Jasmine and why they'd fallen out shortly before Jasmine's river trip. Then she'd drop by Mayang Photo Place and pick up any other files Daniel might have managed to salvage for her.

Angie sat at a small table opposite Holgersen and watched him breaking the poached egg atop his vegetarian "ninja bowl," which had set him back almost twenty-five bucks.

"So how's you doing?" he said as he delivered a spoonful of eggs, brown rice, sriracha, bok choy, and kale to his mouth. "Getting a buncha work from that Brixton at Coastal?"

Angie bit into her breakfast croissant and chewed as she watched Holgersen's eyes. His gaze darted everywhere except to meet hers. He was hiding something. Or he was more buzzed on caffeine and nicotine and lack of sleep than usual.

"Yeah." She swallowed and reached for her coffee. "A bunch of work." She sipped, relishing the hot hit of caffeine and the flavor of a good medium-roast single-source grind.

"So whatcha working on now, exactly? By the way, nice ring you gots around your neck there, Pallorino."

She weighed him, suspicion deepening. "Did Maddocks send you to check on me?"

He finally met her eyes. "Why would he do that? You not seeing him no more or what?"

Touché.

He waited.

She considered carefully what she was going to say, then figured she'd like Maddocks to know what she was doing and to not worry about her being at loose ends while she figured a few things out. She was also warmed by the fact he still cared enough to send the goofball here to check on her. "I got the Moss Girl case. You know the remains that mushroom picker found up at the Nahamish?"

He stilled chewing, lowered his utensils. "Yeah?"

"Body was identified as Jasmine Gulati, granddaughter of retired Supreme Court justice Jilly Monaghan. Coroner is ruling her death as an accidental drowning, but the judge wants me to paint a picture of Gulati's life in the lead-up to the accident and to answer a few questions."

"Shit. For reals?"

She snorted and finished the rest of her croissant. She was hungry for a change and actually looking forward to driving up to Port Ferris and sinking her teeth into some interviews.

"So," Angie said as she swallowed and reached for her mug. "When you do report back to Maddocks, you can tell him I'm going to Port Ferris for a while."

"Fine, you wins. He asked me if I'd seen you around, and I told him that I'd stop by. But I's also got questions of my own for you. Regarding an old sexual assault you worked. So two stones with one bird."

"Two birds with one stone."

"What?"

"That's the saying—killing two birds with one stone."

"Yeah, sure, whatevers." He reached into his jacket pocket and pulled out a photograph. He slid the picture across the table. "Remember her?"

Angie frowned at the mug shot. "Molly Collins. Yes, I remember her. Vulnerable kid from a broken home, her mother known to police. Collins left her home after a fight with her mother one night about three years ago, September 2015. She went to buy drugs from her dealer at a gas station down the road from her house; next thing she was found lying concussed in the middle of the road near the waterfront at around 4:00 a.m. She'd been violently sexually assaulted."

His brows crooked up. "You, like, remember dates and faces of alls your cases and everything?"

"I wish I didn't."

"MVPD never nailed the guy," he said.

Angie studied the image of Molly Collins, her mood darkening. "No," she said quietly. "We never arrested anyone. Collins had been high at the time of her attack. She recalled little to nothing once she sobered up and came round fully. The only information she could provide was that her attacker was big and had been wearing coveralls with some kind of company logo on the chest pocket. He drove a white van with the same company logo on the side. She was assaulted in the back of the van, and when her attacker started to drive off, she somehow managed to get out of the back doors while the van was moving. Six months after that incident, she was found dead from an overdose." Angie paused. "Why the questions?"

"Last December Annelise Janssen allegedly vanished from the university campus."

"Allegedly? It was where she was last seen."

"Until a call comes into the station yesterday. Some dude says he thinks he saw Janssen around 3:00 a.m.—a full ten hours after the campus sighting."

Angie listened intently as Holgersen described what the new witness had claimed.

"And now that this dude's wife has left him anyways," Holgersen said, "he came forward because what he saw has been haunting him all these months. He feels sick about the idea that had he come forward and said something at the time, it might have helped us find Janssen. Maybe alive."

"No fucking kidding. You . . . think these are connected—Annelise Janssen's disappearance and the Molly Collins assault?"

Holgersen scraped up the last morsels from his ninja bowl and delivered the dregs to his mouth. "Could be," he said around his food. "Given the white Mercedes van."

"There's a white Mercedes delivery van on every second street corner, Holgersen."

"Yeah, but there was this other case on the mainland in November 2002. A young woman vanishes off the streets in the Downtown Eastside. Some street worker thinks she saw this woman getting into a white Merc van with a logo on the side. Then in 2009 a young woman vanishes near Blaine in Washington State. Her car had broken down on the highway. The working hypothesis at the time was that she probably flagged down a vehicle for help and was abducted. She was never seen again. Big call for information went out. Cops handed out flyers at road stops. Posters were put up at the border on both the American and Canadian sides. Finally someone who drives that border route regularly comes forward and says he saw the breakdown, and he saw a woman waving down a white van. The vehicle was stopping, so he drove on, thinking she had help. The van model was a Merc, and it had a graphic on the side. The witness *thinks* it had BC plates."

Angie regarded him steadily, a familiar hot rush rising in her chest. "A serial?" she said.

"Maybe."

"How'd you realize a white Mercedes van was involved in those other unsolved cases?"

"Ran the new Janssen information by our crime analyst. White van pops up as a link. The shit them computers can do these days."

"You've got an analyst?"

"Boss man brought one in to help us look at a bunch of cold cases. Janssen was one of the files I picked up first."

"So Maddocks has you working cold cases?"

"New focus or something. Part of iMIT. He's got me and Leo in our own little unit looking at a whole bunch of unsolved shit. The directive comes from brass and police board, and there's new money for it, apparently. They wants to ramp solve rates. Janssen's father has also been laying pressure on the new mayor. Daddy Janssen's got clout."

"Yeah, money has clout. Fuck all the less privileged women who've gone missing. I don't see why you brought this to me. Apart from being an excuse to check on me."

And remind me I'm no longer part of the team.

"You remember anything else about the Molly Collins case?"

"I filed all my reports. My notes are there, too. You have access to everything there is at the station." She pushed her chair back, irritated now because the bug had bitten her, and her hands were tied—she could do nothing about this case. It was like dangling a carrot in front of her nose, just out of reach, before yanking it away again. Just to remind her she once was a cop, and now she was not.

"Thank Maddocks for breakfast," she said as she came to her feet. She unhooked her coat from the back of her chair and shrugged into it. But as she began to walk away, Angie paused. She turned back to face Holgersen. "Did anyone else give a description of this logo? Was it the same on the other vans?"

"It was a dark, kinda boxy, stylized image is alls I gots. That much seemed consistent. Obviously nothing immediately recognizable like a Coca-Cola or MacD's logo or anything."

She held his eyes for a moment. "Good luck, Holgersen. And get some sleep. You look like shit."

He grinned. "Yeah, you toos, Pallorino."

As Angie exited the bistro and headed past the window, she saw Holgersen on his phone inside. She reckoned he was calling Maddocks to report she was busy on the Jasmine Gulati case.

That suited Angie fine. She knew it would put him at rest. He'd know she wasn't taking that close-protection job. The fact he'd sent Holgersen nosing around after her put a flare of hope in her heart.

She was going to make this work.

CHAPTER 22

Angie walked into the teeth of the wind, and as she rounded a corner near the Chinatown area of Victoria, she caught sight of the boutique sign.

Candescence.

She stalled in her tracks and stared up at the hand-painted word. Slowly, she lowered her gaze to the dresses displayed in the bay windows of the heritage building. White lace. Sheer silk. Some designs frothy. Others sleek. Pink and white flowers everywhere.

A bridal boutique? You have got to be kidding me.

She took a deep breath and pushed open the door. A bell tinkled. The interior was small and had been refurbished to highlight the historic architecture of the building. Plaster had been stripped from walls to expose swaths of the original brick. Knotted pine floors had been burnished to a gleam. A wooden staircase with a balustrade painted with black enamel curved to a downstairs area. A glass showcase held tiaras and glittery necklaces and earrings with pearls and diamonds. Music was soft, a female vocalist crooning a song that sounded an awful lot like the one "Jukebox Jill" Monaghan had belted out when Angie went to meet her. Bridal dresses lined racks. Several gowns had been pinned into display alcoves set into the brick walls.

There was no one in sight.

Angie stepped forward cautiously, her biker boots clumping on the wooden floor. "Hello?" she called out. "Anyone here?"

A woman's head popped out from behind a drape that partially screened a dressing room area decorated with Louis XV–style chairs upholstered in gentle florals. The woman, a blonde, removed pins she'd been holding between her lips. "Over here. Come on through."

Angie stepped into the dressing area, immediately catching sight of her reflection being bounced back by a myriad of mirrors. In her black leather jacket, skinny jeans, biker boots, red hair scraped back into a functional ponytail, she couldn't have looked more out of place against all this femininity and softness.

"I was just pinning up a hem for alterations," the woman said as she smoothed down her dusky-pink skirt and draped silk blouse. She looked like a model out of some Calvin Klein ad. A hesitancy crossed her delicate features as she absorbed Angie, apparently coming to the conclusion that Angie was here for something other than a wedding gown.

"What can I do for you?"

"I'm looking for Mia Monroe."

Concern shifted into her eyes. "That's me."

"My name is Angie Pallorino," she said, digging into her pocket for a card. She handed it to the woman. "I'm looking into a cold case from twenty-four years ago involving an old friend of yours, and I think you might be able to help me. Do you have a moment? Is there somewhere we can talk?"

Mia studied the card in her hands. Time had been kind to this friend of Jasmine's. She'd aged remarkably well. Or perhaps Mia had been kind to Mia. Maybe her looks came from eating carefully, sleeping, and exercising well. Maybe it was working with blushing young brides full with the promise of life that kept one peachy.

She glanced up from the card. "Which friend?"

"Perhaps we could sit down?" Angie didn't want to dump the news on this woman that the body recently found on the Nahamish had been identified as her close school friend.

Mia's attention went to the door. "Sure. My first appointment is in only fifteen minutes. And my assistant will be back any second to take over the front. She just stepped out for coffees." She hesitated. "Shall I call and ask her to bring extra coffee?"

"No. I just had some. Thanks." Angie perched herself gingerly on the edge of a Louis XV chair, unzipped her jacket, and loosened her scarf. It was warm in the shop.

Mia sat across from Angie, arranging her legs neatly to the side, hands folding in her lap.

"I don't know if you saw the news about the remains in the shallow grave that was recently discovered on the Nahamish River?" Angie said.

Mia stared at Angie, her eyes widening. "Jasmine?" she said softly. "Is it Jasmine? I wondered if it could be her when I heard."

Angie nodded. "DNA has confirmed it, yes. The coroner is ruling her death as an accidental drowning, but her grandmother has asked me to answer some questions about Jasmine and her life leading up to the trip. I believe you and Sophie Sinovich were her closest friends."

She exhaled shakily. "Yes. Wow. I . . . I suppose her gran can finally lay her properly to rest now. I can't believe it, after all this time."

"If you don't mind my asking, I understand you and Jasmine had a big fallout shortly before her trip. Can you tell me what that was about?"

Mia's shoulders stiffened. "Why?"

"Jasmine's fellow anglers on the trip said she was making a big deal about a supposed secret. Also, when she drowned, she was wearing what appeared to be an engagement ring, but no one seems to know who gave her the ring and whether there even was a significant partner in her life at the time of her death."

Mia looked away. "I see," she said, picking at an invisible thread on her tailored skirt.

"It would really help her gran to have these questions answered. It would help her find closure, Mia."

"I . . . I suppose, if it will help her gran"—she looked at Angie—"there was a significant other. But I don't know who he was. Jasmine was terribly secretive about it. He got her pregnant."

Angie blinked. "Jasmine was *pregnant*?"

"No—no, I mean, she was, but she terminated the pregnancy just before the trip." She rubbed her arm, a nervous gesture. "I think Jasmine was involved with someone who wouldn't commit, but when he learned she was pregnant, he proposed. I suspect it was his way of convincing Jasmine to go through with the abortion. His way of proving to her that he'd still be there for her afterward, that she wouldn't be abandoned."

"What makes you think this?"

She exhaled heavily. "I don't know. I might be way off base, but I just had a feeling that Jasmine was worried she would lose this guy if she didn't go through with it and that he'd be angry. Because part of me believes she wanted to keep the baby."

Angie regarded Mia, an energy, an excitement, building inside her. Jasmine's past—this case—was looking more and more interesting.

"Why did you fall out with Jasmine, Mia?" she asked. "Was it because of the abortion?"

She cast her eyes down. "Jaz wouldn't tell me who the guy was. In fact, she was smug about having a secret lover. Her attitude irked me. Jaz, Sophie, and I had been tight since junior high. We shared and talked about everything. From first cigarette, to first kiss, to first sex. Her big secret lover was a slap in my face. Then, when she asked me to go with her to Vancouver for the abortion nevertheless, I put my foot down and said no. I told her she should think more carefully about her decision to terminate and to not do it simply to hold on to some secret guy. Sophie went with her instead. We never talked again." Her voice caught, and she looked up.

"Not that we even had a chance. Jaz went and disappeared on that river. We were never able to make amends, and I'm deeply, deeply sorry for that."

"Mia," Angie said, leaning forward, "do you have *any* idea who the father might have been? Any wild guesses?"

She inhaled deeply. "No. I don't. Jasmine had a ton of boyfriends over the years. She never hid them. Mostly she had sex with them, got bored, and moved on. This time was different. Whatever she was hiding, she did a damn good job hiding it."

"If she did intend to marry this guy, do you think she would she have slept with others on her river trip?"

"Did she?"

"Possibly."

Mia considered this. "If she did, knowing Jaz, she might have been testing herself or the parameters of her secret relationship. It wouldn't surprise me to hear she'd engaged in casual sex after getting rid of the baby, just to prove to herself that it wasn't the end of the world. That she could still be whoever she wanted. She could have been testing the guy himself." Mia paused. A wry smile curved her mouth. "Then again, knowing Jaz, maybe there was never a secret-ring guy. Maybe she bought the damn diamond ring herself just to fool us all."

Again this possibility was being raised, and Angie took note. It spoke strongly to Jasmine Gulati's character.

"Why would she do that—pretend?"

"Jaz was like that." Mia smoothed away the invisible thread. "The adoration of guys, and sex, was like an addiction to her. She wanted to be Ms. Mysterious, always the center of intrigue and attention." Mia's eyes turned sad. "She was needy. I think deep down Jasmine was empty and afraid, and I wish I'd been there to help her. Instead I pushed her away."

Angie held Mia's gaze and swallowed, thinking of her own issues with anonymous sex. Her own buried neediness. "Was that her first pregnancy?"

Mia blinked. "God, yes. Why?"

"Are you certain? She never carried a child to term?"

"No. No way. We shared everything. All of it. Until the engagement ring and the mystery lover, of course. Even then Jaz still shared her pregnancy with me and Sophie. Like I said, the three of us had been tight since junior high. Jaz and I go back even farther, to elementary school."

"There wasn't a period where Jasmine went away perhaps? For a long enough time that she could have given birth, possibly given the baby up for adoption?"

"Definitely not. She traveled to Europe with her parents one summer after grade nine. But it was for only four weeks. After we graduated, Jaz, Sophie, and I traveled around South America for five months. We were always together. Otherwise any trips Jaz took were short. Never anything to indicate the possibility of a child. Why?" she repeated, concern in her features.

"The autopsy results raised a slight possibility that she might have given vaginal birth. But it's not conclusive. I just thought I'd ask. There was also indication in the postmortem of an old shoulder injury. Do you know anything about that—a dislocation possibly?"

Mia's brow furrowed as she cast her mind back. "No. I . . . I can't recall anything like that."

Angie came to her feet. "Thank you for your time, Mia. You've been a great help. If you do remember anything else, could you please call me?"

Mia stood. "I will. Good luck. I'd love to know what you find out."

"I'm sure Jasmine's gran would also like to speak to you about her granddaughter. I think she's lonely," Angie said with a smile. "You should visit her."

"I . . . I think I will. That's a great idea."

As Angie turned to go, Mia said, "That's a beautiful solitaire around your neck."

Angie's hand flew up to the ring she'd exposed by unzipping her jacket. "Oh, I, uh, thanks."

"Why not wear it on your finger?"

"Needs to be resized."

"Engagement ring?" Mia said, coming forward to examine the diamond.

Angie nodded, her cheeks heating.

"Congratulations."

Angie stepped back abruptly and made for the door, suddenly feeling claustrophobic. Mia hurried ahead and opened the door for her.

"You know, there's a jeweler one block up who can resize that for you in a few hours. I highly recommend him. His name is Dominique. Accent Jewelers. Tell him Mia sent you. Wait—" She scurried over to her desk and picked up a card from the neat display. "Here you go. And do mention my name. He'll give you a good deal."

Angie took the card. Her gaze drifted to the dresses displayed in the alcoves set into the wall. One gown in particular caught her eye. The design was sleek, simple. No fuss or frills. It reminded Angie of something Celtic or medieval in design. Angie had always liked that look. Made her think of Robin Hood's Maid Marian in deep, dark Sherwood Forest, or Guinevere. Of knights and dragons. Mia's gaze followed Angie's.

"When's the big day?" Mia said.

Angie shook herself. "I, uh, we haven't settled on a date yet."

"And a dress?"

Tension balled in Angie's stomach. "Not yet."

"That would look absolutely stunning on you. Especially if you wore your long hair straight and loose. I can just see it. With maybe a small circlet headpiece with a dropped pearl at the brow."

An image formed in Angie's imagination. She shook it off. "Thanks." She pocketed the card and stepped out into the cool air, delighted to have the door of Candescence close firmly behind her.

She zipped up her jacket and hastened up the street, aiming for Mayang Photo Place. Her Mini Cooper was already packed for her drive to Port Ferris.

Angie stopped at a crosswalk to wait for a red light, and she glanced down the street to her right. There it was—Accent Jewelers.

Maddocks's words filtered into her mind.

Just know one thing, Angie—I love you. If you want to stay engaged, if you want what I want, to get married—I'm here. I'm yours. But it's your call . . .

She checked her watch. She had some time to kill before meeting with Daniel. She didn't *really* have to start driving up island until noon or 1:00 p.m. at the latest. What the hell—if she wanted to do something concrete to show Maddocks that she was serious, *this* was a first step. Fit his ring.

A warmth crushed through her chest at the thought of wearing his diamond on her hand. She turned and headed quickly down the street, making for the jewelry store before she could change her mind.

CHAPTER 23

"I'm sorry, Ange," Daniel said. "I got nothing else for you apart from one additional file. The rest is damaged goods. There had to have been a water event, some kind of flooding, maybe a burst hot water cylinder in that crawl space where these tapes were stored. They all got soaked at some point. I suspect they never really dried out properly."

"But the first ones you converted were fine."

"Different box. That one must have stayed high and dry."

"Are you *sure*?"

He gave her a dry look.

"Can you restore the tapes?"

"I can try a few tricks with some of the cassettes, but basically what I gave you is what you're going to get."

Angie inhaled deeply as she processed this fact. "Okay. Can you tell me if the rest of the cassettes at least matched up with the inventory list, apart from those final missing ones you already told me about?"

"Affirmative. Rest is all there."

"Thanks for trying."

"Anytime." He handed Angie an invoice, and she settled her account. As she retraced her steps to the jewelry store, she recalibrated her thoughts. When she arrived at Accent Jewelers, they informed her that her ring was ready.

Dominique himself brought it out and slipped it onto her ring finger. The diamond winked and danced in the light. Emotion threatened Angie's eyes and filled her heart. She wished Maddocks was here. She looked up at Dominique and said, "Thank you. Thank you so much."

He smiled. "Looks good on you. Congratulations."

Angie left the store with the ring on her finger and a cocktail of conflict churning in her gut. Maybe this ring resizing was a fruitless exercise. Maybe she really had pushed Maddocks too far. Maybe she shouldn't be wearing the ring until they'd mended things. His words looped through her mind again.

I'm here. I'm yours. But it's your call.

At the intersection she hesitated once more and stole another glimpse at the diamond on her hand. Her chest ballooned with trepidation. Fear. And a whispering, distant sense of . . . excitement. Of possibility.

Your call.

She steeled her jaw and hurriedly dug out her phone. Quickly, before she thought the idea was ridiculous, before she decided she was overstepping the mark, she dialed a number.

Angie almost choked on a sudden upsurge of nerves, but she tightened her grip on her phone as Ginny, Maddocks's daughter, answered.

"Hey, Ginn, how are you?" She tried to keep her voice light but failed miserably.

"Angie? Is . . . everything okay? You sound odd."

She cleared her throat. "Yeah. Yeah, everything's fine. Have . . . have you got classes this morning?"

"Not until noon. Why?"

She blew out a huge breath. "Okay. Can you meet me downtown? Like, soon? Now?"

"Angie? What's going on—is it Dad? Is he all right?"

"It's . . . I need your help. It's a surprise. And yes, it's to do with your father. But it's all good, I promise."

"Ah . . . sure. Where downtown?"

Angie gave the address without naming the store. "I'll be inside. Ask for me."

She ended the call and sucked in a huge breath as she pressed her hand against her sternum. She then bent into the wind and hurried back down the street. As she shoved through the door of the boutique, the bell tinkled. Mia and her assistant both looked up in surprise from where they were busy at the desk. Angie was breathing heavily.

Mia surged to her feet. "Is everything okay?"

Angie nodded toward the dress in the alcove. "I—I think I'll try it on. That one."

Mirrors covered the walls floor to ceiling, and a thick drape shielded Angie from a sitting area designed for family members or bridesmaids or girlfriends—or whoever brides-to-be dragged along to these things. She stared at her reflection with a sense of surreality swallowing her because Angie did not recognize the woman staring back.

Her red hair hung loose and long about her shoulders, offsetting the clean lines of the gown. It fitted like a glove—like Cinderella's freaking glass slipper, like it was meant to be, just hanging there waiting for her to catch a case that would drive her into the bridal store where she would see the dress.

"Angie?"

She jerked at the sound of the familiar voice coming from behind the drape.

"Ginn, is that you?"

"Yeah, I'm out here. What is this? What in the hell is going on in there?"

Angie drew back the curtain.

Ginny gasped. Her hands flew to her mouth, and her eyes went round. "Oh. My. God. Angie? Is . . . is this for *real*?" She reached out both hands, took Angie's in her own. "Ohmygod, is this going to happen? Is this *really* going to happen?"

Angie felt stupid suddenly. She felt exposed. As if she'd just showed Ginny a secret dream before she was even certain she could attain it.

"I . . . maybe." She swallowed. "Your dad and I have been discussing it for a while, and I came in here for work, and I saw this, and—"

"And you thought you should try it on? Damn right you should have! It's freaking made for you." Tears glinted in Ginny's eyes. "Let me see you. Come out here. Turn around." Ginny stepped back.

Angie came forward and did a slow turn, feeling self-conscious.

Ginny pressed her hand tightly over her mouth and stood there in silence, shaking her head.

"That bad?"

Ginny shook her head harder.

"Ginny?"

"I . . . I can't even talk." She half choked, half laughed the words. "And that ring! Wow, let me see?"

Angie held out her hand, and Ginny examined the ring. She looked up. "Dad didn't tell me. About any of this."

"Ginny, he kinda doesn't know. It's complicated. He . . . we're still working it all out."

"But he gave you a ring. He knows about the ring."

Angie nodded. "But then we had a bit of a blowup. We're . . . taking it slow."

Ginny nodded and blew out a chestful of air, trying to gather herself. She moistened her lips. "Okay, okay. So the dress is a surprise."

"You could say that." Angie snorted, feeling awkward now. "It's a mistake," she said, turning to go back to the dressing area. "I don't know what made me do it."

Ginny grabbed her wrist. "No, Ange, no. It's not a mistake. This is so you. It's beautiful. You'll never find anything like it later. You've got to do this."

"I—I think it really was a mistake."

"No." Ginny's eyes crackled with a sudden ferocity. "I know my dad. I know you. This is going to happen. I know it with all my heart, and I'm going to help make sure it does. You're going to get this dress. And—"

Angie opened her mouth, but Ginny's hand shot up. "No. Hear me out. If you want to argue with yourself, go right ahead. You tell yourself that if things don't work out, you can sell the gown. No problem. But if things do go ahead, you have it. You have something beautiful." Ginny's hot eyes glittered with emotion. She swiped away a tear. "You're doing this, okay? You just are. You called me for a reason, and it's clearly apparent that my reason is to make sure you follow through and order this dress."

Emotion filled Angie's eyes and made her heart hurt. She loved this kid. This kid who would be her stepdaughter if the marriage went ahead. Like Justice Jilly Monaghan had gotten a grown stepdaughter in Jasmine's mother. Jilly Monaghan's words whispered through her mind.

Things happen for a reason, Angela. I firmly believe this. One needs to seize the opportunities where they present.

Angie nodded. "Okay," she said softly. "But it's our secret, Ginn. Just in case things don't work out."

Ginny smiled, a mischievous little glint entering her eyes. "Yes," she whispered. "Our secret."

CHAPTER 24

The cupcake bakery in Ladysmith was tiny, with two sets of round tables and chairs pushed up against a window that looked out into the mall parking lot. Behind the glass-fronted counter, a woman in her sixties was icing a batch of cupcakes.

"Kathi Daly?" Angie said as she approached the counter.

The woman glanced up briefly before returning to piping icing. "What can I do for you?"

"I'm Angie Pallorino. We spoke on the phone."

"Yeah."

"Is there someplace we can talk for a minute?"

"Talk away. If customers come in, you'll have to take a back seat. I don't have anyone to fill in for me right now."

Angie watched as Kathi finished her icing job. Confronted with silence, the woman was forced to look up again. Irritation tightened Kathi's features, which were already pinched with the passage of time and a look of bitterness. Her harshly dyed blonde bob against a dulled complexion further aged the woman. In Kathi Daly's case, the years had not been kind.

"I don't know why you bothered to come," she said, laying down her icing bag and wiping her hands across her apron. "There's nothing I can tell you in person that I couldn't have done on the phone."

"I appreciate you seeing me," Angie said. "I like to talk to people face-to-face." *That way I can tell a whole lot more about you, like whether you're lying. Or hiding something. Or whether you're just a bitter old crone . . .*

"I was wondering if you could walk me through what you remember from that last night in camp before Jasmine Gulati disappeared over the falls."

"Rachel said she told you what happened already."

"Did Rachel call and prep you?"

"Yeah."

"Why would she do that?"

Kathi snorted. "To tell me I was under no obligation to talk to a nosy PI. Because she didn't want her friends to be bothered on her account. This was her trip, she organized it, and she feels bad that you're snooping around interviewing everyone now. Looking for blame."

"Rachel said I was seeking to blame someone?"

"Aren't you? Isn't that what high-and-mighty folk like Justice Monaghan always do—sue someone? Try to blame the organizers, or the guides, or—"

"I'm only trying to answer some questions for a grieving grandmother, Kathi. That's all. Justice Monaghan has questions about her granddaughter and what was happening in her life prior to the accident."

"Well, I'll give you my angle straight, then. I didn't like Jaz. I think a lot of people disliked her. She was an arrogant slut."

"Because she slept with one of the guides?"

"He was married."

Angie crooked a brow. "From the film footage, you looked pretty interested in married Garrison Tollet yourself."

Kathi's eyes narrowed sharply. She said nothing.

"From what the others say, you and Jaz seemed to hit it off on the trip, spent time sharing drinks, talking around the fire."

"Drunks love company. That's all it was."

"She ever tell you who gave her this ring?" Angie set the photo of Jasmine's diamond cluster atop the counter. "Maybe Jaz mentioned a fiancé or significant other while you were having drunken tête-à-têtes around the campfire?"

"You kidding? It was her big secret."

"She write about this secret in her journal?"

"I have no idea. Look—"

"Do you know what happened to that journal, Kathi? It had a purple cover. Here—" Angie laid on the counter the group photo that included Jasmine holding her journal. "She's holding the book in this photo."

There was a flicker in Kathi's eyes. "Wasn't it with her things in her tent?"

"No. It was missing."

She shrugged.

Angie held the woman's gaze. "Were you envious of Jasmine?"

Kathi blinked at the blindside. Her faced reddened. "I'll tell you what, when your husband runs off and fucks every young pussy that hits his radar and leaves you with four kids and no means of an income, you might also have *issues* with nubile young sluts, okay? Do you think I'd still be slaving away in this damn bakery at my age if he hadn't left me in a shithole of debt? Hope that guide's wife gave him hell—she came into the pub, you know? She saw him cozying up to that . . . that woman in a booth."

"I saw that on Rachel's footage, yes. Do you know whether Garrison's wife confronted him about it or spoke to Jaz about it at any point?"

"I have no idea. I think his wife visited one of our campsites one evening. Brought food or something. I think it was the first or second camp. Can't recall. If she did confront Jaz, I wasn't there, because that I would have remembered."

"And your memory of that last night, the hours before Jaz died?"

"All a blur. A nice alcoholic blur. Was my escape from the kids and my fucked-up life for a few blissful days until she went and drowned and ruined it all."

The bakery door opened, and two women entered.

"If you don't mind, I need to get back." Kathi turned and addressed her customers.

"Thanks," Angie muttered more to herself than Kathi. She exited the cupcake shop and walked to her car, the coastal wind tearing at her hair. She felt like having a drink and finding some nice numb bliss herself just to get the bad taste of that woman out of her mouth. She opened her vehicle door, thinking she'd have been tempted to push Kathi Daly over Plunge Falls had she been on the trip. Angie hoped Rachel's daughter, Eden, would be more cooperative when she met with her in Nanaimo, a small city just north of Ladysmith. But Angie had doubts given that Rachel was calling around and giving everyone a heads-up.

As she drove to Nanaimo, rain began to spit against her windshield again, and a dark seed of thought unfurled inside her—she wouldn't put it past bitter and jealous Kathi Daly to have pushed a "nubile slut" into the river.

CHAPTER 25

Dr. Eden Hart's waiting room was empty when Angie entered. Pale-gray walls and large windows filled the interior with natural light despite the dark, moody weather outside. Freshly cut flowers in a vase on a coffee table provided additional cheer. Magazines were lined in neat rows atop the glass surface of the coffee table.

A receptionist behind a counter at the far end of the room peered over the rims of her glasses.

"I have an appointment with Dr. Hart," Angie said as she approached the counter. "Name's Angie Pallorino."

"The doctor is running a bit late. Please take a seat. Coffee is in the urn in the corner over there. Mugs are next to it." She smiled. "The cookies are pecan and white chocolate today."

Angie sat, flicked briefly through a magazine, then turned her attention to the black-and-white prints on the walls. Some were historic photos, others ink sketches and block prints. With surprise Angie realized they all depicted women angling. Intrigued, she came to her feet and studied the first photo. It was signed by Lorian Hemingway. Angie presumed the woman standing proudly beside a swordfish that hung from a scale on a dock in some tropical locale must be one of Ernest Hemingway's twelve grandchildren. Angie moved over to the next image. A block print of a nun in full habit casting a fishing line into the water. A quote beneath the print read:

Si tibi deficiant medici, medici tibi fiant. Hec tria, mens leta, labor, et moderata dieta.

"If you fall short of doctors, physicians will be these three—the happy mind, work, and moderate diet," said a female voice behind her.

Startled, Angie swung around.

A brunette of her own height and age stood right behind her—Angie hadn't even heard her approach. She nodded toward the print. "Dame Juliana Berners, a prioress and noblewoman credited with writing the first fly-fishing essay. Ironic really, considering how long men have dominated the sport ever since." She extended her hand. "Eden Hart."

"Angie Pallorino." Angie took Dr. Hart's hand. It was fine boned, her skin soft, nails impeccably manicured. But her grip was solid. Her gaze was equally firm.

"It was in your mother's VHS footage from the Hook and Gaffe pub," Angie said. "The mention of the nun."

Eden smiled. "You've done research."

Angie laughed, recalling the clip of Trish explaining to Eden why she'd thank her mom for introducing her to fishing. "So your mother made an angler out of you yet?" she said.

Eden's smile did not falter, but something shifted ever so slightly in her laser-sharp gaze. Angie felt a small frisson. There was something enigmatic, forceful about this woman. Something in her smile that while warm and engaging did not seem reflected in her eyes. Her mother's daughter.

"It's really good to meet you," Eden said. "Although I do feel like I know you already, from your story in the news. I'm looking forward to reading Dr. Reinhold Grablowski's upcoming book."

Angie winced. "It's kind of the last thing I'm looking forward to anyone reading. He's written it without my consent."

"I know. True crime is always fascinating to me. The psychological impact on you as a four-year-old victim, losing your twin as well as your mother, the repression of traumatic memory—it must be devastating still."

"A survivor," Angie said crisply. "I'm not a victim. I'm a survivor."

The psychologist's eyes held hers, and Angie felt suddenly as if she'd come to be interrogated by this woman rather than the other way around. Or that Eden was challenging her, laying down subtle lines in the sand.

"Yes, of course," Eden said softly. "A survivor. My apologies. Come on through." She held her arm out toward the door. "I rescheduled my lunch-hour appointment so we can chat in peace."

At least that made a change from Kathi Daly.

"My last patient left via the rear entrance," she said as she showed Angie into a consulting room with comfortable-looking chairs and decor that was easy on the eyes. "Therapy can be an emotionally draining experience for my patients, and no one wants to exit through a waiting room full of people after sobbing their eyes out. This way—" She took Angie into a smaller office that led off the consulting room. Inside was a large desk. Bookshelves lined the walls. Eden shut the door behind them.

The wall beside Eden's desk was adorned with framed degrees, diplomas, medals. The glory wall, thought Angie as she stepped closer to read the inscriptions on some of the medals that hung from ribbons.

"You're a marathoner as well?"

"I completed five. But I prefer the river or ocean to the road. Give me a kayak and a rod over pavement and running shoes any day." She nodded at the medals. "But those races were to prove to myself I could actually go the distance if I put my mind to it. Many things in life are analogous to the marathon struggle. I use the metaphor a lot in therapy."

"These are your kids?" Angie said, moving to the next wall, which was hung with what appeared to be family photographs.

"Two sons and a daughter, yes. I have a stay-at-home husband, or I don't know how I'd manage." Eden gestured to a leather chair. "Please, take a seat."

"Is this him, your husband?" Angie pointed to a photo of a balding male with a beard. The man looked soft in the face, a little flaccid in physique. Gentle eyes.

"Yes. John Drysdale. I kept my own name for my practice since it's how I qualified."

Angie briefly scanned the other images. There were at least seven photographs of Eden and her father at various stages in their lives. No images of Eden with her mother.

Angie stopped at a fading print of a little towheaded boy on a tricycle.

"Is this your brother, Jimmy?" Angie said.

"It is. We lost him that holiday. It's the last picture we have of him."

"I'm so sorry," Angie said as she took the seat being offered her. "Your parents told me about him. It must have been traumatic. Maybe it still is," she said, lobbing Eden's earlier dig back at her.

Eden gave a wry smile. "Touché. It is. Past trauma never really leaves you. You need to make room, a home for it, and learn to live with it and use it in positive ways."

Angie let that sink in because it was true. She was still trying to make a home for her past while at the same time forging a new way into the future, a new way to be.

Eden took a seat opposite Angie and said, "The hardest, I suppose, was that my mother blames me in some ways for Jimmy's death. I was supposed to be watching him, but I'd ventured off the dock to gather the blackberries I could see growing in brambles farther along the lake-shore. While I was picking berries, he went off the edge of the dock with his tricycle. By the time I heard the splash . . ." She fell silent, then inhaled slowly. "Guilt can be a terrible thing. I felt guilt for years. My mother still does, I think. Because she left me with Jimmy, and I was only nine at the time. My mother feels she shouldn't have given me that responsibility at that age."

"What about your father?" Angie said with another glance at numerous dad-and-daughter pictures on the wall. "Was he at the lake that summer, too?"

"He was busy marking papers in the lake house. It was my mother who should've been taking care of us—at least, that's what she'd led my dad to believe she was doing so he could focus on his work. She left us alone often—she was a bad mother in that respect. It's a miracle nothing happened to either of us before then." Eden regarded Angie as if watching for a reaction from which she'd learn more about her visitor. But Angie kept her features studiously impassive. Again, she had a sense the head doc was messing with her mind, testing for something. Maybe that's just what shrinks did.

Eden crossed her stockinged legs and settled back into her chair. Her pumps, Angie noted, looked like they probably cost more than several months' worth of her old MVPD detective's salary. "My mother called to tell me you'd been to see her and that you took her uncut documentary footage. She explained what you were after. How can I help?"

"I suppose she also advised that you were under no obligation to speak to me?"

Eden grinned. "Of course she did. Which made me even more interested to meet you and hear you out."

Angie realized she was a chess piece in some ongoing power game that defined Dr. Eden Hart's relationship with Rachel Hart, the famous outdoor documentary filmmaker and self-professed feminist. "What can you tell me of those last hours in the camp before Jasmine Gulati left to fish alone and before the guides screamed for help?"

"My memory from the trip is spotty. I was only fourteen at the time, and a lot has transpired in my life since then. But I do recall snippets from the turning point events. Like our arrival in Port Ferris and, of course, the night Jaz went over the falls. We'd pulled the boats in for the evening and set up tents. The guides got the fire going. Then Jasmine left with her gear to go fishing. The guides departed shortly afterward to hunt for more wood. Then my mom left to shoot evening footage."

"Which way did your mother go?"

She frowned. "I . . . don't know. I can't recall. I only remember her saying she was going to shoot while the evening light lasted. I went to relieve myself in the woods, but I didn't see her anywhere. Is it important which way she went?"

"Just trying to line up the chronology. There's some discrepancy in accounts. Plus, the VHS footage your mother shot that night has gone missing. Any idea where it might be?"

"Me? Hell no. I never got close to her stuff. There'd have been death to pay."

"What happened next, after you went into the bush to relieve yourself?"

"I returned to camp. It was getting dark. Cold. I went to sit by the fire, where the other women were having drinks and chatting about the day. Then we heard a man scream for help. We all got up and ran up to the logging road. We saw Jessie Carmanagh come racing down the road toward the camp. He said he needed the radio. He said Garrison Tollet had seen Jasmine going over the falls. Garrison was trying to climb down the cliff to the base of the falls to see if he could find her."

"Where was your mother at that point?"

Eden looked up and to the left, thinking. "I don't know. No . . . wait. She was there, I remember her there. On the road with everyone milling about in panic. I don't know which way she'd come from. It was chaos. Jessie radioed for help. We all went downriver with flashlights to see if we could help, but Jessie ordered us back to camp, said he didn't need anyone else falling in and that the cops and SAR would be arriving soon. When they arrived, they tried searching in the dark below the falls with hunting spotlights and then ramped up in the morning. But there was no sign of Jasmine."

Angie opened her sling bag and took out her folder. From the folder she extracted the image of the ring. Like the others, Eden said the same things—Jasmine acted like she had a big secret and had told no one who'd given it to her.

"Jasmine wrote nightly in her journal," Angie said. "Did she ever tell you what was in it?"

"Another secret. She made like it was full of sexy stuff. Her way of messing with the heads and libidos of the male guides who couldn't stop ogling her boobs and her ass and fussing about her."

"Jessie fussed about her, too?"

"Everyone was agitated by Jaz in some way." Eden uncrossed her legs and sat forward, an energy lighting her eyes. "As you're well aware, Angie, given your professional involvement with lust killers during your tenure with sex crimes—Spencer Addams specifically—sex is often simply about power. Control. Ownership. In retrospect, that's what Jaz was all about. Controlling others."

Angie felt her own vibe darken at Eden's mention of the man she'd shot and killed. The event that had cost her her career. She swallowed, holding Eden's eyes. "So you never read her journal?"

"No, I never read it. But I wanted to." She smiled. "I was fourteen and fascinated by Jasmine and what that diary might hold."

"Any idea who took it? It wasn't with Jasmine's belongings after she drowned."

"It wasn't?"

"No."

Eden shook her head and made a moue. "Maybe one of the guides sneaked off with it, and after her death it became too awkward to hand it back?"

Angie chatted awhile longer about the first dinner in the pub, about Sheila Tollet visiting the campsite, about the small blowup between Jaz and the lesbian couple over adoption, about an argument Jaz had with Hannah Vogel and Donna Gill regarding a woman's obligation to support the feminism cause, about Kathi and Jaz's drunken camaraderie.

Angie thanked Eden and came to her feet. "If anything else comes to mind, would you give me a call?"

"I will." She got up and moved toward the door. "Was everything kosher with the autopsy results?"

"Yes," Angie said simply. "Jasmine's death is being ruled as an accidental drowning."

"So . . . Justice Monaghan is just fishing? S'cuse the pun."

"She needs to round out an image of her granddaughter's life before laying her officially to rest. It's her way of coping, I think."

"Or entertaining herself."

"Maybe that, too."

As Angie left Nanaimo and drove the last leg up the desolate island highway to Port Ferris into a darkening bank of clouds, she considered the enigma that was Dr. Eden Hart.

With a mother like Rachel Hart, it was easy to see the forces that had shaped a young Eden. Both were powerful, strong women with sharp feminist sensibilities. It was this feminism that had underscored the intent of Rachel's documentary. Jaz, in her own way, had been a free-spirited, powerful female who wielded her sexuality as a weapon or used it as a tool, sparing neither man nor woman. And as Angie knew well, ambitious and driven women could make a lot of people very, very uncomfortable.

Angie wanted to like Eden Hart. She wanted to like Rachel, too. But there was something about the two she couldn't quite pinpoint. Yet.

Or was she just like the rest—uncomfortable around women who, while holding fast onto their feminine whiles, could also act like men? No. It was more. In Angie's experience, men were generally straightforward. Women were more dangerous—because they were more devious. The aggression was usually quieter. And sometimes darkly passive, hidden like fly hooks in pretty feathers behind smiles and compliments and nice shoes.

CHAPTER 26

The Hook and Gaffe sign Angie had seen in Rachel's footage still creaked in the sea wind above the entrance to the restaurant and pub, but it had long been replaced by a newer version. She parked in the lot outside, checked into the motel adjacent to the restaurant, and dumped her bags on the bed in her room.

The room smelled musty, as places close to the sea often do. She yanked back the drapes, and dust motes floated down. Across the street, through the salt-crusted windows, stood the row of weathered waterfront stores Angie had seen in the digitized footage, including the old Mariner's Diner. Behind the buildings a wooden pier jutted out into a harbor. Gulls darted and wheeled above the pier. Clouds boiled low over a sea dark gray and veined with foam.

This was one of the rooms Rachel Hart had booked for her group twenty-four years ago. Angie suspected not much had been done to spruce up the decor since. She felt as though she'd stepped back in time.

Leaving her gear locked in her room and armed with her recorder, camera, and a folder of screenshots, she drove straight for the Sea-Tech Industries compound, where the aquaculture division was run by Jessie Carmanagh. Jessie had agreed to meet Angie in his office at 5:30 p.m.

Her route took her down to the docks and along train tracks and a rail yard with graffiti-covered silos. The tide was low, exposing rotting pylons and a swath of barnacled and seaweedy rocks that stretched out into the bay. Rain came down softly, and mist blew in. The effect was bleak. Cold. Desolate.

Angie turned into the five-acre compound. The entrance bifurcated. A sign on her right pointed to the Sea-Tech Freight division. Another sign on her left indicated the Sea-Tech aquaculture operations. Angie turned left.

She'd looked up the company before coming. While Jessie Carmanagh ran the aquaculture arm, the freight division—which shipped the live fish and shellfish produced by the aquaculture division across the country and south of the border—was run by Wallace, Mr. Toothless, who Angie had discovered was also a Carmanagh and Jessie's older brother.

She drove toward a long squat building near the water. Men were leaving the building in groups and making for vehicles parked in a lot at the back. It was close of business, and she presumed the men were Sea-Tech employees heading home after their day's work. She parked and found Jessie's office at the end of the building closest to the wharf. She knocked on the partially open door.

"Come in!"

Angie entered to find a woman in her forties seated behind a metal desk with a half-eaten burger in her hands, a supersize drink and fries at her side. The place smelled of fast food and diesel from the boats coming in. Metal shelving filled with binders lined the walls.

"I'm looking for Jessie Carmanagh," Angie said. "I have an appointment with him. My name's Angie Pallorino."

The woman swallowed her mouthful and set her burger down. "Oh yeah." She wiped a napkin over her lips. "He took off down to the wharf."

She rolled her chair back on its wheels, got to her feet, and waddled over to the grime-streaked window. She pointed. "That's him down there by that row of painted bollards. He's fixing the scallop cages."

Angie peered through the window. A large rangy male wearing a bright-orange visi-vest atop heavy all-weather fishing gear bent over what looked like a tangle of nets.

"If ya want to speak to him, you'd better head on down. He'll be a while sorting out that tangle."

Angie exited the building, drew up her rain hood, and walked to the waterfront. A soft drizzle fell, puddles pooled along the concrete paving, and boats jostled along the dock on the rising tide. The place smelled like fish. And diesel engines. Near the dock was a large hangar-style warehouse containing drums. Under cover of the hangar, men in coveralls were busy with the drums.

"Jessie Carmanagh?" she said as she reached the man.

His head jerked up.

A spark of recognition shot through Angie. Although now in his late fifties, Jessie Carmanagh still retained something of the boyish quality she'd witnessed in Rachel's footage. But his eyes belied the rest of his physical presence. They were lined, watchful, calculating. They told Angie she was not welcome here.

Several of the men in coveralls in the adjacent warehouse stopped working. A few grouped together and watched her from under the cover. One lit a cigarette and leaned back against a drum. Jessie flicked a glance at them.

She proffered her hand and a smile. "I'm Angie. We spoke on the phone earlier. My partner and I had the pleasure of doing a Nahamish drift with your son, Hugh, recently, along with fellow guide Claire Tollet. Hugh's a fine teacher and an incredible angler."

"Yeah, I know you were on the river last month. Budge told us." Ignoring her hand, he returned his attention to untangling scallop cages. "And we saw you on the news."

Us.

We.

"You're friendly with Budge Hargreaves?"

"Everyone knows everyone in these parts."

Angie reached into her pocket and activated her digital recorder, keeping it hidden so as not to agitate him further. She eyed the men in the warehouse. She sensed she had a very small window of time to get Jessie to talk.

"Could we maybe discuss this under cover, perhaps in your office?"

"You got something to say, say it here."

In full view of his men. In the rain. He's going to make this as difficult as he can.

Rain started falling harder, and mist blew in thick off the water. Standing in the rain, Angie explained how Justice Monaghan had contacted her and why.

Jessie fiddled with his equipment in silence as he listened, impervious to the increasing rain and mounting wind. Tackle and halyards began to clunk against masts, and water sucked and slapped loudly at the docks. Buoys affixed to the side of the warehouse began to thump in the wind.

"So what does this have to do with me?" He cast another look at the men watching them, smoking, under the cover. They were all big guys. Several with thick black hair. Jaz was right. They did all seem to be bred from a certain mold. Or perhaps this industry and manual labor just attracted the large physical sort. Nevertheless, their presence was hostile, and Angie felt time running out. She cut right to the chase.

"Can you tell me what you witnessed the last night on the river before Jasmine Gulati drowned?"

He came suddenly and sharply erect, all six two and more of him. He planted his stance wide in his fishing boots. Angie tensed, resisting the sharp urge to step backward.

"Look, I've been through this. Twenty-four years ago. And so many goddamn times, over and over—interviews with RCMP, the coroner, the media. Questions from friends, family, everyone in this community. I searched day and night for that woman with the SAR guys until the river got too high and the snows blew in. I volunteered on the searches the following spring when the river got low. She was my—*our*—client, and losing her was the fucking pits. I was *happy* when we could finally put it all behind us, okay? Whole of Port Ferris was relieved to see the damn media circus leave town." He pointed his finger at her. "And no one is welcoming dredging it up again now. Especially me." Hot spots were forming along his cheekbones.

Energy seemed to shift in the group watching them. One of the men ground out his cigarette under his work boot and left the cover of the warehouse. He crossed the paved lot, making for the main building that housed Jessie's office. A sense of foreboding filled Angie's chest. A mental clock ticked fast in her brain.

"I'm sorry, Mr. Carmanagh," she said quickly while keeping the men in her peripheral vision. "But on the other side of the equation is Jasmine's family and friends. They need to process things now that her remains have been found. You're going to have to allow them that little bit of leeway and for them to ask a few final questions. So if you don't mind, I'd like to ask you a few of those questions."

Jessie's mouth thinned. "Make it quick."

She pushed a wet strand of hair off her face. "The reports indicate it was Garrison Tollet who saw Jasmine Gulati going over the falls. Can you tell me where exactly you were in relation to Garrison when that happened?"

He swiped water off his brow with the base of his thumb. "Garrison was up above the talus ridge on the north bank. There was a deadfall up there. He had a handsaw, was cutting some wood. He had a clear view to the falls. I was lower down on the scree, gathering kindling. I couldn't see the river from where I was. My line of sight was blocked by trees."

"How did Garrison know it was Jasmine going over?"

"I don't know that he knew it was her right at that instant. But two and two was put together at some point. Her gear. Her hair—long and dark. He saw it flowing in the white water. We knew from before we left camp that she'd been going downriver alone to fish in the eddies above the falls."

"What happened next?"

"He screamed for me to go radio for help."

"You carried no radio on you at the time?"

His eyes narrowed. "No. I left mine at the camp for the women. Garrison was supposed to have the other one so that the women could call us if they needed. He'd forgotten it. Look, it wasn't a big deal at the time. We went a short ways to find wood. We'd left them all safe at camp."

"Apart from Jasmine."

A flicker ran through his features. "She was an accomplished angler. She knew what she was doing. She was also a client from hell. She wouldn't listen to anything anyways."

"So you kind of wrote her off in terms of protecting her, keeping her safe like the others?"

Tension corded the muscles at his neck, but he said nothing.

"What did Garrison do while you ran back to radio for help?"

"Climbed down the cliff to the base of the falls. Dangerous as all hell, that was. Slick rocks, sheer in parts. That woman could have cost Garrison's life, too."

"When you reached camp, where were the women?"

"Milling about on the logging road. They heard Garrison screaming and came up from the camp."

"All of them?"

"Yeah. All."

"Rachel Hart, too?"

"Yeah, she'd returned from the shelf where she was shooting."

Energy quickened through Angie. "What shelf?"

"We'd seen her from above, her pink hat. We'd all been given Kinabulu toques from the company sponsoring the trip. Some got red hats, some black. But hers was the only hot-pink one. It looked like she'd set up with her tripod on a rock ledge and was filming. From that ledge she'd have had a good line of sight down to the small bay where Jasmine's rod was found, where there were signs she'd slipped."

Rachel's words chased through Angie's brain.

I also left the camp. After the guides. I followed the bank upriver along a promontory of land that jutted out into the Nahamish. From the point I filmed some footage looking back at the campsite. I wanted the ambience of the fire and smoke in the gathering dusk. I was there filming when I heard men screaming.

Had she lied? Why? Had she been filming Jasmine fishing alone in the dying evening light? Is that why the final footage had gone missing?

Or was Jessie lying now?

"Why was it not mentioned in the coroner's and police interviews that you'd seen Rachel filming from the ledge?"

"No one asked me where the other women were while I was gathering wood. It was an accident. We were all doing our best."

"Did anyone else see Rachel Hart on the ledge?"

"I don't know. Probably not."

"So you were the only witness."

"Jeezus, what are you looking for here?"

"Did you like her, Jasmine?"

"Whether I liked my clients or not is immaterial. My son, Hugh, would say the same—whether he liked you and your partner was not an issue. It was his job to show you the ropes and take care of you."

Angie hurriedly zipped open her sling bag and removed her file. Using her body to protect the contents from rain, she took out a screenshot of the group of men at the Hook and Gaffe.

"Could you please identify for me everyone in this photo?"

His body tensed at the sight of the photo. His gaze shot to her face. "Why?"

"Jasmine upset some of these guys. We captured this image from VHS footage that documents the entire exchange between Jasmine and these men. If you don't help me, Mr. Carmanagh, someone else will, and I'm going to be asking what you're trying to hide."

Hostility crackled off him. He flicked a glance at his office, to where the man had disappeared. Returning his attention to the photo, he pointed and said, "That's Budge there at the back of the crowd, standing by the bar."

Surprise rippled through Angie. She peered closer at the image. Jessie was pointing at a huddle of men near the bar, to whom she'd paid little attention. "Budge Hargreaves? He was also there that night?"

"Yeah."

"He looks a lot thinner. I wouldn't have recognized him."

"Lost his wife about fourteen months prior to that day. He'd pretty much been on a bender and in a bad way since her death. After she died, he sold their place in town and moved out onto Tollet land."

"Who's that standing beside him?"

"Darnell Jacobi."

Angie's pulse quickened. "The RCMP officer?"

"He was a rookie back them. Fresh out of depot division. His dad was staff sergeant of the Port Ferris detachment at the time."

"So Constable Jacobi is friendly with Budge Hargreaves?"

"Look, I don't know a guy worth his salt who *wasn't* in the pub that night. It was hometown hero Robbie Tollet's big game in Helsinki. That's a big deal, okay? It was right before the original Jets folded, and it's a small goddamn town. We all know one another."

In her peripheral vision Angie saw a different male exiting Jessie's office. He was big and blond, and he started toward them.

Angie pressed on fast. "And the others in the photo?"

"Behind the bar there, collecting the glasses, that's Axel Tollet. Used to work at the Hook and Gaffe back then. He's a driver for Wallace now. My brother. Wallace runs the freight division of Sea-Tech."

"Axel any relation to Garrison Tollet?"

"Cousin."

She pointed at the big toothless aggressor in the photo. "Is this Wallace, your brother?"

"Yeah, that's Wally."

"And the twins here—they're Joey and Beau Tollet?"

"Yeah. Axel's brothers. They're over there." He jerked his head in the direction of the group watching from the warehouse.

"They work for Sea-Tech, too?"

"Like I said, small town, a few big family-owned businesses. Makes for limited employment options."

Angie stole another look at the men in the warehouse. She could make out two big dark-haired guys among them. She figured they were Beau and Joey. Jasmine must have been out-of-her-mind drunk to mess with this bunch. Hurriedly Angie took out another screenshot, the one where the scrawny older male had joined the group.

"And this older guy?" She pointed.

"Tack McWhirther. Shelley Tollet's uncle. He died some years back. Throat cancer."

"He was protective of Shelley?" Angie asked.

"Shelley was his brother's only child. Tack's brother and sister-in-law died in a small plane accident off Tofino. Tack took care of Shelley until she married Garrison."

Angie sifted through the other prints, everything getting wet in the rain. She held another out to him. "What is Shelley Tollet giving you in this photo?"

His brow lowered, and his jaw tightened. "I don't need to answer this shit."

"No. But what do you have to hide?"

He regarded her intensely. "It was cat medicine. Shelley had come into town to visit a friend who was having a baby, and she also needed to pick up pills from the vet for their old cat. She said she was going to overnight in town because the friend's baby hadn't come yet. She came to the pub to find Garrison so he could take the medication back to the lodge to give to the cat when he drove his clients up in the morning."

"Did Garrison know Shelley had come in and seen him in the booth with Jasmine?"

"I have no fucking idea, okay? This right here is where I draw the line, because none of this shit has anything to do with the accident. If you go up to the lodge asking Shelley and Garrison these questions about adultery after all these years, what in the hell good do you think is going to come of that? What good is *that* going to do Jasmine Gulati's grandmother, eh? When you go telling the old judge that her grand-kid was fucking married men. She was a class-A bitch who begged for trouble."

"Problem, Jessie?"

Angie spun at the sound of the voice. The big blond male loomed behind her. Even twenty-four years after seeing him captured on film, Angie recognized him instantly as Mr. Toothless, who'd gone head-to-head with Jasmine. Wallace "Wally" Carmanagh. Even larger in life. With shiny-white crowns that didn't quite match the shade of the rest of his teeth.

"Wallace Carmanagh," Angie said, turning to face the man squarely. She kept her feet slightly planted apart, her weight positioned more heavily on her back foot—a defensive posture kicking in. She was sud-denly acutely conscious of her knife sheathed to her belt under her jacket. She was also aware she no longer carried a sidearm and was no longer protected by backup. The men in the warehouse shifted closer. Angie mentally calculated the distance to her Mini Cooper parked near Jessie's office.

Wallace ignored her and turned on his brother. "Don't say another fucking word, Jessie. I don't know what the fuck you agreed to talk to her for." He jabbed his finger in Angie's direction. "A PI like her gathers dirt about people. She sweet-talks them into giving information her client will use to file a lawsuit. You mark my words, *that's* what she's looking for. To sue your and Garrison's asses off for some stupid accident on the river a quarter of a century ago."

He faced Angie. "And you—you get your tight little ass the hell outta town before someone gets hurt, you hear me?"

Conscious of her recording device still activated in her front pocket, Angie said with feigned calm, "Is that a threat, Mr. Carmanagh?"

The twins extracted themselves from the group in the warehouse and came toward them fast. Fear curled into Angie. It was getting dark. The other employees had gone. Just this group of big men and her on a wharf in the rain and mist.

"Got a spot of trouble there, Wally?" It was one of the twins, his voice rough, deep.

"Joey and Beau Tollet?" she said with feigned cheer. "I was hoping to chat with you both as well." Angie turned in a slow semicircle, meeting each man's eyes in turn while positioning herself with a clear run to her car.

"The women on the fishing trip said they were being followed by a group of three men while on the river. One might have been carrying a rifle or some other weapon. They also said they heard a banjo at night. Do you know who might have been taunting them?"

Silence.

The buoy banged louder against the side of the hangar.

Angie cleared her throat. "Were some of you perhaps trying to spook the women because Jasmine Gulati was disrespectful in the pub that first night?"

A ripple of energy coursed through them. The wall of hostility thickened. Wind gusted and sent a crate cartwheeling over the paving with a loud clacking sound. It landed in the water and started drifting into the mist. No one moved.

"Look, I know she was difficult," Angie said. "It's all on film what she said to you. It was blatantly rude, so I wouldn't blame anyone trying to teach her a lesson by spooking her."

"That Jasmine Gulati was bad news," Wallace growled. "She needed a warning. If there were banjos out there, it would've been to teach Gulati and her friends that you don't come in here badmouthing locals, I don't care who you are."

"Or you don't go committing adultery with the locals?" Angie prompted carefully, still conscious of her recorder rolling, of her escape routes.

"Thou shalt not lead into temptation," Beau Tollet offered darkly, his voice low. Metal clanked. A horn sounded in the mist.

"So it was *her* fault that Garrison Tollet cheated on his wife? Because he was lured, tempted by a sinful, evil woman?"

Silence.

"And then the sinful woman went and slipped and fell. Right above the falls."

"Sounds about right," Wallace said.

"Okay," Angie said, defusing, de-escalating. "I understand your point of view, I do. She might have needed a lesson. Might have needed to be spooked into her place. Maybe one of you had a banjo. That's fine. No harm, no foul, right? But if you guys *were* out there lurking in the woods, tracking, following, hazing the women, watching them, one of you must have seen Jasmine fishing alone. Maybe you even saw her fall into the river?"

Silence.

"Did anyone see what happened?"

Wallace took a step closer. "I'm going to say this one more time, Miss Private Investigator, and I'm going to say it nice and slow. Why don't you go put your ass back into that little dinky vehicle of yours and drive yourself out of town? You be gone come morning, and nothing goes wrong."

"Thanks. I appreciate your time, Jessie, Wallace, Joey, Beau. And your advice." Angie calmly stuck her photos back into her sling bag as she spoke. She looked up and met Wallace's gaze, feeling a chill inside as she did. "And I will be gone. Soon as I'm done here."

She zipped her bag closed and repositioned it across her body. "You wouldn't know what happened to Jasmine's purple journal would you, Jessie? The one she was always writing in, the one with the sexy content?" She looked into his face, wet with rain. In his eyes, in his stance, she detected conflict.

Something in Jessie Carmanagh wanted to help, but he was afraid. Energy coursed through Angie at this realization. There was a lot more happening here than had at first met her eye. The dynamic of this group of males was charged.

"No," Jessie said. "Last I saw of that diary, the Hart kid was reading it in the bushes."

She stalled. "What?"

"Rachel Hart's kid was reading it. In private. In the bushes."

Eden's words raced through her mind. *I never read it. But I wanted to.*

"Are you *sure*?"

Tension hung thick.

"You calling me a liar?" Jessie said.

"No. I just want to be certain."

"Yeah, I'm sure. Only surprised me that the kid hadn't taken it sooner the way Jasmine was tempting her with it."

Tempting her with it?

"Right. Thanks, gentlemen." Angie tried to walk back to her car in a casual fashion, but she felt the men's eyes boring into her back.

In her gut she knew she had not heard or seen the end of this Tollet-Carmanagh gang. She fully expected the twang of banjos in her own near future.

Back at the motel, Angie took a scalding shower before changing into dry jeans and a comfy sweater. She called Coastal Investigations and left a message for the data clerk, who would be in the office first thing Wednesday morning. She asked the clerk to run background and criminal records checks on Wallace and Jessie Carmanagh, twins Beau and Joey Tollet, Garrison Tollet, Jim "Budge" Hargreaves, and Tack McWhirther, who was now deceased. She killed the call and gathered her files and computer. If any one of those guys had a record, it might speak to a pattern of behavior, show what they could be capable of. Right now Angie wanted to know for her own safety.

So far her biggest takeaway from her visit to the Sea-Tech compound was that either Jessie Tollet was lying and setting up Rachel Hart for something, or Rachel had lied. Regarding Eden having read or not read the journal, in that case a teen's memories might be fickle. It was always a possibility in old and cold cases like this—memory was a trickster. Angie knew this well.

Her other takeaway was a firm belief that Wallace and the Tollet twins had acted all *Deliverance*-ish and hazed the women on the river. The question now was, had one of those men seen what happened to Jasmine?

If so, why had they not fessed up or done anything to help her? Plus a darker question lingered: Could one of them have pushed Jasmine Gulati to her death? Could they have punished a "sinner" who'd lured a man from his wife?

In need of food and a hot drink, Angie took her work and headed across the road to the Mariner's Diner. The eatery still bore the same name as it had in Rachel's footage and looked as though it had not seen new owners or a facelift since. She figured it might be a good place to gather some old-timers' lowdown on the Tollets and Carmanaghs while she grabbed a bite to eat.

CHAPTER 27

Angie took a booth beneath a window that looked out over stormy Ferris Bay. The Mariner's Diner was surprisingly quiet for dinner hour—just two whiskery old men in dungarees playing chess and drinking coffees at a table close to the door and one male on a stool at the counter.

A woman in her early sixties was the lone staffer out front. She took Angie's order and said her name was Babs. She fed her slip of paper through a hatch into a kitchen at the back, where a loudmouthed chef boomed the order out to some minion who did the grunt cooking.

Angie's booth was near the rear of the diner, and she spread her laptop, files, and photographs out over the table. While she awaited her fried chicken sandwich, she sipped coffee and jotted notes in her case book. She'd have her recorded interviews transcribed by staff at CI later, but the physical act of putting pen to paper helped Angie summarize her thoughts, highlight anomalies, and formulate new questions. She was also being purposefully open about what she was doing in this diner. The motel receptionist had told her Babs the waitress had worked at the Mariner's for almost as long as it had been open. Angie reckoned someone like Babs would have a handle on juicy Port Ferris gossip. The old waitress might even get a kick out of being able to help with an investigation.

Topmost on Angie's mind was the fact Jasmine Gulati had offended a lot of people. Jaz had been gasoline to an angry flame, and discrepancies were emerging from witnesses.

In Angie's mind there was a real possibility developing that foul play could have occurred on that river. She decided to test out the notion as she began to jot down names of the people who'd expressed dislike for Jasmine, weighing each against what she called her MOM criteria—motive, opportunity, and means. She started with Mr. Toothless and wrote:

Wallace Carmanagh. *Motive: Jaz was rude to him. Aggressive and vindictive personality. Wanted to teach her a lesson. How far would he go? Opportunity: Did not deny having been on the river, possibly for entire duration of trip—could have been one of the* Deliverance *guys. Could have seen Jaz fishing alone. Was wearing clothes in the pub footage that matched the women's description of banjo* Deliverance *dudes hazing them.*

Garrison Tollet. *Slept with Jaz (still to be confirmed). Motive: Might have wanted to hide this fact from his wife. Had Jaz threatened or blackmailed him with exposure in some way? Sleeping with a client would also hurt his growing tourism business and livelihood if it was made public. Especially on a documentary. Opportunity: Alone on top of talus ridge. Jessie was alibi that he was on ridge, but is Jessie telling the truth?*

Jessie Carmanagh. *Motive: Believed Jasmine was a "class-A bitch," a bad/evil temptress seducing married men. Needed to be punished? Eliminated? Would also hurt Jessie's business if it was made public a guide had slept with a client. Opportunity: Left camp with Garrison after Jaz. Was separated from Garrison for a time shortly before Jaz was seen going over the falls. Did he lie about seeing Rachel on the ledge? Or seeing Eden reading Jasmine's journal?*

Twin Joey Tollet. *Motive: Slighted/humiliated by Jasmine. Aggressive personality. Opportunity: Could have been one of the* Deliverance *guys on the river.*

211

Twin Beau Tollet. *As above. Motive: "Thou shalt not lead into temptation" is how he described Jaz. She needed to be punished?*

Tack McWhirther. *Deceased. Motive: Was highly protective of Shelley, his niece. Had witnessed Jasmine "seducing" his young niece's husband. Wanted to punish Jasmine for seducing Shelley's husband? Protecting niece in some way? Had he been among the group along the river?*

Angie hesitated, then wrote down:

Rachel Hart. *Lied about where she'd been filming before Jaz went into water? Where are the missing tapes from that night? If she was on the ledge filming, she was alone, no alibi at the time Jaz slipped. Motive?*

Eden Hart. *Read diary and lied about it? Or did Jessie lie? Or a young teenager forgot details? If she did read the journal, what did she see in there? Where did journal go?*

Angie chewed on the end of her pen. Her plan was to drive out to Predator Lodge first thing tomorrow and interview Garrison and Shelley Tollet. Next, she'd visit the last campsite and the small bay where Jasmine's rod and the slip marks were found. Angie would then attempt to locate the rock ledge where Jessie claimed Rachel was filming. She'd see if she could get a view from the ledge down to the bay where Jaz allegedly fell into the water.

She'd also check out Garrison's and Jessie's vantage points from the talus ridge. Angie would ask Claire Tollet if she'd guide her around to the other side of the Nahamish for another look at the grave site. Possibly Budge Hargreaves would be home on the Tollet land he rented not far from the grave location. She wanted to talk to him, too. The words the young RCMP officer, Erick Watt, had uttered upon arrival at the grave site sifted through Angie's mind.

So Hargreaves just happened to come this way? He walked right into this remote grove? There's no discernible trail or anything leading into it.

She recalled the look exchanged between Constable Watt and Constable Darnell Jacobi, who'd been drinking in the pub with Budge

Hargreaves that first day of the river trip twenty-four years ago. It all took on a more sinister tone now.

Angie would like to talk to Jacobi again, too, to get his take on Jasmine's behavior in the pub that long-ago night. Given the tiny size of the Port Ferris police force, rookie Jacobi would likely have been involved in the search for Jasmine and in taking witness statements. But neither he nor Budge had mentioned the possibility that the skeleton in the moss could have been Jasmine. Angie would expect a good cop to hold back that kind of hypothesis but not someone like Budge.

Her cell rang. She reached for it, saw it was Ginny's number. She connected the call.

"Ginny? Everything okay?"

"Yeah, yeah—guess what?" Her voice was pitched high with excitement. "I just had choir practice at the Catholic cathedral downtown. I spoke to Father Simon afterward. I told him you and Dad were getting married—"

"Whoa, wait a minute, Ginn. I told you we're still working things out, and—"

"I know, I know. But Father Simon said he'd be honored to officiate, Ange. He said he'd love to marry you guys! How freaking cool is that?"

Memories from more than thirty years ago rushed through Angie. The chilling sound of cathedral bells. Snow. Christmas Eve. Her being stuffed into a cradle opposite the Catholic cathedral in Vancouver. A choir singing the haunting strains of "Ave Maria" in the church as a gun battle erupted outside. Then, last winter, her and Maddocks interviewing Father Simon about a young woman's death.

"Angie? Are you there?"

"I . . . I'm here."

Ginny's tone shifted to one of caution, concern. "Father Simon said he'd do anything to help the woman who fought so hard to find Gracie Drummond's killer, Angie. I spoke to my choirmaster. So did

Lara Pennington. She was one of Gracie's friends who worked for the floating brothel aboard the *Amanda Rose*, remember? She's so deeply grateful that you found the Baptist and stopped him."

Stopped him by killing him. Overkilling him. It cost my career.

"You saved her, Ange. Her life changed because of you. She's become a volunteer at the Haven shelter for street kids. She's started to sing like a pure angel, you know. She's digging deep, and her talent knows no bounds. It's because of you, she said. Because you and Dad helped her back to a solid place, a place where she's starting to let go of fear. Bottom line, my whole choir wants to sing at your wedding."

Emotion sparked into Angie's eyes. These words gave her past value, in spite of the personal cost.

"Ginny," she said, "I'm not ready to even begin to think about these sorts of decisions. I need—"

"Yeah, yeah, you need to talk to Dad and all, and I know you haven't attended a Catholic Mass since you were a kid, but Father Simon says he can work it all out. Just say yes. Let us organize the rest."

Angie stared fiercely at her reflection on the salt-grimed window, her mind spinning.

"Angie?"

She cleared her throat. "Ginn, thank you. This is a wonderful option. When I'm done with this case, I'll see how things stand with your dad, and—"

"I . . . uh, sorta gave Father Simon a date."

"What?"

"Just to block it off on the church calendar. You need to book these things way in advance, Angie. You can always cancel."

Her hand tensed on her phone. "*What* date?"

"April twenty-seventh. It's a Saturday. The cherry blossoms will be out. The streets will be all pink and white."

Shit. She wanted to be mad at this kid. At the same time, she loved the young woman for what she was doing.

"Angie?"

She closed her eyes and inhaled deeply. "I need to think."

"Okay, then think. Work on your case, and leave the rest to me."

"What . . . rest?"

"Just exploring some venues for a reception, that's all. Before you protest, that's all it is, just kicking tires so if it all comes together, we're ready."

We.

She had family in this kid. Ginny was showing Angie that while her past behavior had scored her enemies, it had also made her friends. There were people out there who were grateful, who respected her. That meant the world to Angie. Especially now. It fed her fire to achieve that dream of opening her own PI agency. A firm that would help others find answers during rocky periods of their lives.

Trepidation, nerves, excitement churned through her belly. "I should be furious at you, Ginn."

Ginny laughed a little nervously, and then her voice caught on a snare of emotion. "I know this is going to happen," she said. "You and my father belong together. So if you want to get mad, go right ahead, but I'm going to help this happen behind the scenes."

The waitress, Babs, appeared at Angie's table. "Hey, hon, got your order. One fried chicken sandwich and a side of piping-hot fries."

Angie shot a look at Babs. "Ginn, I gotta go. Just . . . don't do anything you can't take back, okay?"

She hung up and moved her notebook aside to make room for her food.

CHAPTER 28

Mind and emotions spinning, Angie closed her laptop as Babs set her food down. The server's gaze ticked immediately to the row of photographs on the table. "You want any ketchup or vinegar or hot sauce with that?"

"No, thanks, but a coffee refill would be great."

"You betcha." She hesitated, then said, "So you're that PI, eh? I hear you're looking into that woman's drowning from twenty-four years ago, the one found in the shallow grave."

This was what Angie had been angling for—to get Babs talking of her own accord.

"Who told you I was a private investigator?"

She wiped her hands on her apron. "Oh, everyone knows. Right from when you checked into the motel. Town like this? Osmosis, I tell ya. That's how information gets around." She nodded at the photos. "What do those guys have to do with it?"

"You know them?"

A snort. "Who doesn't? Those Carmanagh and Tollet males have been tight for generations. Half of 'em grown up in the woods along the river. Fishers, hunters, loggers. They know the land, those boys.

Right there in that picture, you got the troublemakers. Those twins and Wallace. Feed off one another. You don't mess with that gang."

"Capable of doing someone harm, you think?"

She pulled a face and shrugged. "I dunno. Wouldn't put it past them. There's some whacked-out rumor that one of that bunch, or all of them, killed a kid back in high school. Now there's no proof, mind."

Angie's pulse spiked. "Serious?" she whispered. "They *killed* someone?" She glanced around as if to feign concern over who was listening, then leaned forward and said, "Who? What happened?"

"Babs!" It was the guy who'd been reading the paper at the counter. "Can I get a check over here?"

"One sec," she said to Angie and scuttled off.

Angie took several hungry bites of her sandwich and stuffed hot fries into her mouth as she watched Babs working the till. She was famished.

The two old gents near the door packed up their chess set and went to the cash register as well. They paid for their coffees and waved goodbye to Babs as they exited.

With the diner empty, Babs scuttled back.

"Take a quick seat," Angie said. "Tell me what happened to that schoolkid."

"His name was Porter Bates," she said, sliding into the booth across from Angie. "He was a right bully. Hated gays, lesbians, blacks, the First Nations kids. Always picking on the underdog, always in trouble. He had it in for one of the Tollet boys."

"Which Tollet?"

"Axel. He's the Tollet twins' younger brother. He was a slow learner. He'd been held back several grades, had some writing disability. Like dyslexia but to do with the actual holding of a pen and writing."

"Dysgraphia?"

"It had some name like that. Porter used to call him a fag. Poor Axel. He just used to hang his head down and take it like a giant kicked puppy."

"Is this Axel behind the bar here?" Angie slid one of the screenshots over to Babs.

"Yeah, that's him. Driver for Sea-Tech Freight now. Wallace and Jessie are real good to him. Axel is how it all happened, or so the story goes." Babs cast an eye over her shoulder to be sure they were alone. She leaned forward. "Porter Bates and his two lackeys apparently lured Axel out to this quarry north of town. It's a real dark and spooky place. Dangerous with deep black water. Some of the older guys used to go out there to shoot targets and drink and mess about. When the Tollet kid got there, Porter and his mates jumped him and gangbanged him."

"What?"

"Sodomized him."

A chill rippled over Angie's skin as the horror of it sliced through her.

"Axel had just turned thirteen, and whatever happened out there, he didn't come back to school for the rest of that year. The story goes that Wallace Carmanagh got wind of what Porter did. So Wallace and the Tollet twins, and maybe Garrison, jumped him on a trail in the woods one day. They trussed him up like a rodeo calf and took him out to the quarry. He was never seen again. Just vanished. I used to know Porter's sister at school, Fallon Bates—she's Fallon Rickley now. We were in the same class. She told me Wallace and the Tollet guys drowned her brother."

Angie slowly lowered her sandwich to her plate. Her gaze locked with the server's. "Was Porter Bates's disappearance investigated by law enforcement?"

She gave a huff. "Oh yeah, for sure. Divers went down into that quarry water and everything, but I tell ya, it's black as pitch down there, thick with debris and metal bars and old vehicles. No one knows just how deep that water is. The muck at the bottom is, like, meters thick. They never found his body. Hank Jacobi—he was the top cop back then—he dropped it. I figure Hank had plenty enough worrisome run-ins with Porter Bates to figure sometimes justice ain't all black and white. Sometimes there is evil, and justice is done in strange ways, and whatever happened, Porter Bates got what was due."

Angie stared, a cold thought unfurling in her brain as she recalled Wallace's words.

That Jasmine Gulati was bad news. She needed a warning. If there were banjos out there, it would've been to teach Gulati and her friends that you don't come badmouthing locals, I don't care who you are.

"So," she said, "Wallace and the twins wanted to teach Porter Bates a lesson, so they drowned him."

Babs shrugged. "No proof. Just a story."

Angie inhaled and calmly said, "What about Porter Bates's two buddies? Were they questioned about what happened to Axel?"

"They denied everything. No one pushed further. If you ask me, no one wanted to put poor Axel through more shit by making the fact he was raped public. Poor guy. Wallace and everyone, the Tollet family, they didn't want anyone to know he was buggered. He kinda went into himself after that. As a teen he started building himself a cabin out on Tollet land on the south side of the Nahamish, not far from where Budge lives now. He moved out there not that long after. Still lives there when not staying at the Sea-Tech accommodation while on shift for Wallace."

Angie slid another photo toward the waitress. "Babs, do any of these guys own or play a banjo?"

"Not a musical bone in the Tollet or Carmanagh bodies. But him"—she pointed—"Tack McWhirther. He could play like a wizard. Guitar and piano, too."

A bell tinkled as the diner door opened with a blast of cold sea air. A young couple entered. Babs got to her feet. "Need to go."

"Wait." Angie placed her hand on the woman's arm. "Porter's sister, Fallon—is she still around?"

"Yup, lives in a house off the airport road."

"Thanks for your help."

Angie chewed the rest of her food in silence as she watched Babs seat the couple and bring them menus. It stuck in her craw—if those men had indeed drowned a kid in high school, they were capable of drowning someone again. It spoke to MO. If they'd killed a boy in the past, they were bound to one another by old secrets worth killing for again.

After paying and thanking Barb for her meal, Angie slung her bag over her shoulder and ducked out of the diner. Salty brume off the sea swirled, making halos of light. She ran across the road and through the motel parking lot and stopped dead at the sight of her Mini Cooper.

Angie blinked into rain running down her face, trying to process what in the hell had happened to it. The windows, all of them, front, back, and sides, had been smeared thick with greasy brown muck. Feces?

Her back taillights had been smashed in. Pieces of red plastic glinted in the wet puddles on the pavement. Her heart started thumping. She scanned the lot, peering into the dense sea fog.

All was quiet apart from a soft rush of waves in the distance and the sound of rain dripping. She moved to the front of her car. The headlights and front windshield had been smashed, too. A rock had been placed on the dash with something under it. Angie reached into the side pocket of her bag and took out a pair of blue crime scene gloves—cop habits died hard.

She reached through the broken window and lifted the rock. A piece of wet paper lay folded underneath. She unfolded the paper and read the words scrawled in black capital letters.

GO HOME BITCH BEFORE SOMEONE GETS HURT

CHAPTER 29

WEDNESDAY, NOVEMBER 21

Fury fired through Angie, and her hands were fisted on the wheel as she drove a new Subaru all-wheel drive model out of the auto rental lot in what passed for downtown Port Ferris.

She'd left her damaged Mini Cooper in the motel lot and scheduled a tow company to haul it to a repair shop once the police had taken a look at it. She now aimed straight for the RCMP detachment on the hunt for Constable Darnell Jacobi.

While waiting at the rental dealer, she'd gotten a call from the data tech at Coastal Investigations. Wallace Carmanagh had a record. Aggravated assault seventeen years ago. He'd done some time for it. The CI tech told Angie the assault occurred after a road rage incident. A female resident of a nearby First Nations reserve had cut off Wallace on the highway near Port Ferris. He'd honked and driven his truck up her rear in response. She'd flipped a bird at him and purposefully slowed, which had enraged Wallace. He'd followed the woman off the highway into a parking garage, where he'd struck her with a baseball bat taken from her car. He then took the bat to her sedan, breaking all the windows and the head- and taillights.

This put this sick SOB Wallace Carmanagh at the top of Angie's list for vandalizing her vehicle and leaving that threat. He was also clearly capable of violent assault on a woman. And Jasmine, a woman, had made him mad. Like the driver of that car had made him mad.

According to the CI tech, Jim "Budge" Hargreaves also had a record. A drunk driving charge. He'd been facing additional charges for leaving the scene of a vehicle accident he'd caused while driving under the influence, but those charges had been dropped by then investigator Hank Jacobi, Darnell's father. This was twenty-five years ago. Roughly one year before Rachel Hart had filmed Budge Hargreaves drinking in the Hook and Gaffe with then-rookie cop Darnell.

Hank Jacobi was also the cop who'd dropped the Porter Bates case.

Angie was not liking this nepotistic web of connections.

Wind whipped dead leaves and debris across her windshield as she pulled into a parking bay outside the tiny police station. A Canadian flag snapped alongside a provincial flag atop the building. Adjacent to the complex was the fire station.

Angie entered the reception area.

No one manned the counter behind a screen of bulletproof glass. She hit a bell several times. Finally a cop in uniform came by, yellow stripes down the sides of his pants, a bullet suppression vest over a pale-gray shirt.

"Can I speak with Constable Jacobi?" she said when he asked if he could assist her.

"I'm Corporal LaFarge. Constable Jacobi is busy. Can I help you?"

"I need Jacobi. Tell him Angie Pallorino is here to see him about the human remains found on the Nahamish and a related vandalism incident."

The young man's face changed as he appraised her. He nodded and disappeared down a corridor.

Seconds later Jacobi appeared. He unlocked the side door. "Ms. Pallorino. I heard you were in town in a private investigative capacity."

"Yeah. Osmosis."

"Excuse me?"

"Nothing. My car was vandalized last night. A note with a threat was left inside. I'd like to report it for the record, and I'd like on record that I was verbally threatened by Wallace Carmanagh at his business premises yesterday evening."

He heaved out a sigh. "Come this way."

Jacobi listened to Angie and filled in the requisite paperwork. He set his pen down. "I'll get someone around to look at your car. This is an upsetting thing for everyone," he said, holding her gaze. "Having the past dug up like this."

"I imagine it must be. You'd crossed paths with Jasmine Gulati, too." Angie took out the screenshot of Darnell Jacobi and Budge Hargreaves in the pub. She set it in front of him. He regarded it in silence. His eyes narrowed. A small vein pulsed at his temple.

"It must have dawned on you when you responded to the call about the remains on the Nahamish that they could have belonged to Gulati."

"You were a cop once." He let that hang, the past tense of it, then said, "You know as well as I the tunnel vision that comes with making assumptions about a case too early."

"Budge Hargreaves didn't mention a thing about Gulati, either—he's not a cop." Angie was pushing buttons, primarily watching for reaction.

"Look, I don't know what you're fishing for here, but I don't like the insinuations. Gulati's drowning was ruled accidental, and you're heading toward harassing local residents."

"It was your father who saw to it that additional charges following Budge Hargreaves's drunk driving accident were dropped." She nodded to the picture of him and Hargreaves in the pub.

He came to his feet. "If you'll excuse me, I have work to do."

"One more question. Your father also investigated a case many years back—the disappearance and possible homicide of a high school kid named Porter Bates."

He stilled. His mouth flattened. His eyes flickered toward the door.

"You'd have been Bates's age when he disappeared. At the same school, even, I imagine. Around the same age as Wallace Carmanagh and the Tollet twins, who were persons of interest in Bates's disappearance."

"Look, all my father had at the time were rumors. No evidence. So, bottom line, no charges were laid."

"Or a blind eye was turned? Maybe justice was seen to have been served after the attack on Axel Tollet?" Angie put her photo back in her bag and stood. "I hope you question Wallace Carmanagh about the vandalism to my car and the threat. I left my car in the motel parking lot for you. A tow company will collect it later." She gave Jacobi her vehicle registration. "I'm also aware of Wallace Carmanagh's prior assault charges. I know he wrecked a woman's skull and legs and her sedan with a baseball bat." She glanced at his paperwork on the table. "I'm glad you got this all on record. Thank you for your time, Officer."

He reached out and opened the door for her, his face expressionless, his neck muscles tense.

"Oh—" She paused, faced him once more. "Twenty-four years ago, Port Ferris RCMP gathered Jasmine Gulati's belongings and handed them over to the coroner's service. I checked the evidence list. You were the rookie cop who signed off on those belongings."

Silence.

"Any idea what happened to Jasmine Gulati's journal? It should have been with the rest of the things."

His face tightened further. He tilted his head toward the open doorway. "Good day, Ms. Pallorino. Thank you for coming in."

Jacobi followed her to the exit. But as Angie reached the door at the reception area, he said from behind, "It might not be a bad idea to leave town."

She reached into her pocket and surreptitiously clicked on her recorder. Slowly she turned to face him.

"I'm sorry, what did you say, Constable Jacobi?"

"I said, it might not be such a bad idea for you to leave town."

"Is that some kind of threat, sir?"

"All I'm saying," he said softly, "is that there are things and people in this town I might not be able to control."

"Are you implying that you know of certain people who might be a danger to me if I continue my investigation of the Jasmine Gulati incident?"

"I'm saying it might be better not to stay and find out."

His gaze locked with hers, and silence hung thick. He reached for the reception door, opened it, and waited for Angie to leave.

As Angie drove away in her rental, she cast a look back at the small police station. Constable Darnell Jacobi stood silhouetted in a window, watching her car depart. He had a phone pressed to his ear.

CHAPTER 30

As Angie gained elevation in her rental, the logging track grew steeper, and clouds roiled in thick swaths down the mountain. Rain became mixed with sleet. When she reached the eastern shore of Lake Carmanagh at the top of the watershed, the verge on her left disappeared in a precipitous drop all the way down to the gray-green glacial water. She slowed the car as visibility worsened.

From this point the old logging track hugged the lakeshore all the way to Predator Lodge, which had been built near the western outflow of the glacial lake. The Nahamish River grew out of that outflow, fed by tributaries from the mountains as it twisted its tortuous way down to the stormy and remote west coast of Vancouver Island.

The road turned rutted and muddier. Old-growth cedars and hemlocks grew tall with moss-covered trunks, branches dripping with old-man's beard. Her tires started to slip, and she felt the all-wheel drive engage. Angie was suddenly grateful to have been forced to leave her Mini Cooper behind. She was not convinced her own vehicle would have handled these conditions as well as this Subaru.

Almost halfway along the lake visibility became a serious challenge, and sleet turned heavy.

Lights suddenly appeared in the mist behind her. Angie glanced into her rearview mirror. A big black shape approached fast behind her. A behemoth of a truck.

Her pulse quickened. She tapped her brake lights in quick succession, making them flicker in the fog to increase her own visibility. But the vehicle kept on coming at speed, as if the driver still couldn't see her. Angie's hands tightened on the wheel. She tried to drive faster. Still, the truck loomed ever closer, closer. Her heart pounded.

She flicked on her hazard lights, making them pulse repeatedly in the mist. The black behemoth kept coming. Angie engaged the rear window wipers, smearing an arc through mud and sleet. Through her rearview mirror she saw big silver letters across the grille. RAM. Her mind raced as she absorbed details—Dodge, black, diesel engine. Tinted windows, the passenger cab extended. Wheels had been tricked out with silver spurs and studs. Plate was obscured by mud. A row of hunting spotlights suddenly flared to life along the top of the cab. The diesel engine revved.

Angie clenched her jaw as reality hit—this truck was trying to run her off the road. She pressed down on the accelerator, bracing her body in anticipation of a bang. But the Dodge abruptly dropped back, lights fading into the mist. Her heart slammed against her ribs.

Angie swallowed, tried to breathe. Gripping the Subaru wheel tightly, she bent forward as she peered through the sleet-smeared windshield, trying to locate somewhere she could pull off the logging track and get out of the truck's way.

Part of her also didn't want to stop. The truck's occupants might be trying to force her to do just that, and then she could be in dire trouble, out here alone with them. Unarmed against hunters. Or perhaps it was just someone trying to spook her like Wallace and the twins had spooked Jasmine and the women along the river almost a quarter of a century ago.

But the warning left in her trashed Mini Cooper suggested something more sinister.

GO HOME BITCH BEFORE SOMEONE GETS HURT

She flicked a glance at the drop to her left. She couldn't even see where the water was now, the cloud was so dense, the sleet slashing at her windshield like thick gelatin. Worst-case scenario, the driver of that truck intended to run her off the road and into that frigid lake.

The black behemoth suddenly came racing up behind her again, diesel engine roaring and revving. Her heart stampeded in her chest. She shot another look at the sheer, rocky drop on her left. She knew the lake was deep. Very deep. If her car went over and hit the freezing water, she'd sink fast, drown in the rental. If she could even get out in time, she'd have trouble making it to the surface before hypothermia got her.

The road ahead of her rose suddenly in a sharp incline. Angie took the opportunity, stepping on the accelerator, fishtailing in mud as she tried to gather speed up the hill, revs high, engine whining. Maybe she could put some distance between her Subaru and the heavy truck on the uphill. The rear of her car jacked sideways suddenly, then whipped back. But she kept her foot down, her heart in her throat.

Behind her, the truck began to fall back as she increased the gap between them. Angie hit the summit of the incline. In front of her, the road dipped suddenly. At the bottom of the hill was a tight bend. *Fuck!*

She crested and immediately started gathering speed downhill. But she barely tapped the brakes as she careered down, fists tight on the wheel, teeth clenched, her shirt growing wet against her skin.

As she neared the bottom at speed and the curve loomed, panic licked through her bowels.

This fucking driver is trying to send me into the lake all by myself. It'll look like a total accident in foul weather, with a driver inexperienced in this terrain.

Behind her the truck barreled down the incline, gaining speed now, closing all the distance she'd gained. Angie's stomach turned to water. She hit the curve, slamming on brakes. Skidding sideways, she smacked the right-hand side of the Subaru against a massive tree trunk. The impact jolted her bones, reverberating through her clenched jaw and slamming into her brain. She hit the gas again, fishtailing as she scraped the right side of her car against rocks along the upper bank.

Please, dear God, please let them just be spooking me . . . I'm not ready to die yet. Got a wedding . . . need Maddocks to see my dress . . . I'm going to be a stepmother, can't let Ginny down.

Angie pulled through the bend and rammed the accelerator down again. Behind her the truck slid through the corner, almost smashing against the same tree. It came fast now, looming in her rearview mirror. The grille of the truck blocked light. She couldn't get to her phone. Also knew from her last trip to the lodge with Maddocks that it would be no use. There was no cell reception along this strip, not until the lodge, where a signal could be received from a tower on the other side of the peak.

The logging road dipped sharply again. Angie's limbs shook with adrenaline as she once more gathered speed down the incline. She didn't know how many of these she could pull through alive, how much longer she could stomach the adrenaline, keep up the intense focus. *Fuck!* How could they be so brazen. *Fuckfuckfuck.*

As she closed in on the tight bend at the bottom with a steep drop to the left, Angie was suddenly convinced Jaz had been killed. Someone—or a group of someones—who lived out here in this desolate hillbilly redneck Canadian wilderness wanted to ensure the truth stayed buried. To do that they were prepared to kill her, too.

Who'd known she was heading to Predator Lodge this morning?

An image slammed through her mind. Constable Darnell Jacobi talking on his phone as he watched Angie drive out of the police station lot in her rental. Another image crashed into her brain. A black truck pulling off the verge and into the road behind her as she'd turned north onto the highway earlier.

Had Jacobi called someone and described her car? Given them her rental registration? Was Jacobi in this with Wallace and the gang? Or was it someone else in that truck?

Her car skidded. Jesus. She swerved, almost going over the edge of the bank on the left side. She swung her wheel sharply around another bend to her right. Her heart stopped dead. Oncoming lights in the fog. Fast. Not enough room to pass without one of them pulling over to give way. Or hitting head-on.

The Dodge came up behind her at double speed. It slammed her rear. She screamed as her car veered sideways, sliding across the narrow track, the oncoming lights looming closer. Desperately Angie struggled to spin the wheel the other way.

She went off the road on the uphill side. Through the fog the oncoming lights took shape. A red pickup. With an oval Ford logo on the front. The horn blared as it scraped past her Subaru and rounded the corner, heading straight into the path of the Dodge. Angie heard a bang.

She struggled with her gears and hit the gas again. Spinning her Subaru tires, she skidded back onto the road. She kept her foot on the gas, kept going. No way in hell was she going to stop and go toe-to-toe with whoever was driving the Dodge. They wanted to kill her. She'd call for help for the driver of the red Ford when she reached the lodge.

For the next several kilometers, Angie kept flicking her gaze up to the rearview mirror, fully expecting to see lights reappearing in the fog.

No one came.

Her muscles eased slightly, and that's when the shakes began—big palsied shudders that seized hold of her body and rattled her like a rag doll and chattered her teeth. Fisting her wheel, she swore over and over, yelling every foul word she could think of in an effort to seize back power, to control her mind, to beat down the overwhelming fear that had exploded through her body, to stop the shaking of her limbs.

Teeth still chattering with the effect of adrenal overload, Angie finally saw the dark shape of the big log lodge looming in the cloud ahead. Sleet became fat wet snowflakes as she turned off the logging track and bumped down the rutted driveway into a wide gravel-covered parking area.

In the low cloud and swirling snowflakes, the lodge was huge and gothic-looking. She drew up her hood, opened her door. Her intent was to get inside and call the police to report the truck and crash. But she stilled as it struck her that 9-1-1 would dispatch Port Ferris police. Jacobi. There was no other detachment for hundreds of miles.

Angie exited her vehicle, slammed the door shut, and tried to walk on wobbly legs toward the lodge entrance under a portico. She passed the garage area and froze.

Coming at her through the snow globe of whirling snowflakes and mist was a hooded figure with an axe.

CHAPTER 31

Angie drew her knife, flicked it open, dropped into a defensive stance. Heart thumping in her chest, she blinked into the cold snowflakes. The apparition shifted closer. Fog swirled. The person materialized.

"Angie?" said a female voice. "Angie Pallorino? Is that you?"

"Jeezus," she said, lowering her blade, a whoosh of air escaping her chest. "Claire, God, I . . . I'm so sorry."

She quickly folded and sheathed her knife, secreting it into her pocket. "You spooked the hell out of me. On top of what happened on my way over here." She took a breath and joined Claire under cover of the portico. "Someone in a black Dodge RAM tried to run me into the lake, and then I saw you with the axe. I thought . . . I don't know what I thought."

"I was splitting logs for the fire." Claire propped the axe against a woodpile near the door. "What do you mean, a truck tried to run you off the road?" She looked concerned.

Angie wiped water from her face. "I didn't see the plate. Who around here has a black Dodge diesel engine with extended passenger cab—hunting spots across the top?"

"Just about a quarter of the guys in town." Claire frowned. "Are you okay? You're shaking like a leaf."

"I'm fine. I need to make a call. I need to report the incident. Did someone just leave here or come by in a red Ford pickup?"

"Yeah, my dad just left. He's got a red Ford. He's heading into Port Ferris. He—"

"I think he might have collided with the truck. He almost hit me and then rounded the bend. I—"

"Angie, stop. My dad is fine. He called me like two seconds ago. He was already on the east side of Carmanagh Lake when he phoned. He wouldn't have gotten service between the lodge and the east outflow anyway. It's all a dead zone along the lake."

Which is why it's the perfect place to run someone off the road.

"Did he say anything about colliding with a Dodge?"

Claire scrunched her brow. "No. All he said was that some hunters had run into a spot of vehicle trouble. Their brake line had leaked fluid, and their brakes failed, which had sent them speeding downhill. They couldn't stop on a curve at the bottom, and they smashed into a rock on the bank as he approached. He was giving them a ride back into town and calling in a tow truck."

Angie glared at Claire. *"Hunters?"*

"Yeah."

"He didn't know them?"

"He didn't say."

"How many?"

"I don't know, Angie. He didn't say."

She regarded Claire, not believing a word.

"Look, why don't you come inside? I'll make you some hot tea and something to eat while you dry off by the fire."

Angie's gaze flicked to the axe leaning against the woodpile. Was Claire solid? Could she trust her? Had Garrison honestly not known the guys in the truck and bought into their fake story about brake trouble? Was it conceivable that they actually did have brake line issues, and

Angie had read the incident entirely wrong—imagining she was being run off the road?

"Is . . . is your mother home?" Angie said.

"No. She's in town. My dad's going to bring her back to the lodge after he's done with his errands in Port Ferris." Claire paused. "I imagine you came up here to talk to them about the body in the moss and the river trip all those years ago. I heard you were in town and looking into the accident on behalf of the woman's grandmother."

Osmosis. Babs was right. Angie doubted she could even scratch her own butt without everyone knowing it within minutes. It made her uneasy. Nothing was secret, yet everything was. Like the woods had eyes and the trees were watching her through the mist.

Is that how Jasmine and the women had felt with the men hazing them along the river?

"So when will your parents be back?"

"Late tomorrow afternoon. You should have called ahead," Claire said. "You could possibly have met up with them in town. It would have saved you the drive out here."

"I wanted to come out anyway," Angie said, marshaling herself. *Focus. Claire's a good kid. I'm sure she is.* "I was hoping to visit the campsite where Jasmine Gulati was last seen alive. And to take a walk down to the bay where she slipped and fell into the water. As well as hike up the ridge to where your dad witnessed her going over the falls. I'd also like to revisit the grave site on the other side of the Nahamish and maybe go find Budge Hargreaves or at least see where his place is located. Plus, I'd like to see Axel Tollet's homestead." Angie met Claire's gaze. "I was hoping I could tempt you to guide me, Claire, and have you show me how to get round to the woods on the south side of the river, if not by boat."

"Of course I will." She placed her hand on Angie's arm, kindness in her voice. "But you do need to come in out of the cold and warm up. Maybe we should get you into a hot shower and some dry clothes, too.

The weather is not looking good for the rest of the day, but the forecast is fine for the morning. Why don't you rest up, stay the night? You and I can make a day of it tomorrow. By the time we return to the lodge, my parents should be back."

Angie agreed. Claire gave her a room. Taking the young woman's advice, Angie stripped off her wet gear and took a scalding shower. Once she'd changed into dry clothes, Angie tried to phone Holgersen. She wanted to let someone know where she was, someone other than Jacobi and the local cops, someone other than Maddocks. Just in case she disappeared into these woods. At least Holgersen could initiate a police response if she didn't return home.

But there was no reception.

When Angie asked Claire about the cell connection, Claire explained that heavy weather like this often killed connectivity but that things should improve when the dense cloud lifted and the sleet blew out.

CHAPTER 32

Thursday, November 22

Angie stood in the campsite where all nine women on Rachel Hart's documentary trip had last been together. It was early morning, and the air was like ice against Angie's face. Mist tendrils snaked through the trees, and the falls boomed downriver.

Claire had loaned Angie a toque, and she wore fingerless gloves as she took photos for reference and for the final report she would compile for Justice Monaghan. It was the same campsite where Angie had camped with Maddocks and the old couple from Dallas. It had been raked clean. The fire pit was empty. From the camping area she walked slowly with Claire down a short trail to the river's edge.

Angie raised her digital camera, adjusted the lens, and snapped several more shots of the boat pullout and the swirling water.

"Won't be doing any more guided trips until spring now," Claire said as she stood beside Angie watching the muscled current rolling beneath the smooth, unbroken meniscus of the surface.

"What do you guys do at the lodge all winter?" she asked Claire as she aimed her lens downriver at the boiling cloud of condensation above the falls and clicked.

Claire stuck her hands deep into her pockets. She looked pretty, her nose and cheeks pink with cold, her pale-green eyes the same color as the Nahamish, her thick hair the same rich ebony as her dad's and uncles'. They were good breeding stock, those Tollets—if one defined *good* by being able to guarantee a certain genetic outcome in the appearance of offspring.

"My folks work on repairs, renovations, new plans for the warmer season. We host a few winter guests who use the lodge as base for backcountry ski touring, and I do some ski guiding for them. I've also started volunteering for the local search and rescue crew, and I need to get some winter training in this year. I still need my ground SAR qualification." She smiled. "I'm also waiting on a breeder for a puppy. I'd like to get into canine tracking and air scenting for SAR. Seeing the remains in that shallow grave with you guys, hearing the stories about that woman who went missing on my dad and Jessie's trip—it just fires me up, makes me want to do more." She paused, watching the water. "I can't bear the thought of someone just going . . . missing. Gone. Makes me want to help find them. Search for them. Bring closure, you know?"

Angie shot her a glance. "I know," she said softly. "I always thought 'closure' was an overused and overblown concept bandied about in the media. But it's not. Whether you like the outcome of a mystery or not, you need those answers. The truth. I know because I've been there."

Clair nodded and said, "I know. I read about you, Angie. When everyone started talking about you coming up here to investigate Jasmine Gulati's accident, I looked up everything I could find on you." She fell silent. Wind ruffled the water. "I'm on your side," she said. "No matter what they say, I believe Jasmine would want her grandmother to have answers. I believe she is owed this last look into her grandchild's final days."

Her words reached into Angie's chest and squeezed. "Thank you for that," she said without looking at Claire for fear she'd reveal too much of herself. "It means . . . it means a lot." As she spoke she turned to look upriver. Angie stilled, hot energy coursing suddenly through her. She moved closer to the water's edge, shading her eyes against the morning glare as she peered upstream.

"What is it?" said Claire. "What do you see?"

"There's no promontory. The riverbank to the east curves backward toward the logging track."

"Yeah, so?"

Angie brought Rachel's words to mind.

I followed the bank upriver along a promontory of land that jutted out into the Nahamish. From the point I filmed some footage looking back at the campsite. I wanted the ambience of the fire and smoke in the gathering dusk. I was there filming when I heard men screaming . . .

There was no way Rachel could have headed upriver to get a vantage point that looked back at the campsite that evening. It wasn't geographically possible.

Jessie Carmanagh's words snaked into her mind.

It looked like she'd set up with her tripod on a rock ledge and was filming. From that ledge she'd have had a good line of sight down to the small bay where Jasmine's rod was found, where there were signs she'd slipped.

Angie dug into her bag, which was slung across her torso. She pulled out her notebook and double-checked the campsite coordinates from the coroner's report. "Can you tell from your GPS device if we're right on these coordinates?" She read them out to Claire.

The young woman fiddled with her Garmin. "Yeah, this is it."

"So this is definitely the spot where Jessie Carmanagh and your father brought in the boats and set up camp for the women." Angie turned in a slow circle, then looked up at the talus ridge. "Jessie mentioned there was a rock ledge just west of this campsite, a place where you can see down to the bay where Jasmine Gulati allegedly fell into the water."

"Allegedly?" Claire said.

"Cop speak," Angie replied. "Old habits. They die hard. There's no definitive proof she fell into the river there. Just evidence of her rod being left there and slip marks."

Claire regarded her, frowned, then said, "Well that would seem like evidence to me."

"Do you know where that ledge is?"

"Yes. It's a rock shelf that can be reached via a short path down from the logging track. When the weather is good, we sometimes take guests up there for a picnic. It's a great viewpoint. From there you can really get a good visual of the boiling mist above Plunge Falls as well as a clear line of sight down to the bay where Jasmine went fishing alone." Claire looked at Angie and gave a half smile. "Allegedly."

The sun broke over the mountains as they reached the rock ledge. Angie shaded her eyes against the startling brightness. Kestrels shrieked up high. To their right clouds of condensation roiled like steam from a boiling kettle above the treacherous Plunge Falls. But it was the small bay down below that snared Angie's interest.

"That's it," Claire said, pointing. "The bay where Jasmine Gulati's rod was found. My dad told me there were marks in the slime-covered rocks where her studded wading boots looked to have slipped." She turned and looked uphill. "That talus ridge back there, that's where my dad says he was gathering wood when he saw her going over the falls. There's only one other tiny bay before the water goes over the falls. The river current circles in there before sweeping back out and plunging over the rocks."

Angie shot photos from the ledge. Jessie was right. This would have been a perfect spot from which to film a lone woman casting her line in the evening light below. If Rachel had panned her camera across, she'd also have captured the mist of the thundering falls.

She wondered again how that final footage went missing and why.

From the ledge they hiked down a little trail to the bay. At the water's edge, slick black rocks were coated in slime and moss.

"I wouldn't try to go right to the edge of the bank there. It really is very slippery," Claire said. "You need the right boots. And even so . . ." She let the thought trail off. Angie could see it—how easily someone raising their arm and flicking a rod might unbalance and slide on those rocks. Jasmine Gulati must have been very sure of herself to have ventured so close to the edge to fish alone in the first place. Or the lure of the fish had simply been too great.

Angie looked up. She could see the rock ledge from here. She imagined Rachel upon it twenty-four years ago with her camera and tripod, her hot-pink Kinabulu toque standing out against the sky.

Or not.

"Would you like see the top of the falls, where Jasmine went over?" Claire said. "And where my dad climbed down? We can drive the rig to that point and then continue along the logging road around to the base, where I'll put the boat in and ferry you across the river. Much shorter across the water than driving all the way back to the lodge then around the lake."

"Please. And, Claire, thank you."

She smiled broadly. "My pleasure. This is kinda fun."

Angie followed her guide back up the hiking trail to the logging road. All the while something Claire had said niggled at her brain. It bothered Angie that she couldn't pinpoint why she had this feeling that something was off.

I wouldn't try to go right to the edge of the bank there. It really is very slippery. You'd need the right boots. And even so . . .

Angie and Claire stood on a rock plateau above the booming falls, condensation wetting their faces and forming droplets on their jackets.

Below them the smooth green waters of the Nahamish disappeared into cloud like an infinity pool.

Angie felt anxiety rise inside her chest. It was tense, just standing here in the face of this thundering power, thinking of the unstoppable force, the terror of being sucked up in it, being pulled inexorably toward that precipice knowing you might be smashed to death before you could even drown. Helpless to do anything to save yourself. Yet utterly desperate to live.

Claire pointed to a fern-choked cliff glistening with moisture. "My dad told us he climbed down over there after he saw her go over."

Angie looked to where Claire was indicating.

"When did he tell you this?" She had to speak loudly over the boom of water.

"The other night. After he got news that the skeleton had been identified as his client from twenty-four years ago. He was upset," Claire said. "He needed to talk it through with me and my mom. He climbed down that cliff with no ropes, nothing. He was desperate to save her."

"Dangerous," Angie said, her stomach bottoming out as she imagined herself trying to negotiate that slick rock face alongside that roaring water. Jessie Carmanagh was right. Garrison Tollet could have lost his life trying to help Jasmine Gulati. From where they stood, Angie could also see the tiny bay right before the edge of the falls. She could see the way the current was swirling through there. A massive old tree had fallen into that tiny bay, and debris was stacking up against it.

"There've been fatalities here before," Claire said. "Suspected suicides, some of them, where people drove from the city all the way out here to throw themselves into that water. It's so strange."

Angie nodded. "It's not that unusual. Someone wanting to commit suicide often doesn't want to leave behind a mess at home for their loved ones to clean up. So they go just far enough into the wilderness. Mayne Island is one of those places," she said. "One of the first stops along the ferry route from the populated mainland. Close yet remote enough. People often get off the boat and just go missing in the forests there." Angie wiped her wet face as she spoke, the movement of her hand drawing Claire's attention.

The young woman nodded toward Angie's hand. "That's new, the diamond," Claire said. "Engagement?"

Angie forced a smile, feeling a pang of remorse over her break with Maddocks. She'd kept the ring on after the jewelry store because it was safer on her finger than on the thin chain around her neck, and she'd driven straight from the city up the island.

"Observant," she said, offering no further comment on the state of their relationship.

Claire laughed. "That's an easy one for me. A fishing guide who carefully watches people's hands working their lines notices such things. You weren't wearing it on your last trip. Have you set a date for the wedding?"

April twenty-seventh. It's a Saturday. The cherry blossoms will be out. The streets will be all pink and white.

Angie felt an unbidden frisson of excitement at the thought of Ginny's words, the thought of that dress.

"No," she said. "Not yet." But by damn, she suddenly wanted to blurt out to this young woman, *Yes. I'm getting married in the spring.* That alone was a revelation to Angie. She really wanted this. On some very deep level, she knew this was so right. An impatience sparked through her body—she wanted to get this case over with. Get back and see him. Tell him she was certain, that she now saw a way forward with her job. Plan a future. Together. *If* it was still what he wanted.

Because as she stood here at the edge of this waterfall thinking of what Ginny had told her—that she'd made a difference in people's lives—it struck Angie between the eyes what she'd been running from. Fear of rejection, being abandoned, tossed into an angel's cradle. Fear of not being valued. While she had in fact decided at some point over the past year that she wanted Maddocks in her life, a subterranean fear of rejection still lingered. She hadn't fully trusted his love. In testing him, subconsciously perhaps, she'd driven him to draw his line in the sand. It was so simple, and now that she suddenly saw it so clearly, the paradigm of her world had shifted.

"So did Maddocks get down on one knee?" Claire asked with a grin.

The thought brought a genuine smile to Angie's face. "He might have if he'd had a chance. He had one set of proposal plans that kinda morphed into another when Budge Hargreaves appeared on the bank yelling about a skeleton." She hesitated then said, "He proposed that night while we camped near the moss grave and listened to hungry wolves howling in the hills. Romantic, huh?"

Claire's smile faded, and a seriousness entered her eyes. "I dunno. Sounds romantic to me. And kinda perfect for a homicide cop and his PI."

"Well, it was *supposed* to have been slightly more elegant, back at the lodge with a fire and wine and a warm bed and a hot tub on the deck."

"Either way, I'm happy for you guys. Congratulations. You two really seem suited to each other."

"Really?"

"Yeah. Really. I hope I'm as lucky one day."

CHAPTER 33

It was 11:02 a.m. by the time Angie had crossed the river with Claire in the jet boat and hiked into Budge Hargreaves's spread.

Angie stood on the porch and banged on the door of his cabin. The log structure was nestled near the back of a clearing about a half acre in size. Barking erupted inside, presumably Tucker. But no one came to the door.

Claire, who stood in the mud below the porch, glanced at a black pickup parked under the carport attached to the cabin. "Odd that he's not answering," she said. "His truck is here."

Angie banged louder, using the base of her fist. Still no response other than another explosion of barking from Tucker.

Angie stepped off the porch and squelched through the mud to the carport. Her pulse quickened. The truck was a Dodge. Diesel. Covered in mud. It had extra-large wheels, silver studs. Dirt smeared the plates.

She entered the carport, walked slowly around the Dodge. The right side had been recently dented and scraped.

Claire looked from the truck to Angie, uneasy, which unsettled Angie further. Angie exited the carport and walked into the clearing between the cabin and several outbuildings. The sheds were in various stages of decay. She studied the ground.

"Fresh ATV tracks, do you think?" Angie said, pointing.

Claire came over and examined the grooves in the mud. She then turned to study the dense fringe of conifers around the property. "Maybe he went off into the woods on his quad or something." Her attention returned to the truck. "You . . . don't think it was him, do you?"

"Your father said it was hunters. Plural. If it was Budge he'd run into, he'd have mentioned him by name, wouldn't he?" Angie held Claire's eyes.

Something unreadable sifted into the young woman's features. "Yeah, for sure he would have." She didn't sound so sure. "Besides, like I said, these pickups are a dime a dozen."

"His truck does have fresh damage down the side, though," Angie said, testing Claire's perception of her dad. She felt a resistance rise around Claire. This woman, Angie guessed, if pushed into a corner, would turn against her in order to protect her family. She needed to tread carefully.

"Budge gets dinged up a lot. I reckon he drives after a few too many far too often."

"Despite a drunk driving charge all those years ago?"

Claire's shoulders stiffened slightly. "He has a DUI?"

"You didn't know?"

Claire held her eyes. Wind rushed through the forest. Clouds had started gathering in the north again—the weather in this area as capricious as the terrain.

"Well, it doesn't look like he's here." She jerked her chin at the gathering clouds. "We should get moving before that storm blows in. Could come fast. Snow in the forecast, and we've still got a ways to hike to Axel's place and then to the moss grove before we head back over the river."

Angie nodded. "One last check to be sure," she said. "Why don't you see if he might be in that shed behind his cabin? I'll go over and check those outbuildings on the other side of his property over there."

Angie motioned to three wooden sheds near the forest fringe. She wanted to peek inside them. This place was giving her an odd vibe, her cop sixth sense raising hairs on the back of her neck.

"Sure," Claire said, her voice clipped. She stomped off in her boots. Angie waited for her to round the cabin, and then she made quickly for the biggest shed. She found the door slightly ajar. She stilled, her senses on red alert. Something felt . . . off.

"Hello?" she said, knocking on the shed door. "Budge Hargreaves? Are you in there?"

Silence.

Angie creaked open the door. A few flies buzzed. It was dark inside, but she smelled it instantly. Blood. Warm. Fresh. Meaty. She sensed a presence.

Wind gusted in through the door behind her. A squeaky groan came from her right. Angie swung to face the sound, heart beating fast. As her vision adjusted, she saw what had moved. A buck. It swung from a creaking meat hook. Its throat was slit and gaped raw and red. A glassy eye held hers. Angie tensed. Another gust made it move again, and the dead creature's eye seemed to plead with her. She stepped closer. It had a small wound on the side of its neck. Not a bullet hole. The wound appeared to have been made by a sharp little blade. Arrow, she thought. Her gaze dropped to the concrete floor. Blood dripped and congealed in a puddle below the kill.

Angie placed her palm against the flank of the animal. It was still warm. This kill was very fresh.

She scanned the dim interior of the shed. A workbench ran the length at the back. On the bench lay a hunter's bow and a quiver of arrows with yellow-and-white fletching. To the right of the workbench stood a stained chest freezer. A memory slammed into Angie—the freezer in the basement of serial killer Spencer Addams's suburban home. His mother's dismembered torso inside. She swallowed, a sinister coolness filling her.

She began to back out of the shed.

A sound behind her stopped her in her tracks. Angie froze as she recognized the rack of a pump action shotgun. A sick sensation leaked into her gut.

"Hold it right there." The voice was male, low, quiet.

She didn't dare move.

"Put your hands where I can see them."

Slowly, she held her hands out to her sides.

"Put them on your head, and turn around now. Nice and slow."

She placed her hands on her toque, turned.

Budge Hargreaves. His frame filled the doorway. He wore khaki coveralls. Blood stained his front. A massive hunting knife was sheathed at his side. Light caught the side of his face. His features looked flushed, puffy. His eyes glowed feverish. He aimed his shotgun dead at her chest.

"Budge," she said, keeping her voice even. "Budge Hargreaves. I'm Angie Pallorino. Do you remember me? I was on the river with Sergeant James Maddocks when you found the shallow grave. You were picking mushrooms. You came down to the water and called for our help."

In her peripheral vision Angie noted the implements hanging on the shed wall. A shovel. An axe. A wrench. She wanted something to grab as a weapon because Budge Hargreaves did not look right. Angie edged infinitesimally sideways toward the tools.

"Don't. Move."

She stopped. "Look, it's okay, Budge. I mean no harm. I . . . I'm here with Claire Tollet. She was our fishing guide in the boat when you found the skeleton, remember? I wanted to ask you some questions, and she brought me out here to find you."

Confusion chased across his face. He swayed slightly on his feet, and Angie realized he was three sheets to the wind. She could smell the drink on him from where she stood. Her fear was suddenly that Claire might arrive and spook him from behind, and he'd swing round and pull the trigger on her.

"Claire Tollet went around the back of your cabin to look for you, Budge. She'll be coming down here next. Can we go outside, have a word? Can you lower that gun, maybe?"

"They said you'd come up here." He slurred his *s*'s slightly. "What the fuck you wanna go digging all that old shit out again now, eh? Why you wanna talk to me?"

Angie tried a new tactic. "That's quite the buck you bagged there." She jerked her head toward the animal carcass swinging on the meat hook. "You must have got it this morning?"

He studied her, searching for the trick, then glanced at his buck.

Angie said, "Do you hunt with arrows? That's quite a skill."

Slowly, he lowered the gun. He wiped his sleeve across his sweaty brow. "You spooked me. Didn't recognize you from the back, what with that toque on. Sorry. Jeezus, I'm sorry."

"It's okay." She removed her hands from her head. "Why don't you give me that gun, let me make it safe before Claire comes around and surprises us both?" She tried to keep her voice light as she stepped forward and held out her hand.

To Angie's relief, he let her take the shotgun. She immediately cracked it open, removed the shells, and set the lot on the workbench.

"Shall we go outside? Where it's light. We can talk there."

He turned and exited the shed, stumbling once and catching himself against the wall. She followed and creaked the shed door closed behind her.

"What do you want?" he said, blinking in the light.

"Just a few questions. Is there somewhere we can sit? On your porch, maybe?"

He nodded and started toward his cabin. But he tripped and stumbled again. She caught his arm.

"Had a few celebratory drinks after your hunt?"

"Something like that." He reached the covered porch and clomped up the stairs in his heavy boots. Angie followed.

Claire appeared from around the cabin. "Oh, you found him!" She paused as Budge's state quickly became apparent to her. She crooked up her brows.

Angie nodded. "Just going to have a few quick words with Budge here on the deck," she said as Budge flopped into the only chair on the porch and dropped his face into his hands. Angie sat opposite him on a cut log. Claire remained standing in the clearing in the mud, hands in her pockets, watching, an odd look on her face.

"Who told you I was in town, Budge?" Angie said.

He looked up, assessing her. "Uh, it was just . . . the scuttlebutt. I don't see why you want to talk to me."

"Do you know that the human remains you found have been identified as Jasmine Gulati, a young woman who drowned in the Nahamish twenty-four years ago while on a guided fishing trip?"

He studied her in silence, mistrust entering his bleary eyes. An eagle cried up in the clouds. Wind increased in the conifers, making the forest rush with the sound of a river as branches twisted like skirts about dancing trees.

"Yeah," he said finally. "I heard it was her."

Angie leaned forward. "When you found the skeleton, did you think at the time the body might belong to Jasmine Gulati?"

He raked his fingers through his gray hair, making the front stand up. "I . . . maybe. I didn't think too much about who it was at the time. It was a shock, finding those bones. And that Jasmine woman, she went over the falls such a long time ago. Others have gone missing in these parts since. Other anglers. A jumper over the falls. Hunters. Hikers."

She studied his face. "But you had met Jasmine before she went missing, right?"

"No."

Angie reached inside the breast pocket of her down jacket and took out the screenshot she'd printed of Budge Hargreaves with a young Darnell Jacobi in the pub. She showed it to him.

"You were in the Hook and Gaffe the night Jasmine and the other women were there."

He squinted at the image. The creases in his brow deepened into furrows. "Where in the hell did you get that?"

"I took it from the footage that Rachel Hart shot for her documentary. You're with Darnell Jacobi in that footage. You both saw Jasmine Gulati arguing with Wallace Carmanagh and the Tollet twins."

"I guess I saw her. Was pretty wasted that night. A lot of us were, what with Robbie Tollet's team winning and all. Don't remember much."

Angie turned to study his land. "Your place is pretty close to the section of river that those women were fishing twenty-four years ago. Did you see the women on the river at all?"

He shook his head.

"But you lived out here at the time?"

"Yeah. Been here ever since two years after my wife drowned. I used to work with the forestry service station not far from here."

"I'm so sorry about your wife."

He nodded.

"Can I ask how she died, Budge?"

Claire stiffened in Angie's peripheral vision.

"She drowned."

"You mentioned. How did it happen?"

Claire began to pace up and down near the deck railing. Angie ignored her and focused on Budge Hargreaves. The man's bloodshot eyes went distant. He scrubbed his brow hard, as if it might help clear his head or possibly wipe it clean of bad memories. Angie felt sorry for him.

"We were fishing on Loon Lake not far from here. In my Spratley."

"Is that a boat?"

He nodded. "It was late evening. We were having sundowners. Probably a few too many. I . . . I don't know what happened. One minute, I was standing up to cast. The boat wobbled, and she was out. Splash."

"She fell overboard?"

He looked down at his mud-caked boots. "Yeah," he said quietly. "She went straight down into that black water. Happened so fast. We weren't wearing life vests." He paused. "It was getting dark."

"Can you swim?"

"A little."

"You didn't go in after her?"

Claire cleared her throat and threw Angie a disapproving glare. Angie ignored her.

"I . . . I *couldn't* go in." Budge stared at his feet for a long while. When he met her gaze again, his features were stripped raw, and emotion was naked in his eyes. "Look at me," he said, holding his calloused hands out to his sides. "*Look* at me. I punish myself every day. I try to blind myself with that demon drink. Maybe I'm trying to kill myself, I don't know. A six-pack of beers plus a bottle of whiskey nearly every night, and I'm still fucking here, still fucking standing and walking, and it was my fault. I *am* to blame. I could have done more." Tears filled his eyes. "Maybe I could have saved her if I'd gone in. But I was wasted. Too drunk to try to swim. Or even think straight. I'd have drowned, too, and I should have. I should've gone in and gone down with her—" He began to sob openly, not even attempting to hide the tears streaming down his face. Big, ugly, inhuman sounds issued from him as his body and mind were racked with misery.

"I'm so sorry, Budge." Angie found a Kleenex in one of her pockets and held it out to him.

He blew his nose.

She waited. Wind gusted harder, bending the tips of the trees in the forest all around them. Tiny flecks of snow began to blow in with it. Claire walked to the edge of the clearing, looked up at the clouded sky, then checked her watch.

"What was your wife's name, Budge?"

"Arizona. I always called her Zoe. For short."

"Married a long time?"

He nodded, wiped his nose again, and cursed softly. "When we moved out to Port Ferris, it was going to be a fresh start for both of us. Good things were supposed to come of it. We were closer to outdoor recreation—fishing, hunting. She'd quit her job so I could take the new forestry position out here."

"Why'd you need a fresh start?"

He snorted softly. "Marriage trouble."

Angie studied him. "Bad?"

He shrugged. "Bad enough to make a big move."

Angie wondered if this could speak to motive, whether Budge might have had helped his wife's drowning accident along. Or facilitated it.

"Where did you live before relocating to Port Ferris?" she asked.

"Richmond. In the Lower Mainland. It was a very urban existence. I traveled a lot for work, was away from home for extended periods."

"Yeah, that'd be rough on a marriage, I imagine."

Claire came up to the porch railing. Her face showed anger now. "We should go," she said, her voice tight. "Weather is turning. Still need to hike out to Axel's place and to the moss grove."

Angie raised her hand. "One sec."

The young woman's eyes narrowed sharply. A hostility crackled from them.

"Yeah," Budge said. "Like I mentioned, the move was supposed to be a fresh start. I'd also promised to cut way back on the drinking." He made a scoffing sound. "Guess it all went the opposite way, eh?"

"Had you ever visited that moss grove prior to finding Jasmine's body?"

"What do you mean?"

"I mean, to pick mushrooms or just to visit it. It's a beautiful place. Peaceful."

Comprehension dawned in his eyes. His body stiffened. "You saying that I *knew* she was lying there all these years? Or . . . What in the hell *are* you saying? That I suddenly wanted to show someone where she was buried?"

Angie decided to push his buttons further to see what resulted, given his state. She leaned forward.

"Officer Darnell Jacobi's father, Hank Jacobi, helped see to it that additional charges were dropped after your drunk driving accident."

"What's that got to do with anything?"

"Just wondering if you and the Jacobis were—are—close."

He shot to his feet so fast Angie jerked back in shock.

He pointed his finger down at her face. "You fuck off out of here, okay?" He swung his hand toward Claire. "And you too, Tollet. Don't know what in the hell traitorous shit game *you're* playing by bringing this woman here."

Angie rose up from her stump. Budge took a fast step toward her, forcing her to brace against the deck railing.

"I hope to God that *you* never have to lose anyone you love." He ground the words out, the alcohol fumes on his breath washing into her face. "The only reprieve I found was at the bottom of a goddamn bottle, and those Jacobi men are good men. Good cops. Hank could see what trouble I was having. He *helped* me. He spoke to the other party involved in the accident, told them about the grief that was killing me. They let him drop charges for me not remaining at the scene of the accident. *Nothing* illegal was done, okay? I was still prosecuted for impaired driving. I still paid my dues—I still got the damn criminal record to prove it. I got it the record burned right here in my heart." He bashed his fist against his chest, face red, eyes watering.

"That Jasmine Gulati woman got what was coming to her. She was a sinner. She seduced married men for the fun of it, to test her own power over them, and that's just evil. Funny how justice can work out here, eh? So you go get the fuck off of my property now before you get

253

what's coming to you, too. Or before *I* go mistaking *your* sorry city ass for a bear and shooting you dead."

Shaking, he whirled around and lurched for his cabin door. He yanked it open. Tucker leaped all over Budge as the old-timer entered the cabin, then slammed the door shut behind him.

Angie stared at the door, her pulse racing, her face hot.

"Are you done yet?"

Angie's attention flashed to Claire. She stood in the mud, arms akimbo, anger scrawled across her face. Tiny flakes of snow settled on the dark braids that hung over her shoulders.

"Well, I didn't get to ask him about his truck yet," Angie said, descending the two stairs that led up to the porch. "You okay, Claire?"

Claire spun around and stalked in sullen silence toward the path that led back into the forest. Angie had to hurry to catch up and keep pace behind her. As the path narrowed, Claire pushed branches aside, allowing them to slap back at Angie.

They hiked in this combative fashion for several kilometers into the woods. From the Garmin GPS Claire had loaned her, Angie saw they were almost at Axel Tollet's place.

Claire halted abruptly on the trailhead and spun to face Angie.

"You going to mess with Uncle Axel's head, too? What on earth was all that with Budge anyway? You just trying to hurt him? He's a mess over the death of his wife. He never recovered. What's the deal with all these questions? You think he killed his own wife or something? What does that have to do with your case, anyway?"

"I'm sorry, Claire," Angie said softly. She did feel some guilt over Budge. She'd also hewed very close to having Budge let slip that it was Claire's father who'd been seduced by Jasmine. If and when that got out, it was going to hurt Claire, too.

"Look, it's not my intention to hurt anyone, Claire. But there is a chance that Jasmine Gulati's death was not what it seemed."

Claire stared at her. Wind rushed through the forest. It carried upon its chill winter breath the metallic scent of snow. "You mean . . . it wasn't an *accident*?"

"I mean only that there are some anomalies, conflicting memories around the event. And I want to ask questions that might help throw fresh light on the incident." She paused. "You saw her remains, Claire. You saw Jasmine Gulati's bones buried in the dirt. She was twenty-five when she drowned, around your age. She'd been lying there in the muck, a couple hundred meters away from the river, for maybe two decades after the flooding likely deposited her body there. All alone. No one knowing where she was. Her mother and father were desperate to find her. It almost cost them their marriage."

"If it wasn't an accident," Claire said slowly, "that means . . . someone out here, someone I know, could have hurt her. Is that what you're saying? You think it was Budge? That he drowned her because maybe he drowned his own wife?"

"I just want to hear everyone's story."

"Bullshit. You're off base, way off. You're digging up painful pasts to appease some old woman who's only going to find out that her granddaughter had an accident. What of everyone you hurt in the process? What happens when you waltz out of town leaving a wake of collateral damage? Who picks up the pieces then?"

She pointed into the woods. "Because that back there—that sounded like a fishing expedition, and it was cruel."

"Claire," she said quietly, "I think you're overreacting. Budge was drunk. He's an alcoholic, sounds like he was a drunk before he even moved to Port Ferris. He's probably not even going to remember we visited him by the time he wakes up tomorrow morning."

"I can't take you to see Axel," she said curtly. "Not if you're going to attack him like you did Budge. He's . . . Uncle Axe can be a little slow with certain things. Not because he's stupid, but the education system failed him when he was a kid. He has a learning disability, and because of it he never got proper schooling. And he . . . he's vulnerable. I can't let you hurt him."

"I know what you're worried about. I know what happened to Axel when he was a kid," Angie said gently. "I can't promise to avoid it totally when I talk to him because it could be relevant in unexpected ways. But I've worked for over six years in sex crimes, and I know how survivors of those crimes can—"

"You know *what* about him?" Confusion chased across Claire's face. "*What* happened to Axel when he was a kid—what's this about sex crimes?"

Shit! Angie stared at Claire. She didn't know about the rape. Why in the hell *should* she know? Even if half the old-timers in town did.

"Angie," Claire growled, coming closer. "You better tell me. Now. Tell me what happened with Axel. What is 'it' that you can't promise to avoid?"

Angie inhaled deeply, her brain racing for a way out. "I'm aware that Axel Tollet was bullied as a kid."

"Don't bullshit me! *Tell* me what happened—what does this have to do with your experience in sex crimes? Or I'm not taking you in there. Without me Axel will not talk to you. I guarantee it."

Angie's brain whirled. She owed Claire. She'd dealt her cards by opening this door in error. She now had to play her hand and play it well. And carefully.

"Look, there's no easy way to soften this, Claire, and it's really not my place to tell you." She hesitated. "But you're probably going to hear it from someone in town one day, probably sooner than later now, because a lot of people know about it." Angie cleared her throat. "When your uncle Axel was thirteen years old, he was gang-raped by a group of boys from his school."

CHAPTER 34

Angie's news appeared to physically punch Claire in the stomach. The young woman doubled over and slumped down onto a moss-covered log, her features slack.

"Who?" she whispered. *"How?"*

Angie lowered herself onto the wet fallen log beside Claire. She rubbed her face. There was no way she could put this genie back in the bottle now, not without being dishonest.

"It's the story around town, among the older residents," Angie said gently. "The police do know—I spoke with Constable Jacobi about it. His father was involved in investigating an aspect of the incident. It's not my place to tell you, Claire, but you'll probably hear it as gossip one day, and it's not going to be nice any way you hear it. It's also possible that what happened to your uncle Axel ties into what happened to Jasmine. At least in part."

Because those boys would have bonded tightly over those terrible secrets as they became men, and I'm almost 100 percent certain they were the ones terrorizing Jasmine and the women along the river. And they might also have tried to send me into Carmanagh Lake.

Unless that had been Budge Hargreaves.

Or hunters with brake problems, but Angie was still leaning toward Darnell Jacobi having alerted Wallace and the twins to the fact she was driving a rental up to the lodge. Darnell Jacobi, who'd been at school with them all, and whose father had called off the investigation into the possible murder of Porter Bates.

She cleared her throat. "The story goes that shortly after Axel turned thirteen, a bully at his school, an older boy named Porter Bates, allegedly lured him out to a quarry north of town. Bates and his gang allegedly sexually assaulted Axel there. Bates and his guys had been bullying Axel for a long time before that from what I understand. Axel apparently never officially reported the sexual assault, but shortly afterward Porter Bates was jumped by some local guys on a secluded trail outside of town. These guys allegedly bound him up and drowned him at the quarry. The feeling is that this was done in retaliation for what Porter did to Axel."

"*Murder?* Who . . . who were the guys who jumped Porter?"

"I don't know."

Claire looked as though she was going to throw up. "Not Axel's brothers?" she said. "Surely not the twins—my uncles—and my dad?"

"Porter's body was never found, Claire, and no one confessed to anything. It became a missing persons case that grew cold."

"Is *this* why you were asking Budge about the Jacobis? About them dropping cases?"

"I'm trying to get a sense of where allegiances lie, yes, and how far people might go to . . . avenge things." Angie was treading very close to Claire's father's affair now, and she did not want to be the one to reveal that.

"So what, exactly, does all this have to do with Jasmine Gulati's drowning?"

"Maybe nothing. Maybe everything if the past speaks to patterns of behavior and MO. Even if past events do speak to patterns of behavior, it still might bear no direct relevance to her accident, but I need to ask the questions. Jasmine did anger a lot of people in town. Maybe someone wanted revenge."

"So they pushed her in? Is that what you think?"

Angie gave a half shrug. "Maybe. Some of the people she angered also had opportunity and means. And some of their stories don't add up, for whatever reason."

Claire swore softly, looked away, then said, "I don't know whether I should help you. These are my people you're investigating."

"That's up to you, Claire. Up to your own conscience."

"What about the other guys who allegedly assaulted Uncle Axel?"

"Again, nothing was officially reported or proved."

"So they're out there, maybe? Just walking around while my uncle suffers?"

"I don't know."

She rubbed her knee. "What do you want to ask my uncle?"

"If he saw anything on the river twenty-four years ago and what he remembers of an altercation with Jasmine Gulati in the Hook and Gaffe. He worked there at the time. There is footage of him watching the argument, among others."

Claire opened her mouth, but Angie raised her hand. "Before you say this gives you even more reason not to take me to Axel's place, I promise I will go easy on him. Like I told you, I worked in sex crimes for over six years." She paused, holding Claire's eyes. "I understand the pain, the shame, the confusion, the anger around being a survivor of those kinds of crimes. If anyone wants to do right by a sexual assault survivor, it's me, Claire. I need you to understand that."

Claire kicked her heel against the log. Her hands were balled into fists at her sides, and her jaw had gone tight. Her gaze snapped back to Angie. In her eyes Angie could read hurt, mistrust. But also a hot fire burning.

"Fine," she said. "But if at any time I say we go, we go. Is that understood?"

Angie nodded. "Understood."

CHAPTER 35

The trail opened abruptly into a clearing maybe twice the size of Budge Hargreaves's spread. Angie halted Claire with her hand at the fringe of trees. She wanted to absorb the scope and layout of the place before entering.

Tiny flecks of snow blew sideways in the wind. A cabin squatted in a stand of trees at the rear of the property. Like Budge's home, the cabin had a covered porch out front. Unlike Budge's place, everything looked neat and cared for. Split wood had been piled high along one of the cabin walls. On the roof were solar panels. A rain collection barrel had been constructed to the left of the building.

At the far eastern boundary of the spread, near what looked like a vehicle track leading out between trees, a metal shipping container was set back into a mound of earth. It had been converted into accommodations with the addition of a door and a window. It was painted dark green. A tumble of blackberry bushes and other scrub grew atop the mound that covered the roof of the container. Bramble fronds hung down, partially obscuring the window.

A stone path led from the cabin to a covered carport that housed a dark-gray pickup truck and a muddy quad. A distance behind the carport was an open-sided shed that housed several natural gas cylinders and what looked like a generator plus containers of fuel.

Three additional sheds had been built along the western boundary of the property along with what looked like two big cages, one partly covered with shade cloth.

A raven cawed from atop one of the cages, wings hanging out at its sides like a buzzard.

"Looks like he's home," Claire said with a nod at the smoke trailing up from the cabin chimney.

"What's with those cages?" Angie said.

"Axel built those for two orphaned bear cubs he rescued when I was nine. He's used them for other animals he's rescued since, once for a fawn whose mother Axel was unable to free from an illegal trap. Another time for baby raccoons. And for a beaver one time." Claire gave a wry smile. "I remember those cubs. Uncle Axe bottle-fed them by hand. I used to watch him do it, but he never let me into the cage with him, as much as I begged him to let me help feed them. He wouldn't even allow me to touch the bears. He said he didn't want the cubs to grow habituated to humans, or he'd never be able to fully rehabilitate them." She glanced at Angie. "Before Axel went into the cage, he'd put on this dark-colored coverall that he kept wrapped in smelly old bear hide. He said this was to cover up as much of his human scent as possible. And he'd wear a ski mask. He didn't want the bears to associate his face with food and care." She wiped her nose with the base of her thumb as she returned her attention to the cages. Her skin was going ruddy with cold, and Angie could feel the chill in her own face and fingers.

"Uncle Axe never spoke while he fed them their formula so they wouldn't grow accustomed to his voice. It killed me as a kid—those measures. I just wanted to cuddle those two cubs. Cutest things you've ever seen in your life. They were the size of little shoeboxes, paws that looked too large for them, just like in cartoons."

"Did it work? Was he able to rehabilitate them?"

"Seems to have worked. On the day of their release, Uncle Axe waited for my dad to bring me over the river so I could watch him set them free." She gave a soft snort. "He transported them in smaller cages deep into the woods. When he found the right spot, we carried the cages from the truck farther into the forest and set them on the ground. He made us hide, and he opened the doors and clapped his hands loudly. 'Run, little bears,' he said in his deep Uncle Axel voice. 'Get the hell outta here, be scared, survive, you little critters . . .'" Claire's voice faded. A sad look entered her eyes. "I cried my heart out when they left. Silly, huh?"

"No," Angie said softly. "Doesn't sound silly at all." She smiled at Claire. "I'd probably have done the same. Bawled my face off. You're lucky to have experienced that, to have an uncle like him."

"I know." She met Angie's eyes. "That's why I can't—won't—let you hurt him. Especially not after what you just told me."

The raven cawed and suddenly swooped down off the cage. It landed on the ground and hopped on one leg.

"That's Poe," Claire said. "I named him. He's also one of Axel's rescues. Come." Claire started into the clearing. Angie followed. As they got halfway to the cabin, they heard the shrill whine of a bench saw starting up in one of the sheds.

Claire stopped. "Ah, he's in his carpentry shed." She led the way. Angie followed through the icy wind and spitting snow pellets.

The double shed doors were partially open.

"Uncle Axe?" Claire yelled over the whine as she pushed the door farther inward.

The saw stopped. A giant of a black-haired man swung around, a piece of milled lumber in his gloved hands. His face registered shock as he saw them. He set down the wood and removed protective goggles. Fine sawdust matted his skin and beard. His eyes were icy green, the Tollet family likeness startling. He wore a checked shirt and utility-style dungarees, heavy work boots. His gaze settled on Angie.

"Uncle Axe—" Claire went over to him, leaned up on tippy-toes, and gave him a kiss. "I brought you some company."

The man's attention never left Angie. "Company's not welcome here."

His voice was a rough bass. He took a step forward, his gloved ham-size hands clenching and unclenching at his sides. Angie tensed at the sheer volume of him. He vibrated energy, power, and made Angie conscious of the door behind her and escape routes.

In her peripheral vision she noted leg traps affixed to the walls, traps with big rusted teeth and chains. There was a long gun cabinet with a key in the lock mounted near the traps. A worktable ran along the back of the shed; above it tools hung neatly on a wall. On another table lay a hunting bow and a quiver containing several arrows, some with red-and-white fletching, others with yellow-and-white fletching.

Above the quiver several fly rods rested on hooks. Closer to the door hung two pairs of booted chest waders. The brand logo visible on one pair of waders was familiar—Kinabulu, the company that had sponsored Rachel Hart's documentary. It was, Angie realized, the same brand that Predator Lodge had supplied her and Maddocks on their recent trip. A very common brand for fishing gear, it seemed.

An ATV helmet rested on a bench. Above the helmet shelves were stacked with vintage-looking tins that had once contained Maxwell House coffee, Similac baby formula, Italia canned tomatoes, Gatorade powder, Campbell's Chunky Soup, Harvest Green peas. Beside the tins was a small wooden milk crate that housed four baby bottles with teats. Next to those sat an ancient-looking stuffed teddy bear. Angie was slammed with a sudden memory of the little teddy bear in the angel's cradle where she'd been abandoned. She quickly pushed the recollection down into her subconscious. It was getting easier to do that, thank God.

"This is Angie Pallorino," Claire said. "She's—"

"I know who she is. I said she's not welcome here. They all say she shouldn't be here."

"Who says that?" Claire asked.

"Wallace, Jessie. BoJo. Your dad. She's been bugging Jacobi, everyone. Bringing up bad things. You shouldn't be with her, Claire-Bear."

This beast of a man, while frightening, had kind eyes, Angie decided. She watched him step toward a table near him and reach for a rifle that lay there. Claire tensed. Her reaction made Angie's pulse quicken. She was unsure how to read this sexual abuse survivor who'd never gotten the help he needed and who lived isolated in the forest. In addition to being scary, he looked scared. That could make him dangerous.

"What does she want here, anyways?" Axel growled.

Angie stepped forward cautiously. "Axel, hi. I—"

Claire placed a hand on Angie's arm, stopping her. Claire's gaze was fixed on the gun in Axel's hands. She was reading something in her uncle's stance, and Angie trusted her.

Claire said in a calm voice, "Angie Pallorino just wanted to ask you if you ever saw those women on the river while they were on that trip. She believes you might have met Jasmine Gulati in the Hook and Gaffe, seen her arguing with some of the other guys."

His face turned thunderous. His green eyes flashed back to Angie. He was likely recalling Claire's father, his cousin, cuddling with Jasmine Gulati in that booth, and he wasn't going to let "Claire-Bear" hear about that.

"Get out," he grunted, chambering a round. "Get the hell off my land, and get out of town."

"Uncle Axe—"

"I mean it, Claire-Bear. Take this woman the hell away before I go hurting her."

Claire swallowed and glanced at Angie. The young woman looked upset, nervous.

Angie nodded. She began to back out. "Nice meeting you, sir," she said in an even cop tone. "Maybe we can talk some other time."

He said nothing. Angie exited, but Claire lingered a moment in the shed. Angie heard a muffled exchange of words. Claire came outside with her mouth tight. In brooding silence, she stomped her way back into the forest.

As Angie followed behind, she said, "So Axel really doesn't like visitors."

"No." Claire kept walking, brooking no further discussion. But as they neared the moss grove, she stopped and said, "I can see now why he hates people coming out to his place. I can totally see it, since you told me what happened to him. I bet he knows exactly who drowned Porter Bates, if that did in fact happen. He'd know they did it to avenge his rape, and he'd want to protect whoever that was. If word is out that you're digging up old dirt, that old rape has to be a part of the old dirt. You've got to be threatening those old allegiances."

Angie nodded. "Yes."

Claire glowered at her. "You're pushing people to the edge of comfort, Angie. It . . . could end up going sideways. You could get hurt."

"Are you saying you think your uncle Axel's protectors are capable of hurting me?"

Claire palmed off her hat and turned away, breathing hard. "I don't know." She spun back to face Angie. "But if someone did murder Porter Bates, what do you think they might do if you threaten to open that up again?" Her gaze lasered Angie's. "Is what you're doing worth it?"

"What about truth, Claire? What if that old murder led to another? What if it could lead to more?" She paused. "What about justice?"

Claire inhaled deeply. "What if it was *your* family, Angie? What then? Would you be so hungry for truth then?"

"I've had bad stuff unearthed in my own family. I think you'd know that if you read up on me. It wasn't pleasant to discover the truth, and it was a heinous truth, but I'm better off for it now."

"Are you? Really?"

Angie weighed the answer. Wind stirred the forest, and trees groaned and creaked, releasing pinecones and debris. "I am," she said softly. "The truth doesn't make things easier. But I believe it's necessary. I believe justice needs to come through proper channels, for what kind of society are we without that?" She paused. "Now that you know what happened to Axel, would you—*could* you—just shut your mind and carry on?"

She inhaled deeply. "I don't know," she whispered. "I honestly don't know."

They resumed walking along the trail in silence, and Angie could feel the tension radiating off Claire. She wondered about Axel Tollet. All that she'd gotten out of their visit was more questions. Tentatively, she probed Claire once more.

"Those rusted leg traps hanging on Axel's wall—does he run lines?" she called out as they hiked.

"No," she said over her shoulder. "He found those. He abhors trappers—finds traps cruel."

"Yet he hangs the traps on his wall."

"Kinda like trophies, I guess. His way of keeping score of the animals he's saved from a terrible death by stealing the traps. He told me just looking at the ugly things keeps the fire burning in his belly."

"Yet he hunts?" Angie had seen the rifle, the long gun cabinet, the bow and arrows.

"Subsistence only." Claire clambered over a fallen tree and waited for Angie to follow suit. "He'd rather kill his own meat humanely than support an industry that slaughters terrified animals in an abattoir. And he prefers bow and arrows because it's more of a challenge one-on-one with the animal. Gives his prey more of a fighting chance, he says, makes the kill harder earned. He won't even sell Dad meat for guests at the lodge. He says each man should hunt for his own."

Angie dusted mud from her pants and continued along the trail.

"What were the baby bottles in his shed for?" she asked from behind Claire.

"Feeding formula to the bears. And he used them for the fawns."

"How does he know what kind of formula to use for the different animals?"

"He doesn't really. But he calls the folks at Wild Critter Care—it's a voluntary wild animal rehabilitation center—and they unofficially guide and advise him."

"And the little stuffed bear?"

She stopped and turned. "What bear?"

"The old teddy bear on his shelf next to the baby bottles."

Claire smiled ruefully. "What can I say? He brought the orphaned cubs a stuffed toy in their own likeness. He figured it might help them snuggle and keep warm since there had been three of them—the third cub died." She shrugged. "I know. It seems at odds with his efforts to not habituate the cubs to humans, but he did steep the toy bear in real ursine scent before placing it in their cage. I'm just surprised the little guys didn't tear it to shreds when they started playing with it."

CHAPTER 36

"By next spring moss will have grown back over it," Claire said as they stared down at the scar of black earth marking what was once Jasmine Gulati's grave.

"New brambles will have taken root." Claire looked up at the fish carcasses still hanging from the canopy above. "This forest is pure recycling at work. You won't know that the grave or Jasmine were ever here."

Unless you know what to look for.

A crack sounded, and Angie's hand went reflexively for the sidearm that wasn't there. Claire spun round. They both peered into the surrounding woods, muscles tense. A sense of a presence, of being watched, pricked the hairs up along the back of Angie's neck. She swallowed. It was growing dark in the grove, shadows taking on new shape and menace.

"What was that?" Angie said.

Claire held a can of bear spray in front of her. Angie hadn't even noticed her taking it from her belt. "Nothing. It's . . . this place, I think. Makes me jumpy for no reason." She sheathed the can in a holster on her belt as she spoke.

But Angie didn't think it was nothing. That sense of a sentience lingered, as if they were still being observed from the shadows.

Claire checked her watch as if keen to move. "What did you hope to find here?"

"Context," Angie said, casting another look into the shadows before crossing the grove to the fringe of trees that grew thick along the edge of the clearing. She studied the GPS.

"So the river is that way." She pointed into the woods, speaking more to herself than Claire. "Just over two hundred meters away according to the Garmin."

"Yeah, as the crow flies," Claire said. "But it would be serious bush-whacking on foot. The trail from the river follows natural contours, but it's longer."

Angie checked the contour lines and elevation. "We're standing at almost two meters in elevation above the Nahamish Flats river delta."

"Yeah, so?"

"According to the coroner's report, there were two extreme weather events that caused flooding in the years after Jasmine Gulati went over the falls. The theory is that the floodwaters could have dislodged her body and washed her remains up here. Then, when the water receded, she was left with other river debris in the moss grove. Except"—Angie turned in a slow circle, absorbing the topography of the grove afresh—"this grove is actually on a bit of an elevated knoll of land. If I'm recalling the report correctly, the floodwaters on both occasions crept over two hundred meters from the Nahamish banks but rose only about three feet—or less than a meter—in height. Which means . . . this knoll could have stayed high and dry."

"Are you certain about how high the water rose?"

"No. I'll have to check. If memory serves me, it's not making total sense that Jasmine's body would have been deposited on this knoll of land if the waters didn't rise quite this high. Unless of course there was some sort of surge or the measurements were an estimate and not an accurate reflection of what happened. I'm thinking it would have been a meteorologist's best guess based on extrapolation of historical data."

"Which would mean what, exactly?" Claire said.

Angie worried her scarred lip with her teeth. "The flooding explanation seems the most logical hypothesis for how she ended up here—" A rustle sounded in the bushes. Angie fell silent.

Before Angie or Claire could even turn to look, a *thwock* sounded as something hit the tree trunk behind Angie. She spun around. An arrow with yellow-and-white fletching quivered from impact into bark.

She heard another sound and felt a hot whizz past her ear. She dived to the ground. "Down, Claire, *get down*!"

Another arrow *thucked* into the tree behind her as Claire flung herself flat into the loam. They lay on the ground, breathing hard. Nothing more happened.

Slowly, Claire lifted her head. Mud streaked the side of her face. "Hey! Assholes!" she screamed at the top of her lungs. "There are people here!" She rolled onto her back, yanked her air horn from her belt, and let loose an earsplitting sound. As the sound died and Angie's ears rang, Claire yelled, "You could have killed us, you motherfuckers!"

A human whistle sounded from deep in the trees—three quick blasts followed by one long. An ATV engine roared to life. The sound of the engine disappeared into the forest until all they could hear was the distant boom of the falls and their own heavy breathing. Claire turned to Angie, her complexion sheet white.

"Quad," she said shakily. "Fucking hunter on a quad."

She scrambled to her feet, held out a hand to Angie. "I'm so sorry, Angie. Christ, I'm sorry. I should've given you a blaze-orange vest. We both should have been wearing one. The season is supposed to be over in this area, but there are always some assholes not ready to call it quits yet."

Angie thought of Budge's buck hanging in his shed. He clearly hadn't thought it was over, unless he'd bagged that in some area where the season remained open.

Adrenaline slamming through her body, Angie took Claire's hand and came to her feet. She dusted off, retrieved the Garmin GPS she'd dropped, and went up to the tree with the arrow sticking out of the bark. She examined the yellow-and-white fletching.

Claire came up behind her.

"Both Budge and Axel have arrows like this," Angie said.

"So does half of Port Ferris. And they own quads, too."

"Did you hear that whistle?" Angie said. "Sounded like someone calling for a dog. How many hunt with dogs?"

"A lot," Claire said, voice thick. She wiped her brow. "And there could have been more than one hunter. They could've been whistling to one another, some signal." She glanced at Angie. "It's probably just a close call, someone mistaking us for game. Especially in this light and with no orange vests."

Or not.

Angie blew out a breath she hadn't realized she was holding.

CHAPTER 37

By the time Angie and Claire finally pulled into the Predator Lodge driveway with the boat in tow, it was almost 4:00 p.m. Angie immediately caught sight of Garrison Tollet's red Ford pickup parked under the carport.

Garrison stood beside it, watching them arrive, a lug wrench clenched in his fist.

"Uh-oh," Claire said. "Dad looks like he's on the warpath. I wonder why?"

They exited the truck and ducked through the tiny pelleting snowflakes, making for the cover of the carport where Garrison stood.

"What do you want here?" he demanded of Angie the instant she stepped under the cover. His boots were planted squarely, his weight on the balls of his feet. He looked ready to scrap or strike with that wrench.

"Garrison," Angie said calmly, yet instinctively keeping a four-foot cop distance from Garrison, her hands free and ready in front of her body in the event she'd need to defend herself. This man had been so warm and welcoming on their recent trip, it was like another person had taken over his body. "It's good to see you again. I came up to talk to you about the river trip twenty-four years ago."

"Got nothing to say. You can leave. Now."

"Dad!" Claire stepped between them. "She just wants—"

"The rear left tire of your rental was flat," he snapped, interrupting his daughter. "I put on the spare. Now go. Before the snow gets too heavy and locks you in here."

Angie's gaze darted to the Subaru parked outside the carport. The scrapes and dents were glaringly evident, but Garrison had made no comment about that damage.

"Dad—"

"Shut up, Claire. Get inside. This is not your business."

Claire's jaw dropped. Her eyes flashed with anger. She turned to Angie, the heat of emotion burning red into her face. "I'm sorry about him. I—"

"Get inside, Claire," her father growled. "I'll speak to you later."

"It's okay, Claire," Angie said quickly. "Thank you. For everything."

Garrison showed agitation, shifting his weight foot to foot as he waited for his daughter to enter the lodge and shut the door behind her.

As soon as the door closed, he pointed his wrench to the logging road. "You've got enough light to get back down to the highway before we get socked in. Your bags are in the rental."

"It was you, wasn't it?" Angie said, holding her ground. "In the red Ford truck. You know who tried to run me off the road."

"It was hunters. Brake line failure. That's all."

"Really? What were their names?"

"It's time to leave, Ms. Pallorino." He took a step toward her. Her shoulders stiffened.

"What are you all hiding, Garrison? What's the big secret? Was Jasmine Gulati pushed to her death? Do you know who killed her? Is that what this about? Who are you all protecting? Was it *you* who pushed her?"

"Don't make this difficult. I don't want to have to call the police."

She flicked a glance at the lodge, then lowered her voice. "You slept with Jasmine that night, Garrison. The women in the motel room next door knew it. The guys in the pub knew it. You screwed your client. On the very first night. I think even your wife suspected."

He faltered, blinked. His gaze ticked up to the lodge windows. Angie thought she saw a blind move.

"I have footage of you huddling in that pub booth with Jasmine Gulati. I have footage of Shelley, your wife, entering the pub. I have screenshots of Shelley looking directly at you sitting cozy and intimate with Jasmine Gulati. I've also got footage of Jessie Tollet and Tack McWhirther trying to step in and save Shelley from the indignity of seeing you with Jasmine, unsuccessfully. Because Shelley *did* observe you two cuddling in that booth. Would you like to see the screenshots I took from that footage, Garrison? They're in a folder in my rental."

Blood drained from his face. The paleness of his complexion made his black hair seem darker, his ice-green eyes more stark.

"Or maybe Shelley wants to see the images. Did she perhaps confront you when you returned to the lodge? Did your wife ask if you'd fucked Jasmine Gulati in the motel that night?"

His body language changed. It was as if some of the fight had leaked out of his muscles. Angie had gained the edge. She took it and moved a step closer to him, getting in his face.

"Here's what I know. Tack McWhirther was your wife's guardian, her protector. He cared fiercely about Shelley, and he did not approve of you being with Jasmine that night. I think he blamed the beautiful and provocative Jasmine more than he blamed poor, seduced you for not being able to keep your dick in your pants. Tack's also a fine hand with a banjo, I hear. So he and the Tollet twins—BoJo—and maybe Wallace Carmanagh, too, conjured up scenes of *Deliverance*, terrorizing the women along the river for the duration of their trip. Primarily to teach the wickedly evil Jasmine a lesson about the dangers of mocking the rednecks in these woods. Am I right?" She paused, watching his face.

"One of that *Deliverance* group wore a red hat and a black-and-red-plaid jacket, and the others matched the description the women gave me. I also know Wallace did time for violently assaulting a woman in his past. I know about Porter Bates, too." Her gaze bore into his green eyes. "I know the lengths some of these guys—including you—will go to protect one of their own. Like you protected Axel Tollet."

Her final words seemed to deflate him fully. He took a step back and sat heavily on a willow bench near the lodge door. He dropped his face into his big work-hardened hands and rubbed his skin.

She stepped closer. "Why did you do it, Garrison? Why did you sleep with Jasmine?"

"I was young."

"Forty-two?"

"She . . . she was beautiful. She came on to me. She offered it all to me. I . . ." He looked up, his eyes raw. "Shelley and I were having a rough time with the marriage. We'd just taken over the lodge from my dad, and we were trying to expand the guiding and tourism side of the business. But we were short on cash. We'd also been trying for kids for a long, long time. Shelley had suffered two miscarriages, and she'd collapsed into herself. She'd become distant. She no longer enjoyed physical intimacy. It was just a goddamn fling with Jasmine, something I needed to get out of my system. That woman just handed it to me on a plate, attracted, lured me. Trapped me." He sniffed and wiped his nose.

"She gave me a chance to see if I could still be a man, for Godssakes. I knew I'd screwed up the moment I did it. I knew what was going on with the guys and the banjo on the ridge—I kinda wanted her to pay, too . . . all of those women. I didn't like them. Intellectual, holier-than-thou, rude, feminist liberals from the city. They figured they had the answers to the world and that us rural folk were put on this earth expressly to be used by them. But we also needed them. We needed the documentary to go well. It would've brought huge positive exposure to the region and to our lodge. More business. You can't buy advertising like that. I thought, what harm could it do if Wallace and Tack and

BoJo want to play some stupid head game with them? Jessie and I were in the boats with the women. We knew they would come to no harm."

"Did you really know that?"

Angie let that hang while she filed away his admission that all four men had been stalking the river trip. The women had reported seeing only three at any one time. But with four in play, one could easily have pushed Jasmine into the water that fateful evening.

Wind rushed like the sound of an ocean through pines around the lodge. Flakes shimmied into the carport, turning thicker. A sense of time ticking by fast tightened in Angie's chest.

"Can you be so certain she wasn't pushed? By one of those guys?" she said, less strident in her approach now.

He looked away, avoiding her eyes. "They didn't do it. They wouldn't."

"Did you or anyone actually see her slip and fall into the river?"

He shook his head.

"What about Porter Bates?"

"What about him?"

"Those guys wanted to teach him a lesson all those years ago, too. Didn't they? They delivered to Porter Bates the ultimate justice. Death. Are you so certain they didn't do the same to Jasmine? To save Shelley? To save your marriage?" She paused. "To teach Jasmine a lesson?"

"Jeezus, no, they were just spooking her. She offended them. *She* attacked them in the pub. I simply made a mistake. I don't know anything about what happened to Porter Bates, okay?"

Angie weighed him, wondering how much he really did know.

"Angie," he said quietly, using her first name now, "please, listen to me. Please just let sleeping dogs lie. What good can it do to rake all this up now? What good can it do for Shelley? What good can it do my daughter to know that I was unfaithful to her mother, that I slept with a client? Jasmine Gulati slipped and fell, that's all. Please to God, just leave it where it lies."

"And if she didn't slip?"

His eyes gleamed with emotion. His nose reddened. His voice dropped in tone and turned husky. "It would break my family, Angie. Do you need to break up my family in order to make Jasmine Gulati's old grandmother happy?"

"It's not about happiness, Garrison. It's about the truth. It's about the law, just retribution."

"Is it? Really? Even if everyone has already paid?"

"What happened to her journal?"

He blinked and looked confused. "What?"

"Jasmine kept a diary. Every evening on the trip she wrote in it, claiming it was some titillating exposé. What happened to that journal? Did you take it from her things after she went over the falls?"

"No, I did not. I . . . it must have gone to her family, with her other things."

"But it didn't."

"I don't know what happened to it. I didn't know it had gone missing."

"I've been told Jasmine teased you and Jessie with the fact her journal contained salacious material. Were you worried at any point it might contain details of her sex with you that night?"

"Of course I worried. But no one said anything after she disappeared. It all died down."

Conveniently.

The lodge door swung open wide with a crash. Both Angie and Garrison jerked round in surprise. Shelley exited the door bearing a tray with two steaming mugs. She set the tray down on a small table beside the bent willow bench. She clicked on the outside light. Angie realized how gloomy it was getting already. That clock in her chest ticked faster. She had to get off this mountain before nightfall. She didn't feel safe out here. She should try to check in with Holgersen again.

"Shelley?" Garrison said, looking worried. "Is everything okay?"

Her gaze darted between her husband and Angie, her pale, thin hands fidgeting. "I . . . I thought you guys might be cold out here." Hurriedly she picked up a mug and offered it to Angie. "Hot chocolate," she said.

Angie accepted it gratefully. She was frozen and hadn't eaten since breakfast. But the look on Shelley's face gave her pause.

Shelley said, "Uh, Garrison, why . . . why don't you take yours inside? I'd like a word with Angie," she said. "Alone."

He didn't move.

"Please, Garrison."

He shot a look at Angie, his features tightening, his eyes pleading with Angie to keep her mouth shut. "If you need me, Shelley," he said, his gaze still fixed on Angie, "I'll be right inside."

Shelley waited for her husband to leave, her lips set in a tight line. As soon as the door clicked shut behind Garrison, Shelley opened her sweater and removed a purple book.

"Take it. Just take it, and get the hell out of our lives, okay?"

Angie's jaw dropped. She stared at the book, then looked up into Shelley's eyes.

"Is that what I think it is, Shelley?"

"It's Jasmine Gulati's journal. I took it, and now I'm giving it back so you can pack up, go home, and leave us alone."

CHAPTER 38

Her attention riveted on Shelley's feverish eyes, Angie reached slowly forward and took the book from the woman.

"How did you get it?" Angie said.

"They brought Jasmine's belongings up from the campsite to the lodge the morning after she went over the falls. Her stuff was put with the rest of her gear in one of our rooms. Everyone was out searching. I . . . saw the purple book from the doorway lying on top of her things. It looked like the journal I'd heard the women mention one evening when I took some supplies to their campsite. I went into the room, closed the door, and opened the journal. Just to take a quick look. I'd seen her with Garrison in the Hook and Gaffe that first night, and I . . . I needed to see if she'd written anything about being with my husband. Garrison had denied it, but I . . . I still had this feeling." She pressed her fine-boned hand against her stomach. "Right here."

"*Had* she written anything?"

Shelley's eyes turned hard, and her mouth thinned. She grabbed the edges of her big sweater and wrapped them tightly across her thin frame. Her complexion was almost translucent in this light, and it made her freckles stand out harshly. Flecks of snow danced in under the carport and settled upon her wool sleeves.

"Everything—she wrote it all, every tiny detail." She swallowed hard, rocked in her Ugg boots. "It made me sick to my stomach. She was evil. Everyone knew she was evil—they all said so."

Angie opened the journal. Inscribed on the first page were the words:

A gift for my love and my lover of story. Tell it, my girl. In your own hand . . . with all my heart, Doug.

Angie's eyes flared up, her heart hammering. "What else is in here?"

"Read it. You'll see."

Doug?

Dr. Douglas J. Hart—her mentor and professor, Rachel's husband—was Jasmine's lover? It suddenly all started slotting into place. The secrecy about the ring. The clandestine lover. Terminating the pregnancy. Revealing Doug as her lover would have killed Doug's university career, annihilated his shot at being appointed dean of the faculty. It would have destroyed his marriage to Rachel.

"So you knew?" Angie said. "All these years? That your husband had slept with Jasmine? Why . . . why didn't you speak to him?"

"It was easier, better, for me to pretend it never happened. I don't expect you to understand. Not talking about it, keeping that journal to myself, made it go away."

Like Jasmine went away . . . A new thought slammed Angie. Her mouth turned dry as she held Shelley's gaze. "If this diary contains incriminating information about your husband, wouldn't it have made more sense to get rid of it, burn it or something?"

"Probably. But a part of me wanted collateral. Some control over it all. Something I could use as a bargaining chip with Garrison if I ever needed it."

"You wanted leverage in case he ever hurt you again?"

Her eyes filled with tears. "He'd never want Claire to know, Angie. I . . . if I threatened him with showing Claire—"

"You'd *do* that? You'd show Claire? You'd hurt your daughter to hurt your husband?"

"No. No, God, no. Just to threaten him. I'd never actually do it."

Angie stared at Shelley. So frail and pale, so hard inside. So frightened. Very, very softly, Angie said, "You visited the women's camps in the evening once or twice."

She nodded.

"Were you there on that last evening, Shelley? Did you follow Jasmine to that bay?"

She took a fast step toward Angie. Angie braced in shock. The woman's pale, red-rimmed eyes blared into hers, but her voice came out in a thin whisper. "You're just as much a bitch as she was, you know that? Looking for the worst in people, raking muck out of the past, thinking that we are *capable* of something so heinous as pushing a client to her death. I know what you're thinking; I can see it in your eyes. You're thinking: Could this meek and mild little Shelley Tollet do it? Did she kill the bitch in heat who fucked her husband?"

She spat a harsh little laugh. "Guess you'll never know, will you? You won't get to read what she did with my husband, either, because I ripped out those pages before giving the journal to you. You can have that book, but you can't have those pages. And don't come looking for them because right now they're burning to ashes in the hearth inside." She marched back to the door and yanked it open. Face blotchy, eyes wild and glassy, she turned to face Angie. "Now fuck off the hell outta here."

She slammed the door shut. Angie heard the dead bolt thunk across.

Stunned, she looked down at the book in her hands. She turned to a random page.

Sweet is revenge, especially to women. It's an emotion that outlasts all others.

That night, tucked into her motel room bed, light burning well into the cold darkness, rain pattering against the windows while snow fell at higher elevations, Angie read through Jasmine Gulati's journal. This purple padded book had been a gift on Jasmine's twenty-fifth birthday, July 1994. The year she died. She'd spent that birthday in hedonistic bliss with Dr. Douglas J. Hart, her then professor, mentor, and academic advisor. Doug Hart and Jasmine Gulati had on that day already been sleeping together for eight months.

Angie read further.

Doug was shocked at first when I told him we were going to have a baby. I don't think I intended at that point, or perhaps ever, in keeping it. But I wanted to see his face, feel my power over him. Over his wife. Over his daughter. Over his family, his career, his entire life. It was intoxicating, that look of fear on his face, an emotion that escaped before he managed to control his features and hide it. I near climaxed with the delicious delirium of it.

He called me two days later and took me out to a little cabin, quiet and remote, in Sooke. Right on the sea. There he cooked me prawns in garlic, which I love, and he gave me the diamond ring. Marry me, Jazzie, he said.

Angie turned the page.

I'd won! I guess I'd wanted to see how serious he was. And I'd won. We fucked. This way and that. He was rough. Didn't care about the fact I was pregnant, or he liked it that I was, and it turned him on. He was hard as a rock, harder than ever. Took me from behind like a wild dog. I screamed when I came that day. Never came like that before. It was amazing. We lay there after. Naked. Panting. Bathed in sweat. In a puddle of moonlight.

Then he rolled over onto his side and said, "Why don't we wait, Jaz?"

"To get married?" I said.

"No, no, to have children."

And that's when he said I should get rid of it.

Angie turned to the next page.

I told him I'd consider it. That's when I saw he was really scared. I really did hold all the control now. Over his marriage. His daughter's relationship with him. His work. His promotion to dean of the faculty. He'd told me it was in the works. I knew then I could break Dr. Douglas J. Hart. Or I could allow him to become dean of my faculty . . . It was my choice.

What I also saw in his fear was that perhaps he never truly intended to leave his wife for me. He was fearful that I and some baby would wreck his marriage, his carefully built house of cards. It made this little bonfire of doubt burn inside me. Yet . . . he had given me the ring. I confronted him with this. He claimed I was wrong. It was just a matter of timing. If we waited until after I finished my studies and until after he was appointed dean, the fact I was his student would no longer be an issue. This, he said, was why it would be best to terminate this particular pregnancy, for there would be others, he said, if I wanted.

Angie flipped faster, scanning through the rest of the pages, which were full with details of sexual encounters with Doug and with younger men. Observations about women and sex. About her friends. About Rachel Hart. About her own mother and father. About her grandmother, the judge.

Angie stopped when she came to a page that was blank apart from one simple notation:

Appointment, Women's Clinic. Abortion. Sophie coming with. Mia is so pissed over this. It's fucked up our relationship.

There were no more entries until one that detailed packing and travel arrangements for Rachel Hart's river trip, where Jasmine wrote about how she planned to wear her engagement ring as a symbol of secret power over Rachel Hart, the woman who would be filming her, the woman whose husband she was having an affair with. The arrogant woman who would be divorced.

The rest of the pages were just ragged stubs where Shelley had ripped them out.

Angie sat back against the pillows, Jessie Carmanagh's voice resonating through her brain.

Last I saw of that diary, the Hart kid was reading it in the bushes . . . Only surprised me that the kid hadn't taken it sooner the way Jasmine was tempting her with it.

Poor Eden Hart. If the kid had indeed sneaked a peek, she'd have seen all these salacious details about her own father—whom she clearly adored—having sex with his student. Jasmine. Who was fishing with both Eden and her betrayed mother.

Yet Eden had denied reading it. From those photos on her wall in her office, her father still held pride of place in her heart. So maybe Jessie Carmanagh had been lying, or he'd been mistaken, or maybe Eden had been able to spend only a few seconds with the journal and had not grasped the extent of what lay between these pages.

Angie flung back her covers and began to throw her belongings into her bags. She wanted to be ready to leave at first light.

She needed to confront Rachel and Dr. Douglas J. Hart.

CHAPTER 39

"Reads like an erotica novel," Angie said, sliding the purple journal into the center of the table in the Hart home. She sat across from Rachel and Doug in their dining room. It was just after 1:00 p.m. She'd returned the damaged Subaru rental first thing that morning and dealt with the necessary insurance papers. She'd then picked up her repaired Mini Cooper and driven straight down the island to the Harts' estate in Metchosin.

In her bag at her side, her recording device was running. Neither Rachel nor Doug blinked as they regarded the journal. Neither moved a muscle. Their stillness was unnerving.

A cuckoo clock on the wall ticktocked, the sound growing unnaturally loud as the little pendulum swung to and fro beneath the ornate box. The sense of time loomed large in the room as Angie sat in front of this couple in their seventies, a lifetime of marriage stretching between them. They had a grown daughter. Grandchildren. A lost son. A big home on the water. Career success was notched into their respective belts. They had health, retirement funds, each other. Rachel and Doug had more than a lot of people in this world could only dream of. But that purple book on the table threatened it all.

That book held a secret worth killing to keep.

"Do you know what's in it?" Angie said.

Doug moistened his lips, his gaze fixated on the book. Rachel cleared her throat and leaned forward. She met Angie's gaze, her gray eyes fierce. "I'm sure you're about to tell us, and if you don't mind, please move it along. We have guests arriving within an hour, and I'd like to be ready for them."

Angie turned to Doug. "You gave Jasmine that journal, Doug. For her twenty-fifth birthday. Back in '94."

Rachel stiffened, bracing for what Angie now believed the filmmaker knew was coming. Angie's read on Rachel since she'd put that journal on the table was that the old filmmaker knew exactly what it contained.

Doug's face began to redden as cords of tension swelled in his neck.

"You also gave her this engagement ring." Angie placed on the table the photo of the ring found with Jasmine's bones. "You were her professor. You were sleeping with your student, Jasmine Gulati, for over a year. And you asked your *student*, Doug, to marry you, didn't you?"

Silence, apart from the ticktock of the clock.

"Trouble was, you were already married. To Rachel. Did you propose to Jasmine as some kind of insurance or guarantee that you'd still be there for her after she aborted the baby she was carrying. *Your* baby?"

"It's lies, all lies," snapped Rachel. "That journal contains the fabricated meanderings of a student infatuated with her professor, that's all! Jasmine was a narcissistic sociopath with some sort paraphilia where her sexual arousal and gratification depended on fantasizing about sexually dominating and emotionally controlling men in positions of power. Men like my husband."

Angie picked up the journal and flipped it open to a page she'd marked. "You mean, like in this paragraph?" She began to read:

"I had him, I controlled him by his cock. My Lady Jane in command of his John Thomas, in the terminology of D. H. Lawrence, which he so smugly taught us in first-year English while watching the girls' cheeks warm and the boys shifting in their chairs to adjust space in their jeans for their hardening dicks as he discussed the sex in Lady Chatterley's Lover. *I think it was at that moment I decided I would break him . . ."*

Angie looked up. "How did you know what was written in here, Rachel?"

There was slight flick of her gaze at her husband, a quick glint of panic in her eyes, but within nanoseconds her features were back under control.

"Doug told me." She cleared her throat again. "He confessed he'd had a brief affair with Jasmine but had ended it fast. He told me because he was worried that Jasmine was unstable and that she might go all *Fatal Attraction* on him and his family, and he wanted us prepared up front."

Doug reached for Rachel's hand, covering it with his own as she spoke. She inhaled deeply. "We went for counseling. We worked through it all. It strengthened our marriage and our understanding of each other in the end. But what Jasmine said in that journal—it's not true. The affair was a brief, one-off thing. If she pretended it was more, it's lies."

Angie regarded Rachel, then Doug. "What about the engagement ring?"

"She bought that herself is my guess," Rachel said quickly before Doug could answer. "Like I said, she was playing out a fantasy."

"Why did you not mention this to me when I first asked you about Jasmine's engagement ring and the missing journal?" Angie said.

Rachel gave a derisive snort. "Why do you think? Even now it would ruin Doug's standing in academia. It would hurt our daughter. And it would place me in a somewhat awkward position after Jasmine's accidental death on a trip I had organized. A trip I specifically invited her on."

287

"Awkward?"

"People would think I had motive to hurt her, had there been any doubt about her drowning being an accident."

"You were worried there might be doubt?"

Silence.

"Why did you invite Jasmine on the trip, Rachel?"

"For all the reasons I told you before. She gave me an angle that I wanted."

"But you *knew* she'd slept with your husband?"

"Yes. Like I said, I *wanted* all those elements at play in subtle fashion within the subtext of the documentary. I wanted the divorcée, the adulteress, the lesbians, the single women—"

"The betrayed wife?"

"I was the observer, the recorder. I already had Kathi as the wife whose husband was betraying her sexually."

Angie wasn't buying it, but she played along, casting about for more information. "It must have pleased you greatly when Jasmine slept with your guide on the first night."

Silence.

"That's why you did nothing to interrupt her verbal assault on those locals in the pub, isn't it—you wanted it all to happen? This documentary was, in some ways, going to be your revenge against Jasmine Gulati, wasn't it? You were going to assassinate her in the editing."

Rachel pushed back her chair. "If you're done now—"

"I'm not." Angie leaned forward. "You lied about those final hours of footage. You filmed Jasmine down in the bay where she was angling. You had that tape running when she went into the water. Not only did you see exactly what happened to Jasmine Gulati that evening, you also got it on tape. Didn't you, Rachel?"

All color drained from the woman's face. In the blink of eye, she appeared far older than her seventy-two years.

Angie tapped the table with her finger. "I have a witness who places you on a rock ledge above the bay where Jasmine's rod was found. That witness saw you in your pink toque with your tripod, filming. I visited that ledge, Rachel. From it a person has a clear line of sight down to the bay. But you told me quite clearly that when you left the campsite, you went upriver, in the opposite direction, to film the campsite from a promontory of land. Thing is, I walked upriver east of the camp. There is no promontory. There is no way to get a line of sight to the camp." She paused. "You lied."

Rachel swallowed, shifting slightly in her chair. "Who is this witness?"

"It doesn't matter who it is."

"Look, the only reason I misdirected you was because of this very thing happening now. I was afraid that if you learned Jasmine had slept with my husband and had held fantasies about marrying him, it would've given me motive to hurt her. The fact I was the last person to see her alive would not help my cause. I destroyed those tapes for that same reason."

"What did you see? What did you capture on film? What exactly happened to Jasmine that evening?"

She got to her feet. "That's it. You're done here." She held her arm out toward the hallway. "Please leave. Now."

Angie remained seated. "You watched her struggle," she said quietly. "Did she sweep with that current into the next little bay right above the falls? I visited that bay, too, and that's where all the debris swirls in. A lot of it gets trapped there behind a big fallen tree. Couldn't you have screamed for help, Rachel? Long before Garrison saw her finally going over the falls? Couldn't you have run down the trail to that little bay and tried to pull her out, to save her? Or did you quietly stand back and do nothing and watch her die?"

Doug lurched to his feet so fast his chair slammed back against the glass door. "My wife asked you to leave. We're under no obligation to answer these ridiculous insinuations. You're not a cop. You're a failed ex-cop. A miserable, muckraking disgrace of a detective, and the shit that happened in our lives has got *nothing* to do with Jasmine Gulati's slipping and drowning. Like my wife said, this is *precisely* why she said nothing, because *this* would happen, people would make these horrific assumptions." He reached for the journal, but Angie quickly moved it out of his range and tucked it into her bag.

She hooked her bag over her shoulder and came to her feet.

"We can trace the ring, Doug. You do know that? We can find out if it was you who bought it and where it was bought. We can trace where the diamonds were sourced from and what jeweler made the ring, what store it went to, how it was paid for." Angie knew this was a stretch, especially after all these years, but Doug might not.

"The door is that way," he said, stepping between his wife and Angie, his eyes blazing, his face red.

Angie moved toward the front door. Doug followed at her shoulder, Rachel close behind him. But Angie stopped suddenly and faced them both.

"One other thing. I have witness evidence that Eden read this journal."

Both Rachel and Doug froze. Doug's gaze briefly went to his wife's. Angie waited in silence. The cuckoo exploded from its ornate house and blasted a noise that made them all jump.

Angie said, "This also makes a lie of your claim, Rachel, that you hid everything in part because it would hurt Eden. Because if Eden did read that journal, she already knew of her father's affair with Jasmine Gulati. She knew about Doug's baby that Jasmine aborted, because that's in there, too. Eden knew back on the river, twenty-four-years ago, that her father—whom she adored—was going to leave her and her mother for an obnoxious slut."

Angie was winging it, pushing them as far as she could before they tossed her out because she couldn't be certain Eden had read those parts of the journal. She took a step toward them, getting back into their personal bubbles. "Eden had—still has—quite a thing for her father. This father-daughter relationship is very special to her. How might the news of a looming divorce and the possibility of new children in her father's life have affected a young teenager like Eden?" As Angie said the words, something else struck her. Hard. Her pulse quickened.

"Eden left the camp after you that evening, Rachel," she said quickly, her mind whirling, her body heating. "Allegedly to relieve herself in the woods. Could *she* have perhaps followed Jasmine? What did you *really* see from up on your ledge? Is there a much darker reason that you kept silent and destroyed those tapes?"

Tiny pearls of sweat beaded along Rachel's upper lip, and her skin turned gray. She made a small noise and reached for the wall to brace herself. Doug's gaze shot to Rachel. Shock flared into his features as something dawned on him, too. His attention pinged to a photograph on the wall. Angie turned to see what he was looking at.

A black-and-white photo of four-year-old Jimmy Hart with his tricycle. A photo taken the summer he drowned. The summer Eden had been left alone with little Jimmy at the dock.

Angie's heart began to thump against her ribs as the puzzle pieces clicked into place, Eden's words tumbling through her memory.

The hardest, I suppose, was that my mother blames me in some ways for Jimmy's death. I was supposed to be watching him, but I'd ventured off the dock to gather the blackberries I could see growing in brambles farther along the lakeshore. While I was picking berries, he went off the edge of the dock with his tricycle. By the time I heard the splash . . . Guilt can be a terrible thing. I felt guilt for years. My mother still does, I think. Because she left me with Jimmy, and I was only nine at the time. My mother shouldn't have given me that responsibility at that age.

Slowly Angie returned her gaze from the black-and-white photograph to their faces.

Both appeared to have seen a ghost, some dreadful specter from the past that was rising in the space between them.

"Jimmy drowned," Angie said, her voice hushed. "Like Jasmine drowned. Both were alone with Eden, weren't they? You saw her push Jasmine? You *filmed* it?"

Rachel's legs gave out under her. Doug quickly grabbed her arm and helped her to a chair in the living room. Rachel fell down into the chair like a broken doll. A silent communication passed between Doug and his wife. She nodded, almost imperceptibly. He reached for the back of a chair, holding himself upright, his complexion gray. He appeared utterly and suddenly broken.

Angie guessed this was the first time Doug realized his daughter might have drowned his son. Rachel, on the other hand, had suspected it a lot longer, probably after she saw Eden push Jasmine into the Nahamish River. She'd protected her husband from the horror that one of their children had killed the other.

"You saw Eden, Rachel," Angie said with stronger conviction. "You *saw* your fourteen-year-old daughter pushing Jasmine Gulati into the Nahamish River above the deadly Plunge Falls. You did not call for help. You did nothing and said nothing because it would expose your child to a murder charge. And when you asked Eden why she'd done it, it was her, not Doug, who explained to you what was in that journal and why she'd followed Jasmine down to the bay. Eden was trying to stop Jasmine from destroying her family, her relationship with her father, her life. You were a mother trying to protect both your child and yourself. Because you couldn't allow Jasmine in death to destroy Eden and your family on top of what Jasmine in life had already done."

Tears welled in Rachel's eyes. They slid in a silent sheen down her cheeks. She started to shake.

Doug looked at Angie in horror, his mouth moving, but he was unable to speak. He dropped to his knees in front of Rachel's chair and took his wife's hands in his.

"And you, Doug," Angie said, "had no idea both your daughter and wife knew about your affair and the engagement. You thought your lover had just conveniently slipped away forever, and you were safe."

"Is . . . is it true, Rachel?" His voice came out a rasp. "Please, God, don't let this be true. Did . . . how long have you believed Eden could have hurt our Jimmy—that our own daughter could have killed our son? Why? *Why*, Rachel? Why would she do it? Jealousy? Possessiveness? *Why didn't you talk to me?*"

Rachel seemed to have slipped into some distant fugue state. Doug turned to Angie. "You need to leave. You need to leave right now."

"I need to call the police and report this," she said softly. "You do know that."

He surged to his feet. "Please, please do *not* let that woman destroy my wife, my family, for the mistakes I made with her."

"Your own daughter destroyed your family a long time ago, if she really did do something to effect Jimmy's drowning."

He slammed his fist into the wall that divided the living room and the hallway. The impact shuddered through his body and left a dent in the drywall. He stared at his bloodied hand, his whole body vibrating.

Rachel suddenly spoke in a voice that did not sound like her own. "She needs to tell the police now, Doug. She has the journal. It's all out in the open now. Eden . . ." She shifted in her chair and faced Angie.

"Eden learned from Jimmy's death that drowning works. I . . . I don't know what a parent is supposed to do when they start to suspect terrible things about a child of theirs, yet they're never certain. Things you don't want to . . . can't possibly believe. Can't even ask them about." She swiped the tears from her face with the palms of her hands. "I think Eden learned from her success in eliminating Jasmine that organizing a remote trip works. She . . . the police need to look into another death, the drowning of a woman named Jayne Elliot. She . . . she's Michael's ex—Michael is Eden's husband. I—"

"Rachel! Stop it!" Doug yelled. "Stop right there! Do *not* say another word."

"No. No, I need to, I have to say it. I always wondered. Eden is bad, Doug. She's got an evil seed inside her. Three years ago, she organized an all-girls salmon-fishing trip up the coast. She invited Michael's ex, which surprised me, but Eden said she was trying to make amends and get on with the woman. They'd had issues in the past. Eden feared Michael had never properly gotten over Jayne. Eden invited Jayne and a few other friends, hired a boat and a guide—they all chipped in. On the last day of their expedition up the BC coast, Jayne Elliot went overboard in extremely cold and stormy weather. She was swept away, and a search was mounted. They found her body days later, washed up on an island beach. Drowned. No one saw her go overboard apart from Eden. You need to look into that trip. You need to look."

"*Why* would she do that?" Doug said.

"She's like that, Doug. She has to be the center of attention. She had to be the apple of *your* eye, too—especially you. She couldn't allow Jimmy and a budding father-son relationship to steal that from her. She's possessive and lethal in her jealousy or when betrayed."

Doug sank slowly to the sofa. "I can't believe you never said anything."

"To who? About what? What was I going to say, I *think* my child is a serial killer?"

"You had proof, Rachel. If you filmed her pushing Jasmine into the river, you had proof."

"I hardly filmed her. I froze when I saw it happen, just froze. I let the film run. I didn't scream. I didn't run down to the little bay. That was as much an indictment against me. Then Eden told me why she did it, and I couldn't tell everyone about what you'd done. For Chrissakes, you have *got* to see how that would have all played out. Our life would have crumbled. You would have been terminated at the university. And . . . at the time, I never put two and two together with Jimmy's drowning. That came only later. Even then, I was never certain. It . . . it was just a dark and horrible suspicion, and I'd been a bad mother by leaving a nine-year-old alone with her four-year-old brother in the first place." She faced Angie.

"I looked for that diary, you know? When no one seemed to know where it had gone, I thought Eden had taken it. If Eden had taken it, then she would be safe from suspicion in Jasmine's death and so would I. Because if Eden had it, the contents would never get out. But if anyone else had taken it . . . I worried for years. Then when Jasmine was never found, when the journal never surfaced, I just buried it all away. Deep, deep down in my mind, I compartmentalized it. I went forward believing it never really happened the way I saw it."

"How did it happen? What exactly did you see?" Angie said.

She inhaled deeply. "I'd been filming Jasmine casting alone. The light was so beautiful, the droplets from her line like jewels in the air. I . . . I suddenly saw Eden enter the frame. She was wearing her red Kinabulu toque, and she was carrying a log in her hand. She left the forest fringe and headed directly down the rocky embankment to where Jasmine was casting." Rachel's voice caught, and she took a moment to gather herself. Clearing her throat, she said, "Jasmine turned and saw Eden, and she called out. But Eden was like a robot. She just kept moving down among the rocks until she was right in front of Jasmine. She swung the log. She struck Jasmine hard. Jasmine's boots slid out under her, and she went straight into the water." Rachel started to rock in her chair, her arms wrapped tightly across her chest.

"I . . . I knew how the water swirled back into the next little cove above the falls. I did run down there as fast as I could. I got down to the water to find Jasmine clinging to a strainer—a big tree with a massive root ball that had fallen into the river. But I . . . I . . . All I could see in my mind was Eden swinging that stick, and I knew if I pulled Jasmine out she would tell authorities my fourteen-year-old tried to kill her, and I . . . I just let her slide back into the river." Rachel began to gag.

Doug helped her up and hurried her to the bathroom, where Angie heard the woman throwing up.

Angie blew out a chestful of air and let herself out the front door. She stepped onto the porch and got out her phone. She called the local RCMP detachment. She asked for a detective she knew who worked there.

"I think it's a serial homicide case," she told him. "Possibly three murders so far. All drownings. It'll require an integrated investigation because the cases fall into several jurisdictions. The suspect, Dr. Eden Hart, currently works and lives in Nanaimo." Angie gave the details of Eden's practice and the address of the beautiful waterfront home that belonged to the Harts.

The detective told her to stand by. Units were being dispatched to the Hart home stat. Other units would be dispatched to Dr. Eden Hart's office and residence in Nanaimo.

Angie sat down on the front porch steps and rubbed her face. The weight of what she'd done lay heavy on her shoulders.

Oh, the secrets we keep. And how they keep us. And the havoc the truth could wreak.

The truth wasn't always pretty, but it was necessary. Angie believed that. She *had* to. Truth brought closure. It had brought justice to Jasmine Gulati. Justice to Jilly Monaghan. The old judge would have her closure.

Truth was the one thing Angie had to hold on to.

CHAPTER 40

SATURDAY, NOVEMBER 24

Angie stood on the misty beach alongside Jilly Monaghan watching the sea. It was Saturday morning, and Gudrun had told Angie that she'd find the old woman down here. Cold wind whipped white spume off the waves, and along the horizon the ocean blended gray with the sky.

"So our Jasmine was murdered," Jilly said, leaning heavily on her walking sticks as she braced into the sea wind. "By a fourteen-year-old girl."

"Allegedly so," Angie said. "According to Rachel Hart, Eden Hart followed Jasmine down to the secluded bay and surprised her. She struck Jasmine with a log. It threw Jasmine off-balance and into the icy water, where she was weighted down with her boots and waders. The current swept her into a small bay downriver, right above the falls, where she grabbed onto a fallen tree and tried to pull herself up a slick, steep bank. At this point Rachel Hart might have been able to save her but did nothing. Rachel, Eden, and Garrison Tollet from the talus scree above all witnessed Jasmine going over the falls."

"Rachel caught her daughter's act on film?" Jilly Monaghan said.

"Apparently. Of course this is all hearsay so far; nothing is proven yet. Dr. Eden Hart was arrested in Nanaimo yesterday and is lawyering up. Two additional homicide investigations have been opened, one looking into the drowning death of Eden's little brother, Jimmy Hart. Another into the drowning of the ex-girlfriend of Eden Hart's husband. Rachel, however, is giving a full confession on advice of her own legal counsel," Angie said. "The lead detective on the case told me that Rachel and Doug came to this decision quickly."

"Giving up their daughter in exchange for leniency? Pleading her earlier silence was a mother's need to protect her offspring?"

"I suspect once it hit them, once it was really driven home that their own daughter might have killed their son, they could no longer hide from what their daughter was. And what she could still do. Legal counsel probably convinced them it was in their best interests to come clean and paint themselves as parents victimized by a cunning young sociopath."

"A cold, controlling, narcissistic, and very intelligent personality," Jilly said, her eyes watering in the wind.

Angie nodded.

"So Jasmine must have been trapped underwater by the force of the falls," the judge said, watching the waves and the spray. "Then came the two big floods, and one of the events must have popped her body out and washed her up into that grove."

Angie pushed blowing hair back off her face. "It appears so. The grove where Jasmine was found lies a few feet higher than the estimated rise of the river, but the height that the water rose is just that, an estimate, a meteorologist's best guess given the records at the time. Also, there could have been some kind of storm surge around the terrain. I checked with a specialist at UVic, and he felt it was possible."

"After all these years," the old woman said, "the truth is finally out."

Angie hesitated. "Jilly, it's also going to come out that Jasmine was a . . . complex and somewhat unlikable person."

Jilly Monaghan shot her a look. "I know our Jasmine was difficult. I know she had issues, possibly pathological ones that related to her sexuality." She paused and looked out once more over the gray sea. Wind flapped the hem of her coat. Softly, she said, "But it seems our Jasmine met her match in the young Eden Hart. A serial killer who started at age nine." She turned to Angie. "I wonder if there were others, beyond her brother, Jasmine, and her husband's ex."

"I wouldn't be surprised to learn there are more victims. I'll have my full report to you in a few days in binder form and on a disc."

The judge fell quiet as she watched the waves crunch and churn the pebbles along the shore. A fine mist of rain blew in from the water, dampening her lined face and woolen hat. "You'll find the balance of your fee plus the bonus has already been credited to your account." She met Angie's eyes. "Thank you, Angela. I knew you'd pull through."

"Angie."

The judge smiled. And something unspoken surged between the two fiercely independent women at different points in this stream of life. Looking into the judge's watery eyes, Angie felt the echoes of time, of what had been and what was yet to come, and how it all looped together. The judge had shown her a way forward. She'd shown Angie a way to be. A way to grow stronger and a way to age.

Angie wavered, not quite wanting to say what was on her mind because it would show her vulnerability, but something in the old woman's face made her say it anyway. "Your phone call, giving me this case—it was a lifeline. I'm the one who owes you."

"Ah, but you grabbed that lifeline with both hands. You did the pulling back to shore. It was meant to be that you and I met. I hope you will not be a stranger."

Angie shocked herself by impulsively leaning down and giving the judge a quick hug and planting a kiss on her damp, lined cheek. She left the judge facing the water, her arthritic hands gripping her walking sticks as she stared into the nebulous gray distance.

As Angie hurried along the beach, her hands thrust deep in her pockets against the cold, with the wintery salt wind raw against her face, she considered once more the irony—how media exposure, her notoriety, had tanked both her policing career and her PI job. Yet the media exposure had brought her Justice Monaghan and a tool to seize it all back. But better. Stronger. She would no longer hide from being Angie Pallorino, the cradle baby, the violent cop who'd shot and killed a sick murderer. She'd be all that and more. She'd carry on marching to her own loud drum, and she'd hold her banner high in the name of truth. And closure. For others like herself and like Jilly Monaghan.

Once Angie reached her car, she called Jock Brixton.

His line was busy, so she left a message. "Jock, it's a wrap. You'll find the balance of the Gulati case fee plus a bonus, minus my cut and expenses, in the Coastal Investigations account by close of business Monday. Job's done." She smiled to herself. "A copy of my report will be on your desk in a few days."

She killed the call and sat back, watching the rain wriggle down her Mini Cooper windshield.

Fuckit. She'd won. She'd done it. Her first solo PI case.

Angie started her engine. It had taken the full afternoon yesterday to sort things out with the RCMP. She'd then gone home, showered, and crashed. She'd slept in this morning and then come to see Jilly Monaghan to break the news in person. Next on her agenda was Maddocks. She wanted to see him in person, too.

As she drove she rehearsed in her mind how she'd tell him she was ready. To commit. How she'd ask if he still wanted this—her.

She turned down a street wet with rain and plastered with dead leaves. Slippery leaves. Slippery like those rocks on the river where Jasmine had slipped . . . Something began to niggle in her brain about the Gulati case, something someone had said about her slipping . . . but she couldn't pin it down.

Suddenly, up ahead, she saw the gates of the Mount Saint Agnes Mental Health Treatment Facility. Angie checked the time. Saturday noon. Her dad would be there visiting her mom. He always went on Friday evening and again on Saturday around noon. He'd stay for lunch in the patients' dining room. Angie quickly tapped her brakes and clicked on her indicator. She drove through the massive wrought-iron gates of the Mount Saint Agnes compound.

Angie found Miriam and Joseph Pallorino sitting alone in the glassed-in sunroom. It was darkening outside with lowering clouds, rain flecking against the windows, but logs crackled in a cast-iron fireplace in the corner, making the place warm.

Her father glanced up as she entered. Surprise shot across his face at the sight of her. It was replaced with worry as he came abruptly to his feet, then winced, his hand going to his hip.

"Angie? You—you okay? You look—"

"Exhausted. I know." She smiled and hugged him. "I'm tired but really good. How about you? That hip still hurting, huh?"

He made a face. "Yeah. Same old. Cricks and creaks. This getting-old business is not for sissies, but it's better than the alternative, eh?"

"I guess." She glanced at her mother, who was staring vacantly at her own reflection on the glass pane. "How's Mom?" she said quietly.

"She's okay today. You picked a good afternoon to visit, I think. She might recognize you."

Angie pulled up a wicker chair and sat facing Miriam Pallorino. Her adoptive mom was a faded echo of what she'd once been, her eyes vacant, her face sagging, her once flame-red hair now blending with white to create a clownish pale-orange cloud around her features.

Angie's heart crunched.

Miriam and Joseph Pallorino had kept Angie's past a secret from her. They'd inserted her as a four-year-old into their dead daughter's life, even giving her the same name. But it had been motivated by loss, a desperate act of grief. It was inspired by love in so many complex ways.

Was the motivation behind the Pallorino family secret that much different from those secrets so fiercely guarded by the Tollets, the Carmanaghs, and the Jacobis in protecting Axel Tollet—one of their own?

A whisper of unease darkened Angie's mood as her mind returned to the Tollet and Carmanagh gang. And to the truck that had tried to run her off the road and the arrows fired at her and Claire in the grove.

If it was them who'd done those things, it had likely been an attempt to scare her away from digging up the truth about Porter Bates's murder.

Still, the disquiet lingered, that sense that something was off, unfinished. That she'd missed a critical piece of evidence, and it dangled somewhere in her brain, just out of reach.

She pushed the unease away and focused on why she'd come, on the good things she wanted to nurture in her life now. Reaching out, she took her mother's cold, veined hands in her own.

"Hey, Mom. How are you doing? You been watching the birds out there today? Are they happy with the new feeder I brought last time?"

Confusion chased across Miriam's features, and consternation furrowed into her brow. She shot a desperate look at her husband.

"It's Angie, love," he said. "Our Angie."

Miriam began to rock her chair. "Angie," she said, the frown deepening across her brow. "Angie. Angie. Who's Angie?"

Angie took out her phone. "I wanted to show you something, Mom." She clicked open an image that Ginny had shot with her phone of Angie in the bridal gown. She held the phone out to her mother.

With slightly trembling hands, her mother took the phone and closely studied the image. A look of wonder changed her face. She touched her fingers to the digital image.

"A princess bride," she whispered. "She's so beautiful." Miriam looked up into Angie's eyes. "She's you. She's our Angie. My baby is getting married?"

Tears sprang to Angie's eyes. She cleared her throat. "Maybe. Remember Detective James Maddocks? I brought him here to meet you—tall man with dark hair and blue eyes?" She looked up at her dad, whose eyes glittered with emotion.

"We're talking about tying the knot. Would you give me away, Dad, if it all goes ahead?"

Her father stared at her. He then turned to this wife. Blinking back the tears now leaking from the corners of his eyes, he nodded. When he spoke, his voice was hoarse and soft. "Do you forgive us, then, Angie? For what we did? For the secrets we kept."

She came to her feet and hugged her father. He pulled her close, and he folded his arms tightly around her body. And she felt him cry. He smelled right, like his old sweater, like his aftershave, like her dad, and she buried her face against that old wool sweater with the leather patches on the elbows.

"I love you, baby girl," he whispered against her hair. "I love you so much. I am so, so sorry for not—"

"Shh." She pulled back and placed her hands firmly on his shoulders. Her gaze bored into his. "Don't say it. You're a good man, Dad."

A man so much better than Dr. Doug Hart. Your peer. A fellow academic of around similar age.

"I'm lucky you found me." She kissed his cheek.

He stared at her. Time stretched. Rain began to drum against the sunroom panes, and the sky grew darker. "I needed to hear you say that, Ange—you have no idea how much I needed to hear that."

"I needed to say it, too. I love you." She looked down at her mom, who was staring at the rain running down the window. "I love you both. With all my heart."

Her mother began to rock in her rocker again, and her voice rose softly in song.

> *Ave Maria*
> *Vergin del ciel*
> *Sovrana di grazie e madre pia . . .*

"Maybe Mom can sing that at the wedding," Angie said to her father.

"Maybe." He smiled.

Despite her fatigue, Angie was filled with an incredible lightness of being as she drove for home. She turned down the waterfront road. Lights in the storefronts glowed warm and friendly in the cold foggy evening as bundled-up shoppers made their way along sidewalks, umbrellas leaning into the sea wind. It would be December next month. A full year since she and Holgersen had been called out to the Gracie Drummond sexual assault case. At the time she'd been dreading Christmas, as she always had, for reasons she'd not yet understood. But then she'd met James Maddocks, and he'd turned her life on its head. He'd become her partner, boss, and lover. And now, possibly, husband-to-be. The thought shimmered inside her as she stopped at a red light.

Her phone rang while she watched pedestrians crossing. She answered via Bluetooth.

"Angie here."

"Is that the private investigator, Angie Pallorino?" The voice was female. Hesitant.

Something about the woman's tone made Angie tense. "This is her, yes. Who's speaking?"

A clearing of a throat. "I'm Sophie Rosenblum. Sophie Sinovich Rosenblum. I used to be a close friend of Jasmine Gulati's back at university. I . . . I just returned with my family from vacation. I heard the news that Jasmine's body has been found and identified. My house sitter said you came by with questions and that she referred you to Mia."

"Oh, thanks for calling, Sophie." The light turned green. Angie moved her vehicle forward. "Mia managed to help me out, thank you."

"I phoned Mia. She told me she'd informed you about Jasmine's abortion."

"Yes, she did."

"Jasmine never went through with it."

Angie's chest constricted. Her brain doubled in on itself. She hit her brakes and screeched into a loading zone. "*What* did you say?"

"I accompanied Jasmine to the women's center on the mainland, but she chickened out at the very last moment. She couldn't go through with it that day. Jasmine never had the abortion."

CHAPTER 41

"I need to pick your brain," Angie said as she slid into a booth opposite forensic pathologist Dr. Barb O'Hagan. She placed the coroner's preliminary report on Jasmine Gulati's death on the table between them. "Thanks for meeting me on such short notice." She raised her hand, summoning the server.

Angie had phoned the crusty old pathologist from her car, right after Sophie Sinovich Rosenblum had dropped the pregnancy bombshell. Barb O'Hagan was more than a law enforcement colleague to Angie. She was an old friend and confidante and had jumped at the opportunity to meet with Angie over dinner at Farrier John's, a Tudorstyle pub downtown.

"And there I was thinking you just wanted to see my smiling face."

Angie laughed. The server arrived. "What're you having, Barb, the usual?"

"Why not. Keep the old stomach stable."

"No surprises when they open your tough old corpse on the morgue table one day, eh."

"Got that right."

Angie turned to the server "One Lagavulin sixteen, a double. And . . . what the hell, make that two. Mine with a block of ice. And two Guinness pies with fries and peas." She crooked her brow at Barb to make sure. The morgue doc nodded. The server departed to fetch their drinks.

Angie pulled a face. "My mom used to force me to eat peas, and now I'm ordering them voluntarily?"

"And mushy ones at that."

"Better be good."

"Trust me, best meal you'll have had in a long while. So how you doing, Ange? I heard you scored big on that Gulati investigation for old Jukebox Jilly. Who'd have thought—a fourteen-year-old female? Fascinating pathology there. That's going to be one for the psych students. Then again, I've been in this business long enough that nothing should surprise me."

"Who'd you hear this from? Leo?"

O'Hagan cackled, showing the gap between her front teeth. "No, in this case, Holgersen. He came by to speak to me today about some cold cases Maddocks had assigned him and Leo. They're working in some new unit formed under the iMIT umbrella. Includes the Annelise Janssen missing persons file. Such an oddball, that Holgersen. He said the department was all abuzz with the fact you'd dug a possible serial out of that Nahamish body case and that filmmaker Rachel Hart was giving a full confession to the RCMP, exposing her own kid as Gulati's killer. Well done."

"I don't think it's done, Barb."

The doc's smiled faded at the tone in Angie's voice. Drinks arrived. They fell silent as the server set their glasses on coasters.

"Food will be up shortly," the server said.

Angie reached for her glass. "Cheers." She took a sip. The hot burn that branched into her chest gave an immediate punch of relaxation. She inhaled deeply, relishing it for a moment. A scalding shower and a visit to Maddocks would have to wait, but this drink and some hot food would suffice in the interim. She put down her glass and opened the folder.

"I just received some additional information from an old friend of Gulati's, and it doesn't add up. I need your opinion. Nothing formal, just need to brainstorm some possibilities." She opened to the page with the images of the post parturition scars on Jasmine Gulati's pelvis. She slid the file over to the doc and tapped on an image. "In your opinion, how reliable is this parturition scarring as evidence of a pregnancy?"

"Nice ring," O'Hagan said, noting the solitaire on Angie's hand. "You and Maddocks making it official, then?"

Angie glanced up as her stomach tightened with a sudden burst of both nerves and anticipation. She hadn't taken it off, and she wondered if she should before she went to see Maddocks. Or whether he'd see it as a sign of her will to make this happen if she showed up at his yacht wearing it. Conflict twisted through her chest. There should be a manual for this stuff because it was way out of her realm of experience. "Uh, yeah, maybe. I . . . I'll come back to that."

Barb raised her brows. An odd little smile tugged at her lips. "Congratulations. I'm happy for you two." She drew the report closer, took a sip of whiskey, and set her tumbler down. She fished her small reading glasses out of her breast pocket and perched them atop her nose. O'Hagan fell silent as she studied the pathologist's report, peering closely at the pics.

"Definitely pits, cavities, some depressions located on the dorsal surface of the pubic symphysis," O'Hagan said, leaning in even closer. "Historically, this kind of scarring has indeed been attributed to the trauma of parturition, especially when coupled with reliable information on the decedent's obstetrical history." She glanced up. "But without the individual's particular obstetric history—" She shook her head. "The jury is still out on whether these can be a reliable indicator of childbirth."

"But they *could* be an indication of pregnancy—"

"Not of pregnancy per se, but of having carried a child to term and given a natural vaginal birth. Pregnancy alone does not modify a woman's bones. However, during childbirth, the pubic bones separate to allow an infant to pass through the birth canal. The ligaments connecting the pubic bones must stretch, and they can tear and cause bleeding where they attach to bone. Later, bone remodeling at these sites can leave these small circular or linear grooves on the inside surface of the pubic bones."

She tapped the images of Jasmine Gulati's pelvis. "These parturition pits show that a female *may* have given birth vaginally. But in more recent studies, medium to large 'birth scarring' has also been demonstrated on male pelvic bones and on the pelvises of females known to have not had children." She took another sip of her drink. "Bottom line, these bony changes are being reexamined as an indicator of childbirth, and this is what the pathologist has noted in his report here."

Angie stared at the doc, Sophie Sinovich Rosenblum's words looping around and around in her brain.

She couldn't go through with it that day. Jasmine never had the abortion.

"Do you perhaps have access to this decedent's obstetric history?" O'Hagan said.

"No. The hospital is not obliged to keep records after sixteen years, and it's been far longer than that. But the decedent's closest friends at the time and her only remaining family all said there was no way Jasmine Gulati could have had a baby." Angie reached for her glass and sipped, thinking.

"But hell knows, all families have secrets. Maybe a past pregnancy was just very well concealed. But the thing is—" She set her glass down. "Jasmine Gulati *was* pregnant when she drowned, according to her friend. Yet there was no sign of a fetus found with her remains. If there had been a fetus, there would be evidence, right?"

Barb O'Hagan's eyes gleamed with interest. The doc loved a good puzzle as much as Angie did. "After almost two decades? Part of that time spent underwater, the rest of the time buried in shallow earth?" The doc shook her head. "It's a long period and so many variables. The remains could have become scattered over an incredibly wide area, both in the river and on land. Animal predation could account for missing body parts. The soft parts of the stomach are the first—"

"Look here." Angie turned the page, showing Barb O'Hagan the image of Jasmine Gulati's remains in situ, her skeleton inside the waders exposed by careful excavation of the top layer of soil. "She was fully intact. All her bones accounted for. She was still inside the chest-high neoprene waders that she was wearing when she went over the falls that day. Her engagement ring was still on the bones of her ring finger. So was a cuff bracelet."

The doc whistled softly. "That is . . . indeed interesting. It would be unusual, then, not to find evidence of a fetus if she was in this kind of condition." She looked up. "You're certain she was pregnant?"

"Her friends said she was. She'd scheduled an abortion but apparently chickened out at the last minute before going on the river trip. She'd also written in her journal that she was carrying Dr. Hart's child. But it's all circumstantial, no unequivocal proof. Plus, there is indication that the decedent could have had pathological issues herself—she *could* have been fabricating the whole pregnancy thing. However, she did have the ring, and Doug Hart has confessed to buying it for her—" Angie stilled as she caught sight of two familiar figures entering the dimly lit Tudor pub.

"Oh great," she whispered. "Look who's just come in the door. It's Holgersen and that young female officer Maddocks hired recently."

Doc O'Hagan turned to see. She grinned. "Hardly surprising. This pub is just down the block from the station—you don't expect him to take his date to the Pig, do you? It's Saturday night. Of course the guy is going out for a drink."

"You kidding me? Holgersen doesn't date." Angie watched the pair disappearing into the cluster of patrons gathered around the bar counter. "He's been celibate for I don't know how long."

"Or so he claims." Barb chuckled. "Everyone falls off the wagon now and then, no matter the vice."

"Yeah," she said quietly. "My concern, my question, is why would Holgersen feel that sex for him is a vice?"

O'Hagan watched Angie's face, then tapped the file with her fingers. "Hey, don't leave me in suspense, Pallorino. Talk to me. The case."

"Yeah," she said again, thinking as her gaze lingered a moment longer on Holgersen's head sticking above the crowd. She returned her attention to O'Hagan. "I went back and reread the entries in the decedent's journal. Gulati made a notation of the abortion date but never mentioned anything about the termination after that entry. There was a period around the termination date where she went silent in her journal, but she picked up again with entries about the river trip. No mention of the pregnancy. At first I'd assumed the silence was because it might have been too raw, the termination too recent, and she'd needed time to process. On top of that, Jasmine drank heavily on the trip, and she was promiscuous—slept with her guide. To my mind these were not markers of someone engaged to be married or someone who might still be carrying her husband-to-be's baby. So I assumed there was no fetus."

Angie took another sip of her scotch and gave a rueful grin. "Never assume, huh? I should know better. Because Jasmine's other college confidante, Sophie Sinovich Rosenblum, now tells me that while she went with Jasmine to have the abortion, Jasmine backed out at the very last moment. So where is the fetus?"

O'Hagan paged carefully through the pathologist's report. "If the decedent was indeed pregnant, plus the fact she's exhibiting these scars—"

"You're thinking what I'm thinking, aren't you? You're wondering now if she gave birth to that baby." Angie leaned forward, her blood beating faster. "But *how* would that be possible? Gulati went over the falls in her waders, was never seen again, then is found wearing the gear she drowned in, lying in this shallow grave near the river, which has seen two major flooding events over the past twenty-four years."

The food arrived. O'Hagan quickly closed the file, and the two women fell quiet while the server set steaming plates on the table. As soon as the server left, the doc opened the file again and studied it more deeply. She tapped a photo. "This antemortem scarring at the decedent's left shoulder joint. It's consistent with chronic dislocation of the shoulder. The scarring indicates healing had commenced on the shoulder but in a way that would appear to indicate the dislocation had not been properly reduced."

"Can you tell how long before death?"

The doc pursed her lips and shook her head. "I'd want to see the original radiographs or, better, the skeleton itself. And I'd want an expert forensic anthropologist's input on that."

"But it could have been recently prior to her death, as in not an old childhood injury, for example?"

The doc nodded, reached for her fork, and broke into the crust of her pie. Steam rose from the hole she'd made in the pastry, releasing a fragrance that made Angie's hunger acute. She picked up her own fork, pointed it at the report.

"What about that spiral fracture on her left arm? The pathologist notes it's typical of wrenching force."

The doc nodded. "But that injury is perimortem. It occurred at or around the time of her death—no sign of healing."

"Something that could have happened while going over the falls?"

"It would be consistent, yes, if her arm had gotten caught in rocks or something while the rest of her body was torqued away by currents or by the force of falling water."

Angie tucked into her Guinness pie and delivered a forkful to her mouth, almost burning her tongue in the process. "This is good," she said around her mouthful. "You were right."

"Told you." The doc grinned.

Angie began to wolf down the entire meal as O'Hagan picked at her own plate while combing more carefully through the report, a frown furrowing deeper and deeper into her already lined brow.

Angie reached for her drink. "Is it possible, Barb?" She leaned forward. "Is it remotely possible that Jasmine Gulati did not die going over those falls? But she was injured, and she lived long enough to start healing from injuries sustained going over the waterfall. Injuries for which she never received medical treatment—like a shoulder dislocation. She lived long enough to give birth to the child she was carrying."

O'Hagan bit her lip. "There's nothing here that would be inconsistent with that scenario, Ange."

Angie's heart started to thud in her chest. "But? I can hear the *but* in your voice, Doc."

"But the waders. She's wearing the Kinabulu waders in which she was seen going over the falls."

Angie finished the last morsel of pastry on her plate and pushed it aside. She wiped her mouth with her napkin and sat back. "So help me walk through this. Jasmine leaves the camp with her fishing rod. She goes down to the bay. The two guides, Garrison Tollet and Jessie Carmanagh, leave the campsite to gather firewood. Rachel Hart goes up to the ledge to film Jasmine fishing in the late evening light. Eden Hart says she needs to relieve herself and leaves camp. But Eden follows Jasmine down into the bay. Her mother, filming from above, sees her daughter strike Jasmine with a log." Angie cast her mind back to her own visit to the bay. The cold water rushing by. The shiny, slippery rocks along the bank. Claire's words.

That's it. The bay where Jasmine Gulati's rod was found. My dad told me there were marks in the slime-covered rocks where her studded wading boots looked to have slipped.

That niggle in Angie's subconscious returned tenfold. Her stomach tightened. "Jesus. Give me that, Barb!" She lunged across the table and snatched away the report. She flipped quickly to the page that documented the belongings returned to Jasmine's parents. Among them, two pairs of size nine wading boots. One with felt bottoms, another with rubber soles.

Where her studded wading boots looked to have slipped.

"Different boots. Shit." She looked up, excitement racing through her chest. "The couple from Dallas who fished with me and Maddocks had different boots with them for different conditions. A pair each with felt soles and a pair each with studded soles. Jasmine Gulati also took different sets of wading boots with her according to the inventory of her belongings."

"So?"

"She had to have been wearing stocking-foot waders on that trip. Waders constructed with neoprene booties in their foot sections that slide *into* the wading boots of your choice. Garrison Tollet had told his daughter that the marks left by Jasmine's fall on the slimy rocks indicated they'd been made by studs." She pointed the report. "But look here."

Barb pulled the report close and read the text on the page. "The decedent was found in chest-high Kinabulu boot-foot waders with rubber soles. Size nine."

"*Boot-foot* waders," Angie said. "Where an integral boot is constructed right into the wader. And no studs."

"What?"

Angie grabbed back the file and flipped through it. "It's mentioned here, in the separate SAR report from twenty-four years ago. Signs of her studded boots sliding through the moss-covered rocks." She finished her whiskey and sat back, her brain racing. "Size nine," she whispered, more to herself than the doc. "Jasmine wore size nine boots. She was a tall woman. The boot-foot waders in which she was found accommodated a size nine foot." She leaned forward. "Male size nine?"

O'Hagan checked the report. "Doesn't say specifically whether the boot-foot waders were male or female size nine. You'd have to go back and check. You mentioned this was a preliminary report."

"Yeah, Justice Monaghan got that direct from the coroner. It's not the official final release."

"Maybe that's something that would have been picked up before the final report was issued."

"There's an approximate one-and-a-half size difference between men's and women's sizing," Angie said.

"You're thinking the boot-foot waders in which she was found weren't hers?"

"How is that possible?"

"Hoi, Palloreeeno and the Death Doc. Fancy seeing yous guys here."

Both jerked up their heads at the sound of the familiar voice.

"Christ, Holgersen," Angie snapped. "Give us some warning, will ya. What're you doing here anyway?"

His gaze fell to the open file on the table. "Just having a drink with a mate. Saw yous over here in the corner and thoughts I'd come say hi and congrats on the big solve with the Gulati case."

"What's wrong with the Flying Pig?" Angie said, closing the file on the table to avoid his prying eyes. Last thing she needed was for him to go back to the station and say she'd screwed up and that the case was not actually solved.

A look akin to guilt rippled across his features, and his eyes began darting around the place. "Just talking with a colleague about a case.

Needed to get away from the rest of the blokes. Leo and all, you knows?"

Angie shot an eye toward the bar, saw Corporal Rebecca Webb sitting there. Webb raised her beer bottle and nodded. Angie forced a smile and returned the nod. "Don't let us keep you," she said to Holgersen. "Your company is waiting."

"I'm in no rush. Got two whole regular weekend days off." He grinned. "Boss man took off to the mainland again for a few days on some business thing with the E-division cops."

Surprise pinged through Angie. "He's not in town?"

Holgersen and the doc exchanged a quick glance, and Angie immediately regretted her words.

"Right," she said. "I forgot." It was a lie. But she didn't like looking out of the loop.

"Well," Holgersen said, regarding Angie with an expression of something like sympathy on his face, which irked her. "Good to see ya, Pallorino, Doc."

"Yeah." Angie watched him lope his way through the tables on his way back to Webb at the bar.

O'Hagan studied her. Reading something. "Another drink?"

"I should go. I—"

"We're not done here yet, Ange. Go on, have another drink."

She inhaled. "Okay," Angie said. "Another."

The doc waved to the server, held up two fingers, and pointed to their glasses. She turned back to Angie. "One thing looks to be certain here," she said with a nod to the report. "That blunt-force trauma to Gulati's skull would have done her in. Whether that happened in the water or on land remains a question."

The drinks arrived, and the server took their plates.

"Okay," Angie said, reaching for her tumbler. "If Gulati didn't die in the river, if, say, she was injured going over the falls but washed up and came ashore somehow, and if she lived long enough to bring her baby to term and give birth . . ." She swore softly. "That raises all kinds of questions. Like, where was she all that time? Why was she unable to seek medical attention or come home? What happened to the baby? Did it die in birth? Where is it buried, then? How did she end up in waders with a hole in her head near the river? And *why*?"

"If she didn't die in the river, that perimortem spiral fracture would've occurred on land at the time she incurred the blunt-force trauma to the skull. I've seen those spiral arm fractures before, primarily at a mass grave site in Burundi. The women in a village were raped by soldiers and then killed. Some had tried to escape by wrenching so hard against the hold of their captors on their arms that they broke their arms, resulting in this torque-type fracture."

"So . . . she was trying to escape, perhaps. Running away in those waders that were not hers. She was grabbed. She twisted against the hold. And then maybe she was hit on the head with a sharp object, like a . . . hammer or wrench or something."

"That scenario would be consistent with the postmortem results, in my opinion."

Angie picked up her drink, sat back against the plush leather in their booth. "So what happened to her baby? This makes no sense. This—" Something struck her. Hard.

"What is it?" Barb said.

Another memory. Axel Tollet's place. Which was near the river. Not far from the grove where Jasmine had been found. ATV. Arrows with yellow fletching. Little teddy bear. Bottles for the cubs—

"Similac," she said. "What do you feed bears, Barb?"

"Excuse me?"

"Little orphaned bear cubs that have not yet been weaned—how do you feed them?"

"I don't know. Baby bottles. Some kind of milk replacer."

He calls the folks at Wild Critter Care—it's a voluntary wild animal rehabilitation center—and they unofficially guide and advise him.

Claire's words tumbled through her memory. Angie grabbed her phone and pulled up a search engine. She punched in Wild Critter Care, and the website and contact details came up. She checked her watch and said to O'Hagan, "Hang on. Need to make a quick call."

When a woman answered and introduced herself as the manager, Angie explained who she was and cut right to the chase.

"I have a wildlife question in relation to a case I'm working. What kind of formula would one feed baby bears, orphaned cubs, to replace their mother's milk?"

"A sow's milk is high fat, no carbs. The cubs don't do well on a replacer high in carbohydrates."

"Could you use a human infant formula? Like Similac?"

"Negative. If you were going to use a commercial milk replacer, it would be something like Esbilac powder. For puppies."

Angie hung up, energy humming in her blood.

"What is it?"

"One of the men who lives near the river had baby bottles in his shed and a little stuffed teddy bear. His niece said the bottles and stuffed bear were for the orphaned cubs he'd once rescued. But the old tins on the shelf were labeled Similac—for human babies." She paused. "What if he *was* feeding a human baby. Shit—" Angie sat erect. "Waders. He had two pairs of boot-foot waders hanging in his shed."

"It doesn't prove—"

"I need to go out there. I need to check out his place, ask more questions. He has the right kind of profile, Barb. He's the survivor of a brutal sexual assault in his youth, allegedly perpetrated by a group of boys from his school who used to bully him. He was gang-raped by males, and he never received medical attention or therapy of any kind. The incident was buried. He became even more of a loner, isolating himself out there on that forest property. He rescues things he finds in the woods. Little cubs, fawns, raccoons—"

"And a half-drowned woman? You think *that's* what could have happened? He rescued and kept her? And she gave birth, and the child lived long enough to be fed formula for a time?"

Angie blew out a big breath. "I've got to go see. I need to check if that could be possible." Her gaze shifted back to Holgersen at the bar, and an idea began to formulate in her mind.

CHAPTER 42

SUNDAY, NOVEMBER 25

Angie drove north along the island highway while Holgersen sat in the passenger seat chewing nicotine gum and reading through the coroner's preliminary report on Jasmine Gulati.

"Still can't believe you roped me into this," he said, turning a page.

"Come on, you love it. Admit it—you're flattered. What else were you going to do on your day off?"

"I gots a life, Pallorino, even if you don't."

"That life include dating Webb?

He shot her a sideways glance. "What if it does?"

"You confuse me, Holgersen. I thought you were celibate."

"I didn't say I was fucking her, now did I?"

She gave a half shrug. "Why date if, you know, there's nothing physical?"

"She's a friend. I likes her company. We had drinks, that's all."

"Maddocks know about this? She's in your unit, isn't she?"

"None of boss man's business. Yours, neither. She's not in my cold case division. That's justs me and hairy ass." He sounded irritated or maybe frustrated. Angie let it go. She'd boomerang back to it later, because, yeah, she was curious. Everything about Holgersen made her curious. He was a dark one.

"Okay," he said, flipping a page. "So *maybe* Jasmine Gulati was preggers at the time she went over the falls."

"Yeah, maybe. All I have is her girlfriends saying that Jasmine told them she was carrying Dr. Hart's baby. She wrote this in her journal, too. But how much of that journal is fact or fantasy, I don't know. Jasmine told them she'd scheduled an abortion. She first asked Mia Smith to accompany her for the procedure, but she and Mia had a major fallout over termination. So Jasmine asked Sophie Sinovich to go with her instead, but according to Sophie, Jasmine bailed at the very last minute."

"So, just to be clear, all Sophie Sinovich had was Jasmine Gulati's word that an appointment for an abortion had actually been scheduled?"

Angie nodded. "I called the women's center on the mainland this morning. They confirmed they don't keep records going back that far—sixteen years is the requirement for medical records. So no proof of pregnancy. All just circumstantial."

"And these post parturition scars are not unequivocal proof, either?"

"Correct."

"So given that there was no evidence of a fetus found with her remains, she might not have been pregnant. Everything might be just as it seems. She went over the falls. Drowned. Washed up. Was found twenty-four years later. And the scarring on her pelvis was incidental. She could have hurt her shoulder some time before she went on that trip, maybe. Plus, there's Rachel Hart's confession that her daughter struck and pushed Jasmine Gulati into the river." He powered down his window. Wind blasted into the car as he spat his gum out onto the highway. He dug into his pocket for the pack and started to pop a fresh tablet of nicotine chewing gum out of the cellophane. "That truck chasing you could have just been to scare you away from digging up shit on the old Porter Bates case. And them arrows in the grove, too."

"Or those arrows really could have been hunters shooting at us in error. It happens often enough."

"So it could be like it looks."

"Or not." She shot him a look. "Which is why I need to talk to Axel Tollet and poke around up there some more to be sure."

"You could just let it lie."

"No, I can't. If Jasmine Gulati survived the waterfall, I can't let someone take the murder rap for that."

"They's confessed."

"Perhaps in error. Maybe Eden intended to kill Jasmine Gulati but didn't succeed. Maybe Jasmine washed up, and someone else up there killed her later and buried her kid somewhere."

"Like Axel Tollet, you mean?"

"Yeah. He's a fit for the profile. I think he's capable."

"So he could be dangerous?"

She slowed and stopped for a red light as they entered the outskirts of Nanaimo. "Possibly. I got a weird feeling about him and that place when I went up there. I got a read from his niece, too, that he might have a potential for violence if cornered. I feel for him, though. He's a survivor of a brutal sexual assault and long-term bullying. Ostracized. Shamed. Possibly has weird sexual issues because of it. He likes to rescue things and keep them in cages. But he does set them free after he's nurtured them to health."

"Yeah, but if he rescues a half-drowned woman outta the river and keeps her for long enough to bring her baby to term, he kinda can't set her free because she'd talk. He'd go down for it." He finally freed his piece of gum from the packaging and popped it into his mouth.

"You're going to OD on that stuff," Angie said, stepping on the gas as the light turned green.

"Better than OD'ing on some other shit. And you wanted me to come with you why, exactly?"

"I told you. I might need backup, and I can't go to Corporal Darnell Jacobi for that backup without him potentially alerting Axel and that gang, sending them all into cover-up mode. Plus, I've got nothing concrete to take to Jacobi or to any other cops outside of his jurisdiction that would explain why I'm trying to circumvent Port Ferris police in the first place. If you come with me, and we see something that can give probable cause for a warrant, you're with iMIT, which has interagency protocols. You could officially kick this into motion. Bring in an ident team and search the place, arrest him even, if it came to that."

Holgersen fell silent as he considered the parameters of the case. "You say this Axel Tollet works as a driver for Sea-Tech Freight?"

"Yeah. The freight division of Sea-Tech is run by Wallace Carmanagh, an aggressive dude who might have been the main guy behind Porter Bates's murder. I was told he looks after Axel well at the company. Jessie Carmanagh is Wallace's brother. Jessie handles the agribusiness side of Sea-Tech."

Holgersen fiddled with his smartphone, looking up Sea-Tech. "Hey, lookee here," he said as the company web page came up. "It's one of the ones we're looking at."

She shot him a glance. "What do you mean?"

"I mean, the logo. Look." He held out his phone. Angie cast a quick sideways glance at the screen. It showed a dark-blue logo of a stylized eagle's head with wings stretched out. Like one might find atop a totem pole.

"Remember?" he said. "I told you how's we were looking for white Merc vans that go way back. Ones with logos like this on the sides."

She frowned. "Have you found anything at Sea-Tech that could link to those old cases?"

"Nah. It's just on our list that we gave to the analyst. I don't think she's even got to Sea-Tech yet. There's shit-ton of companies out there—you wouldn't believe how many—that have white vans with dark graphics on the sides in their fleets."

"Sure, I believe it. I told you so myself."

He started to punch a number into his phone.

"Who you calling?"

"Maggie, the analyst who works for our new little cold case division. She's the one combing through the companies, cross-referencing routes, times and dates of shipments, and vehicle models with the various missing persons cases. I'm just gonna leave her a message and get her to puts Sea-Tech at the top of her list when she comes in Monday. Along with this driver dude, Axel Tollet."

"Because?"

"Because you justs told me this driver matches a certain suspicious pervy pathology an' he drives vee-hickles with logos like this on the sides, and this website says Sea-Tech ships all over the island, the mainland, and to destinations in the States an' has been doing so for years. We'd be dumbass *not* to run this first."

His call connected. "Yeah, Maggie, it's Holgersen on a Sunday, and I knows you's off, but I needs something urgent when you gets in." He gave her the details and killed the call. Angie could sense a fresh tension in him. It was infectious. She could feel it inside herself, a charge building as they got closer to Port Ferris and the clouds rolled thick down the desolate and forested mountains.

CHAPTER 43

Garrison Tollet stood looking out the living room window. It was 11:45 a.m. on Sunday morning, and there was a hint of snow in the fine rain falling outside. A fire crackled in the lodge hearth. He, Shelley, and Claire had enjoyed a relaxed brunch of waffles that Claire had made.

He loved this lazy time between seasons, when Mother Nature shrugged her shoulders to roll over and sleep, drawing up a blanket of snow around her. Predator Lodge had tours booked for December and through the winter. Backcountry skiers who would use the lodge as a base for sorties. He might do some guiding if requested, but most of their guests over the winter were self-reliant. Come spring things would get busy again, but from now until then Garrison planned to enjoy the downshift in gears and focus on repairs and some home projects.

Claire was washing up in the big kitchen. Shelley was setting up for a quilting project in her sewing room. Their talk over the table had been about the big news on television—that filmmaker Rachel Hart, seventy-two, had confessed to having witnessed her daughter, Dr. Eden Hart, now thirty-eight, pushing Jasmine Gulati to her death twenty-four years ago.

The reporter credited private investigator Angie Pallorino for unearthing the long-buried secret.

As Garrison watched the weather outside, hands deep in his pant pockets, Claire came up beside him, drying her hands on a dish towel.

"Why do you think she did it? I mean, a fourteen-year-old kid just deciding to attack another woman on the trip and send her to her death? It's insane."

He nodded. "Some people are just insane."

But his daughter's question made him tense. He knew from Jessie that the Hart kid had stolen a peek at that journal while on the river trip. He also now knew from Shelley what had been in that journal—a detailed account of Jasmine Gulati sleeping with him on the first night of the trip. Shelley had told him everything after she'd sent Angie Pallorino packing the other day. He'd been rocked to the core that Shelley had known all along exactly what he'd done with Jasmine. And that Shelley had been prepared to bury it all. Mostly he was relieved Claire had not learned about his affair and that Shelley had ripped those pages out and burned them for good.

But there would be a court case years down the road. Eden and Rachel Hart and the others would take the stand. Eden Hart might testify she'd read those now-burned pages. It might have been why she'd pushed Jasmine into the water, because in the journal, Shelley had said, was a detailed account of Jasmine's affair with the Eden kid's father. Claire might yet learn the sordid truth.

Would it be so terrible if she did? By the time that case made it to trial, Claire would be even older and on her way. She'd have witnessed for herself what a devoted and good husband he'd been all the years since. She might forgive him.

He smiled at her.

"What?"

"I love you, kiddo."

She snorted. "What's with the sudden sentimentality?"

"Just glad it's all over. That we know what happened."

She frowned, then said, "Do we? Really?"

He stiffened. "What do you mean?"

"I mean, we know what happened with Eden Hart killing Jasmine Gulati, but . . . I heard what happened to Uncle Axel."

"What happened with him?"

"When he was thirteen, Dad."

Garrison felt blood leave his head. He reached for the sofa, sat down slowly.

"Angie told me he was gang-raped by some schoolkids. Friends of a boy named Porter Bates. Then in retaliation, some guys lured Porter into the woods and jumped him and allegedly drowned him in the quarry."

He stared at the fire, the crackling flames. This was not over. Far from over. Inhaling deeply, Garrison said, "That's the story, yes. It was terrible, and we don't talk about it. Axel . . . it helps if no one mentions it. He can pretend it never happened."

"Never happened?" Claire seated herself in front of her dad. "That a kid was drowned, *murdered*?"

"He went missing. Nothing was proven."

She eyed him. "So who were the guys who raped him?"

"Porter's gang."

"They were never prosecuted?"

"No one officially reported the rape."

"Who jumped Porter?"

"I . . . I don't know."

Disbelief filled her eyes. "In this small town, no idea? He's your cousin, Dad. He's BoJo's brother. You were all in a gang with Wallace and Jessie Carmanagh. You must have some idea who might want to protect Uncle Axel and exact revenge?"

Garrison heard his pulse boom against his eardrums. He felt dizzy. "I don't. I really don't know."

"Right." She balled and hurled the dishcloth into the kitchen. It fell short near the table. "So many goddamn secrets." She got up, retrieved the cloth, and disappeared into the kitchen.

"Why did Angie tell you!" he yelled after her. "What's it to her, anyway?"

Claire stepped back out of the kitchen. The look on his daughter's face cut Garrison to the quick.

"Angie was trying to figure out where allegiances lie in this town," she said. "I reckon she was asking herself, if a bunch of guys could kill Porter to punish him, then maybe they could have killed Jasmine, too. They'd have been bonded in secrecy over the first murder, so maybe no one would talk about a second, either." She paused, watching him intently. "Apparently Jasmine made some people really angry in the pub on her first night in town."

He stared at Claire, his heart beating into his throat. "Well," he said softly, "turns out Angie Pallorino was wrong, because no one from town laid a hand on that Jasmine woman. It was Eden Hart, and it's all over now."

She held his eyes. "You really don't know who drowned Porter Bates?"

"I know that was over a long, long time ago, Claire. If you go dragging that up and mentioning it around town, it's going to hurt your uncle Axel real bad."

The phone on the oak server near the dining table rang. Claire glanced at it, then turned irritably and went into the kitchen. Garrison got up and saw the caller ID on the landline. He called out over his shoulder, "It's for me. I'll take it in my study."

When Garrison reached his office, he quickly shut the door and picked up the phone on his desk.

The voice on the other end was cold, firm. "Her Mini Cooper is parked in the rental lot. She's back."

Shock rippled through him. He eyed the door and lowered his voice. "*What?* What's she back for?"

"I asked Freddie at the rental shop. He said she and some cop from the city rented an all-wheel drive to head up the logging road on the south side of the Nahamish, but first they called Sea-Tech to check if Axel Tollet was working or at home."

"Fuck," he whispered. "It's supposed to be over."

"She must know something. If they go up there and look around his place, they'll find something to pressure him. You know Axel; he'll talk. And when he talks, we're done. All of us. I mean really done. Prison for life done."

"Bates, I only lured him. I wasn't part—"

"You listen to me, Garrison. You helped Axel bury that woman. You helped him hide everything because he threatened to squeal about Bates. Your helping him was a mistake. *You* got us all tied into this. Now you're in as deep with the Bates shit as the rest of us."

His brain reeled. He was going to throw up. If this got out . . .

"What do you want to do?" he almost whispered.

"What we have to do, Garrison. We have to tie up that loose end."

"Axel?"

Silence.

"Jesus, no. No—"

"It's him. Or us. We're already on our way. Meet us there, because we're not doing this alone. It's all of us or nothing."

Claire carefully replaced the receiver. *Bury that woman? Helped Axel? Prison for life done?*

She heard the downstairs door slam. Claire hurried to the window. She looked down to see her father's truck reversing out of the carport at speed. He turned west on the logging road.

Fear, worry, sickened her stomach.

She'd recognized the voice on the phone. Nothing made sense.

She hastened down the passage and stopped to look in on her mother. Her mom's head was bent over her sewing machine, the radio tuned to some talk show playing loudly. Claire had seen the crazy way in which her mother had sent Angie off the other day. Claire had watched from the upstairs window. She made her way to her room and found the business card Angie had left for her.

Chewing on the inside of her cheek, pulse racing, Claire studied the card. Was it a betrayal? Or would it stop more people from getting hurt? Would it stop her father from doing something else terrible? No, not Angie. Claire had a better plan. She scooped her cell off her dresser and dialed the nonemergency number for the Port Ferris police station. Her call was picked up instantly.

"Hello, it's Claire Tollet. Is . . . is Officer Jacobi there?"

CHAPTER 44

Angie and Holgersen negotiated the rutted logging track in the small Subaru Crosstrek they'd obtained from the rental outfit in Port Ferris. It was cold but hauntingly beautiful along the river. Cloud sifted in skeins through the dense, dripping trees, and as they gained elevation the rain turned to thick sleet that began accumulating on the ground.

Holgersen drove as Angie fiddled with her Garmin satellite GPS, in which she'd preflagged locations. They came upon a track that led into the trees to their left. Holgersen slowed, peering into the woods. "What's down there?" he said.

"Looks like it leads to Budge Hargreaves's spread," Angie said, studying the GPS map. The area appeared unfamiliar to her from this approach. She and Claire had hiked in from the back. "This road we're on should veer away from the river shortly and curve in a big arc. On our right we'll pass a hiking trail that leads down to the grave site. Then should come a smaller vehicle track that'll take us down into Axel Tollet's spread."

"Pretty damn remote out here," Holgersen said as the forest grew denser around them. "Nothing but mountains and rivers for miles from whats I can see. Can't imagine anyone wanting to live out here."

"Apparently that's exactly why Tollet and Hargreaves do. Isolated."

Clouds thickened. The landscape turned inhospitable as trees crowded in tightly along the side of the road, tall, drooping branches draped with old-man's beard. Holgersen turned up the heater and sped up the wipers. Snow was now starting to settle on the track in a slippery, gelatinous layer.

"Whoa, slow down a sec," Angie said suddenly as something in the road ahead caught her eye.

Holgersen eased off on the gas.

She pointed to marks in the slushy surface. "Tire tracks?"

"Sure looks like," he said, bending forward to peer through the arcs carved by the windshield wipers. "Fresh. Maybe made by more than one vee-hickle."

The interior of the Crosstrek started to fog. He turned up the fan. Tension mushroomed softly between them, Angie could sense it. To her untrained eye it wasn't possible to tell whether those tracks on the road had been made by vehicles heading east from whence they'd come or going west in the direction they were traveling. They could have been made by Axel leaving or arriving at his own property. Either way, he'd had company. As far as Angie knew, there was no reason for anyone to drive beyond Axel's homestead. It was just wilderness from his place all the way to the remote west coast of the island.

"Hunters, maybe?" Holgersen said with a quick glance at her.

"I thought the season was done by now, but yeah, maybe."

Holgersen clicked on the headlights and fog lights as they went deeper into a forest that swallowed what little gray daylight remained. It was only around 2:00 p.m., but it seemed like twilight.

"There!" Angie pointed to a fork in the road. "That leads down to Axel Tollet's place."

Holgersen swung the wheel and took them onto a bumpy, narrow track. The indentations from the tire tracks were still apparent under the fresh layer of snow. They saw the trees open up ahead. Her pulse quickened.

"Slow down," she said. "Stop at the entrance so we can get a lay of the land from this perspective and see whether he has company."

Holgersen brought the vehicle to a halt at the entrance to the clearing. Angie and Holgersen oriented themselves, engine running, wipers carving arcs in the wet snow.

To their left, behind a clump of trees, was the converted shipping container set back into the mound of earth and overgrown with berry scrub. Brambles hung down over the window and around the door cut into the side of the container. To the right of the container was the small log cabin. The lights inside glowed yellow in the gloom. Smoke came from the chimney and blew in the wind, melding with the low cloud. The shed doors were all closed. Axel Tollet's truck was parked under the carport, as was his ATV. Snow was turning the ground white, further obscuring the tire tracks that had led into the property.

"Looks like he's home," Holgersen said, watching the cabin. "All cozied up by his fire. But where's those other vee-hickles that left them tracks?"

Angie scanned the area again, this time moving her gaze carefully along the forest fringe around the boundary of the homestead.

"I don't know," she said.

"Is that them cages over there?"

She nodded.

"Freaking weird. Like something outta Grimm's fairy tales," he said. In her peripheral vision, Angie noted Holgersen's hand moving to check the position of his sidearm in its holster under his jacket. He was edgy. She felt it, too—something off.

"Since when do you read fairy tales, Holgersen?" she said quietly as she slowly scanned each of the outbuildings next, checking to see what might have set her warning senses prickling up the back of her neck.

"I knows about Hansel and Gretels. And hows their woodcutter moms and pops tried to kill them kids by leaving them in the dark woods. My gramps read us them stories."

That's when Angie saw it. A small black shape in front of one of the sheds. Wings spread out in the snow. "Poe," she whispered.

"What?"

"Over there. Axel's crow, or raven, or whatever it is. Or was. He rescued it, and Claire Tollet named it. It was a pet. It looks dead. Something happened to it. This place doesn't feel right."

"Not even close. How you wanna do this?"

She worried the scar on her lip with her teeth. Her goal had been simply to talk to Axel, question him further about the old tins with baby formula logos, the bottles with teats, get another look around the property, check out those waders hanging in his shed, see what size they were, see whether there might be something here that would give grounds for a warrant or a more official investigation. Or whether she was completely off about the possibility Jasmine might have survived a plunge over the falls and been brought up here.

"We leave the rental here. I'll walk up to the front door," she said. "Plain sight, hands visible, while you go into the trees behind us and come around the back of those sheds over there. Cover me."

He looked at her. "He's high risk? You think he—"

"I'm definitely thinking he could be a problem if he feels threatened. And I'm uncomfortable about where those vehicles that made those tracks could be. But I'll try to demonstrate to Axel that he's under no threat. Just me out here wanting to play nice and talk to him. Once I feel he's relaxed, I'll tell him you're here, too, and I'll ask if we can look in his sheds. I can get some pics, talk about the waders and sizing and the stuff on his shelf for feeding animals. See if I can get a read on him."

But Holgersen had gone quiet. He was staring at something.

"What is it?" she said.

"That container building," he said. "What's with the mound of earth over top? And all the vegetation shit growing on top? Like he's trying to hide it from the air or something."

"But why would he try to hide just that one building? Not like he doesn't have a bunch of outbuildings on the property."

"Let's ask him. Come, let's do this."

As they'd planned, Holgersen left the vehicle and sifted into the shadows among the trees behind the Crosstrek. Angie approached slowly from the front, hands visible at her sides, boots squelching in the slurp on the ground.

Wind blew icy against her ears. Everything dripped. The woodsmoke from the chimney smelled acrid, and it mingled with the scent of pine and loamy detritus in the cold air. Angie knocked on the cabin door. As she waited, she turned to examine the clearing and outbuildings from this different vantage point. Her gaze settled once more on the corvid lying in the snow. Its neck was broken, head lying at an unnatural angle.

A strange sensation feathered into her. She felt it again. A sense of being watched from the trees. She thought again of the tire tracks.

She knocked once more. "Axel Tollet? Anyone home?"

She smelled gas, sudden and strong as the breeze shifted. Adrenaline dumped into her blood. A crack sounded in the trees. She whirled around, heart galloping, her muscles tense.

Holgersen stepped out from behind a shed. "Pallorino! Over here! Quick!"

As she ran over to him, she thought she saw a shape move in the woods. She hesitated in her tracks. But it was just branches swaying in the mounting storm wind. She hurried over to Holgersen.

He was behind the shed, crouched over a human form on the ground.

Axel.

Her heart kicked.

The big man lay spread-eagled in the snow. Two arrows stuck straight up out of his chest. Yellow-and-white fletching. Holgersen was feeling for a pulse at his thick neck. Axel's eyes, green as the river, stared unseeing into the falling snow. His rifle lay in the snow near his hand. Tension whipped through Angie.

She snatched up the rifle and stepped sideways, her back to the shed. She scanned the shadows in the woods but saw nothing. She checked the rifle. It was loaded, a round chambered.

"He's gone. He's dead," Holgersen said, his gaze darting around, his body tight with coiled energy. "He's still warm. Whoever did this—"

The whirr, the *thwocking* sound, was so sudden neither saw it coming. Holgersen grunted. Angie turned to look at him. He was frozen in place. An arrow—the shaft—had gone clean through his neck. Holgersen's eyes went wide, whites impossibly huge. His hands went to the arrow at his neck. His knees buckled slowly, and he crumpled onto the ground, falling sideways. Before Angie could even process what she'd just witnessed, a whoosh and a bang sounded behind her. The shed burst into a roar of flame.

The force of the explosion threw Angie forward and into the ground, the rifle in her hand going flying. She lay in the slush, disoriented, ears ringing. Time seemed to slow. Slowly, carefully, she turned her head sideways to look at the shed. Black smoke boiled out of the building. Heat radiated from the fire. Flames crackled and hissed in the falling snow. She struggled to come to her hands and knees, head spinning, her vision blurred.

Holgersen.

She crawled to his shape through the slush, hidden from sight of the forest by the roils of black smoke. In the back of her mind she remembered the strong smell of gasoline near the cabin. Someone had rigged this place to blow. She recalled the shed she'd seen earlier with Claire. It was behind the cabin. It housed several natural gas canisters, a generator, containers of fuel. She had to move fast.

Angie reached Holgersen.

He lay motionless, eyes closed, mouth parted. The arrow had gone right through his neck. She reached out to touch him. "Holger—"

Another explosion whammed her into the ground. A second shed went up in flames. The fire roared and crackled. She coughed, eyes watering as she shot a glance in the direction their car was parked. She had to try to get Holgersen to that Crosstrek. A gunshot cracked, and she felt a hot buzzing past her face.

Fuck.

She dived flat again, heart pounding.

Someone was shooting at them from the forest. Wind gusted, and smoke parted, giving her a glimpse of the container building. Angie's heart stalled again as her brain struggled to understand what she was seeing.

A face.

In the small window. A white face.

Surrounded by a wild tangle of hair.

Hands, palms forward, bashing wildly at the glass. A woman. Her mouth open wide in a silent scream.

There's a woman trapped in the container!

A line of flames sparked suddenly to life, racing from the cabin toward the container. Fire whooshed up along the front of the container, igniting the bramble tangles, flames leaping quickly to the dead scrub atop the container mound. Angie's body exploded with adrenaline. Another bullet hit the ground near her hip. Her brain raced. She carefully turned her head in the slush to look at Holgersen. Her old partner lay motionless just beyond her reach, his pistol near her hand.

Another whoosh of flames gushed out of the shed as something else inside exploded. A fresh cloud of black smoke boiled into the air, momentarily screening Angie from whoever was shooting at them from the trees.

Triage. Fucking triage, she thought. She had a woman alive in that container threatened by fire. A fallen partner—arrow right through his neck. Motionless. Not breathing. She'd been trained for this. Your partner goes down, you take what you can to help yourself, and you save those you still can. She reached for his sidearm.

While still covered by the screen of churning black smoke, Angie raced in a crouch toward the container, heart jackhammering. She reached the converted dwelling and pressed herself against the metal side that was not burning. Gun clutched in close near her sternum, she assessed the scene. She tried to stay focused with combat breathing. Four counts as she drew breath in, four counts as she exhaled.

The glass panes of the cabin windows shattered outward in a burst of air and fire. The shed storing the natural gas would go soon, too. She needed to reach that woman and get out of here before that happened.

Angie edged toward the container door. It was locked with a dead bolt from the outside. She struggled with the metal bolt as flames along the front of the container nipped closer, heat intense. Her hand slipped on the cold wet metal. She picked up a rock, bashed the bolt across. Angie yanked open the door.

Smoke was accumulating inside the container. Angie went in, coughing, firearm ready. She had no idea what to expect—friend or foe.

Shock slammed her as she caught sight of the woman. Terrified, she was backed up against the far wall. Angie couldn't tell how old she was. Young. A teen, maybe, or in her twenties. Emaciated, barefoot, she wore a dirty shift dress, and her hair was a wild tangle around her head. Flames crackled outside. It was getting hot in the container.

Angie took in her surroundings fast. The interior was furnished with a bed. Bedding. A tiny kitchenette. Some books on a shelf. A small table with a chair. On the table lay a sheaf of crinkled pages crisscrossed with tiny cursive writing. A pen lay next to the papers. A second door to her right led to what Angie imagined was some kind of bathroom.

She held up her left hand, palm out, gun still at the ready in her right. "It's okay, it's okay," she said, coughing, moving toward the woman. "Is there anyone else in here?"

The woman shook her head, pressing herself tighter against the wall.

"It's okay," Angie said, taking another step closer to the female. Like a trapped animal, the woman sank down the wall and cowered on the floor.

"Sweetheart," she said as she reached the woman. "It's all right. We're here to help. We need to get you out of here before the fire gets in, okay?"

Angie reached for her arm, took hold. The woman didn't have an ounce of fat on her. She was trembling like a leaf. Tears smeared dirt tracks down her face. Angie gripped her arm firmly. "Come, stand up. My name is Angie. I'm here to help you, okay? We're going to leave. But fast. When we get outside, we run. You let me guide you to my car."

The female started to cry. Another whoosh sent a cloud of black smoke filtering into the interior. It was seeping in through the air vents and a pipe that led up into the roof.

"What's your name, hon?"

She shook her head wildly.

"No name?"

Again, a wild shake of the head.

"Okay, come." Angie gripped her skinny arm and led her to the door, but the woman lunged suddenly at the table as they went past. She snatched up the papers from the table, stuffed them down the front of her dress. Angie firmed her grip on the woman's arm and yanked her closer. "No time. Move."

Angie ushered the female to the door and peered out. Smoke roiled, and flames crackled everywhere. The only consolation was that the smoke curtained them from the forest along the property boundary from where the shots had come. She stepped out, dragging the woman with her. The woman's bare feet sank into the slush. Angie held her arm tightly and began to run, tugging the female behind her. Coughing, they reached the Crosstrek.

Thank God, Holgersen had left the keys inside. Angie bundled the woman into the passenger seat while scanning the surroundings, worried the attackers might have come round to this side or that there might be someone else on this end. They'd seen tracks from at least two vehicles.

A crack sounded behind her. A bullet pinged into the car. Angie swore and dived into the driver's seat. Slamming the door, she fired the ignition and swung the car around in a hard reverse turn. She gunned the gas, fishtailing in snow and mud as she aimed for the narrow dirt track that led back to the logging road. The road—if one could call it that—would lead them on a long and treacherous route back down the valley to the highway. Angie doubted they'd make it that far before whoever was shooting at them caught up.

As she swerved around a bend and hit the logging road, a bullet shattered the back window. The woman screamed.

CHAPTER 45

Shitshitshitshit. Angie glanced into the rearview mirror, trying to see through the shattered back window. No lights followed. For now.

"Buckle up," she barked at her passenger as she spun the wheel, skidding the Crosstrek through another bend, wipers flipping madly across the slushy windshield.

The girl or woman—Angie still couldn't tell from her appearance— was shaking so hard she appeared devoid of any fine motor coordination as she struggled to pull the sheaf of papers out from where she'd stuffed them down her dress.

"Stick the papers in the glove compartment," Angie snapped, hands tightening on the wheel as she took the Crosstrek around another curve, trying to remember exactly where along the logging road they'd lost cell reception. It was miles and miles away. She needed help, backup now. "Just put the papers in the damn glove compartment and get that seat belt on." Whatever those papers contained could prove pertinent to this case.

The woman managed to fumble the pages into the compartment and buckle up.

"What's your name?"

She began to cry. "No . . . name."

"You have no name?"

"Nameless. He said I'm nameless. Just called me . . ." Her voice came out in dry rasps, as if unused to speaking. "December."

"December?"

"He . . . he took me in December. Other was . . . was September. I . . . I think there were more before. Signs of them in the cabin."

"He took *other* women? He gave them names of the months in which he abducted them?"

She nodded and began to sob.

"Where did he find you?" The car skidded. Shit. She took her foot off the accelerator, tried to steer into the skid. The action took them almost over the edge. She corrected, getting them back onto the road. The river lay below. They'd negotiated the loop in the road and were now on the section that ran parallel with the Nahamish. It gave Angie a rough idea where they were—somewhere upriver from the falls. She peered into the rearview mirror again. Her stomach bottomed out.

Lights approached. Soft halos were coming through the mist. Two front lights and hunting spotlights across the top of a truck cab. *The Dodge RAM.*

It was coming fast, chewing up the distance between them.

Heart in her throat, Angie put her foot down on the gas. But the truck was faster, looming closer as she sped wildly along the slippery, rutted track. She had no doubt that this time the people in that truck would kill both her and this female. Desperation burned into her. Help was miles away. They'd never make it like this.

Her brain raced. Holgersen's case. Possible ties to Sea-Tech. Freight. Delivery vans. Coveralls. The converted freight container on Axel's property. December—this woman said she was taken in December.

"Are . . . you Annelise Janssen? Is that your name?"

Behind them the lights grew big in the fog. Angie's tires skidded again, and she felt the all-wheel drive engage. But she kept on the gas as they careened along the twisting mountain track with the sheer drop down to the churning river at their side.

The woman nodded.

Her pulse spiked. Fresh energy dumped into her system.

"He's had you for almost a *whole year*? In that container? He took you from the bus shelter near the campus after you had a fight with your boyfriend?"

She nodded, whimpering, tears streaming down her face, her body shuddering. God, this woman was going to die if Angie couldn't get her warmed up and into medical care quickly. She turned the heater and fan on full blast. "There's a coat in the back." Holgersen's rain jacket. Angie's heart crunched at the thought of him, the arrow through his neck. "Reach into the back, put it over yourself. Should be a hat there, too."

The woman struggled to reach for the clothing on the rear seat while the car lurched. She managed to grab the gear, and she pulled on the hat, then covered herself with Holgersen's black raincoat. Angie got a whiff of cigarette smoke off the coat, and tears seared into her eyes.

"*Who* took you? Did you hear his name? Was it Axel? Or . . . Wallace? Or Beau or Joey?"

Another bullet pinged into the back of the car. Shit. The Dodge came closer, closer. They fired again. The bullet hit the shattered back window, and it collapsed inward. The cold and wind inside the car was instant. Angie swerved around a bend. The truck came right up behind her. She saw the silver RAM letters. She saw a hand coming out of the passenger window, followed by a head in a red balaclava, then part of a torso. She saw the gun. The man fired.

The rear tire of the Crosstrek exploded with a loud bam. Angie gasped. The woman screamed. The car lurched into a hectic spin, crashing through brambles, hitting a tree, more trees, a rock, then tipping over the embankment.

Angie squeezed her eyes shut, arms covering her head as the car rolled down, down toward the river in a blur of crashing metal, whirling green and brown, the sound of crunching and screams from Annelise.

They came to a juddering halt against a massive rock and tree trunk. A branch fell. All went silent. Angie was breathing hard. She could smell pine and dirt and gas and metal and grease. She tasted blood in her mouth and at the back of her nasal passages. She could hear the water from the river.

Disoriented, she tried to marshal her brain. A cut on her head leaked warm blood into her eye. Pain seared down her left leg. She forced her head to turn slowly. The woman strapped into the passenger seat stared wide-eyed ahead, unmoving. Blood trickled from her ear.

"Annelise?" Angie whispered. Sound began booming in her ears. It was the sound of her own pulsing blood. Fear rose in her chest. "Annelise?"

No response.

Angie's heart sank.

Then the woman's head turned. She stared at Angie. Angie's heart shocked back into a rapid-fire beat, like a wild animal trying to get out of her chest. "Are . . . you hurt?" she said. "Are you badly hurt? Can you unbuckle?"

Annelise moved her hands in zombielike silence, unbuckling her seat belt. Angie did the same. She managed to crawl out of the broken side window. She went around to the passenger side. The Subaru rested against a rock and a stump of old growth. Below them was a rock ledge, then a sheer drop to the river, which swirled white and green with current. Snowflakes came down through the trees. Angie heard voices up the bank. She saw the beam of a flashlight bouncing against mist. They were coming.

"Shh," she whispered as she helped Annelise Janssen out through the shattered windshield. "Don't say a word," she said as she handed Holgersen's coat to Annelise. "Put this on." Angie didn't want the men to know they were alive down here.

Shivering like a baby bird, Annelise winced as her bare feet sank into snow and pine needles. The small rocks sticking out of the snow dusting the ground looked sharp. Angie managed to reach into the back of the Crosstrek for her overnight bag while Annelise shrugged into the coat. Angie struggled to pull the bag out through the mangled window frame.

"Start climbing down to that rock ledge," she whispered quickly. "I'm trying to find some sneakers for you." Angie always took workout gear when she traveled. She had running shoes in her bag. "Go on. I'll find you. Start moving."

The woman did not want to leave.

"Go!" she hissed. Voices in the trees above grew louder. More flashlight beams bounced through the mist and tree trunks. There were several coming. Armed hunters. Tracking them like wounded prey.

Annelise began to inch down on her butt toward the rock ledge. Angie found the shoes and a pair of gloves. A granola bar. She stuffed the bar and gloves into her pocket where she'd put Holgersen's gun. The only other weapon she had was her knife in the back pocket of her jeans. She reached into the car and retrieved her Garmin and checked that she had her phone. No bars. Still no reception. Voices came closer. Angie froze as she heard a dog yelp. Then the sound of a bear bell.

Shit. They were tracking with a hound? She thought of the whistle the other day when arrows had been fired into the moss grove. Tucker? Budge was with them? Or another dog? She hurried after Annelise, heart thudding against her rib cage.

"Hey, here," she whispered as she reached Annelise. "Put on these gloves and shoes." While Annelise fought her shakes to get the gear on, Angie watched the trees above, listening. She heard the dog yip again, and a yell of encouragement came from one of the men.

Angie shot a glance to her left, then her right. It was all sheer embankment down to the water. They'd never be able to move fast enough along this terrain in either direction, and going back up the bank was out of the question. Plus, the men hunting them had a dog. If the animal was trained to track and got onto their scent, which could be picked up from the Crosstrek—and Annelise sure smelled strong—they stood not a snowball's chance in hell of outrunning their pursuers.

She looked down at the swirling green water and the bank on the opposite side. Could they do it? If they tried to swim at a diagonal across the current, they might be able to reach the opposite shore and get to help. But the waters of the Nahamish flowed out from glacier-fed Carmanagh Lake. The river was the temperature of barely melted ice. They probably would not reach the other side before hypothermia set in and shut down their ability to even pull against the water. Annelise was probably hypothermic already. Not an ounce of fat protected her body.

The dog suddenly started baying like a bloodhound. The men started yelling. Flashlight beams bounced crazily through the mist. The dog was onto their scent. They were coming. Fast.

Angie took Annelise's hand, edging them toward the end of the ledge that hung out over the river.

"Where . . . are we going? What are you doing?" The young woman pulled back, teeth chattering. Angie's heart crunched. The thought of this poor woman being abducted, imprisoned. Assaulted . . . she couldn't dwell on it right now. Now was triage time. Survival. Pure and simple. If Angie could do anything for Holgersen right now, it would be to save this young woman. This woman her old partner had been searching to find. But Angie would bet Holgersen had never expected to find her alive. She had to see this through now, in his memory. She could not let his death be for naught. She *had* to keep this survivor surviving. She had to bring Annelise home.

She touched the side of Annelise's dirt-stained cheek. "Look into my eyes, Annelise. Listen to me. I'm taking you back to your family. I'm going to do my best. And I want you to know something—your father, your mother, they never gave up. They never stopped looking. They're waiting for you to come home. Got that? And you're going to do it. My colleague, Kjel Holgersen, he came up here in part to find you," she said, twisting the truth a little, to bolster both herself and Annelise. To give reason, meaning, to Holgersen's death. "He was hunting down the man who did this. He was going to bring you home. We're going to make that happen. For him. For you. For your family." She would do this. She would do this or die trying. For Holgersen. Emotion surged into Angie's eyes. She sucked in a breath.

Do it. The river is the only chance we have at survival.

She heard the dog baying, coming closer. The drop was about twenty feet to the river. Rock and obstacles downstream. Dense mist shrouding the opposite bank.

Our only chance.

A shot rang out behind them. Angie's heart kicked.

"We jump. Okay? Ready?"

Annelise looked down at the water. Silent. Wide-eyed. Beyond crying now. Angie recognized the blankness of shock.

"Listen to me. We *have* to jump. It's our only hope."

Annelise pulled back, shaking her head.

Angie grasped her wrist firmly, pulling her close. "We *will* die if we don't. Got it? I'll hold on to you tightly."

"I . . . I can't swim."

Fuckfuckfuck. "It's okay. It's fine—" Another gunshot *thwocked* into a tree, exploding bark right next to them. A man yelled as he spotted Angie and Annelise below.

"They're down there! We got 'em!"

Angie leaped, yanking Annelise with her. She heard Annelise scream as they dropped like rocks through the air.

CHAPTER 46

The impact as they hit the water stopped Angie's heart. They plunged beneath the surface, cold crushing through her body, exploding pain through her skull, her sinuses, like the worst brain freeze she'd ever experienced. The coppery taste of blood from her nose filled the back of her throat.

As they sank down, down, down into the frigid depths of the Nahamish River, white bubbles poured up from Angie's nose and mouth, and her red hair streamed around her face. She clutched tightly on to Annelise, who appeared as a waving black shape in Holgersen's voluminous coat. Otherwise, everything underneath was watery green.

As they continued to sink down to the bottom, Angie saw in her mind's eye Axel's open eyes, the two arrows sticking out of his chest. She saw Holgersen's body lying motionless under the cold November sky, the arrow with yellow-and-white fletching piercing clean through his pale, sinewy neck. The snow falling upon his face. She saw Maddocks's smile. She saw Ginny's expression at the sight of the wedding gown. She saw her mother's fingers gently touching the photo of Angie in the dress. She felt her dad's arms tightly around her, and she heard the words of the hymn.

Ave Maria
Vergin del ciel
Sovrana di grazie e madre pia . . .

Angie mentally shook herself. She would not die. She could not. She was going to save this woman for Holgersen. She was going to take Annelise home. She was going to marry Maddocks. She would have that wedding . . . Angie fought to hold on to Annelise as the young woman suddenly began to writhe wildly in search of air, to escape the grip of the current that now swept them fast downstream in the direction of the falls.

Hold on hold on hold on to her . . .

Angie repeated the mantra over and over in her head as her lungs began to burst. Her boots hit the rocky bottom. She pushed off from the river bed, kicking madly and using her free arm in an effort to struggle up to the surface while still maintaining her grasp on Annelise's thin wrist.

The current tossed and churned and hurtled them downriver faster than they were getting any closer to the surface. Angie's lungs burned in pain. Her vision blurred. She reached the surface, and her head popped out. She gasped wildly for air, working her legs like an eggbeater as she yanked Annelise to the surface.

The young woman's head emerged, hair plastering her face as she gasped and choked. The trees on the other side of the bank raced past as they were carried swiftly toward the falls.

Debris swirled about their faces. Water churned white. Annelise was thrashing desperately, slapping at the water, slipping from Angie's grasp. The river was shockingly cold. Angie couldn't feel her limbs.

They smashed into a rock, glanced off, sweeping sideways into a churning gulley of water. Angie's shoulder bashed into another rock, and she hit her head hard. Feeling dazed, she struggled to pull herself back into focus, kicking wildly to stay afloat, to try to steer their drift. They suddenly hit a calm but fast-flowing spot. She took a moment to catch her breath, trying to keep her head above the surface while at the same time pulling Annelise closer. But her limbs wouldn't work. Her fingers could no longer grip things. She had no control. Her mind was going fuzzy. Thinking was hard. She felt herself getting hot, hotter. Angie knew on some level what was happening. Hypothermia.

All her blood was rushing to her core to protect vital organs as other things shut down. In instances like this a person lost in snow in below-freezing temperatures would start stripping off clothes. And when rescuers found the victim, he or she would bizarrely present half-naked.

She could no longer think clearly. No logic. She felt tired, incredibly sleepy. Annelise had gone limp—she looked unconscious now, hair and coat floating out about her on the water. Angie felt the woman slip out of her grasp. She saw her drifting away in the current. Angie tried to raise her hand, to swim. She tried to kick her legs. But the river took her into cold arms, embraced her, and drew her gently down.

"Angie! *Angie!*"

She felt herself being ripped out of the depths. Back up to the surface. Something strong was dragging her free from the death grip of the current and the icy claws of the river. A hand on her arm? More hands? Rope around her chest? Being tugged. She cracked up onto the surface, tried to gulp air but swallowed water. She retched. Another hand. Pulling her up higher. Something hard against her body. She was being hauled over it. Boat. Gunwale. She sucked in air, coughed, threw up foam, bile. Water ran over her eyes. Hair plastered her cheeks. She tried to open her eyes, looked up, saw a face. White face. A face framed by black hair. Green eyes, huge eyes, looked down at her. Pale-green eyes full with worry. Green like the Nahamish River in sunlight, green like spring leaves in sunshine.

"Angie! Can you hear me? Angie?"

Claire? It was Claire. Orange life vest under her face. Her black hair was wet, and water streamed over her creamy complexion. Behind her was another shape in black, also with an orange vest over top. Angie realized she was in one of the lodge jet boats, lying on the bottom. Claire must have gone into the water after her, affixed her to a line. Pulled her in. She heard the roar of the engine, felt the boat rise out of the water. Movement.

Annelise?

"Where . . . Where is . . . A—" She gagged and turned her head sideways. She threw up spittle and water and foam. Claire was wrapping her in a survival blanket.

"We got her, Angie. We got the other woman. What is her name? Who is she?"

"Is she . . . is she . . . okay? Is . . ." Her voice died in her throat, her mind fading again.

Angie heard a man yelling something over the roar of the engine. She blinked, trying to pull into focus the man behind Claire. The man steering the boat.

His features took shape.

A chill shot down her spine.

Jacobi.

The jet boat was racing to shore. On the bank, in front of an army of trees that marched with tips pointing like spears into the cloud, stood another man in black. A rifle in his hands.

"Cl . . . Claire?" she tried to whisper, desperate, her chest filling with fear, her voice fading on her lips in spite of her best efforts. "Where . . . where is your . . . father?"

"Shh," she said. "Don't talk. We'll sort you out. Take it easy."

Jacobi's eyes watched her from above. Like the black gleaming eyes of an eagle up high, circling . . . circling . . . watching, waiting for when best to strike its prey . . . when best to dig in talons and rip the ghost fish from the river. Angie's mind dulled as she stared up into Jacobi's beady eyes, and her world went black.

CHAPTER 47

Angie came around slowly. Groggy, with no sense of where she was or of the past or present, she battled to open her eyes and turn her head. A square of gray light exploded against her retinas. She scrunched her eyes shut against the brightness and lay very still, listening, trying to figure out where she was.

There was a smell. She recognized it . . . *hospital.* Her eyes flared open. Her heart raced. But light sliced pain into the back of her skull like a knife. She shut them again, breathing hard. A hand covered hers. Large. Warm. So warm and strong and familiar. Her breathing eased.

Slowly, she eked her eyes open. She looked up into a face. Blurry. Again, she had to shut her eyes to block light.

"Easy," a male voice said. "Take it easy."

Yes. Easy. His voice . . . so deep and comforting and easy to listen to. He's here. He's here, and I'm alive. I think . . .

Past and present and fantasy and reality stirred together in her brain. A memory surfaced out of the soup of images. The first time she'd laid eyes on Sergeant James Maddocks. She'd been sitting at the bar at the Foxy, hunting for a hot and anonymous lay, desperate to blow off steam and numb her emotions.

The instant he walked into the bar, she knew he was the one. He sifted through the gyrating crowd—it parted for him like the Red Sea to Moses beneath the sparking disco ball. He moved with a command presence . . . scanning the patrons as if searching for someone. He stood a head taller than the crowd, his shoulders broader than average. Light danced off his hair, which was ruffled and the dark blue-black of a raven's feathers. His skin was pale. His eyes . . . she couldn't see the color, but they were wide set under dense brows. Strong features, ones that hovered between handsome and interesting. There was an otherworldly air about him, a vaguely worn yet incredibly alert look.

He turned, caught her eye . . .

Slowly, very slowly, mouth dry, she tried again to open her eyes, to resurface from her dream—or was it a memory?

"Maddocks . . . is that you?" she whispered.

"Shh." He brushed his hand against her cheek. Emotion washed through her chest. "Take it slow, Ange. Take it easy." His other hand was fingering her solitaire ring, moving it around and around her ring finger like a worry stone. His dark-blue eyes glittered with moisture. It made his lashes look dense and long. *So handsome,* she thought. *He's so beautiful. Inside and out.* This person she'd come to love with all her heart, the one person who meant the utmost in the world to her. He was here. At her side. But he looked pale. Worn. Tired.

"Am I—"

"You're fine, Ange. You're going to be fine. You had us all worried there for a while. Your father was here earlier, but he went back to the motel—he's on his way over again. You've been in and out of consciousness since they brought you in. But they got you warmed up. They say you'll be back to normal in no time." He smiled. "You had bad hypothermia, but you've still got all your fingers and toes and limbs. Just a few bumps and cuts and scrapes. You'll be sore for a while."

A chill slid through her as another image surfaced.

Holgersen.

His body. Dead still. The arrow clean through his pale neck. Bile surged up the back of her throat. Emotion flooded into her eyes.

"I—I lost him, Maddocks. I . . . Holgersen. He . . . the arrow, the fire . . ." She couldn't speak. Tears leaked from the corners of her eyes into her pillow, an overwhelming wave of heavy grief swamping her.

"Angie, listen to me."

She shook her head from side to side, moaning as the memory of Holgersen lying in the snow swam into vivid reality in front of her eyes.

"Angie. Focus. Listen." He cupped the side of her face, stilling her head. "Look at me."

She opened her eyes slowly and looked up into his.

"He's going to live. That bastard Kjel is bloody going to live. I swear he's got nine lives, and he's just getting started."

She stared, confusion churning through her brain. "The arrow— it . . . his neck. He wasn't breathing. He—"

"He was breathing. If that arrow had hit him just a few millimeters farther left or to the right or gone in slightly higher or lower, or if the archer had used a more lethal arrowhead, like a broadhead tip, it *would* have pierced a major artery. It would have damaged major working parts. But he was alive when they found him. They medevaced him out, flew him to Vancouver. After scanning him, making sure the arrow hadn't hit any critical working pieces, the surgeons operated and successfully removed it." He smiled, and Angie thought her heart would burst. "He's stable. Recovering." A laugh. "We're not getting rid of that weirdo this quickly, and unfortunately, he will still be able to speak and chew that wretched green gum of his."

"Oh God," she whispered as it dawned on her. "He . . . was alive when I left him. I just left him there. I . . . the explosion. I saw his eyes staring up at the sky. He wasn't moving. They were shooting at us, and the fire . . . I saw a face in the container window—" Angie fell silent, struggling to pull it all back into her memory. "It was her," she said. "It was Annelise Janssen being held captive, locked in that container, and it was catching on fire. Triage. The fire. I had to. I—I just left him."

"Shh," he said again, stroking her cheek. "Claire had called the RCMP in Port Ferris before you even arrived. She phoned the station as soon as she heard her father saying that he was going out to Axel Tollet's place. She feared the worst, and she was right. Jacobi came right away, radioed for backup. They got a chopper into the air, dropped some guys in there. They managed to stabilize Holgersen. If you'd tried to move him, Angie, you *would* have killed him. Some angel up there was looking after that guy. And after you."

Tears ran copiously from her eyes now, and she did not try to hold them back. "Annelise?"

"Serious but stable. She was also airlifted out. They took her to Vic General. Her parents are with her now. Her whole extended family is with her. You saved her, Angie. After all these months, her mother and father had all but given up hope. The odds were stacked so high statistically against her being found alive at this point. A whole media phalanx is camped outside the hospital. Including international press."

"Not me—Holgersen, *he* saved her. He was on it before I even took him up there. He was onto the possibility of Axel, Sea-Tech Freight, putting two and two together that Axel might be the driver of the van that took her from that bus shelter."

Maddocks seated himself beside her bed. Holding her hand, he said, "Yeah, as soon as our iMIT tech got his message this morning, she got hold of Sea-Tech admin and ran Axel Tollet's routes and old delivery records against those cold missing persons cases Holgersen believed were linked. Tollet came up as a match—his delivery routes, the van, the logo, the dates, all of it."

"A serial?"

Maddocks nodded. "I knew in my gut that Holgersen was going to be good on the cold case beat. I just knew he'd pull something out of those files. The mayor and police board are already patting themselves on the backs over the new funding and taking credit."

"So, Jasmine Gulati—"

"Tollet's first, it seems. So far, anyway. He apparently found her washed up downriver below the falls, all broken, and he 'rescued' her. Kept her locked up. No shoes so she couldn't run away. He used her sexually, like a gift from his precious river. Then he found out she was pregnant. He built her that container house, covered it with dirt, and grew brambles over it in some sort of attempt to hide the place or to keep sound from getting out. We don't know for sure yet. She gave birth in that container."

"How do you know all this?"

"Some of it from Garrison Tollet. He came right out the gate talking and denying he had *anything* to do with either death. Not Porter Bates's murder years ago. Nor Jasmine Gulati's death."

"Axel killed Jasmine?"

Maddocks snorted softly and moved a strand of hair off her face. "Yes. When she tried to escape. She had no shoes, but he'd gotten lax toward the end of her pregnancy. He'd apparently been taking her out of the container regularly to sit in the sunshine and to walk about in bare feet a bit. After she'd given birth, Jasmine became fiercely determined to get free. She'd seen the waders hanging in his shed, and she knew they were neoprene and would help keep her warm, even if they were slightly big. And they had boots attached. She made the break when her baby was two months old. Axel Tollet discovered them gone just minutes after Jasmine fled with her infant. He chased her down very quickly because she was having trouble outrunning him in those wading boots. He killed her mere minutes after she'd escaped."

Angie closed her eyes again, trying to process it all. Her head was still thick. She moistened her lips. They were cracked and dry. Maddocks brought a glass of water to her mouth, helped her sip. She lay back on the pillow.

"Who killed Axel, then? Why? Who shot at me and Holgersen? Who set the place on fire?"

"Garrison Tollet claims Wallace Carmanagh killed Axel. He said it was Wallace Carmanagh who shot arrows at you in the moss grove, too." He paused. "Wallace had the most to lose if you found out what happened with Porter Bates because according to Garrison, Wallace killed him, drowned him. In revenge for what Porter Bates did to Axel. The twins helped by carrying Porter Bates to the quarry and standing watch. It was Garrison, however, who lured Bates onto the secluded woodland trail where the others were waiting in ambush and jumped him. They beat him and trussed him up like a rodeo calf, hauled him off to the quarry, weighted him with concrete blocks, and sank him. But after you started poking around, they came to believe Axel would talk, and that would expose them for the Bates murder."

"But the other missing women Holgersen linked to the Annelise Janssen case—what happened to them? How did that all play out? How—"

"The Tollet-Carmanagh gang didn't have a clue there'd been others, Ange. They knew only about Jasmine. They thought Jasmine was a one-off weird sex thing for poor Axel, who'd never had an intimate female relationship in his life after being sodomized by Porter Bates and his boys. They were shocked to find Annelise being held captive in that container—they learned she was in there only when they arrived to eliminate Axel and burn his place down."

"They had no idea at all?"

"Not according to what Garrison is saying. The gang had been going to attempt to make it all look like an accidental fire to hide the murder and to make sure they eliminated any old traces that might have been around from when he'd kept Jasmine. But then you and Holgersen arrived, and everything went sideways. From the detective I've spoken with, the RCMP figure Axel Tollet happened upon Jasmine just after she washed up. A crime of opportunity. But he learned from his experience with Jasmine that he liked female companionship, and he wanted more. He learned that capturing and keeping a woman for a period of time was a way to obtain sex."

"What happened to his other victims? How many were there?"

"No one knows yet. Maybe we'll never know. This investigation will take time. They've got a huge forensic ident crew starting to work on that homestead. Bottom line, the four men—Garrison, Joey, Beau, and Wallace—were all up at Axel's place when you arrived. They'd come in two vehicles, but they all chased you in the one truck. Wallace has a dog, which they used to track you down before you and Annelise went into the river. But Darnell Jacobi and Claire Tollet were already on it from the other side."

He gave her another sip of water and set the glass down again.

"Jacobi had called for reinforcements, which were already on their way. Jacobi and Claire Tollet were driving toward the boat put-out below the falls to go across in the jet craft—they had it on the trailer. They saw you from the road going into the water. Claire got that boat into the river pretty damn fast. Thanks to her SAR training, her swift-water skills, she and Jacobi hauled both you and Annelise out of that water in remarkable time. Jacobi radioed for medical assistance while they both worked to stabilize you guys." He paused. "You owe Claire and Jacobi your lives. You'd have both gone over those falls like Jasmine did."

Angie inhaled deeply. She hadn't been sure where the young woman's allegiances lay. But she'd read Claire correctly. She was an empathetic young woman with a solid conscience. She was just. But now Claire had to face the fact her father had done some very bad things. Poor woman. Poor Shelley. Life in that lodge as that family knew it was over.

He watched her intently as she digested it all.

"Maddocks," she said suddenly, "what happened to Jasmine's infant?"

He held her gaze and took her hand. Tension twisted inside Angie. Something about the look in his eyes made her brace for awful news.

"When Jasmine fled captivity," he said very quietly, "she took her baby all bundled up in a makeshift papoose. When Axel caught up to them in that grove where we found her remains, she set the little papoose onto the mossy ground and spun around to fight him, trying to swing at him with a wrench she'd taken from the shed. But he caught hold of her wrist. She tried to twist free."

Barb O'Hagan's words ran through Angie's mind.

I've seen those spiral arm fractures before, primarily at a mass grave site in Burundi. The women in a village were raped by soldiers and then killed. Some had tried to escape by wrenching so hard against the hold of their captors on their arms that they broke their arms, resulting in this torque-type fracture.

"The spiral fracture on her arm?"

He nodded. "Most likely."

She frowned. "Garrison told you this, too?"

"He told the RCMP. They have him in custody, and he's cooperating fully, hoping for leniency in giving up Wallace and the others. Apparently Axel had described to Garrison how Jasmine died, and it fits the pattern from her postmortem results so far. The shoulder injury was from her tumble over the falls. She never received medical treatment for that. And the wrenching fracture occurred perimortem. While Jasmine was struggling to free herself from Axel and screaming at the top of her lungs, Axel brought the wrench down on her skull. He wanted to make her quiet. He didn't aim to kill her but was panicking and desperate to silence her screams. That blow killed her right there."

Angie thought of the skull lying in the dirt, the soil in the eye socket. A chill rippled over her skin.

Maddocks said, "Garrison told the RCMP that Axel didn't like killing things unnecessarily. He was seriously distressed to have murdered Jasmine."

Angie stared at Maddocks, recalling her conversation with Claire in the mossy grove.

He'd rather kill his own meat humanely than support an industry that slaughters terrified animals in an abattoir. And he prefers bow and arrows because it's more of a challenge one-on-one with the animal . . . won't even sell Dad meat for guests at the lodge. He says each man should hunt for his own.

"What happened to the baby, Maddocks? It wouldn't have been in him to kill an infant."

"You're right. It wasn't in him. Axel took the tiny infant in its papoose up to Garrison and Shelley at the lodge. He didn't know what else to do with it. He begged for their help in taking it somewhere, finding it a home. They were shocked, of course, to learn Jasmine had survived the river and where the baby had come from. Shelley started feeding and caring for the infant. Garrison helped Axel bury Jasmine in the grove. Garrison figured it would be okay after that—everyone thought Jasmine long dead already. And—"

"And he and Shelley had been trying for a child," Angie whispered. "Shelley had had a couple of miscarriages and was struggling emotionally." Garrison's words flooded through her brain.

We'd just taken over the lodge from my dad, and we were trying to expand the guiding and tourism side of the business. But we were short on cash. We'd also been trying for kids for a long, long time. Shelley had suffered two miscarriages, and she'd collapsed into herself. She'd become distant. She no longer enjoyed physical intimacy.

"Claire?" she whispered as the horror sank into her. "*Claire* is that baby?"

He nodded.

Angie's heart beat faster, tension and adrenaline rising hot inside her. It wasn't the Tollet genes that showed so strongly in Claire, as Angie had believed. Claire's luxurious mane of black hair—it came from her mother's genes. Dr. Douglas Hart was Claire Tollet's biological father.

Both Jasmine and Doug Hart must have been carriers of a green eye gene. Claire had technically been kidnapped as a child and raised by another family as their own.

"Shelley couldn't give the infant up, Ange," Maddocks said. "Even if she had wanted to, showing up with a tiny baby in Port Ferris was going to create problems. It would force questions that would tie back to Axel and his abduction of Jasmine. Authorities would have traced things all the way back to the Porter Bates murder. Bottom line, those men were bound to one another for life through that murder. Their secret was only as strong as their weakest link. That link was Axel."

"Bates's victim."

"Yeah. By helping Axel, Garrison effectively tied the whole gang to his crime, because Axel had threatened to tell all if Garrison and Shelley did not help him with the baby. So Shelley stayed away from town the following winter. She emerged in spring with the child. They registered the baby as their own, claiming it was a home birth. All their friends knew they'd been trying for a child. And that family had a history of keeping to themselves and looking after themselves in the woods, especially through the long winters when the roads into the mountains became a challenge. No one questioned it."

Maddocks reached down to a briefcase on the floor. From it he took a plastic sleeve containing papers.

"I made copies for you." He removed the papers from the sleeve and handed them to Angie. They were scans of pages filled with the tiniest cursive writing in tight lines, as if paper had been a scarce commodity and words plentiful.

"What's this?"

"Jasmine Gulati was a journal keeper. She wrote it all down on tiny scraps, and she kept it all stuffed under one of the wooden slats beneath the bed Axel had made for her. In those pages she detailed the events after Axel had found her—her early days in captivity, her pregnancy, giving birth. Annelise found Jasmine's pages under the bed slats. She learned from them that she was not the only one who'd been kept in there. She found comfort in those words from Jasmine. Annelise told the RCMP that Jasmine's words had given her hope, had made her feel less alone, had kept her going, because when she read them she believed—or needed to believe—that Jasmine had managed to escape."

"These scans—they're from those crumpled pages on the table that Annelise had stuffed down her dress?"

He nodded. "We found them in the glove compartment of the Subaru wreck. Annelise had kept them well hidden from Axel. She took them out when the fire started. She wanted to save them."

Angie blew out a heavy breath of air. She looked at the pages in her hands. One sentence had been highlighted.

In captivity I gave birth to You. A tiny baby girl. I survived for You, and I named You Claire.

Emotion filled her eyes. She looked up slowly. "Does Claire know?"

"Yes."

"And that Dr. Doug Hart is her father?"

"Yes. She's been told."

"And you're certain he's the father? I mean, is there any chance Garrison or Axel could actually be—"

"She gave a DNA sample. So did Doug Hart. The RCMP ran an expedited paternity test. She's Doug Hart's child. Jasmine is her mother."

"I want to see her."

"She's not seeing anyone, Angie. She's not talking to anyone. She doesn't want to see you, especially."

Angie closed her eyes. Her world spun sickeningly. "I know how she feels, Maddocks. I . . . I *know* how she feels after learning her entire life, her whole world, was a lie. I've been there. I can help her. I *need* to speak to her."

He stroked the back of her hand. "Don't push it, Ange. She's hurting. Bad. She's been robbed of family. The people she thought were her parents are her kidnappers. Her uncle killed her birth mother. The man she believed was her father helped bury her birth mother. Her half sister—as it turns out—pushed her birth mother into the Nahamish, tried to both kill her and drown the unborn child. Claire knows you did this—you exposed it. She might never take kindly to you. She blames you right now."

A knock sounded. Ginny appeared at the door in her black wool coat, a red scarf around her neck. In her arms she held Jack-O.

"Angie," she whispered. She hurried forward, and Maddocks took Jack-O. Ginny kissed and hugged Angie. "Oh God, thank God you're all right." She flashed a glance at her dad, a look of guilt and worry on her face.

"Ange, I'm sorry. I *had* to tell him. About the dress. I told him on the drive up. After we got the news that you were in hospital—we didn't know if you were going to . . ." Her voice caught. She flicked another look at her father. "We didn't know if you were going to be okay. Dad was so worried. It . . . it was the only thing that kept him going on that interminable drive up the island to see you and until you started coming round. I told him about Father Simon, the church, how my choir wanted to sing at your wedding. I mean—" Her eyes flashed worriedly to her dad. "That is, if you guys are . . . I . . . If—"

"Gin, Ginny, stop." Angie reached for the girl's hand as emotion pricked in her eyes all over again. "I love you, Ginny. It's okay. It's fine. I understand." She glanced at Maddocks, nerves suddenly nipping at her own heart at the strange look on his face. "I love you all so much," she whispered. "Including that butt-ugly mutt." She sniffed, wiped her nose, struggling to contain her sudden overwhelming emotions at just being alive, at having these two and that dog with her now. "I never want to be without you guys."

Maddocks regarded her. Angie swallowed.

"Marry me, James Maddocks."

"Dad," Ginny said, reaching for Jack-O, "I need to step out for a minute. I think Jack-O needs to go pee."

He let his daughter take the dog from his arms. Ginny cast her father a worried look, then turned to Angie. "It's going to be fine."

When Ginny had exited, Angie said, "Talk to me, Maddocks. You're making me nervous."

He took her hand, fingered the ring again. "You had it resized."

She nodded.

His eyes began to gleam with emotion. It twisted his face, as if he was trying to control a tsunami of feelings inside.

"What changed, Angie?" he said. "Has anything really changed? Because maybe it's just the heat of this moment, the euphoria from having survived. Maybe—"

"I did not get that ring resized in some heat of the moment, Maddocks. I . . . realized something over the past few weeks. I always wanted this. You. Me. Together. I thought I'd dealt with my fear."

"Fear of commitment?"

"Fear of being abandoned again. Admitting how much I love you and need you, and then having you walk out on me."

"Angie—"

"No. I need to say it. I thought I'd dealt with it. I really did. But when I lost my policing job, I lost my independence, my sense of self, which was shaky to begin with after learning my past. I was coming to our commitment from an incredibly vulnerable place, and . . . and, yes, it was a scary place. My independence, being able to provide for myself, own my own accommodation, be respected for my job, it was all suddenly gone. I hadn't realized what a deep, subterranean driver that sense of independence and self-control was to me. My PI work was shaky at best, and then I lost that."

"Being with you, Ange, being a couple—it was never about taking your independence. It's about becoming a team. Facing these life challenges together."

She reached for a tissue at the side of her bed and blew her nose. "I know. It was just this resistance deep down. This fear you'd leave me if I gave you everything." She blew her nose again. "It was asking me if I wanted children that blew it to a head because that also terrifies me. The idea that I could be a mother."

"You'd make a wonderful mother."

"Oh please."

A crooked smile curved over his lips, and his eyes gleamed as she held his gaze.

"If you still want me," she whispered. "If you're really prepared to put up with my shit, I want to give this my best shot, Maddocks. I can see it now, a way forward. Come hell or high water. I know . . . I think I really do know in my heart that we can weather anything that comes now. Together. Until death do us part."

His face crumpled. Tears leaked from the corners of his eyes. He leaned forward and kissed her on the mouth, and she tasted the salt of those tears as he whispered in her ear, "You are so stubborn that you had to turn it all around, didn't you? You had to take the proposal into your own control."

She smiled and wiped her cheeks. "Hey, you told me not to come back until I was sure." Her mood turned serious. "This is me being sure, James Maddocks. If you still want this, marry me on April twenty-seventh, a spring Saturday in the city, at the cathedral. I have my dress, and my dad said he'd give me away." She paused, holding his gaze. "And maybe my mother will sing. With Ginny and her choir."

"You told them?" he said quietly.

"I told them maybe it would happen."

He fell silent as he struggled with a surge of emotion. "Yes, Angie Pallorino." His voice hitched. "Until death do us part." He regarded her steadily, moisture glistening in his eyes. "Just hold off from trying to hasten the death part, okay? We need a calm run for a while."

She laughed with relief and love and release, and he kissed her again hard on the mouth, and Angie felt as though she'd come home. She hadn't known until this point what that truly felt like. Now she did. Home was these people. Home was those you loved. And a family could be built of many disparate parts, irrespective of the past. Or because of it.

CHAPTER 48

Star light, star bright, first star I see tonight. I see the evening star from my tiny window in the container where he keeps me . . . It reminds me of long ago nights like this, sitting at a campfire with my dad. He taught me to fly-fish when I was little girl—that was the beginning of a journey that led me to this point, to the river where I thought I was going to die. To this place in this container. Life is like a river, said Rachel. Life is absurd. The only constant is the water of change. She's right. I'm at a different point in that river now, and all that matters is You. I survived—I continue to survive—only for You. I wasn't able to get rid of You. I was going to, but something stopped me that day I went with Sophie. I thought I'd think about it further on the fishing trip. I still had a window of time to do this. And I threw everything against You during that trip—drinking, trying to have sex with different men. I was beating myself up with it all because, I think, I was scared. So very scared. Of losing my independence. Of losing my choices. Of being responsible for a life. But when I looked into the cold eyes of death, when I had faced that temptation to give up or hold on, it was You who took over.

I did it for You. And Your birth changed everything. It made me the most blessed person in the world, even while inside this container. I'd given life. I looked into your little eyes and saw they were green as the river that

changed me, and I named you Claire . . . and one day I will sit at a camp-
fire with you, Claire. One day we're going to get free . . .

THURSDAY, NOVEMBER 29

Angie found Claire on the Port Ferris Bay dock.

The young woman stood right at the very end that jutted into
the gunmetal-gray water. Whitecaps dotted the horizon. Rays of sun
streaked down through a gap in the thick wads of cloud. Claire's long
hair blew loose in the wind, and her hands were buried deep in her
pockets. She was oblivious, it seemed, to the shriek of gulls that swooped
down on the man behind her who was hauling his crab pot up over
the side of the dock. The old man was bent over, sorting through his
catch, casting the undersize crustaceans back into the water. As Angie
approached the man, she thought of forensic scientist Jacob Anders and
his seaside lab and the taphonomy studies he was doing in conjunction
with Simon Fraser University to see how long bodies took to decompose
underwater. And what sea creatures, like crabs, ate at the flesh. He'd
helped Angie in her hunt for her sister. She'd come a long way since her
sister's little foot had washed up on a beach in Tsawwassen.

Like Claire, Angie had been devastated by the revelation she was
not who she'd been told she was, that she'd been raised on lies. That her
entire life was false.

Yet she'd also learned later that those lies had been born out of love.
Misguided love, yes. But love was not simple. Nothing about life was
simple, or black, or white. Life was like that water in the bay and that
sky. Shades upon shades of gray. A continually shifting interplay of light
against dark and, every now and then, a few rays of sun.

Angie had been released from hospital this morning. Maddocks and
Ginny were waiting to drive her back to the city, where she would catch
a plane and go straight to see Holgersen in the hospital in Vancouver.

Before she left, however, she *had* to see Claire. Especially after reading the words Jasmine had written while being held captive in that container.

From the hospital last night, Angie had called and asked Claire to meet her. Claire had refused. Angie said it was necessary in order to tie up some things for the investigation. Claire had reluctantly agreed. But only if they met out in the open. On neutral turf. Someplace where she could breathe fresh air and escape if she needed to.

Angie understood.

Her collar turned up against the cold sea wind, Angie reached the end of the dock and came up beside Claire.

"Thanks for meeting with me."

Claire nodded but said nothing and did not look at Angie. Her profile was strong. Angie was struck—now that she knew the truth—by how much Claire resembled her biological mother in looks. The genetic echoes of both Jasmine and Doug Hart were all there in her height, her long, lean limbs, her smooth and even-toned complexion, her flashing green eyes. Angie's heart crunched with affection for this woman. And with sorrow.

"I wanted to say thank you," Angie said softly.

Claire inhaled deeply as she watched a boat entering the bay, gulls chasing and wheeling in the wake. The faint sound of the engine reached them, along with a tinge of diesel fuel on the wind.

Claire stole a glance at Angie. The young woman's eyes were red-rimmed and full of pain and fury and aloneness. Angie's chest constricted. Guilt whispered.

"Is *that* why you brought me out here—to say thank you?"

"Partly. You saved my life. I need to thank you for that. You also saved the life of another young woman who was lost and held captive for a year. Her name is Annelise Janssen. You brought her back to her parents, Claire, by calling Darnell Jacobi on your father and by pulling us out of that river." She paused. "You could have left it. Let us all be buried and gone with the truth. No one would have known about Annelise. Or what really happened to Jasmine."

She snorted. "My biological mother? Held captive by my own uncle from before I was born?" Tears glistened in her eyes, and her voice turned strident and husky. "I always wondered why he cared so much about me. Loved me sort of like his own. Like he loved his own fucking little bear cubs and fawns. Because I *was* like them, a rescue. I was pulled out of the river inside my mother. And my . . . my . . . I don't even know what to call my parents now. Garrison and Shelley—my kidnappers who I called Mom and Dad my whole life, who I loved with all my heart—are my abductors? Don't bother thanking me, Angie. I have no joy, no satisfaction at all in having turned in my own. I don't even have a home anymore. I can't go back to that lodge."

"Where are you staying?"

"A friend is renting me a basement suite in town."

"You know, Axel Tollet did love you, Claire. Garrison and Shelley really did love and raise you as their own. This is partly why they were all so desperate to keep the truth buried, because they didn't want you to know the truth. They didn't want to hurt you. Or lose you."

"Maybe the truth should stay buried sometimes. Maybe justice was already done. Porter Bates got his due."

"And Annelise? Her parents? And the other women he took—the ones we don't even know about yet? Jasmine? Her parents, her grandmother—what about them?"

Claire's mouth went tight as she tried to control her emotions.

"I understand, Claire. I really do. I know what you're going through."

"You have no fucking idea what I'm going through." She turned, eyes ablaze with green fire. "One minute—no, my entire life—I'm Claire Tollet. That's who I believe I am. Then you show up. And I'm not. I'm . . . I don't know what I am. I don't know how you do it—rip up lives like this and still go to sleep at night."

"I *do* know what you're going through. You know that I do."

Her gaze lasered Angie's. There was combat, challenge in her stance. Gulls swooped and shrieked above.

"I was the angel's cradle baby, remember? I was dumped in a baby box, slashed with a knife, left with no past, no memory. I was rescued and never told where I'd come from. I was inserted into a dead child's life, lied to my entire life. Told that baby pics, birth photos of a dead child were of me. I was even given the same name as that dead child. Until it all came apart, that web of deceit, and I learned I had a twin, that I was the offspring of a heinous sex trafficker and a young woman he'd abducted. A man who tried to kill me and who killed my sister and my mother." Angie paused and continued to hold Claire's gaze. "So I do understand something of what you're going through, and I'm here for you, Claire. I'm here, and I know, and I have walked that walk. In the end, you come to realize that the truth is the best way. That closure rounds the circle. Not just for you but all the others impacted by the ripple effects of crime. Because nothing happens in isolation."

Claire glowered at Angie, her eyes glinting with moisture.

"Here, I brought you something." Out of the front of her jacket, Angie took the plastic sleeve containing the journal pages Maddocks had scanned for her. She handed them to Claire.

"What are these?"

"They're what your biological mother wrote while in captivity. It's evidence that will be used in court, but Maddocks secured copies for me and for you. These pages, these words, belonged to Jasmine. You are her next of kin, so you have a right to them." Angie paused. "She wrote them to you, Claire."

Claire lowered her eyes and stared at the tiny writing. "Next of kin," she whispered. She took the pages from Angie and began to read. As Claire absorbed the first few sentences, strength seemed to whoosh out of her, and she sagged at the knees. Backing up, she sat on a wooden bench along the pier railing. She held her blowing hair off her face as she read the words in an audible whisper.

Star light, star bright, first star I see tonight . . . I looked into your little eyes and saw they were green as the river that changed me, and I named you Claire . . . and one day I will sit at a campfire with you, Claire. One day we're going to get free . . .

She swiped a tear from her cheek. "She named me?"

"She did."

"She died for me. She died trying to get free for me."

Angie seated herself beside Claire. "Hold on to that love, Claire. Secrets are forged and kept in the name of love. And hurt in the same."

Claire looked up and out over the layers of gray upon sea upon cloud upon ocean. The clean, salty wind pinked her nose and cheeks. Tears wet her face. She inhaled deeply.

"What matters, then?" she asked. "What truly matters if life is built on lies?"

"I don't know. But I want to say truth. Truth matters. It's what guides me now."

Claire sat in stunned silence, trying to assimilate what she held in her hands. Her mother's words.

"You need to hold on to that dream of yours, Claire. The SAR, the tracking. Finding the missing. You can help others find closure. In doing so, you will find yourself."

"Is that what you do now? You think you're helping others? Is that what drives you forward?"

Angie smiled wryly. "I don't know. Maybe." She paused. "I want you to meet someone."

"Who?"

"She drove up from the city very early this morning. Wait here."

Angie got up and walked a short way back down the pier. She raised her hand, calling the visitor over.

They watched as a car door opened up on the road. A squat figure exited slowly—a woman in a brown coat and wool hat. She was old, and she steadied herself with two sticks. Bending into the wind, she began to soldier slowly forward down the wooden dock like a crusty arthritic crab, her sticks like extra legs.

I'm Jasmine's only remaining kin . . . I just want some answers before I my lay grandchild's remains properly, and finally, to rest.

"She's your kin, Claire. Your great-grandmother. She's a retired justice of the Supreme Court. Her name is Jilly Monaghan, and she wants to meet you."

CHAPTER 49

FRIDAY, NOVEMBER 30

Kjel Holgersen leaned back against his pillows. His neck was being held steady by a brace. Pain was a constant right now. And his brain was still thick and woozy from medication. Outside it was getting dark, late November rain streaming against the hospital window. December would dawn tomorrow. Then would come Christmas.

He checked the time. Visiting hours were almost over. No one was coming to see him. Why he'd even dared hope was beyond him. He reached for his iPad at the side of his bed and opened the cover. He pulled up a news site and began to read the stories developing around his and Pallorino's discovery of a serial killer's lair at the Nahamish. The media was hailing him as a hero.

He didn't feel like one.

Nothing about his shithole life was heroic. Probably no one would miss him if he'd gone and died out there in the snow. Why he'd been given yet another chance was beyond him.

He shut the cover on his iPad and closed his eyes, thinking of those case files Leo had set to one side as being irrelevant, unsolvable, a waste of time. Maybe that's why.

Because no one should be a waste of time.

He could still make a difference, like he'd made with Annelise Janssen in working with Pallorino to see that she finally came home.

Kjel made a mental note to look at those street kid files again, see what he might have missed the last time around. Because if Leo said they were worthless, Kjel figured they held something that warranted deeper investigation. *Watch Detective Leo. Like a hawk.*

With his eyes closed, he started to drift off to someplace warm, with a beach. A sparkling ocean. With drinks that came in colors like blue and orange and purple and were garnished with tropical flowers and little paper umbrellas.

"Holgersen?"

"A double," he murmured, holding up two fingers. "Make mine a double."

"Holgersen." Someone was shaking his arm. He drifted groggily up from his tropical vacation. He opened his eyes.

"Jeezus, fuck," he muttered when he saw who it was. "I thoughts you was my waitress. Where's my drinks? What in the hells you doing here, Pallorino? You . . . you look like shit." He struggled to sit up higher, but pain stopped him dead. He breathed slowly, trying to moderate the pulsing in his nerve ends. Trying not to move his head.

"Speak for yourself, you ugly old mutt." Angie Pallorino set a packet of nicotine gum on the table next to his bed. "Maddocks found that pack on your desk. Better check with your doc, though, before you go mixing nicotine into that cocktail of drugs they're giving you."

He grinned carefully and whispered, "Sweet mercies. You's doing okay, then?"

She nodded. She looked super pale. She had bruises on her face and a line of tiny black stitches on her brow. And her nose was swollen. He struggled to hold in his emotions at the sight of her alive, struggled to rein in his affection for this hard-ass chick. Who was also so soft. Who he'd really kind of come to love. He'd heard how she'd rolled the car down the bank and gone into the river.

She touched his arm. "And you—how you feeling?"

He almost nodded, wincing again as his slightest movement caused him pain. "Good enough." His voice would be a hoarse whisper for a while, the docs had said. "I'll be back at the station in no time."

She laughed. "Right. We'll see about that. What do the doctors say?"

"They said the only other person they knows about who gots an arrow through the neck like this and narrowly survived because it missed everything important was some Russian dude, a father of two out for a walk in the park near a sports center in Moscow. Someone from the archery club there misfired, and he gots it in the neck. Outta the blue. Life is fucking weird."

She held his gaze, her features turning serious. "Yeah," she said. "It is. But mostly it's better than the alternative."

"Mostly." Although Kjel wasn't so certain about that.

She pointed to a pile of newspapers she'd set on the bedside stand. "Media is hailing you as a hero. The chief, mayor, everyone. You saved what they're calling a daughter of the city, given her dad's high profile."

"Saw on the iPad. It was you who saved Annelise, not me."

"No way. We made a good team."

"Yeah. Maybe."

"Look, I . . . I'm sorry I left you there. I—"

"Hey, I'da have left you, too, Pallorino. Yous did what you was trained to do. You're a good cop."

"Except I'm not a cop."

"Yeah, well. You still gots the bad guys. You still play a good game."

She snorted. "So I've come to invite you to a wedding."

He stared at her, a feeling of joy mushrooming quietly inside his chest. "For reals?"

"For reals." She smiled. Really smiled. And it looked real good on her. And just for this moment Pallorino's honest-to-God smile made the world seem like a better place.

It made Kjel feel just a bit worthwhile. Because he'd helped put that smile there in many tiny, little ways.

Yeah, maybe this was better than the alternative. For now.

CHAPTER 50

Friday, March 1

Angie sat at her desk in her apartment, a hot mug of coffee at her side as she went through files for the new case she was working. Things were going well with Brixton and Coastal Investigations. He'd extended his contractual arrangement with her. He'd pretty much tripped over his feet to do so after the positive results from the Moss Girl case, as he called it, and the extensive media coverage that had flowed out of it. When Brixton had seen all the headlines, he'd seen fresh business. Angie was confident she'd have her full license before long and then her own firm. But for now she was content. She was getting the kind of cases that fired her engine.

The cell on her desk rang. She snatched it up and answered.

"Pallorino."

"Angie, hey, it's Claire. I'm in town to visit my gran. You busy today?"

Angie glanced up, feeling a punch of pleasure at the sound of the young woman's voice. Outside her windows the sky was blue. Spring was in the air. She'd been so absorbed in her case reports she hadn't even noticed it was past noon.

"A woman's gotta eat," Angie said with a smile in her voice. "What do you have in mind?" This was the third time Claire Tollet had called to see Angie when she'd come into Victoria to visit with Justice Jilly Monaghan. The old judge and her great-granddaughter were getting to know each other, one small step at a time, and it warmed Angie's heart. Even while ripping apart one family, Angie had managed to bring this new and disparate family together. It made things seem worth-while. On her last visit, Claire had told Angie that she'd successfully completed her GSAR, the requisite training to become a full-fledged member of Port Ferris Search and Rescue. She was volunteering with the team now but looking farther afield for a new place to live. She'd said she needed to make a full break. Maybe after time she'd manage to go back and form some sort of truce with Shelley and Garrison. Maybe after the trials, Claire had said. But it would still be a long way to trial for Garrison and his wife, and for Beau and Joey Tollet, and Wallace and Jessie Carmanagh. The forensic ident team was still busy carefully sifting through soil on Axel Tollet's property and trying to identify the bones they'd found there so far. At least four more victims had been discovered buried on Axel Tollet's spread, including, as Holgersen had suspected, the remains of a street worker who'd vanished from Vancouver's Downtown Eastside in 2002 and the remains of the female who'd disappeared near Blaine in Washington State in 2009 after her car had broken down on the highway. The other two bodies were yet to be identified. There was a feeling there might be more unearthed yet.

"How about meeting at Fisherman's Wharf?" Claire said. "It's such a nice day, and"—she paused—"this time I have someone I want *you* to meet."

"Who?" Angie said, her interest immediately piqued.

"You'll see. One hour?"

"I'll be there."

Angie shut down her work, grabbed her jacket, and headed to the elevator. When she reached the lobby of her apartment building and saw the fresh green leaves budding on the branches outside, the sun sparkling on the waters of the Gorge, she decided to walk.

By the time she reached Fisherman's Wharf and was making her way down the gangway to the docks, she was famished, and Claire was already there waiting. Angie saw her immediately, sitting in a red jacket at a picnic table near the water's edge, her long black hair shining in the sun, her back to Angie. But there was no one else with her.

Angie paused, wondering if the person she was supposed to meet had bailed.

"Hey," Angie said as she approached the table.

Claire turned and grinned broadly. Angie blinked in surprise. Tucked down the front of Claire's jacket was little hairy black face with liquid eyes. A Labrador pup with a red collar.

Angie stilled, a wave of emotions crashing through her as she stared at the dog.

Claire came to her feet. "Angie, meet Echo," she said. "My new search-and-rescue-pup-in-training."

Goose bumps washed over Angie's skin at the expression of sheer love and pleasure in Claire Tollet's green eyes, and for a moment words eluded her.

"Echo's my second chance," Claire said. "We're going to move north, to Smithers on the mainland, where we'll train in both tracking and air scenting—I've been offered a position on the SAR team up there." As Claire spoke, she unzipped her jacket and took the fat little hairball out. She handed the pup to Angie.

Echo was warm. And soft. And tubby, and had too much skin for her body and smelled just like puppies should smell. She squiggled in Angie's arms, trying to lick her face all over. Angie laughed with unabashed pleasure.

As Claire took Echo from Angie and set the pup down on the dock, she said, "Echo and I are going to start a new chapter." She held Angie's eyes for a beat. "We're going to find the missing. We're going to follow our dream."

And Angie knew Claire was thinking of the words she'd spoken on the Port Ferris pier.

You need to hold on to that dream of yours. The SAR, the tracking. Finding the missing. You can help others find closure. In doing so you will find yourself.

Angie couldn't begin to articulate what this meant to her—that she'd made some difference, had some impact on this woman's life. It made it all worthwhile. It fired her to keep going, follow her own dream, her own new chapter.

Angie and Claire bought fish tacos from one of the stalls and sat in the sun eating their lunch while Echo played on her leash at their feet and gulls wheeled in the clean sea air.

"How's Maddocks?" Claire asked as she chewed.

"Good. Really good. We put in an offer on a place."

"What? Seriously? Where?"

"James Bay. Just up the road from here. It's got a little garden." Angie smiled. "Like I'd know what to do with that."

Claire laughed. "You'll learn. Start with herbs. Can't go too far wrong with a pot of parsley."

"You'd be surprised, given what I know about plants. Maddocks is keen, though."

They chatted awhile about Angie's work, about turning the schooner into an office down the road, about Ginny and Jack-O and Holgersen. And about how Claire was getting on with Jilly Monaghan.

"She's an interesting one," Claire said. "Crusty. But I like her." She reached for her drink.

"I like her, too," Angie said. "She's a strong woman. I'm glad she got to know you, Claire."

Claire nodded, took a sip from her cup. "Me too. What's happening with Eden Hart?"

"She's being charged for attempted murder," Angie said. "She was fourteen at the time, but the prosecutor is seeking an adult sentence, given the nature of the offense."

"What about the investigation into the drowning of her little brother and her husband's ex?"

"Ongoing. No proof so far from what I understand. They might never be able to convict her of those."

"She won't talk? I mean, in exchange for lesser sentencing or something?"

Angie shook her head and popped the last of her taco into her mouth. She chewed and wiped her lips with a paper napkin. "I think silence is Dr. Eden Hart's weapon now. It's her means of maintaining some kind of control. But part of me thinks she will talk one day, especially after doing time for a while. She has a pathological need to be the center of attention, and I heard via the grapevine that she's already made tentative contact with Dr. Reinhold Grablowski."

"The true crime writer? The forensic shrink who did the book on you?"

Angie nodded. "I wouldn't be surprised if Dr. Hart is vying with me for true crime attention now. It's in her nature, this kind of game. I suspect we haven't heard the end of Dr. Hart, not by a long shot."

Once they'd finished their lunch, Claire, Echo, and Angie made their way back up to the parking lot where Claire's car was parked. Claire put Echo into her doggie crate in the back, and she turned to Angie.

"I want to say goodbye, for now."

"When are you leaving?"

"We drive up to Smithers tomorrow."

"You'll come down for the wedding?"

"Of course. I wouldn't miss it for the world. Neither would Jilly."

Claire reached forward and gave Angie a hug. Angie tensed, a knee-jerk reaction to unanticipated physical closeness, but she forced herself to relax, and she hugged Claire back tightly.

Claire looked directly into Angie's eyes and said, "Thank you. For everything."

Angie swallowed. Her eyes pricked. She nodded, suddenly unable to speak. But Claire's words made her world feel right. They gave meaning to what she did for a living now. Angie felt as though she was finally on her true track, becoming the person she was meant to be.

Echo might be Claire's new chapter. This was hers.

THE WEDDING

SATURDAY, APRIL 27

The heavy cathedral doors opened, exposing Angie in her bridal gown, her arm hooked into the crook of her father's. Her dad beamed from ear to ear with pride, and she could feel him shaking slightly from nerves. Or was that her?

The strains of the processional began inside the ancient cathedral. Spring sunlight filtered down through stained-glass windows up high, painting a soft rainbow of color over the wedding guests in the old wooden pews. At the far end of the aisle—in front of the altar, next to Father Simon in his white robe—stood Maddocks in full police uniform.

The sight of her man dressed like that punched Angie hard in the stomach and clean stole her breath.

"Let's do this," her father whispered.

Angie stepped into the church with her dad. As they came forward, the music swelled, rising to the steeples and echoing off the old stone walls. The choice of music was Ginny's, a haunting arrangement Ginn had wanted to sing solo in the *idioglossia* in which it had been written— an idiosyncratic language invented and spoken by only one person or by very few. A private language. Like the "twin-speak" Angie had once shared with her little sister, Mila.

"It's beautiful, spiritual, lyrical, and romantic," Ginny had said. "And it sounds like ancient Latin. It would be a tribute to Mila, your other half, Angie, so your twin can be with you in spirit, too."

Angie did feel that Mila was here with her now. That little ghost girl in pink who'd haunted her from within the deeply buried memories of her childhood, until Angie had dug out the truth, found Mila's bones, and laid her properly to rest along with their mother. In much the same way Jilly Monaghan and Claire Tollet had been able to do with Jasmine Gulati's bones.

Beside Maddocks and Father Simon stood the best man, Kjel Holgersen. In Holgersen's hand was a red lead. At the other end of the lead sat three-legged Jack-O, sporting a red-and-white polka-dot bow tie.

Angie's legs turned to rubber at the sight of them all. It swelled her heart to near bursting and made her falter in step. She could enter a crime scene with an armed gunman, she could fight off an attacker with a knife, she could deliver a solid Muay Thai kick, but this? She didn't know how to do this. She didn't know if she could make it all the way down that aisle in one piece. She clutched more tightly to her father's arm, and he said gently, "Come on, Ange. We can do this."

We.

She drew in a deep breath and continued forward slowly, step by step, keeping pace with the music.

Ginny separated herself from the choir. She looked resplendent in a shimmering golden dress. She began to sing, her solo voice rising in crescendo, reaching to the rafters in that mysterious, haunting language. Like an angel communicating directly to the heavens in the name of all that was love. Angie felt tears prick her eyes. She saw tears glistening in the eyes of all the guests as she passed them.

It amazed her that so many had come. Her old colleagues from the MVPD took up several pews. They stood proud in a sea of neatly pressed black uniforms. With them was pathologist Barb O'Hagan, who'd even donned a frock. Beside Barb was city coroner Charlie Alphonse in his best suit and tie. On the other side of the aisle stood Jock Brixton with Daniel Mayang and a bunch of staff from Coastal Investigations. She was one of them now.

Step by slow step, Angie continued down the aisle toward the man she loved. The man who'd shown her how to be unafraid. How to trust. How to love herself. Watched by these people who now made up her tribe, people who'd helped shape the past year of her life as she'd journeyed into her tumultuous past and come out with a future.

Her therapist and old mentor, Dr. Alex Strauss, was there, too. And so was murder victim Gracie Drummond's mother.

In the second pew from the front, being supported by Claire Tollet on one side and Gudrun Reimer on the other, was Claire's great-grandmother, Justice Jilly Monaghan. Claire was going to be okay. Angie believed that wholly now. She'd be okay because she was helping others.

Miriam Pallorino was seated next to the front pew in her wheelchair, dressed in mother-of-the-bride lilac. She was beaming, seemingly happy to be back in her beloved and familiar Catholic church, reembracing the faith that had once been so deeply rooted in her psyche.

Maddocks smiled as Angie and her dad reached them. It was a deep and pure smile, and it lit his dark-blue eyes, filling them with love, appreciation, and pride. That look of pride meant everything to Angie.

Her father took her hand and placed it into the strong hand of her homicide detective. Her Sergeant James Maddocks.

The music died, and the church fell silent.

Father Simon solemnly joined them in holy matrimony. They exchanged their vows. Then Father Simon said, "You may now kiss the bride."

As Maddocks kissed Angie on the lips, the old pipe organ started up with the strains of "Ave Maria." Joseph Pallorino wheeled his wife over to the choir and handed her a mike. Miriam took it with a trembling hand and began to sing the hymn in a startlingly clear mezzo-soprano, the choir joining her, their voices rising to the steeples of the ancient building, rippling a chill over Angie's skin.

Maddocks whispered in her ear, "Remember, go easy on the death-do-us-part bit."

Angie laughed, emotion filling her soul as she listened to the hymn that had once brought her such strange and dark memories but would now always be remembered for this—a joyous occasion. A promise of a future.

They exited the church and stepped into yellow sunlight. The cathedral bells started to clang, their peal ricocheting up and down the city streets as cherry petals blew from trees in the soft sea breeze.

Uniformed officers lined the stone stairs. Baskets were handed out, and fistfuls of petals were cast into the air, settling like spring snow on Angie and Maddocks and falling in a pink-and-white carpet on the pavement outside the church.

There was a gaggle of journalists out on the street. Cameras flashed. But this time the headlines would tell of a happy-for-now for an ex-cop and her clan who'd brought home alive one of the city's daughter's—Annelise Janssen.

Maddocks took Angie's hand. The light in her man's eyes as he looked into hers said it all. Love.

Maybe it wasn't just truth. Maybe at the heart of it all, at the heart of all that was human, even in the dark, was love.

ABOUT THE AUTHOR

Loreth Anne White is an award-winning, bestselling author of romantic suspense, thrillers, and mysteries, including *The Drowned Girls* and *The Lullaby Girl*, the first two books in the Angie Pallorino series. Winner of the Daphne du Maurier Award for Excellence in Mainstream Mystery/Suspense, Loreth is also a three-time RITA finalist, plus a recipient of the Romantic Times Reviewers' Choice Award, the National Readers' Choice Award, the Romantic Crown for Best Romantic Suspense and Best Book Overall, and a Booksellers' Best finalist. A former journalist who has worked in both South Africa and Canada, she now resides in the mountains of the Pacific Northwest with her family. When not writing, she skis, bikes, and hikes the trails with her dog, doing her best to avoid the bears (albeit unsuccessfully). Learn more at www.lorethannewhite.com.